Glenice Crossland lives in Sheffield. She has loved writing from an early age, only taking it seriously after early retirement from her job in a leisure centre. She has read one of her poems on BBC2, had several read on Radio Sheffield and more published in various anthologies. She is well known locally for her watercolours of churches and local traditions. Married with one son and grandchildren she still lives a few hundred yards from the house in which she was born. She is also the author of *The Stanford Lasses* and *Christmas Past*.

Praise for Where the Heart Is

'Shows she could be a major new player in the Josephine Cox and Katie Flynn field. Fans of this genre will quickly warm to the three Yorkshire girls and enjoy sharing their trials and tribulations'
Peterborough Evening Telegraph

'A poignant and mesmerising story of tragedy and triumph from the author of *The Stanford Lasses*'
Country Gentleman's Association

'This charming tale will be perfect for when you want to escape the festive preparations'
First magazine

Where the Heart Is

GLENICE
CROSSLAND

1 3 5 7 9 10 8 6 4 2

Arrow Books
20 Vauxhall Bridge Road
London SW1V 2SA

Arrow Books is part of the Penguin Random House group of companies
whose addresses can be found at global.penguinrandomhouse.com.

Penguin
Random House
UK

First published as *The Ever Open Door* by Arrow Books in 2008
This edition reissued as *Where the Heart Is* in 2019

www.penguin.co.uk

A CIP catalogue record for this book is available from the British Library.

ISBN 9781787463219

Typeset in Times by
Palimpsest Book Production Ltd,Grangemouth, Stirlingshire
Printed and bound in Great Britain by Clays Ltd, Elcograf S.p.A.

This book is dedicated to the memory of my parents and grandparents, all of whom lived in houses with an ever open door

Acknowledgements

With thanks as always to Georgina Hawtrey-Woore and all the team at Random House for their guidance and support.

Chapter One

The key was inside the letter box, hanging from a string. It was a heavy old key, turning rusty from lack of use. Neither Sally Butler, her husband Jim nor little Daisy saw any reason to lock anybody out and, since they hadn't much of value, didn't think it necessary to lock anything in either. On the rare occasions the door did happen to be locked, any neighbour in need, indeed any Tom, Dick or Harry, would know where to find the key to number nine Potters Row. Usually visitors would simply tap on the door and enter the house with a call of 'It's only me' or 'Anybody in?'

The first caller of the day would be Nellie the postwoman. With telephones a luxury, only for the likes of doctors, business folk or the very wealthy, not many days would go by without a visit from Nellie. There'd be letters from aunts inviting them to stay, others announcing forthcoming visits, and especially welcome would be the ones easily recognisable as being from Sally's airman brother, Ernest. Nellie would be fortified with something hot in winter, and on high days and holidays a drop of port wine.

'It's only me,' she announced herself. 'One from your Ernest this morning unless I'm mistaken.'

'Oh, at last.' Sally sighed with relief as she unfolded the flimsy sheet of paper. It was mainly thanking them for the parcel of knitted socks and gloves that Ernest had received. He sent his love to all the family and said he hoped little Daisy was being a good girl, then gave a glowing description of yet another new girlfriend.

Sally guessed things wouldn't be nearly as rosy for him as her brother made out; nevertheless her mind was set at rest that so far he was still in one piece. After Nellie had been given the letter to read and then continued on her round, Sally unknotted the scarf from the top of her head, took off her pinafore, and raked a comb through her mop of chestnut curls. Then she hurried along to number five where her sister Enid Cartwright would devour the contents of the letter eagerly, also very relieved that their brother was safe.

The next caller of the day was Mr Harrison the milkman, who found the house deserted except for Dippy the black-and-white mongrel. The dog sniffed excitedly round the caller's legs before returning to his mat. Mr Harrison usually enjoyed a gossip with Sally, but not to worry; the money and the jug were waiting on top of the sewing machine as usual. He measured out the milk with his gill measure and poured the dregs into the dog's dish before he left, closing the door behind him.

No doubt he would catch up with Sally at her sister's if he put a spurt on.

He smiled to himself. If he'd been twenty years younger, Mr Harrison could have fancied Sally Butler, who was quite a looker, with her trim figure and what the lads used to describe as 'legs up to her armpits'. Of course, he would never have got a look in when Jim Butler came on the scene, and nobody would begrudge the amiable young couple their obvious happiness together.

Little Daisy was playing shop with a couple of tin lids, a pile of stones and a few leaves when the milkman arrived at Enid's. He began to sing 'Daisy, Daisy' and the child smiled shyly. Daisy liked the milkman. He could hear the two women laughing through the open door and as he popped his head in, Enid called, 'Oh, aye, timed it right again, have yer? I don't know how you manage it.' He knew that meant she had just brewed up. 'Sorry there's no sugar,' she said as she poured three cups of tea, 'but at least we won't be short of milk.'

'Eeh, thanks, that's welcome.' He poured milk into the measure and transferred a drop into each cup. 'What about the little lass, will she have a drop of milk?'

'Thanks all the same but she won't touch the stuff, I only wish she would.' Sally frowned. 'I've never known such a faddy little devil.'

Her sister grinned. 'She'll have no option when she starts school, they have a bottle every morning playtime whether they like it or not.' Enid was a cleaner at Millington Council School, a few minutes' walk away.

'Well, I only hope she isn't sick if they force her to drink it.' Sally held out the letter. 'We've heard from our Ernest at last.'

The milkman acknowledged the news with a smile.

'That's good, I wish I could say the same about our Frank. There's been no news for weeks.'

'Oh, I'm sorry.' Sally frowned. 'Still, no news is good news, or so they say.'

'Not much consolation that, though, when your son's somewhere out there,' Enid pointed out.

Mr Harrison put on a show of bravado. 'They say the mail's not reliable, I expect that's it. Oh, well, I'd better get a move on.' He turned back at the door to say, 'Thanks for the tea.'

'Me and my big mouth!' Sally sighed. 'And the lad only just eighteen.'

She closed the door behind him and went to the window, standing looking out at the hardened earth that served as the road for Potters Row. On the opposite side a gap in the dry stone wall led to a path across the field, where in summer a profusion of meadow flowers would bloom.

Millington was a good place in which to live. Its main shopping street and the long, sprawling steel-works down in the valley were hidden from view by the trees in what was known as the Donkey

4

Wood, lower down the hill. At the bottom of Potters Row ran the loop of St George's Road, which curved at either end to join the main road. Potters Row and two other similar rows of houses, Barkers Row and Taylors Row, all led off St George's Road and were separated from each other by open fields. Beyond the rows the first of the council houses, built in the twenties, could be seen, and the square, tiled roof of the council school. And in the distance the wide-open moors of the Pennine hills stretched for as far as the eye could see.

Sally frowned as she looked at the brick and concrete of the recently erected air-raid shelter at the bottom of the field, next to which a footpath known as the Donkey Path provided a short-cut to the main road.

'It doesn't seem two minutes since young Frank was doing the round with his father in the school holidays. The poor man must be out of his mind with worry.'

'And his wife,' Enid said. 'Is this what we struggle to bring them up for? To send them off to be killed?'

'Don't say that, Enid.'

'Well, it's true. All I can say is, I'm glad mine are both girls.'

Sally placed her arm round her sister's waist. 'Well, at least our men are safe in the steelworks.'

'No one's safe, love, not even us. In fact, it's all the steelworks that are making our city a target.'

'Well, we're not really *in* the city, are we?' But Sally sounded uncertain.

She went outside on to the flagged causeway where Daisy was tearing up dandelion leaves to use in her shop. She picked up her daughter and held her close as if to protect her from everything evil, saying a little prayer for Ernest and Mr Harrison's son to be kept safe, and for the rotten old war soon to be over.

Jim Butler glanced at the sweat-stained face of his watch. Half-past nine . . . only another half-hour and he would be clocking off. He shook the perspiration from his face. God, he could murder a pint, and then home to supper, Sally and bed. He watched the next steel billet leave the roughing as a square and made ready to turn it up diamond-shaped. Experience made him do this at the double, otherwise the immense heat would scorch the seat of his working trousers. He passed the six-foot turning-up fork to his mate Tom, who would turn the next billet which would possibly be turned into war weapons.

A man arriving for the night shift touched him on the shoulder so that Jim turned and read his lips: 'Come on, Jim lad, get thy sen home to bed.' Conversation in the billet mill was impossible due to the noise there. Jim mouthed his thanks and grinned as the man advised him what to do to that lovely young wife of his. Then he snatched up his snap tin and left the hellish heat and noise behind him.

Millington at ten o'clock at night would have been a quiet place had it not been for the sound of the steelworks and the clatter of working boots as the afternoon shift tramped wearily up the hill past the old smithy. The stream of buses were nose to tail, taking home the workers to outlying towns and villages; those they'd just brought in would already be hard at it on the night shift. The men who had left to join the armed forces had been replaced by women for jobs such as crane-driving, and now they too were wearily making their way home.

Jim called in at the Rising Sun and downed a pint in one go, bade the barmaid goodnight then made his way home. Sally scooped a ladling can of water out of the boiler by the fire and into the washing-up bowl as she heard her husband's boots on the step. By the time he had washed at the pot sink in the corner, his meal of fried cheese and a pile of bread was waiting for him on the table. Only then did she speak of Ernest's letter and her worry over the lack of news from young Frank Harrison.

Jim read the letter from his brother-in-law with relief and hoped a young man like Frank, who had everything to live for, would come through this war safely. He couldn't help feeling grateful that his was a reserved occupation. Then he went outside and round the corner to the block of lavatories with its two rows of three cubicles. On the way he breathed in the cool night air, which was welcome after the filth and heat of the mill.

He went back in to Sally and the promise of his warm bed. As usual he peeped in on Daisy first, who lay sucking away at a pink dummy in her sleep. He considered removing it but decided against risking waking her. He was unwilling to share Sally with anyone tonight, not even his beloved daughter.

'It's time our Daisy threw that hideous old dummy away,' Jim told his wife the next morning. 'She's going to have the bloody thing when she starts school, if we're not careful.'

'I have tried.' Sally frowned.

'Well, tell her she's a big girl now, not a baby.'

'I've done that.'

'And?'

'She informed me she likes being a baby and doesn't want to be a big girl.'

Jim laughed. 'She's an answer for everything, that one. Try bribery then.'

'Hmm, I've already decided on that. Today, as a matter of fact.'

Daisy loved the sycamore tree that stood near their house at the edge of the field. In spring the twittering of the birds on its branches woke her, and in autumn the leaves formed a red and gold carpet at its foot. She and her cousin Norah would crunch them and kick them in the air so that they rained down like the confetti at Aunty Betty's wedding.

The little girl had felt like a princess then in her pink satin bridesmaid's dress with head-dress and muff to match. Aunty Betty had looked beautiful, though Grandma Butler didn't seem to think so; in fact, she'd shouted and bawled at Aunty Betty when she'd come downstairs dressed in her lovely white dress and veil. Grandma had said it was a sin to wear white in her condition, and how the girl had the cheek to go to chapel veiled she couldn't believe. Daisy didn't know what condition she meant and had asked her dad, which hadn't helped much as he'd told her to ask her mam, who had changed the subject.

Now Daisy couldn't make up her mind what to do. Mrs Porter next-door had a new baby; it had come yesterday in the nurse's black bag. Daisy really, really wanted to go and look at it, but Mam said that if she did, she had to take her dummy and give it to baby Celia. Daisy looked down at the soother which hung from a ribbon fastened to her cardigan by a huge safety pin. She looked over to Mrs Porter's door, standing invitingly open, and could no longer resist the temptation. She fumbled with the pin until finally she managed to undo it, then she ran into Mrs Porter's house.

'Hello, Daisy,' said a woman in the kitchen. 'Your mam said you were coming to see our new baby.' She nodded. 'Come on then.' The woman took Daisy upstairs. Mrs Porter was sitting up in bed, looking very pale.

'Hello, Daisy,' she welcomed the little girl gamely. 'Your mam said you were bringing something for baby Celia.' And Daisy handed over her precious dummy to Mrs Porter.

'Right, thank you, I'll give it to her later. Now would you like to hold her?'

Daisy nodded again, speechless at first to be trusted to hold the baby girl. She gazed in awe at her tiny fingers and nose. 'Isn't she little?' she said. 'Just like my Baby Doll.'

'That's because she's come very early.' Mary Porter lifted her daughter from Daisy's lap, and frowned worriedly. 'I'm going to try and feed her now but you can come and see her again another day. Thank you for the dummy.'

Daisy ran home then, eager to ask her mam if the nurse would bring them a new baby just like Mrs Porter's.

The next day Potters Row and all the rows were plunged into mourning when baby Celia died. Daisy immediately said she would go and fetch her dummy back.

'No,' Sally told her daughter. 'Baby Celia has taken it with her to heaven.'

Daisy cried that night in bed.

'Don't be sad,' Sally told her, 'Jesus will look after baby Celia. He'll help her grow into an angel.'

'But what about my dummy?' the little girl asked. However, that was the last time it was ever mentioned. Baby Celia's short span on earth had succeeded where two years' coaxing had failed.

Mary Porter had been Sally's best friend since school days. The loss of baby Celia affected Sally almost as much as it did Mary and her husband Tom. Sally knew words of sympathy wouldn't help so set about helping to arrange the baby's funeral, ordering flowers, and making meals for the distressed couple and their son Stanley, who was a few years older than Daisy.

Mary's labour had been a difficult one and her grief at losing her daughter had rendered her almost useless from weakness and shock. On the day of the burial Sally coaxed her into her best coat, on which she had sewn a black armband, and a black hat borrowed from Enid. Almost everyone in Potters Row turned out to attend the funeral and follow the tiny coffin down the hill to Millington Parish Church. Jim stood shoulder to shoulder with Tom, his fellow worker and friend, knowing words would be of little consolation but hoping his presence might help.

Afterwards the living-room and kitchen at Mary's were overflowing with relatives and neighbours, and by the time a few gallons of tea and even more pale ale had been consumed, Mary and Tom were looking and feeling a little better. Mary even confided in Sally that she would be trying as soon as possible for another child; she also told her friend that if she had a dozen more babies, none could

11

ever replace the little one she had buried on this day.

Then, for the first time, Mary let loose the dam of tears she had stifled, as her friend held her in her arms. Sally knew that Mary would come through the darkness, and she knew her friend Sally would be there to guide her into the light.

Betty Hayes' *née* Butler's condition continued to shame her mother, no matter how anyone tried to console her. Eighteen now, Betty had always been a flighty piece, according to the locals. In fact, Mrs Ramsgate at number one expressed surprise to all and sundry that the girl had got away without becoming pregnant for as long as she had.

'One lad after the other since the day she left school,' she said. 'I wonder if that new husband of hers knows her reputation.'

Amy Butler was having none of that. *She* was entitled to call her daughter all the names she could think of, but that didn't mean anyone else had the right. She limped painfully along the row and hammered on the door to number one so that faces appeared at the windows and doors of all the other houses and ears strained to hear what all the commotion was about.

Mrs Ramsgate was only just five foot tall and as round as she was long. She was also the worst gossip this side of Sheffield. Usually she would spread her scandal then scurry off indoors, but there was no hiding from Amy Butler, who stood on her doorstep, arms firmly folded and a cloth hanging over one of them.

'Amy?' Mrs Ramsgate addressed her neighbour of many years.

'Mrs Butler to you. What's this you've been saying about my lass?'

'What?' The other woman shuffled her feet uncomfortably in their filthy old carpet slippers, wondering what Amy had heard. 'I 'aven't said owt except how lovely she looked in 'er wedding gown and veil.'

'Yes, she did. In a white gown and veil she should never 'ave been wearing, seeing as she's almost six months gone.' Amy raised her voice then so that all the neighbours could hear. 'But at least she *had* a wedding gown and veil, and a ring on her finger – which is more than can be said for your Florence, who went sneaking off to Blackpool or somewhere on pretence of being a waitress when all the time she had gone to bear a child, a poor little mite she had to give away to strangers – all because she didn't 'ave a mother who'd stand by her.

'Well, I'll tell you this, Kitty Ramsgate, wedding ring or not, no grandchild of mine would ever be parted with, even if I 'ad to bring it up meself. And just because me daughter's misbehaved herself, it don't give *you* the right to call 'er names, because it isn't any business of yours or anybody else's!'

Amy Butler unfolded her arms and handed the

cloth to the red-faced woman before her. 'And *here's* a floor cloth. Yer filthy doorstep 'asn't seen a bucket of water for weeks!'

Kitty Ramsgate waited until her neighbour had made her slow departure then called after her, 'Say what yer like, she's still a flighty bitch.'

Amy continued imperturbably on her way as she answered over her shoulder, 'Maybe, but at least she's a clean one.'

Confrontations such as this were commonplace on all the rows but never before had Amy Butler or any of her family been involved in one. Scenes like this had always been beneath them previously and Amy felt secretly ashamed that she had lowered herself. Even so, neighbours who had respected her as a good friend for years were delighted by the way she had put the Ramsgate woman in her place; her shoddy ways and scandal-mongering were felt to have lowered the tone of Potters Row.

Mrs Firth nodded to Amy as she passed her door. 'You're right, Mrs Butler, she is a dirty bugger.'

'I didn't call her that.'

'No, but she is. I bet if she took 'er curtains down they'd drop to bits. Eeh, but I didn't know about their Florence. I thought she was such a nice lass.'

'She is, but what chance had she got with a mother like that?' Amy sighed. 'I reckon the poor little mite she had was better off adopted. Though I'm sorry I said what I did now.'

Then she went home, put the kettle on and mashed

herself a pot of tea. She was still trembling, glad she'd put the woman in her place but just as ashamed of their Betty. The awful thing was that she knew the other woman was right. Her daughter *was* a flighty little piece, and the man she'd married didn't seem much better either. In fact, Amy doubted he had wanted to marry Betty at all. Well, at least he had done what was right and made an honest woman of her, but marriage shouldn't be about doing the right thing, it should be about love – the kind of love she had felt for her George. Right up to the day he died they had loved and cherished each other, as they had promised to on their wedding day. *Through sickness and in health . . .* and God knows there had been enough sickness on George's part, what with his weak heart and his lungs full of coal dust.

She could almost hear him now, sighing, 'Eeh, Amy lass, I'm neither use nor ornament.' Through all the pain and weakness he had apologised to her, when in truth he had been the love, light and mainstay of Amy's life. She would give both her legs to have him back – not that they were much to write home about these days.

That was what love was all about: putting somebody else first; knowing them as well as you knew yourself; loving them the same in the morning while scrubbing the pit muck from their clothes as you did at night when each warm body was comforting the other. That was love.

15

Oh, well, it was no use crying over spilled milk now. Their Betty and Clarence Hayes had made their bed and they'd have to lie on it. Amy giggled to herself at last. At least she'd done the row a favour if Kitty Ramsgate had been shamed into cleaning her doorstep. It had shown them all up for long enough, that doorstep. Amy might take her a wash leather if that had worked and tell her about her mucky windows. Potters Row was a nice, respectable place in which to live . . . Amy frowned to herself. Even with their Betty in it.

Daisy watched Norah and Pat cross the field to school. Then she saw the Dawson boys from Taylors Row and Stanley Porter, all running at the last minute. How she wished she could go with them. When she started school Daisy would never be late, she wouldn't want to miss a minute of it.

She wandered over to the sycamore tree and began to sing as she circled the old weathered trunk: '. . . the *mulberry* bush, the mulberry bush.' She hated school days when there was no one to play with. Next she skipped along the row to Mrs Firth's. Daisy loved Mrs Firth, who always had either puppies or kittens in the cupboard beside the fire. Once Mr Firth even brought a piglet from his father's farm and kept it until it was strong enough to go home. The Firths loved all living things, and Daisy loved them.

Once she had taken Baby Doll and her nightdress

and gone to live at their house. That was because of the dirty dumplings. Mam had said the dirty bits were just herbs, to add flavour, but there was no way Daisy was going to eat dirty dumplings. Dad said she could either eat them or go without dinner, and no wonder she was all skin and bone. So Daisy had gone to live with the Firths.

Mrs Firth had let her stay until teatime and then sent her home as Mam and Dad would be missing her. Mrs Firth had given her a rolled-up brandysnap to take back for tea. Leaving home hadn't done any good. Mam said if all Daisy would eat were things with no goodness in them she would have to have a tonic, so every day now she had to take a large spoonful of Virol. She thought even dirty dumplings might taste better than that horrid, brown sticky stuff.

Mrs Firth was out today and Daisy was feeling bored. She went through the gap in the dry stone wall and picked some fluffy pussy willows, then she saw some pretty yellow flowers further along the row and decided to pick some for Grandma Butler. They looked lovely with the pussy willows. Grandma asked where she had found them and cringed when Daisy showed her.

Of all the gardens on the row, Miss Appleby's was the most perfect. Each plant was set an exact distance from the next, each row colour-matched so that the flowerbed formed a tidy pattern of purple crocus and golden daffodils. Now there were spaces in the border where Daisy had plucked her flowers. Spaces that stuck out a mile.

'Oh, love,' Grandma sighed. 'Why did you have to pick them from that particular garden?'

'Because they were the best flowers,' said Daisy.

Sally smacked her daughter's leg and took her to apologise to Miss Appleby, who looked as though she might have a seizure as she surveyed the ruined border.

'Well, I don't know what our Donald will say, I'm sure.'

It was Miss Appleby's nephew who had planted the spring bulbs. Sally could have pointed out that as the woman's nephew called so rarely, the flowers would probably be dead anyway by the time he next visited. But all she said was, 'Well, at least the bulbs aren't damaged for next year.' She hurried Daisy home then, gave her a glass of milk and threatened to hold her nose if she didn't drink it. Then she took the sulking child down the Donkey Path to buy a nice bunch of flowers for Miss Appleby.

The poor woman had looked so pained that Daisy felt remorseful.

'I'm sorry,' she said when they gave her the flowers, 'but it's my mam's fault for not letting me go to school.' Then she turned an accusing eye on Sally.

Miss Appleby took one look at Daisy's indignant expression and smiled. Sally was astounded. In all the years she had known her, the woman had never been seen to do that before.

'Our Daisy's getting spoiled,' Jim informed his wife when he heard about the shenanigans.

'No, Jim, she's just bored. Ready for school, that's her trouble.'

'Well, she'll have to wait, and boredom doesn't give 'er the right to go helping 'erself to owt she fancies.' His mouth twitched. 'Especially the Appleby woman's treasured blooms.' He couldn't help grinning then. 'I'd 'ave given owt to see her face when she surveyed the damage.'

'Well, at least she smiled later, which in itself was a miracle.' Sally frowned. 'She's nobody to play with when they're all at school. Our Daisy, not Miss Appleby.'

'No, she needs a brother or sister.'

'Really?' Sally's face lit up. 'Wouldn't you mind?'

'Well, the way I see it, the way we've been carrying on it's a wonder it hasn't happened already.'

'But after our Daisy was born, you said one was enough?'

'Aye, I did, but the death of Tom's baby made me realise how precious a child can be. Besides, what if anything happened to our Daisy? I know we could never replace 'er, and it doesn't bear thinking about, but aye, I think we should 'ave another.'

'Oh, Jim, I'm so glad. And our Daisy'll be made up.'

''Ere, hold on, it 'asn't happened yet. Besides, what about old Walter? You've got your hands full enough there.'

Sally's eyes filled. 'I don't think he'll be here for much longer, Jim. He's just sleeping the whole time now.'

'I suppose it'd be a blessing if he went then. What about that niece of his? Has she been to see him yet?'

'No! Do you think I was right to let her know? My mother said I should.'

'Maybe. After all, he is ninety-nine, can't 'ave long left.'

'But she knows that, and despite the letter I sent she still hasn't bothered to get in touch.'

Sally finished ironing the pillow cases off Walter Jessops' bed and hung them over the fireguard to air. She had been looking after old Mr Jessops for ten years now; had done his shopping from being a little girl not much older than Daisy was. Sally's grandmother and Mrs Jessops had been lifelong friends, and Sally had been treated almost like a daughter by the lovely old couple, the child they had always wanted but had never conceived.

Years before, their niece Charlotte had filled that gap in their lives. Then, in their twilight years, just when they had needed her, she had deserted the old couple. Mrs Jessops, partially paralysed by a stroke, had longed for contact with her niece but her letters had been ignored. Sally had done the best she could to comfort her late grandmother's friend. A fading Mrs Jessops had begged her to look after her beloved Walter. Of course, Sally had agreed, little realising the number of years her promise would have to be kept. So for the last ten years she had cleaned, shopped and cooked for him, and brought home his washing, even putting Jim second on occasions, much to his dismay. Especially during their courtship when he had wanted Sally all to himself. Being an unselfish soul, however, and knowing her generous nature could never be changed, he had accepted that old Walter would have to be cared for as long as he survived.

'If he gets any worse, I'll send for her again,' Sally decided, referring to Charlotte.

Jim shrugged. 'Doubt if she'll take any notice,' he said. 'Besides, if he gets any worse, he'd be better off in hospital.' Though he knew deep down that Sally would carry on looking after the old man to the bitter end.

Amy Butler hobbled along the row on her morning visit to see her daughter-in-law and grand-daughter. Daisy would no doubt succeed in taking her mind off their Betty. The little girl ran to meet her and threw her arms round her grandma's legs.

'Hold on! Wi' my legs, I'm likely to topple over if you unbalance me like that.' So Daisy took her hand and carefully helped the elderly woman up the step and into the kitchen.

'The kettle's boiled, you've just come right.' Sally poured the water into the teapot and stood it on a tray.

'We've got some biscuits!' Daisy stood up on a chair and brought a biscuit barrel down from the cupboard as Amy flopped on to a kitchen chair by the table.

'You look tired,' Sally said. 'Didn't you sleep again?'

'Not a wink. Hadn't a chance wi' the row going on across the landing.'

Sally frowned. 'What was it about this time?'

'Money, or rather the lack of it. Betty wants to give up work, says she's too tired . . . more like too idle, if you ask me! I mean, it's not as if she's a heavy job. All she does is work one of those adding machines, settling the wages and things. He says she could work for at least another month. After all, she's not very big yet. I agree with Clarence, for once. It would buy a few things for the baby. Besides, they need to start getting things together for when they have their own place. Though God knows when that'll be, with a war on.'

'There's bound to be somewhere to rent some time soon,' Sally reassured her. 'She should get their names down on the council list anyway.'

Daisy thought Grandma Butler looked sad and climbed on her knee to cuddle her.

'Oh, Sally, I don't know how they'll end up! Arguments every night . . . that's if he hasn't stormed out and gone to the pub. What an atmosphere into which to bring an innocent child. And that's another thing . . . neither of 'em seems to want the baby.'

Daisy lifted her head from the comfort of her grandma's ample bosom. 'Can we have it, Mam? If Aunty Betty doesn't want it, can we have the new baby? We've still got my cot and pram.'

Amy's face brightened up; Daisy always cheered her. She nibbled at a digestive biscuit. 'We'd better be careful what we say from now on. Little pigs 'ave big ears.'

'What little pigs?' Daisy enquired.

Grandma slithered her down to the floor. 'I'd better be off, there's the washing to peg out. And that's another thing . . . all't washing and ironing. Betty never strikes a bat when she comes 'ome of a night, and 'im with a clean shirt on every day. All that standing ironing plays 'avoc wi' my legs.'

'She'll have to be told, Ma. You don't need that at your age.'

'Oh, I'm all right, apart from me legs.'

'Are they worse? The ulcers, I mean.'

'No better, lass. Well, I'd best be off.'

'Can I come?' Daisy pleaded.

'Not today,' Sally said. 'Grandma needs to rest.'

'Aye, yer can come another day,' Amy said, sighing wearily as she hobbled off along the row.

Sally vowed to have a word with Jim about their Betty. She must be told to pull her weight. Though she feared it would take more than words to get his sister to mend her ways. The rumours were right: Betty Butler always had been a flighty little piece, and Sally doubted if Betty Hayes would ever change for the better.

Sunday school wasn't nearly as exciting as day school, or so Daisy imagined, but today there was a special Easter service which was to take place in the big chapel instead of the dark, dismal lecture room. Each child had made crosses out of card and decorated them with catkins and flowers, in Daisy's case some purple primulas from the garden. The children were to present their handwork to all the parents and grandparents.

Daisy looked like an angel in her shortened pink bridesmaid's dress as she tripped down the aisle by her cousin Norah's side, carrying her crosses in a strawberry basket. She loved the big chapel with its coloured windows casting reflections on the wall, and the smell of polish, dusty old hymn books and flowers, though usually Sunday school meant boring stories and boys who pulled her hair and tipped the girls' chairs backwards.

Mam looked pretty today in her best dress and hat, standing with Aunty Enid and Grandma Denman who came to chapel regularly, following in the long tradition of the Denman family whose graves took

24

up a large section of the graveyard. Grandma Butler was also in the congregation, standing with her friends from the Sisterhood.

Daisy took a cross to Grandma Butler, who gave her a hug and a kiss. Norah gave one to Grandma Denman, who didn't hug and kiss as much as Grandma Butler, though Daisy loved her just the same.

After the crosses were handed out the rest of the service was boring, except for the hymns, and even then Daisy didn't know the words. When she went to school she would be able to read the hymn books. Today, however, Daisy was happy. For two weeks in the holidays she would have Norah and Stanley to play with. In the meantime there was Sunday tea and the evening walk to enjoy.

Usually on Sundays Aunty Enid and Uncle Bernard and their daughters Pat and Norah would accompany Daisy and her parents on a walk. Daisy's favourite was to Sheepdip Wood, where they could throw leaves into the muddy stream and watch them float away all the way to the sea or fairyland or other wonderful places. Tonight, however, they were going in the opposite direction, up past the golf club and the flat-roofed house where Daisy had always thought Jesus lived, until Mam explained that Jesus lived in Heaven with baby Celia and the angels. It was all most confusing, due to the picture given to the children at Sunday school: Jesus' house definitely looked like the one on the way to the common.

When they reached the farm Dippy had to be put on his lead until they'd left the cattle behind, and once they climbed the stile out on the moor Daisy clung to her mam's hand. She had heard Aunty Enid talking about a ghost lady who walked here, and though Daisy didn't know much about ghosts it always seemed scary when Stanley and Norah talked about them. Out on the common Jim always crouched down on the rocks to breathe in the pure Yorkshire air and drink in the view.

It was certainly worth drinking in. Fields of every shade of green were dotted here and there by grey farmsteads and bordered by dry stone walls. In the distance tall crags towered upwards, reflecting the colours of the setting sun. The whole scene was seen in reverse reflected in the long, shimmering reservoir, painted in the evening glow of gold, orange and warm, rosy purple. Even Dippy seemed content to lie down and gaze out at the scene. Only Daisy and her cousins were impatient to be off, knowing that Sunday walks always happened to lead in the direction of a country pub, and lemonade and crisps.

As the Red Dragon came into view Daisy would be hoisted up on to the shoulders of either Jim or Bernard so that they could hurry on to quench their thirsts. When they got home again, sometimes Daisy would be allowed to stay up and listen to *Community Hymn Singing* on the wireless; another treat would be the slice of bread and dripping which would always be served for supper on Sundays. Sally would scrape the black layer from the bottom of the roasting tray as this was considered the best bit. Daisy would make her slice last as long as she could; she didn't like bedtime with the scary cupboard to one side of the room and the shadows cast by the tree's branches on the wall. Tonight she would be thinking about ghosts too.

Sally said, 'When you start school there'll be no more dawdling about over supper, so make the most of it while you can.'

Usually on the day after Sunday school the kitchen walls and windows would be dripping with steam by the time Daisy came downstairs. The white clothes would be boiling in the copper and Sally would be bent over the washtub, scrubbing the coloureds on the rubbing board. The wringer would be waiting, with a bucket beneath it, and on the table would be a bowl of starch for the shirts and tablecloths and another containing dolly blue. When the coloureds were done, Jim's stained working clothes would be given a scrub and hung away beneath the tree branches out of sight.

This morning was different, though. When Daisy pattered down with Baby Doll under her arm, the table was laid for breakfast and Mam was toasting bread on the long-handled fork. On the table was a boiled egg with a face painted on it.

'That's your Easter egg.' Sally smiled.

'Can I save it?' Daisy was delighted with the red cochineal-coloured egg with its painted black eyes and hair. It would be good to keep with her collection of leaves and pebbles.

'No, you can eat it.' Mam cut the toast into soldiers and sliced off the top of the egg, causing Daisy to start whining.

'It's no use crying. Besides, we shan't go to the crags if you don't eat your breakfast.'

'What's crags?' At the mention of going somewhere Daisy had stopped crying.

'You'll know when we get there.'

'Are our Norah and Pat going?'

'Probably.'

'Can I take Dippy with me?'

'Yes, if you eat your breakfast.'

'And Baby Doll?'

'We'll see.'

Jim arrived then and Sally placed two more eggs in the pan, thinking how fortunate they were to have neighbours like the Firths whose parents sometimes had a glut of eggs and were willing to share them, especially now they had gone up in the shops to three shillings a dozen.

Jim was carrying a rabbit by its tail. He and Bernard often went rabbiting over Longfield. Bernard had recently acquired a ferret and their expedition had obviously been a successful one. Sally thought it was a cruel carry-on, but with the rationing would have been a fool to refuse the extra meat. She did, however, put her foot down at having it in the house with its skin on.

'Take it outside,' she told her husband. 'You know what happened with the last one.'

Jim did remember; he had laid a hare on the wooden drainer before realising it was alive with fleas. They had been hopping all over the sink and curtains!

'Get it out!' Sally shooed him out of the house. He grinned as he hung the rabbit off the hook supporting the washing line.

'By gum! That's a beauty, Jim,' called Tom Porter. 'Tha must've been up wi't lark this morning?'

'Aye, Tom. It's always the same after't night shift, I can never sleep so I might just as well get up.'

'Aye, it plays havoc wi' the system. Still it seems a shame not to 'ave a lie in when tha gets a day's holiday.'

'Well, tha knows what they always say . . . yer die in bed. And I don't think I'm ready for that just yet.'

'I should 'ope not!' Tom said, and made his way round to the lavatory, pulling on his flat cap as he disappeared round the corner.

Jim cursed himself then as he realised that death was a subject best avoided so soon after the passing of Tom's little daughter. He ought to apologise but wondered if that would just make things worse. He went in to breakfast, thankful for his own little girl who rushed to sit on his lap and urged him to hurry so they could go to the crags. Daisy showed him her painted egg shell. She would keep it anyway, even with the top chopped off.

Jim hugged her close as he thought back to the time she had weighed a pathetic three and a quarter pounds, just after birth. Their worry over whether she would survive or not. He knew he was over-protective of her, but to be left in Tom Porter's position must be a nightmare. He drank a pint pot full of tea and finished his toast. 'Come on then!' he said, throwing Daisy into the air and catching her as she squealed with delight. 'Let's get ready. It's Easter Monday and there'll be everybody and their grandmothers out for the day.'

Daisy found Baby Doll's bonnet and Dippy's lead. She was ready for the crags, whatever they might be.

When they came back, tired and aching from the long trek to the crags and back, Betty Hayes had made herself at home in her brother Jim's front room. She quickly turned on the tears as they came in the door. Sally's heart sank as she wondered if something had happened to her mother-in-law.

'What's up?' Jim asked. 'What's happened, our Betty?'

'I've left home, Jim. I can't stand it any longer.'

He frowned. 'Why? What can't you stand?'

'Mam . . . going on at me all the time, telling me how wicked I am for having to get married. *Now* she's on at me about the ironing and she knows how ill I feel.' Jim thought his sister's acting could have matched Vivien Leigh's any day of the week, but Sally rushed to her sister-in-law's side to comfort her.

'Oh, Betty, your mother doesn't mean it. It's just that she's not well at the moment, with her bad leg and that.'

'Hmm! And THAT ... it's THAT she's worried about! My being up the duff and what the neighbours think. Well, I don't care a bugger what the neighbours think, I love Clarence and that's all that matters.'

But Betty didn't love Clarence, and never had. Oh, she had liked the sex at first, the admiration in his eyes when she wore the pretty cami-knickers he'd bought her. And Clarence had been good in bed ... better than the others. Not any more, though. Her becoming pregnant had put them both off. As for the baby, who needed a crying, smelly brat? Certainly not Betty. She turned on the tears again. 'So I've come to stay here for a bit, just till I feel a bit better. The nurse said the sickness should go soon, then I'll be all right.'

'And what about Clarence?' Jim's expression was thunderous.

'He won't mind, he'll be just as happy here with you as at Mam's.'

'No!' her brother snapped. 'We 'aven't room, Betty.'

'But you've only got our Daisy, can't she go in with you for a while?'

Betty turned on the tears again, so convincingly that Sally said, 'It might be better, Jim. If it's upsetting your mother, I mean. We could manage, just for a while.'

Jim stormed out and set off in the direction of the Rising Sun, even though they had promised each other an early night. Besides, he didn't usually drink at all when he had to be up for the morning shift.

Sally took the kettle from where it was simmering over the fire and mashed some tea. Then she lifted Daisy from the sofa where she had fallen asleep as soon as Jim had laid her there. Sally put her back down again, uncertain where the child would be sleeping if Betty had taken up residence in the second bedroom. She swore under her breath. Where was her husband? He couldn't just turn his back on this. More importantly, where was Clarence?

Sally fetched cups and saucers from the cupboard and poured the tea. 'Sorry, we've no milk left. I used it all in the picnic flask.' Betty sniffed, pulling a face as she took a sip of black tea.

'What happened to make you leave?' Sally asked, for something to break the uncomfortable silence.

'The ironing. Me mam told me if I wanted a clean blouse for work I'd better iron one, and that I must do my own ironing from now on. So I told her I didn't want a work blouse because I wasn't going to work any more. I handed in my notice last week.'

'But why? The money would have helped – you must need loads of things for the baby, quite apart from what you'll need when you get a home of your own.'

'What, with fourteen thousand people on the housing list? Why kid ourselves? We haven't a chance.'

Sally frowned. 'Well, we don't have room for you permanently.'

'Oh, no, it's only till I feel better, and till *she* comes round.'

'*She* is your mother, Betty.'

The girl blushed. 'I know, but she's so straight-laced. I am married, for God's sake.'

'Your mam's not well, she shouldn't be standing much with an ulcerated leg. You should be helping more. Well, you'll be able to now if you've given up work. You would have found your wages handy, though, what with needing a pram and everything.'

'Oh! I thought we could have yours . . . can't we?'

'No, I'm afraid not. We're trying for another baby, and anyway my parents bought that pram, I couldn't give it away.'

'Oh, I only meant borrow it. I mean, my kid'll have done with it by the time you need it.'

'No, I'm sorry.'

Betty burst into tears again. 'Why is everybody being so mean? I can't depend on anyone any more.'

'You've got Clarence.'

At this Betty Hayes wailed louder than ever, waking Daisy who began to cry too at the sight of Aunty Betty's tears. Sally carried her upstairs and put her in the middle of her and Jim's bed.

'Can I sleep in here tonight then?' Daisy's tears disappeared as if by magic.

'Just for tonight.' Sally kissed her daughter good-night and wished Jim or Clarence or anybody would come and sort things out because she certainly didn't know what to do.

When Jim did come home he took off his jacket and went straight upstairs, swearing silently when he found his daughter in the middle of the double bed. Sally followed him but he made no attempt to discuss the problem of Betty. He undressed and got in to his own side of the bed, with his back to Daisy.

'What are we going to do?' Sally attempted.

'You've already done it. I told her she couldn't stay, you should have backed me up.'

'But I felt sorry for her, feeling ill, and I know how upset your mother's been. She can't be expected to cope with too much at her age. Not after the hard life she's had.'

'Sally, it isn't our problem. It's our Betty and Clarence's. Besides, she isn't ill – she's pregnant and bone idle. Well, she needn't think she's living the life of Riley here because she isn't! In fact, she isn't living here at all, we've no room.'

'I know. So what are we going to do?'

'We're going to get some sleep, I've to be up at five.'

Sally attempted to hold his hand but he pulled it away. 'Goodnight then,' she said.

She didn't hear Betty come up to bed and spent the rest of the night worrying while listening to Jim snoring like a pig, as he always did after a couple of pints.

'It's only me.'

Sally smiled to hear Mary Porter's voice. This had been their usual morning routine in the days before the loss of Mary's baby. Sally would sit for ten minutes chatting to her friend before beginning on the day's work. Mary's visit this morning was the first in weeks, a sure sign that she was getting back to normal.

'Oh, well, that's our Stanley organised for the day.' Stanley had gone to his grandma's. 'He doesn't know what to do with himself in the holidays.'

'I know, our Daisy can't wait to start school.'

'Where is she?'

'Still in bed.'

'That's unusual. She's usually playing out before nine.'

'She was up late, there was a bit of an upheaval.'

'Oh! Is that why Jim was at the Sun? Tom said he was downing them a bit, with the morning shift to come.'

'Yes, their Betty's left home. She's upstairs in our Daisy's bed.'

'Oh! And where's that husband of hers? Fed up of her already?'

'I'm not sure. I only know it's causing trouble between Jim and me.'

'*She'll* cause trouble for anybody, you know that. She's a wrong 'un, Sally, always has been. Tried it on with my Tom when she was no more'n fourteen.'

'I didn't know that.'

'No, because I nipped it in the bud before it got properly started. Well, I know Tom likes to flirt a bit . . . in fact, he thinks he's God's gift to women sometimes . . . but even he would never stoop to kid chasing.'

'What happened exactly?' Sally could hardly believe what she was hearing.

'It was when I was expecting our Stanley. Betty went to meet Tom outside the works, off the afternoon shift. Said she fancied older men, and would he like to go for a walk in the Donkey Wood? He told her it was time little girls like her were in bed. It happened three nights in a row! The other men were noticing by then so he came home and told me what was happening. The next night I went to meet him, casual like, after I had been to the chip shop. Betty began mouthing off at me, calling me a fat bitch, so I smacked her in the face with a parcel of cod and chips!' Mary grinned at the memory.

'Oh, Mary!' Sally couldn't help laughing. 'I didn't know about that. Why didn't you tell me?'

'It wasn't your problem, love. Just like she isn't your problem now, so send her packing.'

'Yes, she'll have to go. Anyway, we haven't room.'

'You certainly haven't, and I know one thing for sure: if your Daisy's in your bed every night, Jim'll be the one to go. He's like Tom, he needs his home comforts. Don't let her drive him to the pub, 'cos that'll be what happens.'

Daisy came running in then, Baby Doll under her arm.

'Where's your slippers? You shouldn't be on the cold lino with bare feet.'

'In my bedroom, but Aunty Betty's in there. She told me to go away because she's tired.'

Mary raised her eyebrows. 'There you are, she's taking over already.'

Sally frowned. 'I'm mashing again, do you want another cup?'

'Hmm, the cup that cheers, my mother always says, and you really need cheering this morning, my love.'

Sally smiled, but it was a forced smile. Then she realised how much better Mary seemed. That was one consolation among all the upset. Sally had her friend back at last, and just when she needed her. She made Daisy some jam sandwiches and as a special treat brought out the digestives. Mary's return was worth celebrating.

'Are we having biscuits for breakfast today?' Daisy enquired.

'Aye, just for today.' Sally grinned.

When Mary had gone, Sally dressed Daisy and took her over to grandma Butler's. Amy was sitting on the window ledge, cleaning the outside of the bedroom window.

'Don't fall, Grandma,' Daisy called worriedly.

'What on earth are you doing?' Sally called up to her. 'The window cleaner only came last week.'

'Aye, it's Charlie Firth's pigeons. Bird muck all down the winders. I couldn't leave 'em like that.'

'Get down, I'll do it for you,' Sally offered.

'Nay, lass, it's done now.'

But Sally went upstairs and carried down the bucket of water for her. Amy hobbled downstairs, left foot first all the way down.

'How's your leg today?'

'Oh, me leg's a lot better. That new salve Dr Sellars gave me seems to be drying it up a bit. It's me mind that's ailing me this morning.'

'Due to Betty, no doubt. You know she's at our house?'

'Oh, thank God for that. The way she stormed out, I didn't know what had become of her.'

'She can't stay, we haven't room.'

'And even if you 'ad, I shouldn't imagine you'd want 'er.'

Sally felt her face grow hot. She couldn't lie, she wasn't good at it. 'No, I admit we don't. I know she's Jim's sister but we really want to be on our own.'

'Of course yer do, it's only natural.' Amy turned to Daisy who was sitting patiently on the pegged rug. 'Do yer want to sort out my button box?' Daisy's eyes sparkled. Grandma's button box was Daisy's favourite thing in the whole world. She emptied the box on to the red plush tablecloth and began finding buttons that matched. Grandma broke off some lengths of cotton for Daisy to thread them on. There were mother-of-pearl buttons, tiny cloth-covered shirt buttons, glass buttons, and pretty buttons off dresses and blouses, saved for more years than Amy cared to remember. She could tell Daisy who she had danced with while wearing a blue dress adorned with tiny blue and silver buttons, and which buttons were off the green coat she had worn for her honeymoon in Southport.

There were not only buttons but hatpins, too. One had a pearl on the end, and there was a brown shiny one which Grandma said was made of amber. Then there was the silver spiral one that was Daisy's favourite. There was also a button hook and a number of shoe buttons from shoes and boots worn by Aunty Betty and Grandma, as well as some thimbles, one with a picture of Queen Mary and King George on it. Daisy was so enthralled rummaging among them that she forgot to listen to the conversation going on over her head.

'She'll 'ave to come home, what will folk think? They'll say I've turned 'er out, me own daughter. I wouldn't do that, no matter what.'

'It doesn't matter what folk think, that's not important.'

'It is to me.'

'Still, you're right, she'll have to come home. And she's got to pull her weight. She can't just sit there while you do all the work. I'll go tell her now.'

'She won't like it.'

'Then she'll just have to lump it! If it's going to cause trouble between Jim and me, she can't stay.'

'Quite right, lass. Where's that husband of hers got to?'

'I've no idea. Come on, Daisy, put the buttons back in the box.'

Daisy began to protest but Sally manhandled her into her cardigan and replaced the box on the mantelpiece.

'You can play with it another day.' Grandma kissed her grand-daughter and wished she would get some more colour into her pretty little cheeks.

Back at home Betty was still in bed. 'Right!' Sally strode purposefully up the stairs and into

Daisy's bedroom. 'Come on, Betty, time you were going home.'

'I'm not going home!' She pulled the patchwork quilt over her head. Sally pulled it down again.

'Yes, you are, your mother's worried about you.'

Betty sniffed. 'Pull the other one.'

'Well, you're still going home. This is Daisy's room.'

'I'm not feeling well.'

'No wonder. It's not good for expectant mothers to lie about. You need to exercise or you'll have a terrible time at the end.'

Betty didn't want to think about the actual birth; if she didn't think about it, it might go away.

'Come on, get your things together. I'll make you some toast.'

'You don't know what it's like, living with my mother.' Betty told Sally as she ate the toast. 'Nothing I do is ever right.'

'Then you'll just have to try harder, she's a lovely mother really. You should be proud of the way she stood up for you against Kitty Ramsgate.'

Betty didn't know about that. 'My mother stuck up for me? When?'

'One day last week, on Kitty Ramsgate's mucky doorstep, with all the row listening.'

'Really? That must have taken some doing, my mam having a set to with everybody listening.'

'Yes, it must, but she did.'

Betty remained silent as she absorbed the latest

news. Then she went upstairs and fetched the bag containing her things. 'Right then, I suppose I'd better go. Clarence should have come home by now.'

'Where will he have been?'

Betty shrugged. 'Oh, working on something or other. He doesn't tell me what he gets up to. I know he works at the pit, it's his spare time that's a mystery to me.'

'Perhaps you should talk to each other more, that's if you want your marriage to work. You do, don't you?'

Betty didn't look bothered one way or the other. 'I suppose so. Thanks anyway. Sorry I put you out last night.'

'That's okay. We really don't have room, Betty. Besides, your mother could do with a bit of help just now. Her leg's quite bad, you know.'

'All right, I'll do my share, I promise. It's just that I hate bloody ironing.'

'So do I,' Sally told her. 'It's one of the prices we pay for being a woman.'

Betty waved as she went back home. It had shaken her to know her mam had had a go at Kitty Ramsgate on her behalf. She thought back to all the other times Mam had been there for her when she was small. Oh, well, maybe she wasn't such a bad old stick after all, even if she couldn't forgive her daughter for marrying in a veil and virginal white. Betty would help out with the housework more and give her a rest. After all, she would need to know how if they ever managed to find a house of their own. Besides, she didn't want to fall out with her mam, not when they would need a baby-sitter come July or August.

Chapter Two

Sally's parents lived down a lane overlooking the Bar Mill. It was a pretty little house in the wrong setting. Joe Denman had an allotment with a fast-flowing stream on one side and the chapel on the other. The trouble was the noise from the mill and the locomotives, which were working day and night.

Daisy liked Tuesdays, when they always went to Grandma and Grand-dad Denman's for tea. If Grand-dad was on the right shift he would cook bloaters over the fire on the brass toasting fork. Grandma would nag at him not to let the oil from the fish drip on to her black shiny fireplace or the brass fender, but Grand-dad never seemed to take any notice. When the bloaters were cooked he would open them and remove the long bones from the middle. In Daisy's case he would take out all the tiny bones too, so that she could eat the fish without anybody worrying.

Daisy would sit and watch Grand-dad, and stare into the fire which would flare up as the oil dripped into the flames. Sometimes she saw pictures in the fire, like figures dancing and laughing faces. After they had eaten the fish and Grandma's home-made bread there would sometimes be stewed rhubarb from the allotment and nice creamy Bird's custard.

Grand-dad Denman had a piano, a walnut one with candlesticks set on the front. He was teaching Daisy to play scales and had promised her that as soon as she could read, he would teach her to play real tunes. Just as he had Sally, except that she had never really been interested in learning to play. He was also teaching his grand-daughter to read and write her own name.

After tea Grand-dad would take Daisy to the bottom of the lane and lift her on to the high wall which separated the houses from the works. She loved to watch the locomotives transporting metal from one place to the other and listen to the gossip between Grand-dad and some of his neighbours who would join them. They would talk about the pit where most of them worked, or the war some of their sons were fighting. At eight o'clock he would take Daisy back to Grandma's and go with the other men to the works club for a pint or two to 'slaken the dust' – well, that was the excuse they made. It was also Daisy's bedtime. Today Grandma Denman had taught Daisy how to do French knitting. She had knocked four tiny nails into an empty bobbin and threaded pink wool around them. She showed Daisy how to make stitches with a pin so that a long trail of knitting came down the hole in the bobbin. Daisy was fascinated. Grandma Denman always thought of some different way to entertain her grand-daughter. No wonder Daisy loved Tuesdays.

Every day Sally would visit old Mr Jessops and take him a drop of soup or something, even though he could eat nothing any more. She kept his house and bed clean and tended the sores on his back. Mr Jessops lived on Taylors Row and had bought the house when it was built in the 1880s. It was a good house, built of the same local stone as the school at Longfield. Because there was a tunnel-like entrance leading to the back of the row, Mr Jessops' house had an extra bedroom above this. The Dawsons, who lived next-door, were also fortunate enough to have an extra room. In the third house lived Emily Simms. Mrs Simms was spending a lot of time at present sitting with Mr Jessops, but it was Sally he looked for on the rare occasions when he opened his eyes.

Today she had had to do the washing. It was usually considered a sin not to wash on a Monday but the Easter visit to the crags had played havoc with this week's routine. Now, with her washing wafting on the line in the spring sunshine, she was ready to visit the dying man.

Mary Porter was sweeping her flags. 'Are you going to see old Walt?' she enquired.

'Yes, I'm late today,' Sally answered.

'Why don't you leave Daisy here? I'm sure it's not healthy for her to see him lying there so ill.'

'Oh, you're an angel, Mary.'

'Any time. Besides they're playing nicely together, her and our Stanley. He'll only start pestering me if he's on his own.'

'Thanks anyway.'

Sally hurried off across the field. Poor old Walter wouldn't have known if she had been a day late or not even turned up at all. She bent and stroked the wispy hair from his cold, pallid forehead. Emily Simms came and stood beside her.

'How's he been, Mrs Simms?' Sally enquired.

'Not worth a row of pins, if you ask me.'

'Well, you can go now. I don't know what would happen to him without your kindness.'

'Nay, lass, I haven't done much. The nurse came and brought him some more dressings and ointment, but I couldn't get 'im to eat owt. I couldn't even get a drop of water down 'im.'

'I'll have a go, see if he'll take anything.'

'It'd be cruel, if you ask me, just prolonging things.'

'Yes, maybe you're right. I'll just sponge his lips then.'

'I'll go and 'ave a bit to eat and be back at teatime so you can get off.' Emily Simms frowned. 'I don't think he should be left on his own at this stage.'

'No, I've been thinking . . . I'm going to stay the night.'

'What about your little lass?'

'Our Enid will take care of her. She can go in with our Pat and Norah.'

'Won't yer 'ubby mind?'

'Who, Jim? Oh, he might moan a bit, but he knows how much Mr Jessops means to me.' Sally was suddenly overcome with emotion and began to sob.

Emily wrapped her in her arms and cuddled her. 'Now then, you're bound to be upset but 'e's 'ad a good innings and I don't think 'e's aware of any pain. You've done more than anyone could 'ave been expected to do. Come on, love, 'e wouldn't like to think you were upset because of 'im.'

Sally smiled, a weak watery smile. 'Go on, go and have something to eat, you must be famished.'

'Aye, I am a bit peckish. I'll be back about four. I'll bring me embroidery so yer needn't come back till bedtime. You've got a family to consider, I've nobody but meself.'

Sally went to see the kind old woman out, then she went to find a bucket and cloth and set about cleaning the windows. She looked out at the garden, which at one time would have been a mass of colour. Clara Jessops had tended it lovingly over the years. Now it was neglected, although Jim had kept the grass down. He was good like that.

She could see down the valley from this side, down the Donkey Wood and beyond to the tops of the smoking chimneys of the works. It was a well-built house and must be worth quite a bit now, even though it was in need of decorating. It must be ten years since Mrs Jessops had died and very little had been done since then. Nevertheless Sally had kept the place immaculate, just as Mrs Jessops had before the stroke had taken the use from her legs and almost paralysed her. Her death had been a merciful release, as would Walter's, she supposed.

Only last year Sally had told him they would have a party when he reached his century. Now, if there was any organising to be done, it would be for his funeral. Sally felt his niece should have been thinking about arrangements, but she had never replied to Sally's letter asking her to visit the sick man.

Sally went to check on him, glad that his bed had been brought downstairs. That had been Jim's idea, too, he and Bernard had moved it one Sunday afternoon. He really was a good man, her husband. The only time Jim grumbled was when Sally insisted on doing everything for everyone. Sometimes he thought other people were more important to her than he was. She frowned. He wouldn't like it tonight when she told him she was staying here.

Mary popped in while Sally was making a pie for tea.

'It's only me, can I come in?'

'Looks like you're already in.' But Sally grinned to see Mary back to her normal cheerful self.

'Want to go to the pictures?' Mary asked.

'Sorry, I can't, I'm going to stay with Mr Jessops.'

Jim came in then and hung up his coat. 'Perhaps another time,' Sally said.

'Oh, well, it was just a thought.' Mary looked disappointed, though. 'It's just that it's so long since we went anywhere, that's all. Is he worse, Mr Jessops?'

'Yes. I doubt if he'll see the morning.'

'Oh, dear. Well, I'll see you later then. Perhaps another time . . . the pictures, I mean.'

Sally would have loved to go to the cinema, especially as it was the first time Mary had suggested it since Celia had died.

Jim put in looking rather glum, 'What was that about staying with old Walter?'

'Oh, Jim, I have to. Mrs Simms thinks he could go at any time. She can't stay up all night at her age.'

'I know that, Sally, but *you* can't be staying up all night either. What about our Daisy?'

'She'll be all right with our Enid.'

'I know, but that's not the point. Besides, I want you here with me. You can't be looking after the old man and our Daisy all day, and staying up all night. I'm thinking about your health, Sally. I know yer think a lot of him – I do too, he's a lovely old thing – but he isn't yer father. He should be in hospital.'

'It won't be for long. He can't live without some form of nourishment. Besides, I promised Mrs Jessops, and I can't break a promise to a dying woman.'

'It wasn't a promise, it was a bloody life sentence! You weren't to know he would live to be ninety-nine. All those years you've been fetching and carrying, even at weekends.'

'I didn't mind, Jim. He appreciated everything I did, and making him a bit of dinner at weekends wasn't any hardship.'

'I didn't mind that. I didn't mind you bringing his washing home. I didn't even mind fetching him across to spend Christmas with us . . . but I do object to you staying up all night!'

'It won't be for long, and it's a lot easier now you've brought his bed downstairs.'

'Okay, I know I'm wasting me breath. I don't expect you'll ever change. I don't suppose I'd even want you to. I just wish you'd put us lot first for a change. What with our Betty coming waltzing in uninvited, I sometimes think we live in a house with an ever open door. Still, I don't suppose I'd 'ave fallen for yer if you'd been any different.'

Sally felt the tension slip away from her. 'Sorry I can't change.' She pulled a face at him.

'Hmm, I am too.' But he grinned as he spoke.

'What time are yer off then?' Jim asked a few hours later.

'I ought to go now and let Mrs Simms go home.'

'Come on then, I'll walk over with yer.'

'Thanks, Jim. Though I'll bet that's an excuse to set off to the Sun.' Sally attempted a smile as she put on her coat and picked up her *Red Letter* magazine. 'Oh, and Jim?'

'What now?'

'Don't think I shan't miss you 'cos I shall.' She reached up and kissed him.

'Come on, or are yer trying to make me change me mind?'

Mrs Simms rolled up her embroidery and gathered up her silk threads as she heard Sally coming through the entry.

'How is he?'

'Not on this earth, if you ask me. I thought he'd gone once and then all of a sudden 'e sat bolt upright, nearly gave me a heart attack! Told me to switch off the light . . . and 'im blind as a bat for all these years.'

'Goodness, I didn't think he had the strength to move, let alone sit up.'

'Oh, he's on his way, love. The light always comes to show 'em the way. It 'appened to my Albert just the same. You mark my words, 'e'll be gone by morning. If I were you, I'd open that winder. Yer don't want 'is soul trapping in 'ere. Somebody else'll want to live in this 'ouse once 'e's gone.'

Sally almost smiled, but the look on Emily's face told her she was deadly serious so instead Sally said, 'Yes, well, seeing as it's not a very warm night, I think I'll leave the window closed. Besides, I don't think a stone wall'll prevent his spirit leaving if it's a mind to.'

Sally wished Emily hadn't started on about ghosts and things, though, not when Sally was to spend the night with a dying man. Emily, however, believed in all things of a psychic nature and swore her late husband had been in contact with her on a number of occasions, through a medium at a spiritualist church she sometimes attended.

'Aye, well, if yer'll be all right, I'll be off to me bed then.' And think on – if yer need me, come and knock me up.'

'I'll remember, and thanks for staying with him.'

'You're welcome. Like I said, he'll be gone by morning.'

Sally sighed as she slipped on the bolt. It was going to be a long night. She boiled some water and bathed the old man's face, then she made some tea and settled in a chair to read her magazine. The words were leaving no impression on her, despite her reading them over again. She put down her reading matter and closed her eyes, her mind flitting from the organising which would soon need to be done to the fact that Mr Jessops' only relative couldn't be bothered to visit him and hadn't even answered Sally's letter. Well, at least *her* conscience was clear.

She saw the covers on the bed moving then as his cold, claw-shaped fingers clutched them. Sally reached his side just as he whispered her name.

'Sally?'

'Yes, it's me.'

53

'Sally, lass, my will . . . everything yours, Dunstone and Sedgewick.'

'Shush, you'll wear yourself out.'

'No, listen. Don't let that niece of mine 'ave owt.'

'She's entitled, she's the only family you've got.'

'I've told yer, she got everything she could out of us then never came near.' Walter's voice seemed stronger now. 'How long is it since she came?'

'According to Mrs Simms, it must be twenty years. Even so . . .'

Suddenly a rattling noise began in Mr Jessops' throat but still he struggled to speak.

'Nothing . . . Charlotte Scott gets nothing.'

Sally held his hand as he took his final breath. Walter Jessops had spoken his last words.

She sat for a while, stroking the fine, white hair from his forehead. A tear dripped on to the blue satin elderdown and still she waited, wondering what to do, unwilling to let this gentle old man, who had been like a second father to her, go. Then the realisation that he had already departed from this life seemed to hit her for the first time and Sally laid her head on his chest and sobbed.

She was stripping the bed the next morning when Emily Simms arrived. 'Why didn't yer fetch me, yer silly lass?'

'There was no point in waking you. Mr Baraclough let me use his phone . . . the shop was just opening anyway for the men going on the morning shift. Dr Sellars came as soon as I called, there was nothing for you to do.'

'Well, how are yer feeling? In shock, I expect. It's always the same. You're waiting for it to happen, and then when it does it hits you just as hard. Did yer get any sleep?'

'Not really. I got home about quarter to six, just as Jim was setting off for work. I'm okay, but I'm going to miss him. The Jessops sort of adopted me when I was a little girl – I suppose it was with them being childless.'

'And no wonder they took to you. I don't know what they'd 'ave done without yer when that poor woman lost the use of her legs. All the same, Clara shouldn't 'ave expected yer to see to him for all those years.'

'It was a pleasure, Walter appreciated everything I did.' Sally bundled up the bedding, then she picked up a vase from the window ledge and stroked the cream, rose-patterned porcelain lovingly.

'Almost a hundred years of memories in these ornaments,' she sighed, 'and what's to become of them now?' She replaced the vase and picked up a copper kettle from the hearth. 'And those brasses, they were Mrs Jessops' pride. She used to Brasso them every Wednesday.'

Emily sniffed as she placed a cup of tea in front of Sally.

'I expect that greedy bitch Charlotte'll not wait

long to get her hands on everything, especially the pictures. Do yer know, she even had the cheek to bring a valuer in once to see how much they were worth? Her uncle soon showed him the door. She'll 'ave everything sold off in no time, just you see.' Emily took a sip of tea. 'Still, I blame them really, they allus spoiled her rotten. Do yer know, they even put her through art college, and what a waste of money *that* was!'

'Art college? I didn't know about that.'

'Well, she told 'em she wanted to be a dress designer. Oh, aye, full of big ideas Charlotte was. Supposed to be artistic. Well, she ended up traipsing about 'aving her picture taken in all the big shops such as Cole Brothers. A model, that's what she called 'erself. Oh, I'm not saying she wasn't beautiful enough, but so vain with it! Happy as a pig in muck when she was parading about all dolled up.' Emily lowered her voice. 'Especially in front of young men. The rumour was that she took 'er clothes off for 'em to paint pictures of 'er. She was no more a dress designer than I am.'

Sally couldn't help smiling at Emily's indignant expression.

'By the looks of your embroidery, I bet you'd make a marvellous dress designer.' Then she frowned. 'They never mentioned paying for college for her.'

'Well, they wouldn't. Bought her a gold watch – second-hand, I admit – but still. Paid for holidays too. And just look how she repaid them. Neglected them completely in their old age. Have yer let 'er know 'e's gone?'

'Yes, and what a performance that was. The number I had was for Brady Scott, Charlotte's husband. Well, the man who answered wasn't Brady Scott but her *new* husband. She's divorced and married again apparently. Well, I apologised for ringing so early and he fetched Charlotte.'

'And I bet the first thing she asked was how much had Walter left?'

'Not quite, but she didn't sound very upset. I asked her about making arrangements and told her he wanted the Co-op. She just slammed down the phone. Probably thought it was nothing to do with me. Well, I couldn't just leave him lying there so I contacted them myself. I did give her the name of the solicitor he mentioned, so what she does now is no concern of mine.'

'Except that if you called the Co-op, you'll be lumbered with the bill.'

Sally was horrified. 'Oh, Mrs Simms, how much will it be?' She wondered what Jim would say.

'Well, when I buried my husband it cost twenty pounds but that was six years ago. I dare say it will have gone up quite a bit since then.'

'So much?'

'There's the coffin, the grave opening, bearers and the gloves for them to wear. Then there's the funeral cards and flowers.' Emily was on her favourite subject. 'It soon mounts up. No doubt there'll be some insurance money, though.'

'Oh, I do hope so.' Sally could control her emotions no longer. What with being up all night and the uncertainty over what to do, she suddenly began to panic. Emily recognised the symptoms of delayed shock and brought out the bottle of brandy, kept for emergencies. 'Here, get some of this down yer, then we're going to lock up and go home. You've a dinner to cook for that husband of yours, and your little lass'll be wanting her mam.'

'Yes, you're right.' Sally was still trembling. 'But I ought to ring the solicitor Walter mentioned. The trouble is, Charlotte's the next-of-kin and might take offence if I interfere.'

'Interfere? He'd still be laid 'ere in his blooming bed if yer hadn't! You're right, though. He can't stop in the chapel of rest for ever. Somebody'll 'ave to arrange his funeral.'

'Oh, Mrs Simms, what if he was just rambling on and he hasn't made a will at all?'

'Oh, he has, love. I remember I was witness to it, soon after Mrs Jessops died. Not that I know what was in it, I never was one to pry.'

'Goodness. And I thought it was just talk. Do you know what else he said? He said Charlotte Scott was to get nothing.'

'Eeh!' Emily had a huge grin on her face. 'That'll be an eye opener for her. There'll be ructions when she finds out . . . a right nasty piece of work, that one.'

'I've never met her,' Sally said, nervously.

'Well, you won't 'ave. As soon as they had to tighten the purse strings, you couldn't see her for dust. Never set foot in the door again. Mind you, that should 'ave been a relief. My Albert wasn't far wrong when 'e said Charlotte 'ad a few slates missing.'

'She couldn't have been that daft, if she knew how to get everything out of them.'

Emily gathered up the tea cups. 'No! But the way she carried on . . . stamping her foot, paddying . . . I felt so sorry when I heard she'd married young Brady Scott, and him such a talented young man. Trouble was, with her being so beautiful and 'im being an artist, 'e must 'ave found it difficult to resist her.'

'I've seen photographs of her. They must have doted on her once, they had an albumful.'

'Aye, well, I imagine she'll be past her best. She must be in her fifties by now.'

Sally went towards a picture hanging in the alcove. 'Are these the ones she had valued?'

'Goodness me, no, they're just prints. Not that I know much about such things. The ones of value are the watercolours on the landing, in the gilt frames.'

'Oh! Well, I much prefer these.' The two prints Sally found so fascinating each portrayed a pretty girl in twenties-style clothing with a dog at her heels. At the bottom of each picture were the names,

Blanche and Joyce. 'The girls are pretty but it's the dogs I love,' Sally said. 'I don't know much about art but I reckon the artist must have been extremely talented. Mr Jessops told me the originals were watercolours. I'd have loved to have seen them.'

'Can't say I'm keen on 'em meself.' Mrs Simms thought there was something a bit weird about the way the eyes of the dogs seemed to follow you round the room. 'Shouldn't want 'em on my wall.'

'Well, I love them, even if they aren't worth much.'

Mrs Simms sighed. 'I remember Charlotte had her eye on the vases, too. Austrian Crown porcelain, they are.'

'Goodness!' Sally gasped. 'Then there's the jewellery . . . let's have a look at it.'

'Don't tell me it's still 'ere?' Emily's mouth gaped open. 'The times 'e's told yer to take it 'ome for safe-keeping.'

Sally went to the old chair in the corner. 'I couldn't,' she said. 'It wasn't mine to take.' She lifted the cushion from the chair bottom and felt inside the upholstery underneath, foraging about and bringing out a small leather box. Emily came and sat beside her as she opened it.

'Just look,' Sally whispered. 'These rings must be worth a fortune, especially the engagement ring. Seventy years old at least. And the gold chains . . . feel the weight of them.' She handed the chains to Emily. 'How much do you think they're worth?'

'I've no idea, but with those half-sovereigns . . . I remember Clara once saying that because they were Australian they were more valuable.'

'Goodness!' Sally said as she replaced the jewellery in its hiding place. 'Mrs Simms . . .'

'Yes, love?'

'Mr Jessops said everything was to be mine. I expect he was delirious.'

'Eeh, lass, I 'ope it is. There's nobody more deserving of it.' She glanced round the room. 'Eeh, and all this lovely furniture. Well, I know most of it is past its best but other pieces, like the bedroom suite, now that's lovely. I've never seen one as nice in all me born days.'

'Do you really like it?'

'Oh, I can see it now after Clara had polished it. It used to shine like glass.'

Sally frowned. 'I suppose I ought to have polished it more often. Anyway, if it is mine, you shall have it.'

'Eeh, no, I wasn't hinting at that.'

'I know, but Mr Jessops would have liked you to have it.'

'Well! I don't know what to say.'

'No good saying anything; they're probably Charlotte's anyway. So what shall I do? Go to the solicitor or leave it to her?'

'Go and see 'em, I would.'

'It seems a bit mercenary, so soon, but someone will have to arrange things.'

Emily fetched Sally's coat. 'Come on, yer going 'ome now. I'm surprised that man of yours 'asn't found 'imself another bedmate, the way you carry on.'

Emily's attempt to take Sally's mind off things seemed to work. 'Come on then, I'll go to the solicitor's later.'

'And I'll see yer tomorrer, unless that spoiled bitch has decided to take charge.'

Emily picked up the almost-full brandy bottle. 'Here, take this home. It'll warm you up on cold winter nights. Mind you, you've already got Jim. We could all do with a nice handsome lover to put us cold feet on!'

Sally laughed. 'Well, you can't have mine.'

They locked up carefully; they wouldn't like anything to happen to old Walter's belongings. Sally carried the bundle of bedding. Nobody would want it after it had been on a dying man's bed. Although, if she washed and ironed the sheets, they could come in handy for Betty . . . They were all good quality stuff. She smiled to herself. On second thoughts, she would leave the ironing of them to Betty – she knew how much her sister-in-law enjoyed that.

Amy Butler had to admit Betty was making an effort. She'd decided to learn how to cook and was in the process of mixing a batter for Yorkshire puddings. She emptied flour into the mixing bowl and added the egg and milk and water. Daisy was standing on a stool, watching her critically, Amy hovering nearby waiting.

'Oh, Aunty Betty, you won't be able to get the lumps out now.'

'Of course I shall, I haven't mixed it yet.'

'Yes, but you've put all the water in at once.'

Betty began to beat as vigorously as laziness would allow. The flour had congealed into hard lumps which wouldn't dissolve, no matter how she tried.

'You should mix the egg in first until it goes smooth. Then the milk and water, a little bit at a time. It won't work now.'

Betty felt her face growing hot. She could have slapped Daisy. It wasn't fair, a four-year-old telling her how to cook!

Amy listened to what was happening and felt proud that her grand-daughter had obviously helped her mother to cook Sunday dinner. She also felt ashamed that she had never taken time to do that with her own daughter while she was Daisy's age. But then, she had had other things occupying her mind. She wondered how she could salvage her daughter's pride, knowing just like Daisy did that no amount of mixing would remove the lumps from the batter at this stage.

'Betty,' she called, 'I forgot to tell yer not to use the flour out of the old bag. Oh, well, it's my fault, I should 'ave told yer. You'll just 'ave to throw it away and start again. A shame to waste it but there it is.'

Betty didn't need telling twice. She was out of the door and pouring the batter down the drain before her mother noticed the lumps. She began again, under Daisy's instruction. The batter turned golden-coloured and smooth as silk.

'What was the matter with the old flour?' Daisy asked.

'Oh, it might 'ave been my imagination but I thought it looked as though a mouse had been at it.' Amy smiled to herself. If the lass was willing to learn it was up to her to encourage, not embarrass. A good thing Daisy had been here, though, otherwise Betty would have been beating till kingdom come.

Daisy liked sleeping at Aunty Enid's, even though Pat and Norah talked about scary ghosts and told her a story about a wicked witch who locked children in a cage. She wasn't scared when she was in bed with Norah. Besides, there was no tree outside the window to send scary shadows swaying on the wall, or cupboard where Daisy imagined all the monsters in Millington lived. Last night they had played dressing up, with curtains and nightgowns and Aunty Enid's high-heeled shoes. They had used the paper flowers as a bouquet and Pat had pushed Baby Doll down her knickers and pretended to be Betty Butler getting married.

'Why is Baby Doll making your tummy fat?' Daisy didn't like Baby Doll being hidden away like that.

'Because your Aunty Betty's having a baby!' Norah said. 'She doesn't know where babies come from,' she giggled then.

'I do! They come in the nurse's black bag. Baby Celia did.'

The two elder girls rolled about laughing at this.

'Babies grow in your stomach, from a teeny-weeny seed.'

Daisy didn't know if Pat was teasing her or not. 'Well, who planted the seed in Betty then?'

Pat smiled knowingly but Norah looked uncertain.

'You'll find out when you're bigger,' her older cousin said.

'But where *did* the seed come from?' asked Norah.

'I've told you, you'll find out sooner or later.'

Daisy didn't mind not knowing so long as Norah didn't know either.

'Can I have Baby Doll back now?' she said. 'I'm going to sleep.'

Before she dropped off she told her cousins sleepily, 'I expect Aunty Betty ate the seed by mistake, that must be why she doesn't want the baby.'

Charlotte Kaye paced the living-room, impatient for her husband to come home. Her new husband was becoming as unreliable as her first. At least with Brady Scott she'd known where he was; the studio had been his second home. Charlotte smirked. By the time she'd dragged him through the divorce courts, it had become his *only* home. She glanced around her. Oh, yes, she'd landed on her feet here all right, and it had been so easy. All she'd had to do was put a few bruises about her body, turn on the tears – and lie through her eye teeth. Poor Brady, who wouldn't hurt a fly, had been devastated and almost ruined. And all the time she had been carrying on with Mark! Of course, divorces still took a long time to finalise, but Brady's money had hurried things along nicely, and now she was married for the second time.

Mark was more exciting than poor, boring Brady, whose only interest had been painting. The trouble was, Mark hadn't the talent for making money that Brady had had. That was why she needed Uncle Walter's inheritance. She had depended upon it, relied on it being there as soon as he had gone. And now that Butler woman had fallen for the lot!

Where was her husband? He was too handsome, that was the trouble, not to be trusted. She went to the mirror over the fire. The lines on her face stood out in the electric light. There was a lot to be said for gas light, it was kinder. A few years ago it had only been daylight in which those lines could be detected. Charlotte was ageing. Would her husband still want her when her looks were gone? After all, she was forty-seven, and he was twelve years her junior. Where the hell *was* he?

She heard his key in the door and Mark came in, grinning and rubbing his hands, smelling of alcohol. 'What's for dinner?'

Charlotte picked up a Capo di Monte figurine off the display cabinet and threw it at the wall. 'Dinner? Get your own bloody dinner.' Her voice rose to a screech. 'The bastard . . . the spiteful old bastard!'

'Who? What are you ranting on about?'

'Uncle Walter. He's died at last, after ninety-nine bloody years. I've waited and waited, and then he's gone and left it to *that woman*. Not even a relative, and he's left her the lot.'

Mark sank lazily into the deep leather sofa. 'I thought you said there was no money left?'

'I'm not on about the money, that was the least of it. The house, that's what I'm on about. Then there's all the stuff in it. Some of the things in that place are worth a small fortune. Aunt Clara's jewellery alone . . . then there are a couple of paintings, books – some of them first editions, more than a hundred years old – and the porcelain vases and clocks, one with masonic symbols. I tell you, they're worth a fortune.'

'You could contest the will.'

'No good, I've already tried. The old fool's definitely stated that I'm to get nothing.'

Mark laughed. 'Well! Could you blame him?'

'I'll tell you this for nothing, *she's* not getting away with it.'

'What do you intend doing?'

'I don't know yet, but I'll think of something.' Charlotte went to the cocktail cabinet and fixed herself a gin and tonic. She never even considered making one for her handsome young husband. Charlotte Kaye never thought of anyone except herself.

Sally was washed, changed and had dinner prepared when Jim came home.

'How are you?' he enquired as he took off his jacket.

'Okay,' she said. 'Apart from the shock.'

'Well, you're bound to be shocked, even though it was expected.'

'Well, yes ... it was a shock when Walter died, but I've had an even bigger one since. I'm the sole beneficiary in his will.'

'What?'

'He actually rallied enough to tell me himself, but I thought he was just hallucinating. Then I went to see the solicitor and he told me everything's mine! I mean, there's not a lot of money, but there are some lovely old things which are worth quite a bit.

'Mind you, I'm expecting Walter's niece to put up a fight. In fact, I couldn't blame her if she did. Everything should be hers by rights. I told the solicitor that and he said it's not possible to go against

Walter's wishes. It seems he actually insisted she was to inherit nothing.'

'Good Lord! Well, you certainly deserve anything you get.' Jim picked up his knife and fork and put them down again. 'Oh, Sally, I feel so guilty now for grumbling about yer looking after him.'

'Well, you've no need, you did enough for him too. No, Jim, it's me who should feel guilty, for neglecting you like I did.'

She started to cry then and Jim jumped up, knocking over a chair as he reached out to hold her. 'Oh, come on, love, it's over now. Walter's out of his misery, the poor old thing. Look, once we get the funeral over we'll go away for a few days. Well, it'll 'ave to be just for the weekend, but still, it'll be a change.'

Sally wiped her eyes on her sleeve. 'We'll see. Come on, the dinner's going cold.'

Jim started on his rabbit stew but Sally sat staring at her plate. 'What's up?' He looked worried. 'Come on, love, you'll 'ave to eat summat. Where's Daisy?'

'At our Enid's. Jim, do you realise what this means? How much is involved?'

'Well, we won't know exactly until we clear the house, but what does it matter?' He suddenly thought he understood. 'Do yer mean, it's going to cost us, for the funeral? Oh, Sally, you do realise you might have to part with some of the old man's things to pay for it? I don't know if our savings'll run to all of it.'

69

'No, the insurance should cover that. What I mean is, everything has been left to us – and that includes the house.'

'What?' Jim's fork hung in mid-air, a piece of rabbit leg still attached to it.

'He owned the house, and now it's ours.'

'But I thought . . . well, I didn't really think about it at all. I just surmised it was rented, like ours.'

'Well, it wasn't. Walter had owned it for fifty-three years, ever since it was built. He wanted something to pass down to his children, Mr Dunstone told me.'

It was suddenly all too much for Sally. She could hardly continue speaking for the lump in her throat. 'The children they wanted so much and never had.' She did her best not to cry.

Jim put down his cutlery and came towards her. 'Please don't, Sally. I can't bear it when yer cry.' He held her close, rocking her like a baby. 'Come on, love, look at it this way. They obviously looked upon yer as the daughter they'd wanted so much. You certainly looked after them like a daughter would, so what is there to cry about? Oh, but Sally, are yer certain about the house? It isn't all a mistake?'

'No, it's ours, Jim. According to Mr Dunstone nothing can change that. Though Charlotte what's-her-name will no doubt try.'

Her husband's face brightened. 'Let her try her damnedest! If it's our house, nobody's going to take it away from us.' He looked at Sally then. 'Sorry, love, it's yours, not ours. What are yer going to do with it? You could always sell it and be a woman of means? Put it in the bank for a rainy day.'

'No, Jim, what's mine is yours, and always will be. We're going to live in it! Just think, no more rent to pay *and* an extra bedroom in case we have a son. Oh, Jim, I do feel so guilty about being excited when Walter is barely cold . . . Let's eat our dinner, and then there's the house to clear.' She began to laugh. 'What am I on about? We've no need to clear anything, it's all ours, and Mrs Simms and I have actually started packing things up. Even so, there's still a funeral to arrange . . .'

It was a beautiful funeral – according to Emily Simms who was a connoisseur, having attended every one taking place in Millington for years, regardless of whether she knew the poor departed soul or not. There were no more than a couple of dozen mourners in the church, which was all Sally had expected seeing, as Walter Jessops' friends and workmates had passed on years ago. Nevertheless, there were representatives present from most houses in the rows, and Mr Baraclough had even closed the shop for an hour so that he and his wife could pay their respects.

Sally noticed a stranger standing at the back of the church and would have invited him back for refreshments had he not hurried away. Afterwards

Mrs Simms told her it was Brady Scott. 'Fancy him turning up, and her not having the decency to attend her own uncle's funeral. Mind you, he always was a gentleman. Too good for the likes of Charlotte, even if he was one of them theer artists.'

'Well, with her not being left anything, she must be absolutely devastated.'

'Devastated? She'll be more than devastated.'

'I hope she doesn't cause any trouble. After all, she had a right to expect more, as his only relative.'

'Then she should 'ave acted more like a relative.'

By seven o'clock everybody had left for home except Mary and Tom. It was the first funeral they had attended since their daughter's, and even though it must have been an ordeal for them, they were doing their best to cheer up Sally and tuck into the leftovers.

'That's it, eat as much as yer can,' Jim begged them. 'Otherwise I shall be taking dry sandwiches to work for the next three or four days.'

Sally was glad of Mary and Tom's company, too, and very relieved that the sad occasion was over.

Charlotte Kaye was too busy scheming to attend the funeral, even if she'd wanted to. The van was hired and Mark had been ordered to collect it after work. He wasn't at all pleased with her plan but knew better than to refuse to indulge his volatile new wife. Sometimes he wondered what he had ever seen in Charlotte. She was definitely a beauty – well, had been. Still was when she was all done up. It was at times like these, though, that he saw beneath the surface. Her mood swings could be frightening. Then she would forget to apply the Pond's cream and powder to her face and the crêpey skin would be visible. He had to admit the stronger attraction he'd felt hadn't been to Charlotte anyway, he had needed a home. And some home it was too. All paid for by Brady Scott's remarkable talent.

The fine house had come at a price, though. Charlotte Scott needed a man, and not just any man – one she could flaunt to her so-called friends. A young man, a good-looking man, a stud. So they had both got what they wanted, and now he was paying. Charlotte was a strange woman; sometimes he thought her unhinged. The best thing to do would be to fall in with her plans. He'd learned by now it was the only way to keep the peace.

Jim had written to his Aunt Jane and Uncle Jack, announcing they'd be coming for a visit at the weekend. They didn't need an invitation, the elderly couple were always delighted to see them, and Daisy loved the time spent with her great-aunt and uncle. Their little cottage at Springvale was just a short walk from the river and in summer it was great for picnics and paddling. Daisy would help Jack to feed the chickens and spoil the many cats who were in and out all day, regardless of whether they belonged there or not.

Sally loved Aunt Jane, and when Jim and his uncle were not slaking the dust at the Britannia close by with a pint or three, they would bring out the huge compendium of games and keep Daisy occupied with Snakes and Ladders, Ludo and Happy Families. Uncle Jack was also a big fan of *ITMA* on the wireless. The programme had been taken off for a while the year before and its return had been a great boost to his spirits. Uncle Jack liked to make Daisy laugh by eating mixed-up things, like kippers spread with jam, and she was so enthralled by his odd habits that she usually ate everything put in front of her on these visits.

Uncle Jack's chickens appeared to be permanently on his mind and during the night he seemed to wake up every hour to remind his wife about them. They would all hear him.

'Jane lass, are yer awake?'

'I am now you've woke me.'

'Aye, well, don't forget to feed them theer hens in't morning, will yer?'

'No, Jack, I won't forget.' Then after a while, just when everyone had dropped off to sleep, 'Jane lass, are yer asleep?'

'Aye, what now?'

'Don't forget to feed them theer hens, will yer?'

'Jack, it's two o'clock in't morning.'

'Aye, well, I thought I'd just remind thee.'

'Yer've already reminded me. Go to sleep.'

'Goodneet then.'

'Goodnight.'

Sally and Jim would be trying to stifle their laughter as the conversation penetrated the thin walls. Then, on the third reminder, 'Jane lass, are yer waken?' Jim could control himself no longer.

'Jack!' he called.

'Aah?' Uncle Jack asked.

'Have yer ever thought about feeding them theer hens yerself?'

'Aah,' Uncle Jack answered, 'I all's feed 'em meself. I'm just reminding our lass, in case I forget.'

Sally and Jim by this time would be nearly in hysterics.

Sometimes they would all walk to Ingbirchworth to visit another aunt of Jim's. Aunt Lizzie's house was opposite a farm and the cattle would stand gazing in at the window. Daisy and the children of Jim's cousins would be allowed the run of the farm and spent many happy hours sliding down the hay in the Dutch barn and playing rounders in the field, not that Daisy played a very active part in the ball games, preferring to watch her cousins as she picked flowers from the meadow.

Daisy always came back with a little more colour in her cheeks after those happy weekends away. This time, though, it was Sally who seemed to reap the most benefit from the change. She had recovered her spirits after the anxiety of the past few weeks.

When they left Springvale for the long trek back to Millington, Uncle Jack told Daisy she looked just like Shirley Temple. Oh, she did love Uncle Jack, and didn't in the least mind him waking her up in the night, talking about his chickens. She ran her fingers through her hair. It did feel curly, like on the picture she had seen of Shirley Temple. She would ask Mam to buy her a Shirley Temple frock, like Una Bacon's on Barkers Row, and a new dress for Baby Doll too.

The only one who didn't benefit from the weekend away was Dippy the dog. He was used to the peace and quiet of number nine, and being placed in the care of Bernard and Enid meant two boisterous, giggly girls to contend with as well. He sulked the whole time and ate nothing, not even a biscuit, and if he could have talked he would have complained about Daisy taking that pampered Baby Doll with her and leaving Dippy in lodgings.

Charlotte had a key to Uncle Walter's house; had had it since Aunt Clara was alive. She'd been able to come and go as she liked in those days. In fact, they had doted on her then, and nothing had been too good for their niece. It was only when Uncle Walter had hinted that the money was about to run out that she'd stopped visiting. After all, with only their pension left to live on there would be no more holidays forthcoming for her, no more handouts for birthdays or Christmas. Just tokens, not worth the boredom of having to sit and listen to their endless conversation about the old days. Why should Charlotte care about what her mother had got up to as a teenager? Or how her grandmother had had to walk several miles to work each day in order to keep her children fed after she was widowed? Charlotte had only been there for the money, and when that was gone, so was she.

Still, she had kept the key, there in the bottom of her handkerchief box. The only thing that would stop her now was if the lock had been changed, which would have been extremely unlikely at Uncle Walter's age. She would keep everything she took for a while, in case there was any trouble. She didn't envisage any, though. She had planned everything perfectly and found a secure hiding place, behind a false wall Brady had fitted to cover the alcove in their bedroom. It had been easy for Mark to remove it, and once it had been replaced nobody would detect a thing. The whole lot would be safe there until she was sure the police hadn't been involved.

Charlotte wasn't anticipating any trouble from that Sally woman; she had a feeling she was far too soft-hearted to cause any. She'd sounded so apologetic on the phone for ever bothering Charlotte, and judging by the way she had devoted her time to Uncle Walter, must be too obliging for her own good. She was just the type to believe all the stuff should be Charlotte's anyway! No, that meek little woman was unlikely to cause a fuss, and if she did, there would be no sign of the stolen property anyway. It was all down to Mark now, and he had better not let her down, or else.

'There's a funfair down in the field at Don Farm,' Alfie Ramsgate announced. He always struck up a conversation halfway down his second pint; if he made it last it would be time to go home by the time he'd finished it, and then he could escape without buying a round.

'Ger away!' Tom exclaimed. 'I never thought they'd be allowed in wartime.'

'Well, I don't know about that, but anyway they turned up yesterday.'

'Good job the nights are lighter,' Tom said. 'They certainly won't be allowed to show any lights.'

'How long are they 'ere for?' Jim looked thoughtful.

'Don't know. If they're not 'ere legally, they might be gone by tomorrer.' Jim downed his drink and picked up his jacket. 'Right, I'm off.'

''Ere, hang on, it's not closing time for another quarter of an hour.' Tom wondered if Jim had a promise on and was eager to get home to bed.

'And it's Saturday,' Alfie reminded him.

'I'm going to take our Daisy to't fair.'

'What, at this time of night? She'll be fast asleep.'

'Then she'll just 'ave to wake up. I doubt she'll complain. We might not see another for years.'

'Aye, yer right, Jim. Hang on, I'll come with yer and take our Stanley.' Though Tom wondered what Mary would say to that.

Alfie thought he might as well go with them, seeing as he'd have to buy his own beer if he stayed.

Sally was listening to a scary play on the wireless and nearly jumped off the sofa when Jim came home so early. 'What's the matter, has the Sun burned down?' she quipped.

'No, I'm taking our Daisy to't fair.'

'Oh, no, you're not, it's nearly ten o'clock.'

'So? It'll make it more exciting for 'er.'

Jim went upstairs and shook his daughter gently. 'Daisy, come on, wake up, love.'

'Daddy, I thought you were a monster.' She was immediately wide awake and inquisitive about what was happening. Jim lifted her out of bed, put on her slippers and carried her downstairs. He put her gabardine coat on over her nighty and lifted her up on to his shoulders. Sally thought he must be drunk.

'Are you mad?' She tried to lift her daughter down.

'No, just giving me daughter summat to remember when she grows up. Are yer coming with us then?'

Sally shook her head vigorously. 'One idiot in the family is quite enough,' she said.

Tom and Stanley were already waiting, Stanley jumping up and down with excitement. Alfie tagged on behind.

The funfair wasn't much of one, but to the two children it was the best fair in the whole world. They rode on the Noah's Ark, Daisy squealing with delight as the ride went faster and faster and not once complaining about feeling sick. They dodged each other on the dodgems, and went higher and higher on the swing boats.

'You ought to 'ave brought your Kitty,' Jim told Alf. 'Yer could 'ave snuggled up in't Ghost Train.'

'Our Kitty in't Ghost Train? They'd think she wor one of the ghouls. Wi' a face like hers, she'd frighten anybody to death.'

Jim and Tom laughed and enjoyed cat-calling at a group of teenage girls who were flaunting themselves at the three men. Jim won a fairing for Daisy, an ornament in the shape of a cottage.

'It's my favourite thing in the whole world,' she exclaimed. She fell asleep on the way home but Jim knew she would remember this night for the rest of her life.

Stanley had won a pot dog. It was a hideous-looking thing but he carried it home carefully. He would save it till Christmas; it would make a good present for his mam.

'It's the best night I've had in my whole life,' he told Tom.

'Come on, little lad,' Alfie said. 'Jump up on my back and I'll give yer a ride.' Alfie was glad he'd mentioned the fair. Seeing the excitement on the kid's faces had been grand. He wished he'd thought of summat like that when their Florence was little.

His face clouded as he thought about the grandchild they might have had, had it not been for that bloody wife of his letting his daughter down. Then he realised he was as much to blame as she was, for not standing up for their Florence in her time of need.

Mark Kaye drew up outside the empty house. All was quiet. Once he had made sure all the neighbouring houses were in darkness, he had driven round the back. Even if anyone had still been awake, their blackout curtains would prevent him from being seen. Charlotte had told him it was the back door key he had. He held his breath as he tried it in the lock. Yes! He fumbled for the light switch and let out a string of expletives as he realised what a fool he was. Of course the houses had no electricity – not everyone could afford a house like Brady Scott's.

He went out to the van to look for a torch, without success. He dug in his pocket for his lighter instead. Things weren't going to plan.

He almost fell once inside as his foot caught the edge of a box. He lifted a flap and felt inside: crockery, Charlotte hadn't mentioned any crockery. Clocks, jewellery, pictures, yes. He could make out the shapes of some pictures still on the wall. He opened the blinds to let in the moonlight. He plucked the pictures from the wall and placed them near the door. Clocks! There was nothing resembling a wall clock, but wait . . . there were some vases, standing wrapped tightly in tissue paper, their shapes clearly visible. He found the stairs next and fumbled his way up, then he tried the lighter again. He could see the clocks standing in a row, covered in cloth. He lifted off one of the covers and found one of them still ticking merrily. Suddenly the tallest of them chimed, almost giving him a heart attack. He carried them, one at a time, downstairs, still trembling from the shock. Bloody hell, why had he ever agreed to do this?

The jewellery next, the main thing he was to look for, where was it likely to be? Upstairs, that was the usual place, on a dressing table. He made his way back up. It was easier now as his eyes became accustomed to the darkness. The dressing table was bare except for a cardboard box containing a glass trinket set and, miraculously, a small wooden box. He lifted the lid and the tune 'Greensleeves' rang out. He closed it hurriedly and took the box downstairs with him.

Then he remembered the books. Charlotte had specifically mentioned those, leather-bound ones she had told him. He flicked the lighter. Now where would books be kept? There were boxes and sheet-wrapped objects everywhere. Suddenly his eye caught a bookcase in the corner. He could make out books behind its glass doors. He found at least a dozen leather-bound volumes, emptied a box on to the floor and dropped the books inside.

That was everything. If Charlotte thought of anything else, she could damned well fetch them herself. He carried the books outside, tripped over a picture and stumbled his whole length on to the stone flags outside the door. The pain as he hit his nose caused him to black out for a few seconds. Blood poured from his nostrils as he rose shakily to his feet. Bloody Charlotte! He found the box and the pictures and went back for the rest of his haul. Still agonised and drenched in sweat and blood, he locked the door of the house and drove home, cursing his wife for being the cause of his broken nose.

'Have you got everything?' Charlotte asked, not in the least concerned at the sight of her husband's wounds.

'If I haven't, you can get it yourself. Where's the first-aid box?'

'The bathroom cabinet.' Her eyes gleamed at the sight of the masonic clock. She went from one thing to another like a child on Christmas morning. Then she opened the wooden jewellery box. 'What the . . . ?' Her fingers plucked out a cheap silver-plated chain. She remembered buying it once from a gift shop in Barnsley for Aunt Clara's birthday, considering her aunt too ignorant to be able to tell the difference. A string of yellow beads and a couple of brooches made up the rest of the contents.

'You stupid, stupid man!' she raged. 'Can't you ever do anything right?'

Mark had managed to stem the bleeding but felt as if he'd just done twenty rounds with Charlie Parkin. He managed to reach the lavatory before vomiting, dropping to his knees in his weakness. He could hear Charlotte still ranting on. Apparently he had brought the wrong pictures, the cheap prints, the ones of the dogs, and left the ones of value. He rose to his feet and made it well into the lounge just as she was accusing him of being a bastard and an idiot, along with a string of other obscenities.

'Shut up!' His voice was hoarse. 'One more word out of you and you'll pay for this night's work.'

Charlotte didn't seem to hear, but kept raging at the injured man. Suddenly Mark's hand lashed out and slapped her so hard she was sent reeling. As the shocked woman flopped backwards on to the sofa, Mark looked down at his wife, the woman he realised for the first time he actually hated, then he left the room, slamming the door behind him, and went to sleep in the spare room.

Daisy put Baby Doll to bed for her afternoon nap. Sometimes she lay beside her with her picture books and told stories about Red Riding Hood or Goldilocks until she herself fell asleep. Today she told Baby Doll about the Three Little Pigs and then went out to play. Stanley was hanging about in the field so she went to join him. 'Shall we play school?' Daisy said.

'All right, if yer like.'

'I'll be teacher.'

'No, you can't, you don't know what teachers do,' Stanley said, but Daisy looked so miserable that he gave in. 'Oh, go on then.' Stanley began to say the alphabet. 'A for apple, B for ball . . .'

'C for cat.' Daisy knew all her letters. 'D for dog,' she said.

'Please may I leave the room?' Stanley put up his hand. Daisy was confused.

'We're not in a room,' she said.

'No, but that is what you have to say when you want to wee.'

'All right,' Daisy said.

Stanley walked over to the long grass and began to urinate.

'What's that?' Daisy said, pointing at his little private parts.

'That's my willy.' Stanley buttoned up his trousers. 'Now you've seen mine, you've got to show me yours.'

'I haven't got one of them.'

'All right then, you can show me yer knickers.'

Daisy lifted up her dress and Stanley had a peep. 'Una Bacon wears pink knickers,' he informed her.

'How do you know?'

'I saw 'em when she was doing handstands.'

'Yes, but did you show her your willy?'

'No, she didn't want me to. She said she'd already seen one when they went paddling in the river. She said willies were boring.'

'Yes, they are,' Daisy said. 'E for egg. F for fish.'

'I'm fed up of this game,' Stanley said. 'Let's play Cowboys and Indians.'

'Another day. It's time for Baby Doll to get up.' Daisy ran home and up the stairs to her bedroom. Then she screamed. Sally took the stairs two at a time to reach her distraught daughter. There on the bed was Daisy's beloved celluloid doll, its face completely chewed away so that it stared grotesquely out of one blue eye, the only part of it still recognisable. Sally covered the doll with the quilt and picked up her little girl.

'It's all right,' She tried to console Daisy, but it was impossible. The sobs were continuing deep within her.

'I don't want her to go to heaven like baby Celia!' she cried.

'No! We'll take her to the dolls' hospital and see if they can make her better.' Sally hoped to God they could find a replica of the doll that had been just as loved as a real baby.

Jim wondered what the hell had got into Dippy. The dog had never done anything like this before. Dippy lay on his mat in the corner, his nose on the floor. He knew he had done wrong but it was worth it to be rid of Baby Doll. Daisy came and sat on the pegged rug and he slithered over to her and rested his head on her lap.

Daisy cuddled him. She didn't know it was Dippy who had hurt her baby. Otherwise, like a mother, she would never have forgiven him.

Chapter Three

The view from Miss Appleby's house was of the field, the air-raid shelter, and a pair of semi-detached houses on St George's Road. She spent most of her day watching the comings and goings at those two houses. Ida Appleby was a miserable, bored and utterly selfish woman. Nobody had ever known her join in any of the neighbourhood activities and until recently her house had been kept immaculate. Now she had decided she needed some help to keep it in that condition. When Sally Butler had brought her the flowers as a peace offering, she had wondered if the young woman would take on the task of cleaning for her, especially now she wasn't doing for Mr Jessops any more. When she saw the eldest Cartwright girl coming home from school she had a letter waiting for the girl to deliver to her aunt. Now all she could do was wait and see.

Sally and Jim were making love for the first time in weeks, what with Jim's shift work and Betty moving herself in, then the death of old Walter and the weekend at Springvale with Daisy sharing their bed. Now at last Jim had his wife in his arms and her body was responsive and eager for love. He slid the Celanese nighty over her head and stroked the smooth, firm silkiness of her breasts until her nipples stood erect. He had just penetrated her moist inviting body when the sound of somebody downstairs completely deflated his ardour. 'What the hell was that?'

'Nothing.' Sally was too aroused to care what was happening anywhere else, but Jim was already out of bed and climbing into his trousers. He moved silently downstairs and opened the door of the living-room.

'Ernest! Bloody 'ell, man, you didn't 'alf give me a fright. Oh, but it is good to see you!'

'Aye, you too. Sorry to drop in like this, I didn't intend to wake yer, I was going to kip down on the sofa. I didn't want to knock the old folks up at this time of night, and I knew where your key would be.'

'Oh, aye, ever open door ours is.' He suddenly noticed Ernest's arm bound up in a sling. 'What's up with yer arm, lad?'

'Pulled me shoulder out't socket. Bloody painful, but worth it to get leave.' Ernest grinned and Jim could see why all the lasses fancied his brother-in-law. The door opened then and Sally came running in and gathered her brother into her arms.

'Ouch!' Ernest moaned. 'Watch me arm.'

Sally looked concerned. 'Sorry, what have you been doing?'

'Dislocation. Took two men to get it back in again.'

She pulled a face. 'How long are you home for?'

'All depends on when I can use it again, but at least a fortnight.'

'Oh, well, it's good to see you. Are you hungry?'

'No, I had fish and chips. Stood at the counter and ate 'em. Couldn't carry 'em wi' me arm and eat at the same time.'

'Ah, poor you! Anyway, we'll have some tea and then you must get some sleep.'

Ernest looked tired out and seemed to have lost a couple of stone in weight. Sally supposed it was due to the pain from his injury. Little did she know the conditions he and his RAF comrades were about to be subjected to. Ernest knew, and realised it would be no picnic, but he was trained for the job and couldn't wait to get on with it. In fact, his injury was not just a pain in the shoulder but a pain in the arse to him. And though the leave was welcome, he couldn't wait to be back to the job of winning the war.

When Sally was given the letter asking her to visit Miss Appleby at her convenience, the first thought in her head was to wonder what Daisy had done now. However, her brother's arrival meant the visit to their neighbours was put off until another day. Ernest set off for their parents' home early in the morning, and because Daisy couldn't bear to be parted from her uncle, he took her with him. Jim volunteered to pick up his kit bag from the station.

Lizzie Denman burst into tears at the sight of her son's injury, but the tears were really of relief that her cherished boy was safe home again.

Joe Denman was a man of few words but Ernest knew how his father felt. Words were unnecessary between them. The two men merely set off to the allotment, where any man on the night shift would usually escape while the women completed their daily chores. Today, Ernest was the centre of attraction. Although the older men questioned the airman all about his injury, Ernest made light of it, unwilling to cause anxiety to his father and the other men who all had sons serving their country. Instead he led the conversation to the fact that Chamberlain had resigned.

'Aah, it'll all be over in no time now Churchill's in charge,' Ben Hoyle predicted. 'Our lads'll be 'ome before we can say Charlie Chaplin.'

Joe Denman wasn't too sure. He began talking about knurr and spell, on which Mr Hoyle was quite an authority, being a champion player of the game.

In Ernest's kit bag were three pairs of tiny wooden Dutch clogs for his three nieces. Daisy's were yellow with floral decorations and she thought they were the prettiest things. They even succeeded in taking her mind off Baby Doll for a while. Ernest had also brought her a small fur-lined helmet, similarly shaped to the ones pilots wore. Despite the fact that it was July and quite warm, she insisted on wearing it to go home in.

'That'll keep you warm on the way to school in winter,' Grandma Denman told her. When Stanley saw the helmet, Daisy was pestered with requests to let him try it on. Then the Dawson boys came over to look at the treasured garment. By the time she had given them all a turn at wearing it, she was the most popular child in the whole of Millington and the helmet, because a real airman had brought it home, was the envy of all.

Sally was itching to start work on the cleaning and decorating of Mr Jessops' house but was not permitted to do so until the letter from the solicitor arrived, confirming her inheritance. Betty, on the other hand, was becoming more and more impatient, having decided to apply for Jim's house as soon as it became vacant. Sally had promised not to tell anyone else so that she and Clarence had the first chance.

Clarence didn't want the house, he didn't want the responsibility. Nor did he want Betty because he didn't want to be married at all. And, most of all, he didn't want a baby, especially one he wasn't even certain he had fathered. He didn't tell Betty any of this because Clarence didn't like confrontations, all he wanted was a quiet life to do as he pleased. Clarence Hayes was a weak, easygoing man so he went along with Betty's plans while all the time he was making plans of his own.

Ida Appleby was sitting in her usual place by the window when Sally came on the row. Ida went to put the kettle on; she must be sure to be on her best behaviour. If she wanted Sally Butler's services, she must make a good impression. She even managed a smile of sorts as she answered the door. 'Come in, come in,' she enthused. 'Thank you for coming so soon.'

Sally would have liked to tell the woman to get on with whatever it was she wanted, but Miss Appleby rambled on about the shortages.

'I don't mind the sugar so much, but why they had to ration our butter and bacon I'll never know.' Anyone would think she was the only one affected by the rationing. 'And how are we expected to manage on five ounces of meat a week? We can't keep healthy on that.'

'Well, not just five ounces, we are entitled to three-quarters of a pound of imported meat as well,' Sally volunteered.

'Oh, foreign muck! They won't catch me eating that, we don't know who's been handling it. I'll go without first.'

Sally took the cup of tea she'd been offered, which was barely coloured, and sat down at the table opposite Miss Appleby.

'Right, what I wanted to ask you was if you'd

come and help me out wi' a bit of cleaning and shopping and such?'

Sally was stunned and didn't know what to say.

'I'll pay yer well, if that's what yer wondering.'

'No, I wasn't . . . I just wondered, why me?'

'Well, I know yer did well for Mr Jessops, and now he's gone I thought you might consider giving me a few hours.'

'Well, I don't know. I've got our Daisy, and until she starts school I can't leave her with just anybody.'

'Oh, no, I wouldn't expect yer to. Yer could bring her with yer if yer were stuck fast.' Ida put on a pained expression. 'It's me poor legs, yer see, the rheumatics.'

'Oh, I see. Well, when would you want me?'

'There won't be any washing, it goes to't laundry. All except me private bits and pieces, which I like to do meself.' Ida lowered her voice to a whisper. 'Knickers,' she said primly. Sally almost giggled.

'But there will be some ironing. Then there's the bed to change and the floor to mop and me furniture to polish . . . that's all really. Oh, and me shopping.' She looked expectantly at Sally. 'And there'll be't lavatory to put Izal down.'

'Well, I don't know how many hours that'd need . . . and I'd have to see what Jim says. He doesn't like women working, not with children involved.'

'Oh, I quite agree, but that's in peacetime. Women have to sally forth during the war.'

94

She wondered how doing Miss Appleby's ironing would benefit the war effort but kept her thoughts to herself. Besides, the money would no doubt come in handy with all the decorating they'd to do. Then they would need some new carpet squares . . . it would all need paying for. They might even afford new curtains with a bit of extra money coming in. She thought about the valuable things in the Jessops' house but knew she could never bring herself to part with them. They were all she had left of the old couple. Sally finished her tea.

'Right then, I'll let you know.' She stood up to go.

'How much an hour would you expect?'

'Oh, I don't know, what do you think?' Sally felt embarrassed at being asked about wages.

'We'll see.' Miss Appleby followed her to the door. 'Yer'll let me know then?'

'Yes, I'll let you know before the weekend.'

It wasn't until Sally was opening her own front door that she wondered why she was even considering taking the job. She didn't think she liked Miss Appleby very much, though she did feel sorry for her. The fact was, Sally Butler's was a soft heart, just waiting for anybody to take advantage of it.

Joe Denman heard the news that Anthony Eden had decided the Local Defence Volunteers were from now on to be known as the Home Guard. It had irked him that he hadn't done his bit towards the war, even though he was knocking on a bit and his job as a miner wasn't an easy one. Anyway, now they had stopped buggering about with fancy names, he decided he'd join. When he was on the right shift, of course. Knowing his son was injured had made Joe's blood boil. The lad wouldn't let on how it had happened but it was obviously summat to do with the war.

Joe knew he was too old to go to war himself but he would show willing here in Millington. There were the pit, the steelworks, the reservoirs, and most important of all his own family to guard.

He knew Ben and John Thomas would join the Home Guard too now they had called it summat sensible. Like Ben had said, it would be an excuse to pop into't club after practice. Ben's wife was a right owd battleaxe who timed him to the minute when he went to slaken the dust with a pint. Joe grinned. The Home Guard would put paid to that. Owd Ben'd be let loose at last.

He sauntered on to the allotment, where he could sit and enjoy a Woodbine without Lizzie complaining about the smoke. It was nice here, with the chapel on one side and the stream on the other. He never noticed the noise from the steelworks or the coke ovens; Joe had been born here and had become immune to the clanging and screeching over the years. All he was aware of was the trickling stream and the bird song in the trees above the graveyard.

He gazed with satisfaction at the beans climbing

up their sticks. They hung, green and tender, waiting to be gathered. Peas were filling out nicely, too, Lizzie would enjoy those. He grinned. That was, if his grand-daughters didn't get to them first. Eeh, but the joy those three lasses gave to Joe Denman was worth all the peas in Millington, especially little Daisy. Just the thought of her made him smile.

Ernest Denman hadn't told anyone what had happened to dislocate his shoulder. Nor did he let on that he was training with Fighter Squadron and that, provided his shoulder allowed it, he was waiting for the call to action at any time. It was because Ernest was outstandingly fit and intelligent that he had been selected. If his shoulder didn't regain full mobility all that training would have been in vain.

To tell the truth, though, he wasn't the cool, confident young man he presented himself as. In fact, as he manoeuvred his equipment – which weighed sixty pounds – on board a Spitfire, he, like most of his fellow fighters, was usually so scared he was almost shitting himself. But he and his comrades were willing to forfeit their lives for their country.

For a week Ernest wasn't allowed to use his shoulder at all. After that he was determined to work the bloody thing back to its original strength. The enemy had to be defeated and Ernest Denman would never shrink from the task.

*   *   *

Betty had found her mother's old *Bestway Cookery Book* and was itching to try out some of the recipes, but of course it was impossible with rationing. However, she was proud of the corned beef pie she had made. She had managed to buy a couple of onions by queueing at Mr Baraclough's door, waiting for the delivery of the greens. She had discovered some old dried herbs in the back of the cupboard and experimented until the seasoning was just right; her pastry was as good as it could be with the limited amount of fat available. Even Clarence complimented her on the finished meal, and Amy said her daughter had turned out a better pastry cook than she herself would ever be.

'You've a pastry cook's light hand,' she praised her daughter.

The truth was that Betty Hayes had at last discovered her forte. She loved cooking. She had even begun sewing, and had made a couple of tiny bibs for the forthcoming baby. The thought that she might soon have a home of her own seemed to have boosted her household skills no end. She also felt more kindly disposed towards Clarence. Amy thought it was a bit soon to sigh with relief but at least things were looking brighter.

If she had but known it, this peaceful interval was just a lull before the storm.

Clarence watched Ernest Denman visiting his sister, marching straight and proud despite the sling on his arm. Clarence pulled back his own shoulders and wondered how long it would be before he developed the hunched back some of the older miners were lumbered with. He hated that mine. Hated working ankle-deep in water, and in seams so low that the men's backs were permanently stooped. He hated the coal that ground itself into the skin and worked its dust deep into the lungs of the colliers. Clarence had had enough.

On pay day he handed in his lamp and collected his wages, then he went home to the meal Betty placed proudly in front of him which he devoured with relish, praising her for her culinary efforts. Then he went upstairs, packed a bag and told his wife he was going to the Miners' Club for a bath. He placed his wages and the money he had made on the side, illegally, on the dressing table where she wouldn't find it until bedtime.

He kept little for himself; she would need it all for the kid. He couldn't think of the child as his, too many men had been there before him. He didn't think badly of Betty, though. All she had wanted was a good time, just like him really. He doubted he would have a good time where he was going but at least he would see some action. If he was killed in the process, so be it.

Clarence kissed Betty warmly, went to the Miners' Club and rid himself of the bloody coal muck, then he caught a bus to Sheffield and enlisted.

*   *   *

99

Jim didn't like the idea of his wife being a servant to Miss Appleby; he didn't like the thought of her working at all. He just knew what would happen next. Sally would start by working the hours agreed upon, then she would begin bringing washing home, then she would just be popping over to take Miss Appleby this or fetch Miss Appleby that. His wife, of course, had an answer to every argument he raised.

'I promise I won't bring work home,' she said. 'And where else would I find a job where I can take Daisy with me?'

'She won't like it, cooped up with that woman,' Jim pointed out.

'Well, our Enid's offered to have her. After all, she doesn't work in the school holidays and they're almost upon us. Break up this week actually.' The one argument Sally didn't put forward was about the extra money. She had the sense to know her husband wouldn't like that. Jim liked to be the breadwinner, and if he thought he couldn't provide for his family it would be a blow to his pride. 'I feel sorry for her, she's lonely.'

'And who's fault is that? She's never put herself out to mix wi' the neighbours or owt.'

'I know. I'd like to give it a try, though, see how it goes.'

'All right, all right. Have it yer own way, you usually do.' Then he added, 'On one condition.'

'What's that?'

'That our Daisy doesn't suffer.'

'Of course she won't, what do you take me for?'

The wage offered to Sally was quite fair, compared to Enid's for school cleaning. It was agreed that Sally would begin the following Tuesday by working two hours and they'd go from there. In the meantime she wondered how long it would be before she could safely say she was the owner of the Jessops' house. The boxes she and Emily Simms had packed remained where they had left them. Or so they thought.

It was eleven o'clock before Betty found the letter. Because she was used to Clarence disappearing for hours on end she hadn't missed him. Amy had just dropped off to sleep, having left her daughter reading her *Secrets* and *Flame* by the fire.

Betty let out a shriek fit to wake the dead so that Amy almost fell out of bed in her haste to reach her daughter. Betty's face looked ghastly in the candlelight.

'What is it? Is it the baby?'

Betty shook her head. 'Clarence . . . he's gone.'

'Gone? Gone where?'

'He's joined up, left the pit and joined up.'

'Oh, well, we've got to admire him for that.'

'Admire him? What about me and the baby? And what about the house?'

'You 'aven't actually got the house yet, love.'

'But we would have! Oh, Mam, he must not care about me at all, to go away and leave me now.'

''Course he cares about yer. You can't condemn him for going to war. Thousands of wives are in the same position.'

Betty opened the other envelope and looked at the money.

'Well, at least he hasn't left yer destitute.'

'No, he's never been mean, I'll say that for him. Oh, Mam, where do you think he got all this money from? Not from the pit, I'm sure.'

'No, no, lass, not from't pit. I'd say 'e's had 'is fingers in some other little pies, by the look of that lot.'

Betty seemed a bit brighter. 'He could just have left me his wages from the pit and I'd have been none the wiser about this. So he must have cared about me, mustn't he, Mam?'

''Course he cared, love, and for the baby. Well, it's obvious, isn't it?'

Betty grinned then. 'Being as he was never at home, I'm not going to notice much difference, am I?'

Amy drew her daughter towards her. 'That's my lass,' she said, hugging Betty close. 'I should get that little lot in't bank tomorrer.'

'After I've bought a pram,' Betty said.

Jim got up after the nightshift on Saturday and said he was going to Sheffield. 'Are yer coming? It'll be an outing,' he said.

Sally got herself and Daisy ready and they took

a short cut down the Donkey Path to the bus stop. Daisy – as usual – made it impossible for them to complete the journey and they had to get off the bus just past the Infirmary, due to her travel sickness. It would be the same on the return journey when they would end up walking the last few miles.

In town, Jim made his usual visit to the book stall in Norfolk Market where he allowed Daisy to pick a book for herself. He also enquired about a book called *Brother to the Ox*, by Fred Kitchen. The bookseller promised to order it for him in time for next week. Apparently it was one of the year's bestsellers, and written by a Derbyshire farmer.

Daisy chose a brightly coloured picture book and Jim also purchased a second-hand copy of *Tom Sawyer*. 'Our Daisy'll enjoy that in a few years' time,' He told Sally. She thought about all the books at Mr Jessops'. Jim would be thrilled with all the classics there such as *Uncle Tom's Cabin* and *The Coral Island*.

After a walk round the Rag Market, Jim took Daisy to the pet stalls. She was delighted with the pups and kittens. He lifted her up on his shoulders so she could see the budgerigars and canaries. Sally refused to go near the pet stalls, making the excuse that the smell made her feel ill, but Jim knew it was the sight of the poor creatures shut up in cages that upset his sensitive wife.

He took them next to one of the cafes that had begun selling wartime lunches, then said he would see them later. Curiosity almost got the better of Sally, but she resisted questioning him about where he was off to. She took Daisy to Lewis's instead, to look at the fashions, hoping they were still advertised at being at pre-war prices, but she was out of luck there. Unperturbed, she bought a dress of blue crêpe-de-Chine for Daisy, adorned at the bodice with pretty pink rosebuds. She also bought navy blue knickers in readiness for her starting school. Daisy hated navy blue, but if they were for school she decided she wouldn't complain. She wondered if Una Bacon would change from pink to navy when *she* started school. Their next call was to Walsh's where Sally was fascinated by the famous gypsy, Leon Petulengro, who was giving a talk about Romany folklore. The talk was almost at an end when suddenly he left the stragglers and approached Sally.

'I hope you don't mind,' he said, 'but I feel I must warn you that you're in for a disappointment. Somebody has taken something away from you, something you hold very dear. Beware. The woman is out for revenge and will stop at nothing.'

Sally felt a shiver run the length of her spine.

'A woman?' was all she managed to say.

'A beautiful woman on the surface, but ugly to the core.' The gypsy looked at Daisy and smiled. 'Your daughter is a child of fortune and a gifted one at that. She will see the inside of a hospital soon, but all will be for the best. Ah, you are indeed a gifted child.'

He ruffled Daisy's curls and walked away. Sally felt as though a cold hand had descended upon her and ruined her day. On the bright side, her daughter had been promised good luck. *A gifted child of fortune.* If Daisy was all the gypsy had promised, no ugly-hearted woman could take that away from Sally. Her daughter's future was all she cared about. They went to meet Jim then, Sally still curious to hear about his whereabouts in the meantime.

He came towards them, all smiles, and handed Daisy a brown paper bag. She looked inside. Her eyes gleamed as she lifted out her beloved Baby Doll. 'She's all better.' Daisy cuddled the perfect doll.

'Yes, she's been to the hospital, they can do miracles at the doll's hospital.'

'What's a miracle?' Daisy enquired.

'What they've done to Baby Doll, that's a miracle.'

'Ah, like making her eyes a different colour?'

Sally and Jim looked at each other, then at the doll which had been fitted today with a brand new head. Baby Doll's face was identical to the ruined one except for the eyes which were now a beautiful, warm brown. And Jim had never noticed.

Early on Sunday morning a knock on the door startled Sally, who was only half-awake. There was another more urgent one, and then a voice calling,

'Sally . . . Sally, are yer there?'

Jim was sitting up by this time. 'What the . . . where the bloody 'ell does she think yer are at this time of the morning?'

'It's Mrs Simms,' Sally informed him as she struggled into her undies. 'Something must be wrong.'

'Aye, summat is. She's spoiled our Sunday morning lie in, that's what's wrong. Ever open bloody door, that's what ours is.'

Sally hurried downstairs. 'What is it? What's happened?'

'Eeh, lass, it might be nothing. On the other hand, I'm sure summat's not right at Mr Jessops'. Yer know how we made sure all't windows were blacked out and curtains drawn?'

'Yes, we did.'

'Well, they're not. Curtains, I mean. And there's what looks like blood on't back doorstep. Well, it might be from a cat or summat, but a cat can't open't curtains, can it? I wouldn't 'ave noticed if I 'adn't done the step.'

'I'll come with you.' Sally didn't stop to comb her hair but set off across the field with Emily still chattering beside her.

'I wouldn't 'ave noticed . . . I mean, I'm not one to pry . . . but I thought while I was doing me steps and lav I might as well do Walter's as well, like I 'ave for years. But this time I could tell summat wasn't right. Well! I thought. It's none of my business. But when I got in bed, I couldn't sleep for thinking about it. I made me mind up that first thing

106

this morning I'd come and tell yer.' Emily paused to draw breath as she tried to keep pace with the younger woman. 'I forgot that not everybody rises with the lark like I do. I hope your Jim wasn't annoyed?'

'Not at all,' Sally fibbed. 'You did the right thing.' She knew as soon as she unlocked the door that someone had been in here. The strong smell of men's hair oil or some kind of toiletry permeated the air and the broken crockery spilled over the floor caught her attention immediately. A trail of blood from the door and across the kitchen floor stopped her in her tracks. 'Oh, God, someone's been in!' She knew even then who that someone was, either Charlotte or someone sent by her.

At that moment Jim walked in. 'What's wrong?'

'Someone's been in. Burglars, I shouldn't wonder,' Mrs Simms said.

Jim looked at the bric-à-brac broken and strewn in a heap on the floor.

'Charlotte,' Sally said.

'What? Who's Charlotte?'

'The niece,' Emily explained.

'I've told you about her,' Sally snapped. 'Surely you were listening.'

'Yes, 'course I was. I didn't know her name, though.'

'The vases have gone, and look at the book-case . . . it's almost empty. We never left it like that.' Sally hurried to the old chair in the corner and searched underneath the cushion until she found the leather box. Sighing with relief, she checked the contents.

'At least she hasn't got her aunt's jewellery.' She sat down, her hands trembling.

Jim went towards the door. 'I'm off to the police station.'

'No!' Sally jumped to her feet. 'No, everything should be hers by rights. I said from the beginning it should all be hers.'

'Don't talk daft, Sally.' Jim was livid that the old man's wishes had been thwarted in this way. 'He gave it all to you. You can't let her get away with this. Besides, it might not be her. Burglary happens all the time.'

'Not round here. It *is* her, I know it is, and if it isn't, it's someone acting on her behalf.' Sally wearily climbed the stairs, wondering about the beautiful clocks and the watercolours on the landing. The pictures were still hanging there. The clocks were gone. She came downstairs, tears blinding her at the thought of the old gentleman's treasured possessions ending up in some stranger's home. Then she noticed that the pictures of the girls with the dogs had gone. Those pictures were the only thing of Walter's Sally had coveted, not for their value but because they would always remind her of the wonderful old couple. She sat down and cried for their loss. The events of the last few weeks had suddenly become more than she could bear.

Emily Simms hurried out, intending to mash a pot of tea. The lass needed a good strong cup to buck her up. Eeh, but that bad bitch had a lot to answer for! She would go to the devil, that one would, and it wouldn't be a day too soon when she did.

Jim knelt before his wife and hugged her to him. 'Don't, Sally.' He was overcome himself and pressed her head to his shoulder so she wouldn't see his own tears.

He was rocking her gently when Emily returned with a tray. The break-in hadn't really been a surprise to her. 'I said all the time she'd be trouble, that one. All the same, you should let the police know.'

'No.' Sally was adamant. 'I don't want anything she's handled. Just leave it. At least I've got the rings. I couldn't bear knowing she was wearing those.' She stood up, drank the tea Emily had made, and pulled herself together. 'Come on,' she said, 'it looks like the sooner we sort this house out the better. If Charlotte had heard from Dunstone & Sedgewick, she wouldn't have needed to nick her uncle's things, so it looks like what's left is ours.'

Jim began to clear up the broken crockery.

'There's one consolation,' Emily said. 'Whoever it was'll not be feeling too good. It looks like a slaughterhouse round the back.'

Mark Kaye wasn't feeling too good at all. He'd had to cancel his appointments until further notice; after all, he couldn't face the public in his work at the Town Hall with a great wad of lint covering half his face. He had also needed a dentist to cap two broken teeth. In fact, he looked more like a gangster than a civil servant. On top of that, he was far too jittery to drive to the city, expecting the police to stop him at any time.

He wouldn't have minded if his wife had shown a little appreciation but all she had done was complain. The jewellery in the trinket box was just useless trash. The pictures were the wrong ones, and he must have done something to one of the clocks as the bloody thing kept chiming even though nobody had wound it for days.

'How am I supposed to sleep through that racket?' Charlotte complained. 'On the hour, every hour, from one o'clock onwards. It's driving me mad.'

'You're imagining things,' Mark said. 'I've never heard it.'

'Well then, you're going deaf. Besides you're not in my bedroom any more, though I don't know why.'

'Don't you? Use your imagination, woman. You're turning into a miserable old nag. Nothing I do pleases you.'

Charlotte sat looking shame-faced. 'Well, yes, I admit I lost my temper a bit. I'm sorry. Come back to my bed, I miss you.' She hitched her skirt up over her thighs, knowing her legs were now her best feature and hoping to entice him back to the intimacy they had previously enjoyed. Mark looked at her with disdain.

'I'm going out for a breath of air,' he said. 'I'll see you sometime.' He knew he never wanted to sleep with her again. Charlotte was, in his opinion, long past the age at which she should consider herself desirable.

When Sally woke Jim was feeling amorous. 'Come 'ere,' he said, gently pulling her towards him.

'For five minutes, then I'll have to get up.'

'Why?'

'It's my first day at Miss Appleby's.'

'Well, if you're a bit late you can make up the time later.'

Jim ran his hand up beneath the silky nightdress and stroked Sally's thigh, climbing his fingers upwards until they reached their goal. They were like a pair of spoons, she with her back to him, as he slid himself inside her, continuing to massage the firm globes of her breasts. Sally's intention to stay no more than five minutes went completely out of her mind and it was twenty-five minutes later when she finally separated herself from her husband. Even then, she was still in a daze as she went down to the kitchen to wash and came back upstairs to dress.

'My first day and I'm going to be late.'

Jim turned on to his back and watched her. He could lie in until Daisy woke. The afternoon shift was the one on which the shift workers caught up on their sleep. 'Just tell her you were unavoidably detained. Or, better still, give her a graphic account of what you were detained by.'

Sally giggled. 'I'll bet she's never seen one. I'll bet she's the only virgin in Millington over the age of twenty-one.'

'Oh, I'd make that eighteen if I were you.'

'See you later.' Sally hurried away. She would have to forgo breakfast, but who cared about that after what had just taken place?

She was only five minutes late and didn't apologise even though Miss Appleby looked pointedly at the clock.

'Oh, you 'aven't brought your little girl then?' Sally thought she sounded relieved.

'No, her dad's looking after her, he's on afters this week. Right, where shall I start?'

'Well! Seeing as I 'aven't changed me bed for two weeks, I thought yer could do that and get it ready for't laundry.' Sally made for the stairs. 'Yer'll find clean sheets in't cupboard in't back bedroom.' Once that was done Sally swept the carpet square and carried the pegged rug outside to give it a shake. A cloud of dust spread around her and she guessed it hadn't been shaken for some time.

'Have you a mop and bucket?' she asked.

'Aye, it's on't cellar steps.' The mop was dry and stiff, and when Sally dipped it in water and wrung it out she found it so thin she felt she was scraping the bottom of the handle on the lino. 'We shall need another mop head,' she told the older woman who was watching every move she made.

'Well! I don't know ... I 'aven't had that one very long.'

'There's nothing left of it.' Sally thought it must have been on the cellar steps since before the last war, never mind this one. 'I can't clean if I've nothing to clean with.'

'I used to 'ave to get down on me knees when I was a housekeeper.'

'Really?' Sally had no intention of rising to the bait. She remembered Emily's advice to start as she meant to go on: 'Otherwise the woman'll make yer life purgatory.' Emily had known Ida Appleby from school days, and though she rarely spoke ill of anybody – except Charlotte Kaye – she had given Sally a warning of what Ida would try to get away with given half a chance.

'You can make us some elevenses if you've a mind to,' Miss Appleby said, even though it was only ten o'clock. 'Yer'll need a break after working so hard.'

Sally put the kettle on and made up her mind to give it a good scouring when she'd been here a bit. Anyway it was praise indeed if the woman thought she was a good worker. Sally relaxed a bit.

'Don't use more than one spoonful of tea between us.'

Sally cringed. It would be like drinking coloured

water. Nevertheless she did as she was told, adding a bit more between her fingers.

Then Miss Appleby started on about the rationing. 'It was bad enough before but now they've gone and rationed our tea! Then there's the marge and cooking fat . . . I don't know what'll happen next, I'm sure.'

'No, it is a nuisance, but I don't suppose the war'll last much longer.'

'I expect I shall be dead by the time this war's over, what wi' my legs.'

Sally hurriedly finished her tea – if you could call it tea – found a duster box under the sink and began polishing the furniture. Everything was of good quality, old, but the type that polished up until it looked like new. Sally wondered how Miss Appleby managed financially if she'd never had a husband. Maybe she'd been a well-paid housekeeper during her working years, that would account for it.

Sally was relieved the first day was over. It wouldn't be too bad once she got organised. One thing she would insist on, though, before she did any more floor-washing, was a new mop.

Sally agreed to Miss Appleby's suggestion that she should come again on Thursday for another two hours, when she would go to the shops and clean the windows, lavatory and the doorsteps. She hoped there wouldn't be any queues at the shops or the steps would have to wait. It wasn't until she got home that she realised she had been at Miss Appleby's for an extra fifteen minutes. So much for a five-minute tea break, and it wasn't even tea!

Jim and Tom Porter went off to work and Daisy went out to play. Mary brought out two chairs and coaxed Sally into sitting outside after her first morning as a working wife.

'I'll tell you what,' Mary said, 'we'll go to the pictures on Saturday. I can't remember the last time we went out.'

'I ought to be getting something done at the Jessops',' Sally said.

Mary laughed. 'It isn't the Jessops', it's yours.'

'I know, but I keep imagining something going wrong so that it isn't ours. I suppose it's because of the break-in.' Sally smiled. 'Actually it wasn't a break-in . . . whoever it was just unlocked the door and locked it again behind them, proof enough who was responsible.' She sighed. 'Well! They won't get in again, Jim's changed the locks. Oh, Mary, are we doing the right thing? Moving, I mean.'

'Well, I don't want you to go. It won't be the same without you next-door. But, yes, of course you are. It's a better house altogether. Nice garden, extra bedroom . . . you'd be crazy not to move.'

'You're right, I know you are, but in all the years we've lived here we've never had to lock the door, and if we've gone off for the day the key's been there for any visitors. I can trust everybody on Potters Row.'

'Well, you can trust the Dawsons and Emily. Taylors Row is a lovely place to live.'

'Yes, you're right, and you won't be far away.'

'What's your Daisy doing?' Mary shielded her eyes from the sun to peer at her.

'She's supposed to be dancing. They're going to have a concert. She's been practising all week. She wants to dance like Marjory Bacon's little girl. Apparently she's quite a little performer, I doubt if our Daisy will ever make a dancer but at least she's enjoying herself. Oh! And our Daisy wants pink knickers because Una Bacon wears them, and she knows they're pink because your Stanley's seen them.'

The two friends giggled like schoolgirls as they soaked up the sun. It was good that Mary was content again. Life was lovely at the moment even with the war, and it might never reach Millington. Sally watched the crowd of children from the three rows. Oh, yes, it was a good place in which to live. Please God, keep it that way.

When Sally invited Betty to accompany them to the cinema she refused, saying she couldn't possibly as her skirt was held together with a safety pin and she wouldn't be seen dead out in public in a maternity smock. She did, however, suggest she sit with Daisy and Stanley so that Jim and Tom could go too. 'It's no good us all sitting here miserable,' Betty said.

Sally was thrilled that Betty seemed to be becoming less selfish. Jim was more suspicious. 'She'll be looking to the future when she needs a baby-sitter herself,' he said.

Rather than waste an evening at the cinema it was decided they would all go to the Empire Theatre in Sheffield.

'I hope Elsie and Doris Waters are on,' Mary said, 'I've heard they're a right laugh.'

Sally didn't mind who was on as long as it was an excuse to get dressed up for a change. After they'd gone Betty settled down with her *Family Star*. With Daisy tucked up in bed and Stanley occupied with Jim's Meccano set, she was prepared for a quiet night with her feet up. Stanley had just moved to the sofa and fallen asleep when Ernest Denman walked in.

'Oh, Betty, long time no see.'

'Well, you can certainly see me now,' She laughed, and patted her lump. 'You'd have a job to miss me.'

Ernest grinned. 'Well, I must say, you look well.' It was true. He was astounded at how much Betty had changed. Gone was the heavy make up she had been wearing the last time he had seen her. The perm had grown out of her hair, which now waved loosely round her face. 'In fact, I'd say you were blooming.'

'Oh, I'm blooming all right, big as a blooming elephant!'

Ernest looked round. 'Where are they all?'

'Our Daisy's in dreamland, just like Stanley here. The others have gone gadding off to the Empire.'

Ernest opened a carrier bag and brought out a couple of bottles of stout. 'I'm not carrying these back home, so how about joining me?'

'Well, I'm not drinking at the moment, but I'm sure half a glass won't do any harm.' Ernest struggled with the opener on his pocket knife.

Betty took the bottle from him. 'Here, let me. How is your shoulder by the way?'

'Not bad, it's just that I don't seem to have much control over my hand.' Ernest frowned. He was more worried than he would admit about how he would cope back at base. 'I'm joining my unit on Monday,' he told Betty when they were seated one at either side of the kitchen table.

'Oh! Are you well enough?'

'I've to see a doctor, I'll know more then.' He paused then asked, 'How's Clarence?'

'Gone.'

'Oh, he'll be back, don't you fret.'

'No, he won't. He's not just left the pit, he's left me too.' Betty looked close to tears. 'Everybody always leaves me.' She gave a nervous little laugh.

'I'm sure that's not true.' Ernest was concerned for her.

'Oh, but it is. The story of my life.'

Ernest thought she must be feeling vulnerable

because of the baby. He didn't know what to say and Betty continued talking.

'Even when I was a little girl, like our Daisy.'

'Who? Who left you?'

'The babies, one after the other, two brothers and a sister. I'd just get used to them being there when they'd die.'

'I didn't know that. But they didn't leave you . . . I mean, they died, they didn't have any option.'

'One tiny coffin after the other, taken to the grave-yard.' Ernest reached across the table and placed a hand over Betty's.

'Then the next ones were twins, a boy and a girl. Fine, healthy babies this time, according to the midwife. Not like the other poor wee things. By that time I was eight. I doted on them, nursed them when they cried, helped to bathe and change them.' Tears were streaming down Betty's face by this time.

'So, what happened?'

'One day I came home from school and they were being taken away, wrapped in blankets. Red blankets, the colour of blood. I've hated anything red since then. They had diphtheria. They were taken to the fever hospital . . . you know, the one on the edge of the moor? I was taken to see them one day. A nurse stood at an upstairs window with a baby in each arm. All I could see were two little faces, pale against the blankets. I never saw them again.'

'Oh, Betty!' Ernest came round the table to comfort her. She held up her hand to prevent him.

'Please, Ernest, let me finish. My mother seemed to shut me out after that.'

'But it must have been worse for her. Your mother, I mean.'

'Yes, I see that now, but I didn't then. She didn't even let me go to the funeral. Said it was no place for a child.'

'She was just protecting you.'

'But I needed to talk about them, take flowers to the grave, and I wasn't allowed even to mention their names.'

'What about your dad?'

'Oh, he understood, we talked when we were able. My dad gave me the affection I was seeking, but then he left me too. My dad died as well.'

'Oh, Betty, look . . . you're upsetting yourself too much. It can't be good for the baby, or for you.'

'It is. You don't know how long I've needed to talk about it.

'Well, after Dad died I started going out more, hanging about round by the clock, the life and soul of the gang. Or so they imagined. I got the reputation for being easy when all I was craving was affection. I thought I could buy it by giving them sex. I thought Clarence was different. I thought he respected me. Now he's left me too. Oh, I don't blame him, it was all wrong from the start, we should never have married without love.'

'You'll still have your baby,' Ernest said. 'You'll have someone to love you then.'

Betty frowned. 'Yes, but I'm scared about that. I'm scared to love anyone now. In case they leave me too.' She made an effort to smile. 'Sorry,' she said. 'What a way to spend Saturday night, listening to sob stories! Why aren't you at the Sun?'

'I don't know. I seem to be out of touch with the lads who are still here. All my mates from school have enlisted. Besides, I'm used to some right old booze-ups when we're off duty. Though that'll have to end soon, it'll be lemonade only once we start . . .' Ernest daren't say any more, in fact he'd said too much already. In any case, Betty suddenly let out a groan and clutched her stomach.

'What's up? Is it the baby?'

'No, it isn't due for another week.'

'All the same, perhaps I should fetch somebody?'

'No, I'm okay now, probably wind. So are there none of your mates left at the Sun?' Betty was embarrassed now to be alone with Ernest, not counting little Stanley who was fast asleep.

'One or two, but like I said, I'm not on the same wavelength, I don't know anything about mining.'

'You always were a cut above the rest of us, Ernest.'

He looked uncomfortable. 'How do yer mean?'

'After you went to grammar school. Well, you have to admit, it was unusual for any of us from the old church school to pass for the grammar.'

'I can thank me dad for that. He used to say, "Always mek most of thy sen, Ernest lad. If tha doesn't, no bugger else'll bother."' Ernest was a good mimic.

'Good for him.' Then Betty unexpectedly let out another groan. 'Oh! That really hurt.'

Ernest was out of the door and on his way to fetch her mother before she could stop him.

'What's up? Is the house on fire, lad?' Mrs Firth was standing at her door, getting a breath of air.

'No! It's Betty, Mrs Firth. I think the baby's on the way.'

'I'll come, lad. I shouldn't get 'er mother up, she's bound to be asleep at this time.' Mrs Firth was on her way before Ernest could argue. 'We'd best get yer to bed, love,' she said, seeing the stage she was at. Betty was bending over the table, moaning. She sank to her knees as she went towards the stairs. Ernest went to help her up but made the mistake of trying to lift her and found it impossible with his injury.

'Bloody shoulder,' he muttered.

'Now then, don't you be so daft or yer'll cause yerself no end of damage. Let's get 'er on't sofa, if yer can just shift young Stanley,' ordered Mrs Firth.

Ernest couldn't lift Betty but he scooped the boy, still miraculously asleep, in his good arm and deposited him upstairs on Jim and Sally's bed.

'Can yer make sure we've got some hot watter,

Ernest lad? And do yer think yer can find some towels to protect the sofa with?'

Ernest wasn't one to panic. He went calmly through the cupboards until he found whatever was needed.

'She'll not be long now. Eeh! It saddens me that all the fathers are away at times like these.' Mrs Firth began examining Betty then and Ernest made himself scarce to the kitchen. He could hear Betty crying out, and Mrs Firth talking soothingly to her the whole time. He had to laugh as he heard the woman telling Betty about the lovely calf she had recently delivered, and how it had come out the wrong way round: 'But this little mite's the right road round, no doubt about that. Now, let's 'ave a good strong push when yer feel as if yer need to.'

Betty must have felt it was needed because Mrs Firth said, 'That's a good girl . . . and now another. There it is! I can see the head. Come on now, just one more. That's it, easy as shelling peas.'

Then Ernest heard the cry of a new baby and Betty's voice exclaiming, 'Oh, Mrs Firth, it's a boy! Oh, isn't he beautiful? I never knew it would feel so wonderful.'

'Eeh, love, you'll never know joy like this if yer live to be a hundred. So let's have a pot of tea and enjoy the feeling.' Then her voice boomed out, 'Ernest, is that kettle on't boil? Can yer make us all some tea?'

123

'Yes, Mrs Firth. But can I come and look at the baby first?'

'Aye, come on, lad. Eeh, I bet yer right glad yer did yer shoulder in, aren't yer? After all, it's worth a bad shoulder to see a bonny new baby like this.'

Ernest grinned and looked at Betty, sitting up on the sofa, pretty as a picture with her new son in her arms. 'Yes, Mrs Firth, it certainly is.'

Betty Hayes *née* Butler looked happier than he could ever remember seeing her; she had always been a sulky young miss, from what he could recall. Now, though, he felt he could understand why. Betty, however, seemed a bit embarrassed as she remembered the things she had told him earlier.

'Thanks, Ernest, for listening,' she said shyly. 'And I'm sorry I've spoiled your Saturday night.'

'Spoiled it? I wouldn't have missed this experience for anything.'

Ernest found that he was glad she'd confided in him about her childhood. One thing was clear: *this* hale and hearty little one wouldn't be leaving her for a long time. His face clouded over then. At least, he hoped not. No one knew what would happen from one week to the next in wartime, but Ernest Denman knew a bit more than most. He realised things were about to get worse before they got better.

Betty never did find out who had been on at the Empire; nobody bothered to tell her, they were all too busy admiring the new baby, who by all accounts was also to be called Ernest.

'And what will his dad have to say about that?' Amy asked, in between cooing over her grandson and making sure her daughter was comfortable, after they had carried her on a chair back to her own bed.

'He isn't entitled to say anything,' Betty told her mother firmly. 'It wasn't him who was here for me, it was Ernest.'

Clarence Hayes had never even bothered to write to his wife, and since she didn't know his whereabouts, she couldn't let him know he was now a father. Betty didn't mind. She didn't want to share her son anyway. She wanted him all to herself.

The letter confirming Sally's inheritance had not yet arrived and she was becoming impatient to start work on the house. She knew the work might be in vain if anything went wrong, but decided to take off the wallpaper, which she placed in sacks ready for collection, and bought some distemper. She chose lemon for downstairs and pale pink for upstairs, then reversed the colours to stipple the walls with the aid of a sponge. She was delighted with the results and how much lighter the house now looked.

She daren't part with any of the furniture in case Charlotte became the new owner, against the odds, but Emily Simms had taken possession of the bedroom suite *pro tem*, on condition that it might have to be returned. The best of Mr Jessops' furniture would be retained and the rest given to some needy family, when the letter from the solicitor came through.

Sally enjoyed cleaning the house and making it attractive but was in no hurry to move in. The truth was she was nervous about taking her daughter to live in a house that had recently been entered and burgled.

Chapter Four

Daisy didn't want to go to the new house, not now
there was a new baby at Grandma Butler's. Sally
was having trouble keeping her daughter away –
Baby Doll had almost been abandoned once a real
live baby was on the scene. It was only the forthcoming concert that drew Daisy away from baby
Ernie and back out to play.

Pat was the organiser. Being rather big-headed
now she had passed for grammar school, she had
pronounced herself the boss. All the kids from the
three rows were roped in to take part in the show,
which would be staged on the flat piece of land
by the air-raid shelter. Nobody had any real choice
in what they would be doing except for Pat
Cartwright. She, of course, had the biggest role,
and since she was the best singer nobody
complained.

Pat would be singing three songs. One was about
a tree, and another about nymphs and shepherds –
not that any of them knew what a nymph was, not
even Pat. Norah was to sing about an aspidistra in
a pot. Daisy knew what that was because Grandma
Denman had one. The Dawson boys were to form

a trio and sing a George Formby song as well as 'Underneath the Arches'.

Most of the songs had been learned from records in the Cartwright's front room. Bernard complained that his precious 78s would be worn out by the time they had finished. Stanley didn't want to do anything at all, so he was elected to help with the costumes, the chairs, and to go round with a hat during the performance. Daisy, because she had Baby Doll, was to nurse her and sing 'Go To Sleep, My Baby'. She already knew that, as Sally had sung it to her every night, without fail, from the day she was born.

The star turn was to be Una Bacon who would wear the costume she wore when she attended her dancing lessons. She was to sing 'Horsey, Horsey, Don't You Stop'. In the middle of it she would stop singing and do a dance routine, including cartwheels. For someone not yet of school age this was a remarkable performance and Una was the envy of the whole gang.

All the mothers were in charge of costumes. Stanley, who'd thought he was being let off one responsibility, was disappointed, though. Pat decided he had to dress up as Charlie Chaplin, complete with moustache and cane. The hat would be just right for collecting money in because it would hold a lot.

On a glorious August Sunday afternoon, with a sky as blue as the dress Daisy was wearing, chairs were brought out of all the houses and a screen borrowed from Mrs Firth. This was used as a backcloth, behind which the performers made their entrances and exits. The concert was timed to coincide with the men arriving home from their lunch-time pints and promised to be an entertaining afternoon for performers and audience alike. Everybody who wasn't at work attended – apart from Betty, who had been forbidden to leave her bed for ten days, and Miss Appleby, because of her legs.

First on stage, of course, was Pat, whose clear melodious voice rang out across the field. By the time she had finished singing about a thing so lovely as a tree, a crowd of passers by, out for their usual Sunday afternoon walk, had joined the audience and their applause could be heard all the way down St George's Road.

Next were the Dawson lads and because their choice of songs was so popular, they were forced to add on another at the end. Fortunately they all knew another song and the audience joined in so that any forgotten words went unnoticed. 'Strolling' had everybody swaying along with the three lads from Taylors Row.

Next little Daisy brought forth cries of 'Aah' and a few tears to the eyes of her parents as she stood centre-stage – if there had been one – and sang to Baby Doll.

Then it was Pat's turn again, this time with 'Nymphs and Shepherds', which wasn't quite so popular, and then Norah. Her 'Biggest Aspidistra' was better received.

Little Una, of course, should have been top of the bill. She actually received a standing ovation when 'Horsey' finally stopped. Then it was Pat's turn again. She had certainly planned the programme well, as she ended with a medley of songs such as 'Tipperary' and about another half-dozen wartime favourites. At the end of all this she was joined by the other performers for the finale with 'Land Of Hope and Glory'.

The whole crowd rose to its feet and sang along with gusto, and Sally wasn't the only one crying by this time.

Charlie Chaplin made sure he approached the visitors from St George's Road first. They were the ones from the big houses and were probably the wealthiest. The ones who gave the most generously, however, were those who had come straight from the Rising Sun. They would no doubt wonder where their money had disappeared to, later on when they had sobered up.

Pat proudly thanked everyone for coming and begged them to give generously for the Sheffield Newspapers' War Fund.

There were no prouder parents in England that afternoon than Bernard and Enid Cartwright, and with good reason.

Sally had just finished the ironing when Miss Appleby looked at the clock.

'You should 'ave time to put a bit of polish on the furniture before yer go. I hope yer not going to be sneaking off before twelve.'

'Now, Miss Appleby, you know I never sneak off anywhere. If I wanted to go early, I should tell you and just go.'

The older woman was sitting as usual in her chair by the window. Suddenly she sat bolt upright, on the alert. 'Hello, it looks like she's expecting another caller. Almost midday and she's drawing the curtains.'

'Who?'

'The one on St George's Road. The one with the window box.'

'Well, it is rather sunny, maybe she doesn't want the furniture to fade.'

'Sun, rain or snow, makes no difference to that one. Always entertaining one man or another. Two she's carrying on with at present. There's a young one . . . nice-looking he is, too . . . then there's the other one who seems old enough to be her father. Looks to be on his last legs to me.'

'Perhaps he *is* her father,' replied Sally, thinking, what a vicious old woman you are.

'Of course he isn't! Her parents moved down south years ago. Ashamed of 'er, I shouldn't wonder.'

'She seemed a lovely lady when I spoke to her.'

'You spoke to her?' Miss Appleby seemed surprised to hear it.

'Yes, about music lessons when I was fourteen, but she was booked up solid. That proves how good she is.' Sally grinned. 'A good thing, really. I lost interest as soon as I left school so it would have been a waste of money.'

'No staying power, you young ones. Anyway, she'd 'ave fitted you in if you'd been of the opposite sex, no doubt. I 'aven't seen any pupils there for months. Must be making enough out of her man friends,' said Miss Appleby spitefully.

'She didn't seem that type of person to me,' Sally protested.

'Well! You can't go on appearances is all that proves.' She moved closer to the window. 'Isn't that Dr North over there? I hope 'e isn't coming 'ere. He isn't a proper doctor like Dr Sellars. Oh! You'll never credit it . . . he's going in. Don't tell me she's got 'er eye on him too!'

'Maybe she's ill.'

'Dr Sellars used to come and see me every week about my legs,' Miss Appleby said, unconcerned whether the poor woman was ill or not.

'Well, she never seemed to do you much good. Dr North told you to walk more. Said a walk to the surgery would do you good.'

'You know very well I can't walk. It takes me ten minutes to get out of me chair. Anyway, what does *he* know? Not long out of school, by the looks of things. At first he seemed quite nice, then after a bit 'e didn't seem to want to listen. I offered 'im some tips on 'ow to run the surgery better, but in my opinion 'e wasn't interested. Some people won't be told, even when it's for their own good. I mean, I should know 'ow surgeries work when I 'ad a cousin who cleaned in one.'

Ida's face suddenly took on a condescending expression and she gave a little wave like the Queen. 'There, he's going now. I told yer he wouldn't call.'

Sally gave an exasperated rub with the yellow duster. 'You said you didn't *want* him to call.'

'I didn't, but it's the thought that counts.'

Just then Sally knocked over a framed photograph with a clatter.

'Go on, go on, break up me happy home now,' Miss Appleby said sharply.

Sally replaced the photograph, muttering to herself: '*Happy* home . . . with you in it?'

'What did yer say?'

'I said, I'll make you a drink in a minute.'

'Go on then, and make one for yerself. And mind how much tea you use.'

Sally went to the kitchen and filled the kettle, placed it on the gas ring and prepared a tray. In her absence Ida Appleby stood up, walked over to the ironing board and began examining the pile of ironing. Sally stood by the door and watched her.

'I thought you couldn't get out of your chair,' she said. 'And why are you counting the handker-chiefs? Don't worry, I shan't pinch those. I could start a market stall with the ones I've had bought.

133

Besides, we never seem to need them at our house. I can't remember when I last washed one.'

Miss Appleby moaned and made a performance of looking crippled and in agony as she made her way back to her chair. 'That doesn't surprise me,' she said, referring to the hankies. 'Too lazy to wash them, I expect. Now when I was a housekeeper things were different. Everything had to be boiled, starched and dolly blued. You wouldn't have lasted two minutes in that job. You'd have been scared of the steam ruining yer make up.'

Sally brought the tray in from the kitchen and slammed it down on the table. 'I still boil and dolly blue, I'll have you know. Here's your tea. I won't have one myself, thank you. In case you haven't noticed, it's ten-past twelve.'

She picked up her bag and stormed out, leaving Ida sitting there open-mouthed. By the time Sally had walked the few doors home she had calmed herself down, but wondered why she felt sorry for such a miserable, self-centred old woman as Ida Appleby.

Nellie delivered the letter from Dunstone & Sedgewick on Friday morning, which announced that probate had been granted. At last Sally let herself become excited at the prospect of moving house. Little did she know that her rival was still planning revenge on her for her temerity.

Mark Kaye had begun to wonder if Charlotte

needed some treatment for mental disturbance. For two nights she had woken him up with the story that there were dogs in the room. He had returned to the marital bed, not because he desired the closeness of her body, but to put an end to her constant nagging.

'Look, there are no dogs! There have never been any dogs in this house.'

'There are! They're the dogs out of those cheap prints you brought from Uncle Walter's. You should have brought the right pictures.'

'Yes, well, as I told you before, I'm not a bloody owl. If you'd wanted me to see in the dark, you should have supplied a torch or fed me more carrots.'

'They're big dogs . . . menacing.'

Mark looked at her with incredulity. 'You're stark raving mad.'

'I want you to get rid of those pictures.'

'Oh, you do, do you? Well, you wanted them, you got them, so shut up! I've got work in the morning.'

'The clock strikes as well.'

'What?'

'The clock . . . I can hear it strike one, as if to wake the dogs. Then they come for me.'

Mark laughed. 'You really *are* mad.' He turned over, pulling the eiderdown with him. 'And if you aren't careful, I shall soon be back in the other room. For good.'

Charlotte huddled closer to him.

'Don't leave me, Mark, I'm scared.'

'Go to sleep.'

She's insane, was the last thing he thought before he dropped off to sleep. The sooner she got rid of her ill-gotten loot, the sooner she would shut up.

Charlotte lay there, staring at the blank wall behind which stood Walter's clocks, silent and unwound.

Ernest arrived back at his base on the Lincolnshire coast, intent upon proving himself fit for action. During his medical examination he gritted his teeth and told the doctor he was ready for duty.

The doctor was an expert at weeding out malingerers. In this case, he knew Ernest Denman was lying in order to be back in action. He was quick to note the colour drain from his patient's face as he prodded and stretched the offending shoulder, however. 'Two more weeks,' he diagnosed.

That decision was probably to save Ernest's life. In the following few days, the RAF lost twenty-seven of its own aircraft, shooting down more than a hundred enemy raiders. The plane Ernest Denman would have been flying was one of them.

Friday afternoon was one of Daisy's favourite times, when her mam and Aunty Mary took the two children to Millington market. All the mams seemed to get dolled up a bit for their visit there and Daisy was washed and changed into a clean dress. The mams always had a gossip and admired new babies, as well as queueing up for any biscuits or sweets that happened to be available. The sweets were usually pear drops or humbugs which would be shared out over the next week, a few every day. Daisy had noticed that on Sunday afternoons she usually got a few extra to keep her quiet while Mam and Dad went for a lie down upstairs. Today they were going to buy her new socks for school. Mam said she would get them from Old Misery's stall as his were cheaper.

The market was a cheerful place. There was jolly Mr Capstick who sold shoes and menswear. There was the fruit and vegetable stall where the stall holder juggled with potatoes. Old Misery's stall, where Sally bought underwear, a fancy goods stall, and best of all the toy stall where Stanley and Daisy would no doubt be bought a paint book or windmill, or, in Stanley's case, stamps for his album.

Sally perched Daisy on the edge of the stall while she and Mary examined the goods. Suddenly she heard her daughter talking to the stall holder and was mortified to hear her announce: 'I've come for some new socks, Mr Misery. Can I have some with stripes round the top, Mr Misery?' Of course the man had only been nicknamed Old Misery because he had a face as long as Woodhead Tunnel, but Daisy wasn't to know that.

Sally was in such a hurry to escape the embarrassment that the socks were forgotten as she scooped her daughter up in her arms and hurried her from the stall and out of the market. 'But I haven't got my socks or a windmill,' Daisy complained.

The windmill-buying was usually left until the end of their visit, in order to bribe the kids to behave in the meantime. Today, however, no brightly coloured celluloid toy was forthcoming. It wasn't until they were halfway up the Donkey Path that Sally looked at Mary and they both began to chuckle. Before long they were convulsed with laughter.

'I shall never dare show my face there again,' Sally said when they had calmed down.

'Well, Daisy wasn't to know it wasn't his real name. Besides, he may take the hint and smile sometimes now.'

'I don't think he knows how. Tell you what, him and Miss Appleby ought to get together.'

That set them off again and they were still laughing when they reached Potters Row. Stanley made a gesture to Daisy that indicated they were both daft.

'It's all right them laughing but I haven't got my socks,' she complained.

'And I haven't got any stamps for my album. Good job we went to the sweet stall first, or we wouldn't have got any sweets either!'

Betty placed Ernie in his smart new pram, carriage painted in navy and cream, and wheeled him proudly down St George's Road. People paused to admire the fair-haired little boy and remark on how closely he resembled his mother. She could see no resemblance at all, in fact, and believed he was the image of Clarence. If he grew up to look like his father he would certainly be a handsome man, though Betty realised now it was too late that looks were the least important thing in a husband. Clarence had given her security, though, by leaving her financially independent; she was grateful to him for that. But the money wouldn't last for ever. She didn't dare to think what would happen when it was all gone.

She turned the corner towards the Co-op, just as Florence Ramsgate got off the bus. The other girl was wearing the uniform of the Women's Army Corps. She looked so smart it was a few seconds before Betty recognised her friend of many years' standing. On the other hand, Florence had to look twice at Betty, what with the change of hairstyle and the big new pram.

'Florence!' Betty stopped in her tracks. 'What are you doing here?'

'Betty, this is never yours?' Florence pulled down the pram cover and peeped at Ernie. She looked so sad then as she congratulated Betty on her beautiful little boy. Betty knew Florence must be remembering her own baby, and because she and Florence had been friends from the day they were born she couldn't not mention it.

'Yes, it's mine. What about yours, Florence, or would you rather not talk about it?'

'No, it's quite all right . . . I had her adopted. They took her away when she was born. It wasn't easy, but the best thing for her. Well, I didn't want to bring her back to my mother's place, you know what *she's* like. Oh, but it is good to see you, Betty!'

'You too. How long are you home for? Hey, and how about this?' Betty patted Florence's uniform.

'Yes, well, I didn't want to come back here, so joining up seemed my best way out. I'm here for a few days, though, duty visit. I do miss my dad, you see.' She pointed at Betty's wedding ring. 'So you married Clarence then?'

'Yes. Mistake, though.'

'I thought you and he were well matched?'

'Oh, we were well-matched, all right, for a bit of fun, not for life.'

'So where is he? Still at the pit?'

'Gone to do battle, don't ask me where.'

'Well, I'd better go, but we'll catch up later.'

'Yes, come on and see my mam, she'd love to chat to you.'

'Sure will. After tea maybe?'

'Yes, that'll be okay.'

Betty felt sorry for Florence, having to part with her baby, but she envied her all the same. She looked so good in that khaki uniform. If only Betty could be free to do something, go somewhere. Then she looked at Ernie, staring up at her with big blue eyes, and knew she wouldn't swap him for all the fancy costumes in Lewis's, let alone a dull, brown twill cotton thing with no shape at all.

All the same Betty was itching to become part of the outside world again, and wondered now why she had found her job in the wages office so boring. There had been the chats with the other girls, the jokes the men had told, and the tricks they had played on the young lads on their first day.

Betty giggled as she remembered the day young Derek Flint had begun work. Mabel the canteen lady had brought a neatly folded overall for young Derek to wear as he cleaned the machines. 'Go behind the filing cabinets and take off yer shirt and trousers,' she had told the shy young lad. 'Pass them over and I'll give yer the overall.' Young Derek had passed his clothes to Mabel and then stood waiting, wearing nothing but a string vest and underpants. No one had taken any notice as he stood there, shouting for Mabel to come back. It had been an hour before she decided he had waited long enough.

The fun had lasted much longer than an hour, though, as one of the office girls had sneaked a picture on her Brownie box camera of Derek cowering behind the filing cabinets in underpants down to his knees! Betty wondered what the people at Kodak had thought about that photograph. At least it would have given them a laugh.

She continued her walk to the Co-op, where she bought Johnson's baby powder and Dettol in readiness for Ernie's bath. She decided to treat herself to a new lipstick, the first thing she'd bought for herself since Ernie was born.

It would be nice catching up with Florence's news. She'd missed the friend who had shared all her secrets, though Betty was secretly ashamed of some of the things she and Florence had got up to in their early-teens. Well, they had both paid dearly for those mistakes and one thing Betty was sure of: from now on her reputation would remain unblemished. She had made enough mistakes to last her a lifetime.

Millington Council School was built in four wings surrounding a central garden plot. The garden had been taken over by the senior boys as an allotment for the duration of the war.

It was Daisy's long-awaited first day at school. She set off excitedly with Norah in charge of her. The baby class was bright and cheerful, and Miss Robinson the mistress in charge of it was kind to Daisy. The walls were hung with colourful pictures and the letters of the alphabet, which Daisy already knew from beginning to end. In the corner was a sandpit, and little fold-up beds where the children were expected to rest in the afternoon. What Daisy liked best of all were the boxes of crayons. They were each allowed to choose two colours to make a pattern on grey paper; she chose purple and orange. Later Miss Robinson pinned the pictures on the wall.

On her first day Daisy made a new friend called Carol, a beautiful child with long, golden curls. Daisy's own curls were rapidly turning mousey-coloured. Carol and Daisy soon became inseparable and were firm friends.

Daisy loved the baby class, especially Friday afternoons when they were allowed to bring in a toy each to play with. Sometimes Daisy would take in two after she'd noticed one of the other children didn't seem to have any toys. This little girl came from a very large family and Daisy enjoyed lending her a toy; it made them both happy. Carol lived close to the school in a large, stone-built house with a wonderful overgrown shrubbery. She had a little sister, whom she mostly ignored, and a whole family of cats whom she adored. It wasn't long before Daisy was invited to play at Carol's. Their favourite game was dressing up the cats in baby bonnets and bootees – that was, until one of them weed on Daisy's new gaberdine coat.

She took it home, hung it on the hook behind the door, and every day afterwards Sally complained about the smell. She scrubbed out the doorway with Dettol, cleaned the doormat, and bitterly blamed Mrs Firth's cats. It wasn't until one rainy day some time later that she realised it was the coat that stank.

By that time the cat game had been forgotten but the friendship between Carol and Daisy was to endure for the rest of their lives.

Daisy skipped happily along to school every morning, wearing her gymslip and blouse. She also wore a V for Victory badge and carried a tiny shoulder bag containing a clean handkerchief and, on Mondays, two shillings to be invested in the school bank. Miss Robinson found Daisy advanced for her age, due no doubt to Grand-dad Denman having already taught her to read short words and to write her name.

The only lesson Daisy didn't like was Physical Training. She found the exercises difficult and couldn't catch a ball, no matter how hard she tried. It wasn't long before she was having nightmares about cart-wheels she couldn't turn and forward rolls in which she never got off her feet. She soon learned to sneak to the back of the queue to avoid her turn. How she wished she was Una Bacon, who could manoeuvre her body any way she chose. Daisy worked hard, though, especially on her reading books, and soon left Dick and Jane far behind. She was reading anything and everything she could lay her hands on.

Sally was determined to keep cheerful as she let herself into Miss Appleby's one morning. 'Hello,' she called, 'and how are you this lovely morning?'

'Oh, yer know, usual.' The woman's already gawky neck stretched like a giraffe's as she attempted to catch any sign of activity down on St George's Road.

'Look, there's *another* visitor down there . . . that's him I was telling yer about, the young one. Wearing sunglasses so that no one will recognise him, I expect. He's probably got a wife and kids at home.'

'Good morning, Sally. How are you feeling today?' she mouthed to herself as she washed two days' worth of dishes that had been waiting for her. 'If he's driving he'll need sunglasses on a day like today,' she said out loud.

'I've heard that car drawing up in the middle of the night sometimes.'

'How do you know it's *that* car?' Sally glanced out of the window at it.

'Well, it sounded the same to me. She wants reporting . . . men coming and going at all hours of the day and night.' Ida Appleby suddenly moved closer to the window, eyes gleaming. 'Look, they're getting into the car together, bold as brass! Just look at her, dolled up like the woman of the streets she is. Look at the height of them heels.'

'I've never seen her in the same outfit twice. Slimmed until there's no flesh left on her, and I bet she's put her make up on with a shovel. Spends money like water does that one. Still, we all know where she gets it from, don't we?'

Sally knocked the photo frame over as usual and stood it up, only for it to topple over again.

'You did that on purpose! I don't think you'll be satisfied until you've broken that frame.'

'You need a new one, it's unsteady.'

'No, it isn't! I'll bet it cost our Donald a lot to have that framed.'

Sally continued with the dusting, muttering her thoughts to herself.

'It's a pity he doesn't come and visit instead.'

'What did yer say?' Miss Appleby was supposed to be deaf but she never missed a thing.

'I said, Mrs Simms said his hair's an unusual shade of red.'

'Hmm, now, where were we? Oh, yes, her going gallivanting in that car . . . Well, we all know how she earns them treats, don't we?'

Sally put away the Mansion polish and got out the clean sheets and pillow cases to change the bed. 'From what I've heard she comes from a very well-to-do family, and she's certainly a very accomplished pianist. A member of the examining board too, which could account for her income. Not that it's any of our business.'

'Some folk'll believe owt! I *know* how she comes by her money. You've only to watch the men going in and out. A disgrace to the neighbourhood, she is.'

Sally took out her anger on the pillows. 'I think you're imagining things. You spend too much time by that window. When was the last time you went to the shops?'

'I don't think I shall ever get to the shops again, not with my legs.' A knock on the door prevented Sally from protesting at this.

'That'll be Emily Simms,' Miss Appleby said. 'Nobody else comes here any more – and *she* only comes round nosing. I don't think I like her discussing our Donald wi' folk.'

Emily came bustling in then and Sally thankfully prepared to leave, relieved that she'd managed to keep her temper with the spiteful old woman.

Charlotte Kaye heard the clock strike one. She moved closer to Mark but daren't wake him in case he decided to move to the spare room again. She heard the dogs snarling, and then the sound became more aggressive and she felt the eiderdown being tugged as they approached her side of the bed. Charlotte screamed in fright and her husband jumped out of bed and switched on the light.

'What the hell's the matter?'

'The dogs! They were coming for me, trying to climb up on to the bed . . .'

'Where? Just show me these dogs.' Charlotte was silent as she stared around the room, perplexed.

'You can't, can you? Because there are no dogs. There have never been any dogs in this house.'

'I told you, they're the dogs from the pictures. I want you to take them away!'

'They're yours. Do what the hell you like with them, but don't involve me.'

Mark Kaye had had enough of hearing about the pictures, the clocks, the books, the jewellery he'd stupidly left behind. And, most of all, he'd had enough of his wife mithering about the non-existent dogs. He switched off the bedroom light and went back to the spare room. She'd had her chance; he was out of her bed for good this time.

Charlotte cowered beneath the eiderdown, trembling with fear. She heard the clock strike two, then three, then four. When daylight came she was still staring at the wall, already dreading another night spent listening to the dogs.

As soon as autumn came and the colder weather set in, Daisy started with her sore throats again. Sally hoped it wouldn't be a repetition of last winter, when nearly everyone in Sheffield went down with influenza. Daisy was dosed with Veno's and, when that didn't work, with balsam and aniseed. She was muffled up in a warm new Liberty bodice from which were suspended her long, black woollen stockings. She moaned because Norah had brown ones, which Daisy considered more grown-up.

She also hated the pixie hats that Grandma Butler busily knitted in order to prevent her fingers from stiffening up with the rheumatics. Daisy wished she dare wear the fur-lined hat Uncle Ernest had bought her instead, but it was too precious to risk losing. So she conveniently 'lost' the dreaded pixie hats by dropping them behind the hot water pipes in the school cloakroom. The sore throats didn't stop her from playing out with the big boys and girls, and Sally threatened to keep her indoors unless she took more care of her clothing and kept warm.

At the end of October the Dawson boys announced that it was Kay Kay Night.

'What does kay kay mean?' Daisy always liked new words.

'Don't know.' Trevor thought about it. 'It's just an owd rhyme that we sing at doors at this time of year. Me dad used to do it, and me grand-dad before that.'

'Can I come?' Daisy asked.

'If yer like.'

The children went from door to door, singing at each one:

> Kay kay kay,
> Hole in me stocking,
> Hole in me shoe.
> Please can yer spare us a copper or two?
> If yer haven't a penny,
> A halfpenny'll do.
> If yer haven't a halfpenny,
> God bless you.

Daisy knew if her mam found out she wouldn't let her join in, so she didn't tell her. Instead she followed Norah, Stanley and the Dawsons. Most of the neighbours parted with a penny or two or even a threepenny bit, fondly remembering the times when they themselves had gone kay kaying, many years ago. Shared amongst six of them the money didn't amount to much but Derek Dawson said that didn't matter.

'What matters,' he said, 'is that we get our own back on the ones who were too skinny to give us owt. We'll do that on Mischief Night.'

Mischief Night was the last night of October. As soon as it was dark enough they set off along the rows, starting with Barkers Row. 'That Mrs Broomsgrove never gives us owt,' Trevor moaned. 'She doesn't like kids, she's scared of us muckying her doorstep. I know . . . we'll tie all the doors on her side together so they can't get out.'

'But all the folks who did give us summat won't be able to get out either,' Norah pointed out.

'Oh, no, but that'll only be for fun. When we've tied all the doors together we'll do the bull roar at owd lass Broomsgrove's.'

'What's the bull roar?' Daisy didn't like the sound of that.

'Wait and see,' Trevor told her. He looked at the bag his brother was carrying. ''Ave yer got the string?'

'Yer, it's 'ere.'

Trevor took the large ball of string, which had been found – or so he said – in the allotment at school.

'You lot, keep hidden,' he said. The rest of the gang crouched behind a wall and Trevor set off along the row, where he fastened the string tightly to the first door handle and threaded it through each of the snecks, all along the row, until he reached the last one where he tightened it and made it secure. Then he dashed back to the others. 'Right,' he said, 'did yer bring the papers?'

'Yer, they're 'ere,' Derek answered, him.

'And the matches?' His brother handed the bag to Trevor, who dashed off in the direction of the Broomsgroves'.

It was a dark night and they could just make him out as he stuffed all the paper up Mrs Broomsgrove's drain pipe. Then he lit it and dashed back to their hiding place behind the wall. They waited in anticipation. Suddenly the paper began to roar up the pipe. Mrs Broomsgrove was the first to try opening her door, next was Mr Bacon, but the doors were held firmly shut by the taut string. Suddenly Mrs Broomsgrove appeared round the corner of her house, having used the back door. This was the signal for the gang to disappear across the field, enjoying the thrill of the chase and hysterical with laughter. Little Daisy was terrified of being left behind but revelled in being included in the gang. Their next stop was Potters Row.

'It's no good going to our row,' Trevor said, 'one house is empty and the other one's Mrs Simms.

We're not scaring her, she gave us sixpence. Besides, she's an owd woman.'

'Mrs Broomsgrove's an owd woman,' Stanley reasoned.

'I know, but she's a miserable owd woman.'

'Whose house is next then?' Norah hoped it wasn't theirs.

'That Miss Appleby's. She gave us nowt.'

'Not the bull roar, not when she lives by herself. She'll be too scared,' Norah pointed out.

'Oh, no, summat better than that for her.' Trevor ran round the corner by the lavatories and came back with an old, dead rabbit. Norah backed away. 'Don't bring that thing near me,' she whispered.

'No, Daisy can do this, she's the littlest.' Daisy looked terrified. 'But I don't like dead animals,' she said.

'Well, you've only to 'old it by the ears, open the door, throw it in and run away. Being the littlest, she won't notice you.'

'Oh, I don't know.' Norah looked scared. 'Because she's only little, our Daisy won't be able to run away in time.'

'That's okay, that owd woman won't even notice her, she'll be too shocked. Go on, Daisy.' Trevor held out the flea-ridden carcass. 'Just run and open the door and throw it in. Then off, as fast as yer can. We'll wait for yer.'

Daisy was trembling with fear: fear of the thing in her hand, and fear of Miss Appleby. She had heard her mam saying what an awful woman she was, but the little girl was even more scared of being excluded from the gang, so she did what she was told.

Holding the rabbit at arm's length, she tiptoed to Miss Appleby's back door, opened it and threw the creature into the kitchen. The scream the woman let out could be heard from one end of Potters Row to the other.

Daisy made off in the direction of the gap in the wall but the rest of them were nowhere to be seen. The only one left was Daisy Butler, who sank down into the long grass and began to cry.

'What the hell's going on?'

Jim saw the open door and dashed into Ida Appleby's, the first time he had ever set foot in the place.

Mr Firth followed close behind. 'What's up, Ida?'

But by this time both men could see and smell the furry corpse on the pegged rug in front of the fire.

The shock had rendered Miss Appleby speechless. Just then Alfie Ramsgate tottered in, wearing only a mucky white shirt, fortunately a long one, his thin bare legs sticking out beneath it. Alfie was still drunk from his drinking session at dinnertime.

'I thought bloody 'ouse was on fire,' he grumbled. 'I'd just managed to get our Kitty to come to bed for an hour – and then you 'ad to go and disturb us. Yer daft owd bat, making a racket like that!' He glared at Ida from beneath shaggy eyebrows.

'Go back to bed, Alf, your Kitty'll still be waiting for yer. There's nowt to get alarmed about,' Jim assured him. 'Who did it?' he asked the trembling woman.

'Y-Your little l-lass,' Ida stammered.

'What?' He couldn't believe it.

'Never!' Mr Firth thought the world of little Daisy.

'She did, she threw it at me. I saw her.'

'If she did,' Jim said, as though the woman might be lying, 'I'll tan her arse, I promise you. *And* she can clean it up.' He stormed out of the house. By this time Enid and Sally were out and about too.

'Daisy!' Jim's voice echoed along the row. The field was empty. The Dawsons had skedaddled. Stanley had gone home and sneaked off to bed without being told. Norah was sitting quietly, white-faced, her head hidden in a book. Only Daisy was still cowering behind the wall.

'Daisy, wherever you are, yer might as well come out.'

She came slowly through the gap in the wall, her face a ghostly white in the darkness. She had never seen her dad so angry.

'Did you do this?'

Daisy nodded and wished she could make herself invisible.

'Go and get a shovel.'

She ran home to fetch the coal shovel, then ran back. She was crying harder now. She knew she had done something really dreadful.

'Get rid of this,' ordered Jim, glaring at her. Daisy shovelled up the stinking mess which immediately fell off again, on to a different and clean bit of rug, making another wet, dirty patch which was further embellished by the muck on the coal shovel. Miss Appleby screamed again at the sight.

'Tell Miss Appleby you're sorry,' Jim ordered.

'I'm s-sorry, Miss Appleby,' Daisy sobbed.

'Now,' Jim took the shovel from his daughter, 'get home and wait for me there.'

Miss Appleby looked a little calmer by now. Mr Firth had filled the kettle and placed it on the gas ring. 'I'll mek yer a cup of tea, Ida,' he said.

'You . . . er . . . you won't smack her, will yer?' Ida asked Jim.

'Aye, I will. She's got to be punished. It'll hurt me more than it does her, but she can't get away with summat like this.'

'But . . . I mean, she's only a little lass. I daresay it were the big ones who put her up to it. So I'd prefer yer not to hit her.'

Jim looked at her. He'd never really taken to this woman but maybe she wasn't so bad after all. Even so, Daisy couldn't go unpunished; she needed to learn right from wrong.

Bernard Cartwright had come to see if there was anything to be done. 'Our Norah's as bad as her if she was with her at the time, which I suppose she was. She'll have to be punished as well.'

'Nay, it were our Daisy who did it.'

'But I imagine our Norah stood by and watched her. She should have set an example, her being the eldest.'

'No, don't smack either of them.' Miss Appleby seemed upset by the thought of the children being hurt.

'I'll see,' Jim said, as he made his way out with the shovelful of stinking fur. 'I'm sorry,' he said. 'I don't know what got into her.' He pointed at the rug. 'I expect Sally'll be able to clean that when she comes next time.'

'Aye, I expect she will. She's a good cleaner, I'll say that for her.'

'I'll say good night then.' Jim wished he was miles away. Any other night he would probably have been at work and Sally could have dealt with the problem. No, that was a cowardly way of thinking. What the hell was he to do, though?

At home he was met by the sound of Daisy crying and Sally shouting at her, 'If you don't shut up, you'll get another one.' Daisy's cries turned into strangled sobs. She was rubbing her leg where Sally had slapped her. Thank God it was over and done with.

'Get undressed and up them stairs,' Jim snapped.

Daisy took off her jumper and skirt, still sobbing as she stood there in her knickers and Liberty bodice. She took off her stockings and Jim noticed that her leg was unmarked. Sally took a nighty off the fireguard and slid it over her daughter's head.

'Now, to bed,' Jim said. 'We'll say no more about tonight, but just remember never to do anything so cruel again.'

The sobbing increased as Daisy told them, 'They t-told me to do it . . . I d-didn't want to.'

'Then you should have ignored them. Don't blame anybody else, it was you who did it. Now, upstairs!'

'But I haven't had me supper.'

'Upstairs.'

Daisy disappeared without another word. Her mother didn't often smack her but she realised she'd deserved it this time. Besides, it would have hurt a lot more if her dad had hit her. She didn't take much notice of her mam, but punishment from her dad really upset her. The worst punishment of all was having no supper . . . that and the look on poor Miss Appleby's face. She would never do anything so bad again, ever.

'Poor Miss Appleby,' Sally sighed after Daisy was fast asleep.

'Aye, and poor Kitty Ramsgate.' Jim grinned.

'What?'

'Being deprived of a good seeing to from owd

Alf.' The sight of him in his nightshirt, and the thought of Kitty lying there waiting, was worth all tonight's upset. Alfie would never hear the last of it when the tale was told in the Rising Sun.

Chapter Five

At last Ernest Denman was back in action, just in time to help defend London from a night attack on 15 September. It had been anticipated that the German invasion would take the form of an attempt to destroy the RAF. Instead the capital and other major English cities were to be targeted in a series of raids by the enemy. On the first night Ernest was back with his squadron the Luftwaffe lost fifty-six of its planes.

One of the Messerschmitts shot down over the south of England was brought to Sheffield a few days later and put on display at Barker's Pool. Jim took Daisy, Stanley and Norah to see the plane. Within a week 40,000 people had paid to view it. This helped to raise £1,000 for the Sheffield Newspapers' War Fund. The sight of it made Jim realise just how vulnerable Ernest must be to attacks from these precision-made enemy fighters. He was relieved that Sally had been too busy to come with them.

The three children were thrilled by the trip, especially Stanley, who was allowed to be lifted aboard. Thank God the children were unaware of the blood, sweat and tears the courageous young RAF men expended on their behalf. Jim said a silent prayer that the war would soon be at an end and all the brave fighting men home safe and sound.

It was not to be. In November 1940, in the city of Coventry, hundreds of civilians were killed in the worst air raid of the war so far.

Betty Hayes had been unsettled by Florence's home visit. Amy had looked after her grandson so that Betty and her friend could enjoy some time together. They had gone to the Palace to see a film, and bought a bag of fish and chips afterwards, to eat sitting on a seat in the Memorial Gardens. Betty hadn't had much to talk about; in fact, nothing really except for little Ernie. It had brought home to her just how a monotonous a life she was leading.

Florence, by comparison, was in touch with all kinds of people, doing a worthwhile and interesting job, and going out dancing most nights she was off duty. Betty kept reminding herself that her son was more important to her than anything or anyone in the whole world, but it didn't take away her desire to be doing something other than just being a mother.

Amy recognised the new dissatisfaction within her daughter and wished she could give the girl a bit more leisure time, but the pain in her leg and the rheumatism in her hands and arms meant she was almost incapable of handling Ernie safely.

When Sally heard about Betty's night out, she said she should do it more often, even offered to care for little Ernie the following Saturday, to give her sister-in-law a break.

Betty wondered where she could go. Florence had been her only friend apart from the girls at work. There was always Doreen, she supposed, who was in the same position as herself. Her husband was in the Navy and she was the mother of a little girl. Betty and Doreen had worked together since leaving school. Maybe she would like to meet up again. Of course, there was the baby-sitting problem but Betty would pay her a visit anyway.

Doreen was thrilled to see her. 'Come in, it's been ages.' She peered at Ernie in his pram. 'Oh, Betty, he's gorgeous. I'll put the kettle on.' Doreen's mother worked in the forces canteen in Sheffield. Doreen herself was quite content at home with little Alice to keep her company. Betty played with Alice while Doreen made the tea.

'She's going to break a few hearts, just look at those eyes.' It was true, Doreen's little girl was beautiful.

'What are you doing with yerself these days?' Betty asked her friend.

'Not a lot.' Doreen pulled a face. 'Get up, eat breakfast, clean up, eat dinner, take her for a walk, eat tea. Then I listen to the radio until bedtime. I know I should feel like running away, but actually I'm quite content as long as I've got my baby.'

Betty laughed. 'Just like me. Except, I must admit, sometimes I could scream.' She rocked Ernie's pram as he began to stir. 'It's just, I feel so useless.'

'We could go out one night. Me mam'd mind our Alice.'

Betty frowned. 'I'd love to, but my mam isn't so well. She's not as young as yours. Though my sister-in-law did offer . . . Anyway, where would we go?'

'Well, there's the dance at Victoria Hall.'

'Really! I didn't think they'd still have them, with all the men away.'

'Oh, you'd be surprised. The soldiers stationed in Sheffield come out here. Then there are the poor things convalescing at the Wharncliffe after Dunkirk, they're encouraged to go out, not that many of them are up to dancing. Then there are the miners and steelworkers . . . they still need cheering up. Anyway, we could always dance together.' Doreen laughed. 'Even dancing wi' you'd be better than sitting here every night!'

'You're not kidding. If I don't get a social life soon, I shall end up like a cabbage.'

'Well, you always were a bit green,' Doreen teased. 'Look, do try and get a night out, it'll be a laugh. Here, 'ave a biscuit.'

Betty nibbled at a Marie biscuit and pulled a face.

'Hmm, I know, they are a bit soggy. Me mam

brought them home from the canteen, they were supposed to chuck them away.'

Betty dunked it in her tea and giggled. 'Won't know the difference now. Oh, I am glad I came.'

'So am I. I can't wait to get dolled up and shake a leg.' Doreen grinned. 'I might even get some of that leg paint and colour them.'

'Yes, we both will. We'll paint 'em. Just wishful thinking, though; I can't leave Ernie. Still, nice talking to you. Maybe we could take them for a walk one afternoon?'

'Yes, we'll go up the moor towards Longfield, take a picnic. It might be a bit cold but it'll blow the cobwebs off us.'

'Great. Well, I'd better be going. He'll want a feed as soon as he opens his eyes.' Betty kissed Alice and waved goodbye to her.

'Call for me on Sunday, then.'

'Yes, I will. Oh, and by the way, we won't bother with the biscuits.'

Laughing, together, the two girls felt happier than they had for ages, like carefree young women instead of housebound mums. Betty thought she might take advantage of Sally's offer, just the once.

Amy Butler didn't look very pleased when she saw Betty colouring her legs. 'I 'ope yer not turning all common again,' she said.

Betty looked indignant. 'Well! I've been called some things in my time, but never common. I've been called Sexy, Flirty, and once at school I was even called Sugar Tits. But I'm *not* common, Mam.

'I'm not going to misbehave. Not tonight, not ever again. I won't do anything to make my son or you ashamed of me.'

Amy believed her. Betty had shaped up nicely since Ernie had come on the scene; she was a good mother and doted on the little fellow. Even so, she hadn't exactly been anywhere where she could be tempted. The Victoria Hall dance would definitely be a temptation, Besides, there was no reason to be dyeing her legs. Who'd be looking at them anyway? Still, the lass deserved a night out. After all, you were only young once. All the same, Amy couldn't help feeling uneasy and wished the lasses were going to the pictures instead. A dance hall was no place for a married woman, in her opinion, but there again she was old-fashioned, or so their Betty said.

Sally was looking forward to minding Ernie. He was a placid little thing and usually as good as gold. Jim whistled at Betty when she wheeled in the pram.

'Wow, you look stunning!' Sally said. She was right. Betty was a good-looking girl even on her worst days. Tonight she looked absolutely scintillating with her sparkling blonde hair, blue eyes, and figure to die for. Yes, scintillating was a good description.

164

'Are you sure he'll be all right?' Betty sounded unsure. 'He's had his bath and his feed. He usually sleeps through now, so he shouldn't be any trouble.'

'Go on, stop worrying, and have a good time. And don't do anything I wouldn't do.'

'I won't.' Betty took a last look at her sleeping son and hurried out.

'She'll be up to no good now she's been let loose.' Jim hadn't agreed with Sally minding the baby while his sister gadded about.

'She'll be fine.'

'Well, on your head be it if she doesn't behave. Besides, now you've done it once, she'll take advantage. I know my sister of old.'

'Of old maybe, but she's changed, Jim. Besides, everyone needs a break occasionally.'

'Okay, you've been warned.' He had only just got the words out when Ernie woke up. He looked around for his mother, saw the strange surroundings and let out a wail. Sally nudged the pram but he wouldn't drop off. Jim turned up the wireless so he could hear it over the cries and Sally lifted the baby out and began to rock him. Nothing worked. Daisy came downstairs and tried to amuse him, but he just cried louder. Then Dippy began to howl in sympathy. Jim could stand it no longer. He combed some Brylcreem into his hair, put on his tie and jacket and went to the Sun.

'He'll settle down,' Sally promised as her husband went out.

'Probably,' Jim moaned, 'but until he does, I can think of a better way of spending Saturday night.'

Ernie did settle eventually, but by that time Sally was left on her own, apart from a sleeping baby and a little girl who wanted a story, then a drink of water, and then had a coughing spasm and needed Veno's. Sally could think of a lot better ways of spending Saturday night herself, but unlike Jim, she was here and must make the best of it.

The reason Daisy couldn't settle was because her dad was out. If Sally and Jim ever argued – which wasn't very often – Daisy knew it was usually on a Saturday night. Sally didn't mind Jim going off for a few pints with Bernard and Tom, to slaken the dust. Jim would grin as he kissed her and went off to the Rising Sun. If she was in a reasonable frame of mind, all would still be well. Jim would come home, switch the wireless over to *Saturday Night at the Palais*, and they would dance round the living-room, ending up in a passionate embrace before they went to bed for the lovemaking his shift work played havoc with during the week. But on other occasions Sally would berate him for staying out too late, and for spending too much on his beer.

It never occurred to Jim that Sally might have good reason to be annoyed, for once he got a few pints inside him he was generous to a fault. Any of the lame – which Sally didn't mind – and the lazy

– which she did – knew he would give away his last penny once he had had a few drinks. Jim had never been known to turn nasty in drink, indeed it seemed to enhance his generous side, which some of his fellow drinkers never failed to take advantage of.

This meant that after Saturday night and another session on Sunday dinnertime, Jim would often be left with nothing with which to buy his packet of five Woodbines a day. Sally didn't mind paying out for him. It just maddened her that his hard-earned money was being handed over the bar at the Sun instead of being put towards doing up the new house. It also maddened her that he would never change. In fact, despite the way he annoyed her, she didn't really want to change him. She loved Jim, just the way he was.

The house was coming along nicely. All the painting was completed, and the walls had been finished off with a pretty inch-wide strip of border. Sally had stuck this on about a foot from the ceiling all the way round the living-room. She had bought some lino from the Co-op which would match the carpet square they already had. Her mother had pegged a new rug on the pegging frame, helped by Pat on her weekly visits to her grandma's.

The house was cleared now of all but the things they could use. Bedding, towels and some of the crockery still left intact after the break-in had been stored at Amy Butler's in case Betty ever needed it. Furniture that was surplus to requirements had been given to a grateful family of ten in one of the houses down by the works.

Now, all was ready for them to move in. But still something seemed to be holding Sally back. She continued to find one excuse after the other and knew Jim was becoming impatient with her. She would arrange for the move immediately after Christmas, she decided, and felt better now she had set a definite time. January for certain.

Betty had really enjoyed her night out. The band had been passable even though some of them were stand-ins, due to the war. Once she and Doreen started dancing they couldn't have cared less who the musicians were, though. One or two of Betty's former boyfriends thought they might be in with a chance and offered to walk her home, but she made it quite clear that she was a married woman now, and soon put them in their place.

One of Clarence's mates from the pit had a few dances with her but only talked about things in general, such as Clarence's whereabouts. Betty simply told him she wasn't allowed to say. He enquired about the baby, and her brother Jim, and then moved on to Doreen. Neither girl gave any encouragement to their partners but simply enjoyed the dancing. Betty Hayes had certainly changed.

The night out still didn't satisfy her need to be

doing something useful, though. She really had to do something about that.

When Daisy ran through the gap in the wall on her way home from school the following Monday, there was a woman knocking on their front door. Daisy had never seen her before and couldn't help staring. The woman had long black hair curling over her shoulders and was wearing a fur coat. She had bright red lipstick and black stuff round her eyes. She was also wearing the highest heels Daisy had ever seen.

Sally opened the door and her mouth dropped open at the sight of the other woman.

'Is Jim in?'

'No,' Sally said. 'What do you want him for?'

'I just wanted to talk to him.'

'What about?' Daisy noticed her mam didn't seem too pleased to see the new arrival. 'Look!' Sally continued. 'If it concerns my husband, it concerns me.'

'Oh,' the other woman hesitated, 'I . . . er . . . it's all right. It wasn't important.' She went tottering down the row, stumbling in her impossibly high heels in the effort to get away. The scent of Californian Poppy lingered behind her.

Daisy could tell by her mam's face that she wasn't in a good mood and took refuge under her tree. When Jim came back from visiting his mother, Sally was waiting for him.

'You've had a visitor.'

'Oh?' He sat down and took off his shoes. 'Who?'

'One of your fancy women, by the looks of her.'

'What? Oh, aye. Chance'd be a fine thing.'

'Black hair, fur coat and no knickers, I shouldn't wonder.' Sally's face was scarlet with rage.

'What are you on about?' Jim asked, but he looked as though he'd already guessed.

'You know very well what and who I'm on about. What I want to know is, why she should come looking for my husband?'

'Well, I don't know. I just bought her a drink on Saturday in the Sun. She started chatting to me at the bar. Pleasant enough, she seemed. That's all.'

'Propping up the pub bar, on her own? You should have *known* what sort of woman she were, just by looking at her! Still, I expect you admire that sort. Not somebody like me, who goes out mopping floors and cleaning lavatories. So that *you've* got money to spend on the likes of *her.*'

'Look, Sally, I bought her a drink, that's all. I suppose I felt sorry for her, with nobody talking to 'er.'

'And why do you think nobody was talking to her?'

'I don't know.'

'Well, I do! You great, gormless idiot. Because she's a . . .'

Daisy ran into the kitchen, interrupting this conversation before Sally could speak her mind.

170

'Mam, who was that lady?'

'Lady?' Sally gasped.

'Yes, who was she? I liked her shoes.'

'Oh, did you?'

'Yes. And, Mam, will you grow your hair like hers?'

Sally's face was such a picture that Jim had all on to stifle a smile.

'No, I certainly will not.'

'And, Dad, will you buy my mam a coat like hers, all nice and warm and furry?'

Jim's face finally turned serious. 'What, yer mam in a fur coat? Aye, if she promises to wear it wi' no . . .'

'Jim!' Sally put a stop to whatever he was about to say. Then she looked at him, and couldn't help it – she began to laugh, he did, and then neither of them could stop.

'Let's get our teas.' Sally went to the oven and brought out a tray of jacket potatoes. It wasn't until Daisy was in bed out of the way that Sally asked her husband, 'Did she know you were married?'

Jim looked up from his book. 'What? I don't know, I don't suppose so. Why should she? I told yer, I just bought her a drink, that's all. I'd forgotten all about her. Why she should want to see me, I don't know.'

'Well, she obviously fancies you, and I expect you encouraged her. Jim, you'll have to stop buying drinks for all and sundry! We can't afford it.

Besides, it's going to get you a bad name, drinking with women like her. It's a waste of time me trying to earn a bit extra if you carry on like this. Do you think you're being fair?'

'No, I'm not,' he sighed. 'Oh, lass, you know what I'm like? Too soft for me own good.'

'Yes, well, it's got to stop.' Sally suddenly grinned. 'Oh, Jim, you should have seen her face when I said you were my husband. She nearly fell off her heels, hurrying away.' Sally felt the heat rise to her face then. 'Oh! I hope Miss Appleby didn't see her . . .'

'Bugger Miss Appleby! Anyway, she'll only think I've got meself a fancy woman.'

'Don't even think about doing that.' She picked up the ball of wool she'd just wound and threw it at him. Sally might be putting on a good face but she couldn't shake off the feeling of jealousy. How she wished she was a bit more glamorous, especially as Daisy seemed to admire that woman so much.

Sally still wished Jim wasn't quite so generous with his hard-earned money, then she might be able to afford a few glamorous adornments for herself. Then she realised that if that was Jim's only fault, she had a lot to be thankful for. Besides, she supposed *she* wasn't perfect herself, always being there for everybody and their grandmothers. It was right what Jim always said, theirs was a house with an ever open door. When they moved to the new house, Sally vowed to change that – to lock people out occasionally.

She grinned, knowing it would never happen, neither of them would ever change . . . except that after today she would try and do herself up a bit, make herself a bit more attractive. She might even become a bit more of a fur coat and no knickers type – without the fur coat, of course, they couldn't afford that.

Preparations for Christmas were in progress, even though everything was in short supply. The cakes made by Betty were more carrot than fruit but she had insisted on baking Sally one too, so rations had been pooled and the results looked quite satisfactory considering the circumstances. Jim was busy making a doll's house and Amy Butler knitting for Daisy and Ernie.

Joe Denman was enjoying being in the Home Guard – not that they saw much action in Millington, except for their right arms which received a fair amount of exercise lifting pints, in order to slaken the pit dust at the Miners' Club after the meetings.

Betty was preparing for another night out, this time with Florence who was home again for a few days. She had been invited to a dance with a couple of soldiers and Betty was to make up a foursome. She had declined the invitation at first but had been persuaded when Florence assured her there would be no hanky-panky. They met on Coles corner and the foursome decided to go for a drink before moving on to the dance.

Betty liked the soldiers on sight, they were easy to talk to and had a good sense of humour. Both of them were married, and though they were obviously attracted to the two girls, made no attempt to seduce them. They were also good dancers. Just as Betty began to relax and feel comfortable, the air-raid warning sounded. Nobody seemed worried at first except Betty herself, who wanted to leave immediately and get home to Ernie.

'It'll be a false alarm,' Florence assured her. 'We'll be all right.'

'No! We ought to make for the shelter.' Betty was beginning to panic.

'I think Betty's right,' Ron said. 'We ought to play safe.' He took her arm and made for the door. Florence decided to follow her friend, but as the four of them hurried along the street an almighty blast shook the building on their left as a bomb hit the shop. Betty and Ron were lifted off their feet. He threw Betty to the ground and himself on top of her. She saw the shop front explode and then the whole window was shattering in their direction.

'I'm sorry, Ernie,' Betty whispered as she was buried beneath Ron and a mountain of glass and brick.

*   *   *

174

Sheffield was ravaged by a raid for nine and a half hours that night. Walsh's store burned throughout and almost 3,000 houses were demolished. The fires could be seen miles away in Millington, and when Betty failed to come home Amy lifted little Ernie from his cot and rocked him until the light of the winter morning showed through a gap beneath the blackout. Then she placed him in his pram and wheeled him the few yards to Jim's. She didn't want to wake the family and went quietly into the house to sit by the smouldering cinders of the fire, feeling comforted just by being in the same house as her family.

She placed a few new coals on the fire and lifted the half-full kettle on to the bars. It would be singing by the time Jim and Sally left their beds. Then she began to worry lest any news was brought and she wasn't home to receive it, and that was followed by anxiety about her grandson. What would happen to him when her limbs became useless, as they threatened to do more often these days?

Sally was first up. Seeing Amy startled her so much that she dropped the cold bed brick she had been carrying.

'Oh, Ma, whatever's wrong?'

'It's my lass,' Amy said. 'She 'asn't come 'ome. Summat's happened, I know it 'as.'

Sally placed her arm round her mother-in-law but could think of no words of consolation. All Millington had heard the bombing and watched the blaze over the city. Some had taken to the shelters for the first time. The Butlers and Cartwrights had gone to Enid's cellar for a while, and had a sing-song to take the children's minds off the noise. Jim had checked on his mother, who had promised him she was not shifting anywhere and would go to bed directly their Betty arrived home. Betty clearly hadn't.

'Look!' said Sally. 'No news is good news. She probably couldn't get home. The buses would have stopped running.'

'No, she'd 'ave come 'ome if she'd 'ad to walk it. She would never 'ave abandoned our Ernie.'

'No, no, she wouldn't, if she'd had any choice, but she probably didn't have one.' Sally made some tea. Just then Mr Harrison arrived.

'It's only me.' He looked at Amy. 'Oh, yer there, Mrs Butler. I've left yer a gill, is that all right? Only you 'adn't left a jug out so I got one out of the cupboard.'

'Aye, lad, thanks.'

''By, but what a night that's been! They say city's naught but a bomb site.'

'Aye, and our Betty's somewhere amongst it.'

'Oh! Eeh, yer must be worried sick. Well, I dare say she'd 'ave got to a shelter or somewhere safe. There'll 'ave been no transport or owt.'

Jim had heard their voices by now and appeared at the bottom of the stairs.

176

'Mother?'

'It's our Betty. She's not come 'ome.' It was all too much for Amy then. She broke into sobs. 'Summat's happened, I know it 'as. And what's to become of the bairn?'

'Don't worry about Ernie. He'll be cared for,' Jim assured her. 'But don't let's imagine the worst.' A knock on the door silenced him then and Sally hurried to open it.

'Florence! Thank God you're all right.'

'Yes, but it's Betty, Mrs Butler. She . . . she's hurt. We were on our way to the shelter . . .'

'Hurt? How bad?'

'I'm not sure. She's been taken to the Infirmary, but they're so run off their feet, it's just chaos there.'

'What 'appened, love? Here, get this down yer.' Jim had brought out the brandy.

'We were making for the shelter when a shop front was blown out. Betty was the nearest. She would have been much worse off if it hadn't been for a soldier throwing himself on top of her. He protected her from the worst of the blast. Unfortunately, he didn't survive.' Florence began to shake then. Sally recognised the signs of shock and forced some of the spirit into the girl's mouth. Jim had already put on his overcoat. 'I'll go see if the buses are running. If not I'll get a taxi.'

'Shall I come?' Sally enquired.

'No! The bairns'll want seeing to.'

'I'm coming,' Amy insisted.

'No, Mother. Wait till I get back, then we'll see. I doubt if they'll let two of us in until visiting time.'

'I'd better go and let them know at home I'm all right.' But Florence doubted her mother would even have missed her. Betty didn't know how fortunate she was, having such a caring family. She started to cry. Partly for Betty, partly for Ron, and partly for herself and the baby she had never even held in her arms.

'Come on, love, I'll take you home,' Sally said. Florence didn't want to go home, to a mother who had forced her to give away her own flesh and blood. What kind of a mother would do that? She decided she would go away again, as soon as she knew Betty would be all right. There was nothing for her in Millington any more.

Fortunately the buses between Millington and the hospital were back on the road. The conductor told Jim that dozens of trams and buses had been destroyed and tram wires broken. Fortunately the steelworks targeted in the east end had been largely spared, but the city centre was a no go area.

'I know,' Jim told him, 'my sister was in the thick of it.'

'So yer off to the Infirmary then, are yer?'

'Aye. I don't know what I'm going to find, though.'

'Chaos, lad, bloody chaos. Some's 'ad to be took to the Sally Army Citadel and other places.' He wound Jim a ticket off. 'Anyway, I 'ope yer find her not too bad.'

'Thanks,' he said as he waited for the bus to reach its destination.

Betty had just regained consciousness when Jim arrived. She had a lump on her forehead the size of a golf ball and one arm had been stitched from elbow to shoulder. Her emotional state seemed to be the biggest problem. Betty began to cry as soon as she set eyes on her brother.

'God, Betty, are yer okay? I thought you were a goner, love. How do yer feel?'

'As though I've been rolling naked through a razor-blade factory.'

'Your arm's a mess, love, but it'll heal.' Betty folded down the sheets and showed her brother her ankle. He couldn't see the wound for a huge wad of lint and bandage.

'What about the rest of yer?'

'He saved my life, Jim. He died saving me. They've only just told me.'

'Who was he, do yer know?'

'No. Only that he was a friend of Florence's and his name was Ron. I saw the blast – well, felt it really – and then the glass and bricks, I don't know what, and then his body was on top of me. That's all I remember. I thought I was about to die. I thought I was leaving Ernie.'

'Come on, Bet. You're going to be all right.'

'I am. Ron isn't.'

'What happened to 'im? Do yer know?'

'A piece of glass severed his main artery. They say he was dead by the time the ambulance arrived.' She shivered. 'It would have been me, but for him. It *should* have been me. He was a married man. He survived Dunkirk and then died in the bloody Sheffield blitz, saving me.'

'He was a brave soldier, Betty, and must have thought yer were worth saving or he wouldn't 'ave done what he did.'

'He didn't even know me. We'd only met last night.'

Jim struggled to find words to console his sister. 'Well, at least he wouldn't have had time to suffer.'

'How's Ernie? Where is he?'

'He's at our house. Mother wanted to come but I thought she'd be better away until I saw what you were like. Sally'll bring her at visiting time.'

'What about Ernie?'

'He'll be well looked after, don't you fret. Enid or Mary'll be glad to 'ave 'im. I'd like to come back meself but I'm on afters.'

'I'm coming home.'

'Oh, I don't think so.'

'Go and find a nurse, I'll ask her.'

Sister was at a bed by the door when Jim enquired about Betty.

'She's to stay until tomorrow at least. You never know when they've been concussed. Not only that but she's still in shock. We need to observe her for a while.'

'That's what I thought,' he agreed. 'She looks awful.'

'She'll be fine. She can't go home, though. Now I must get on, we're having all on to cope.'

When Sally and Amy arrived at visiting time, Betty was giving a baby his bottle. 'His mam's in a bad way,' she explained as she removed the bottle to wind the little mite. 'They were bombed out, lost everything.' Betty was obviously upset but Sally didn't think she looked too bad, considering.

'I can't come home yet.' Her eyes filled with tears. 'I'm sorry to be a nuisance, I should never have left Ernie.'

'He's happy as a lark, with our Daisy and Dippy fussing round him.'

'All the same, I should never have gone out.'

'Has he finished?' Sister came for the baby. 'If you feel up to it there's a little girl who could do with a bit of coaxing with her food. We can't get her to eat and we haven't the time to spare for persuading her.'

'Sure, I'd love to. If I'm to stay, I might as well make myself useful.'

'We're going to miss her when she goes home,' Sister told the visitors. Just then the bell went, signalling the end of visiting time. Betty didn't mind. There was a little girl somewhere who needed her. It was good to be needed. Besides, she hoped that if it had been Ernie, some kind patient would have done the same for him.

Jim was minding Daisy and Stanley while Sally and Mary were at the pictures. He had taken the kids down the Donkey Wood, searching for holly to brighten the walls. They had brought home pockets-ful of fir cones and Jim had made some flour paste. They were dipping the cones in it and sprinkling them with glitter. They had also cut out stars and bells from an old Rinso packet which looked pretty, painted red and sparkling with more glitter. Daisy was excited at the thought of decorating the tiny Christmas tree in readiness for the family get-together on Christmas Day.

Jim glanced at the clock. The wives should be home any time now, freeing him and Tom to spend a couple of hours at the Sun.

Alfie Ramsgate was propping up the bar when they arrived. He quickly emptied his glass and began tapping it on the bar, attracting Jim's attention.

'What'll it be, Alf?' he enquired.

'Pint o' bitter, Jim.'

'Three pints o' bitter, Connie, please.'

The conversation was of course concerning Christmas. 'What're you buying Mary, then?' Jim asked.

'Scent, I expect. She likes scent. How about you?'

Jim grinned. 'I might get her some nice frilly knickers from Judith McCall's.'

'That'll be cheating,' Tom laughed. 'They'll be for your benefit, not Sally's.'

Alfie had never bought their Kitty a Christmas present in his life. He could imagine Sally Butler in a pair of sexy frillies though. And then contemplated the sight of their Kitty's belly, with all the layers of flab hanging down, and the great, floppy breasts drooping over the top of it. She might look better if she wore one of them brassiere things . . . then he realised she would need a bloody crane to lift a pair like that, never mind a brassiere! The conversation had changed back a couple of minutes ago and they were now discussing the death of Neville Chamberlain from cancer when Alfie suddenly announced, 'I know what I'm buying our Kitty for Christmas.'

'What?'

'I'm buying 'er one of them pink shiny brassieres from Miss McCall's.'

'Oh, aye? Do yer know what size she is then, Alfie?' Alf hadn't thought about size. 'No,' he said, 'but I can just get one in two hands.'

Jim and Tom almost choked on their beer, before realising that Alfie Ramsgate wasn't joking. He had never been more serious in his life.

* * *

Considering all the upset Betty's accident had caused, the Christmas Day party was enjoyed by all. Everyone from both families was invited. A table was borrowed from Enid's so that the meal could be served in both the kitchen and sitting-room. Some of the cooking had been undertaken by Betty at her mother's house so that everything was ready at the same time.

Mr Firth had turned up trumps again and supplied a couple of fowls. Joe Denman supplied the vegetables from his allotment and declared the sprouts would be all the better for being out in the severe frost of the last couple of weeks. Betty had made the stuffing, and since rations hadn't run to a traditional Christmas pudding a huge tin of prune pudding sufficed. A bottle of whisky brought from Mr Jessops' put the men in a jovial mood, with a bottle of port for the ladies.

Father Christmas had paid his annual visit bringing a home-made doll's house for Daisy and enough books to keep her happy for weeks. Norah, a budding artist, had requested paints and sketch books. A home-made easel made her the happiest of girls. Pat, who considered herself too old for toys, was showing off her new wristwatch and making Grandma Denman sneeze with all the perfume she was wearing. Baby Ernie was testing his brand new tooth on various teething rings and rattles. Jim said he couldn't wait to buy Ernie a train set, after all the dolls and other feminine things he usually had to pay for.

With the meal cleared away and everybody full to the limit, Grand-dad Denman thought they should sing a few carols and things. Pat was happy to give them a solo of 'In the Bleak Mid Winter', and her lovely, clear voice could be heard by Tom and Mary next-door. Of course carols soon gave way to some war-time favourites. The songs of Vera Lynn, George Formby and Gracie Fields were sung with gusto.

Then Grand-dad Denman said 'Who wants a piana?'

'What?' Sally was taken aback that her dad should be considering parting with his beloved instrument.

'I said, who wants a piana? Do you want one, our Enid?'

'Not likely. We haven't room for the furniture we have already. Besides, neither of our two wants to learn. I've offered them piano lessons but they aren't interested.'

'I should 'ave thought our Pat would be musical, with a voice like that. How about you, Sally?'

She had been through a phase during her childhood when she had begged for lessons. Joe had taught her the easy exercises and scales, but when the music teacher on St George's Road had been unable to take her she had lost interest. She'd love Daisy to play, though.

'Are you sure you want to give it away, Dad? You pass many an hour on it in the dark winter nights.'

'Aye, I did, but with the Home Guard I 'aven't time any more. Besides, I'd rather listen to't wireless. I fair enjoy *ITMA* and *Band Waggon*. Then there's *Music While You Work* – I can listen to that when I'm on nights.'

'Our Ernest might want it.'

Lizzie Denman laughed. 'Our Ernest? 'E's been grumbling about that piano for years. Said if we got shot of that we could 'ave a nice sideboard.'

Sally looked at Jim. 'What do you think? Should we have it?'

'Not here, but we'll 'ave room at the other house, it's up to you. Daisy, do you want a piano?'

'Yes!' She jumped up and down with excitement. 'Can I learn like Carol?'

'Oh, so that's why you want it? If Carol jumped in the dam you'd have to do the same. All right, then. But I'll write and ask our Ernest first.'

The mention of him put a dampener on things for a few minutes as they all wished he was here to celebrate the festive season with his family. Jim decided to pop next-door then and invite the Porters round for a drink. 'The more the merrier,' he said.

When they were all settled again and a few more drinks had been consumed, a game of blind man's buff followed by postman's knock livened up the proceedings, and everybody pronounced it the best party they'd had for ages.

'Right then,' Joe Denman said, 'before we go,

let's all raise our glasses to the absent members of our family, namely Ernest and Clarence, and may God bring them home safe. As for all the poor blighters left homeless in our city, may it please God to help them through this terrible time and put an end to all the suffering soon.'

Betty couldn't help shedding a tear at this. She hoped Clarence was safe. Even if she didn't love him, he was still Ernie's dad. Nobody who looked at the little boy could ever doubt it.

When Kitty Ramsgate emerged from her front door after Christmas, nobody on Potters Row could believe their eyes. While Kitty was still outside number one, her chest was already at number three! She had hitched her new brassiere up so high that her chins were almost resting on her cleavage. Unfortunately she hadn't bought new clothes to go with her voluptuous new body and the middle two buttons on her frock had to remain open, revealing the pink satin brassiere.

'It won't be long before that brassiere's the same colour as 'er doorstep,' predicted Mrs Firth.

'And 'er winders,' added Amy Butler.

With Christmas over, the next bit of excitement for the kids was a trip to the pantomime at the Empire. This year it was *Cinderella*, starring Adele Dixon, Jack Buchanan, Nat Jackley and Fred Emney. Daisy was mesmerised by the magic of the theatre, and playing at pantomimes became the favourite game for the kids of the rows until it was time to return to school.

Fortunately Millington School was kept open while the ones in the city centre were taken over as billets and rest centres for bombed-out families. Forty thousand people were known to have lost their homes in the blitz. Several of the large city shops were damaged, though most managed to relocate to cinemas and other such premises.

Stanley was most disappointed that school was to resume as normal. Ironically, Daisy, who couldn't wait to get back to her lessons was suffering from another sore throat which was diagnosed as tonsillitis, so she was unable to return.

A few days later a taxi drew up at number nine Potters Row. It was such an unusual sight that everybody came out to see what was happening. When Sally bundled her daughter into the back seat, Daisy almost danced with excitement.

'Where are we going, Mam?' What a treat to be riding in a car! She only hoped it wouldn't be spoiled by travel sickness. When the car stopped they were outside the hospital.

'Come on.' Sally hurried her inside. The stench of antiseptic and carbolic greeted them.

Daisy was suddenly filled with apprehension. 'What have we come here for?' But children weren't told about such things in the 1940s. Daisy was undressed and wrapped in a red blanket. Then Sally decided to explain what was happening.

'You've come to have your tonsils and adenoids out. We won't be long, we'll be home by teatime.'

'What's tonsils and adenoids?' she cried, clinging tightly to Sally's coat, burying her head in the June-perfumed cloth.

Then a nurse came and dragged her away, screaming blue murder, to the theatre where they put her on a trolley. Somebody placed a pad or something over her nose, making her struggle violently. The ether filled her nostrils with a sweet, cloying, hideous smell – and then the nightmare began.

The trees came for her, black branches reaching out long, twig-like fingers towards her. Closer and closer they came, clawing at Daisy's face, until she awoke with the smell of ether still filling her nostrils. She was lying on a rubber sheet on the floor, head to toe with other children, and by her side was a bowl of something red and terrifying.

A stiff, starched nurse came to take her to the end of the room where a doctor was waiting with a scissor-like instrument in his hand. Waiting – or so Daisy thought – to cut out her tonsils and adenoids, whatever they might be. She tried to scream for her mam but her throat was too sore.

'You're fine,' the doctor said, after examining inside her mouth and her ears. 'You can go home now.'

Daisy slept the whole way home. What a waste of a taxi ride! However, there were other treats in store: jelly and custard, new crayons and drawing books. A fire in the bedroom and, best of all, no more tonsillitis. But the smell of ether and the tree nightmare were to haunt Daisy for many, many years.

The new house was ready for them to move into. Even the piano had been brought on the back of the coalman's lorry. The move was to take place at the weekend, after fires had been lit every day in order to air the place. Jim was convinced that Potters Row had contributed to Daisy's ill health, what with the damp walls and the draughty windows.

Daisy herself wasn't at all sure about the move; she didn't want to leave Mrs Firth and Grandma Butler, and especially not little Ernie. Nor would she like being away from Norah or Stanley. She looked up at the damp patch on her ceiling which had spread out so that it resembled an angel. She was convinced it protected her from the monsters in the cupboard.

Then she realised that there wouldn't be a cupboard at Taylors Row, just a lovely wardrobe Dad had built into the alcove near the fireplace. She would miss her sycamore tree, though, except on moonlit nights when its scary shadow swayed on her wall. There wouldn't be any tree shadows at Taylors Row. Maybe it wouldn't be too bad living there after all. Besides, it was nearer to school and to Carol's house.

Between St George's Road and the Donkey Wood stood an old sprawling house in a large overgrown garden. This house belonged to Dr Sellars and, unknown to their parents, Carol and Daisy had found they could climb through a hole in the garden's stone wall and lose themselves in this mysterious place. At first their games just consisted of hide and seek or climbing trees. Then they decided to make a house for themselves in a dark hollow, amongst the holly bushes and rhododendrons.

Every day something else would be added to their hideaway. An old piece of carpet, unwanted in the new house; Daisy's doll's teaset with pandas on it; old curtains from Carol's. A tea chest used in the move from the old house served as a table, and a couple of cushions completed the furnishings. All might have been well if the pair hadn't found a tin of paint behind the shelter – in fact, a dozen tins of paint. Carol brought a paint brush from home and they set about painting the bushes surrounding their house bright blue.

Daisy came home from school one day to find the policeman, known to everyone locally as Bobby Jones, sitting in their kitchen enjoying a pot of tea. Bobby Jones was feared by all the kids, who would scatter in all directions once he came into view. So Daisy decided to try and sneak out again even though she couldn't think of anything in particular she had done wrong. However, she had already been seen.

'Hello, Daisy,' the policeman said to her departing back.

'Hello.' Daisy began to tremble.

'Have you or your friends seen any tins of paint anywhere?'

Daisy thought he must know they had or he wouldn't be here.

'Yes,' she said. 'But we found it, it was thrown away.'

'It's all right, you're not in trouble. Can you just show me where you found it?'

Daisy didn't believe she wouldn't be in trouble if he knew about their secret hideaway, and could feel her heart beating like a drum. She imagined herself in prison, or something even worse. But she led Bobby Jones down to the air-raid shelter, behind which a dozen tins of the blue paint had been hidden by a local burglar, apparently stolen from the local decorator's store room. Until the girls had removed one. Bobby Jones didn't comment on this.

'Right, that's a good girl. You can go home now.'

Daisy ran all the way home in case he should change his mind. Nothing was ever said about the bright blue bushes behind Dr Sellars' house –

perhaps he didn't know about them. They were abandoned by the girls along with the carpet, curtains, and worst of all the teaset with the pandas on it. Daisy never dared go back through the wall to rescue it. Bobby Jones might be watching.

Chapter Six

Amy was worried about Betty. Not that she was doing anything to cause concern, it was more her state of mind. Just the slightest thing, a sad song on the wireless or the news of yet another raid, could reduce her to tears. She didn't want Ernie out of her sight for a moment, even taking him across the field with her for the bread.

'I don't know what to do about our Betty,' Amy told Sally. 'She won't even go out to't pictures, the lass's worriting herself to death.'

'She needs something to occupy her mind,' Sally said. 'She's probably worrying about money too.' Neither Betty or Amy had told anyone about the money Clarence had left. Sally considered the problem.

'She needs to be doing something useful, Ma. Did you notice how she was in the hospital when she was helping with the children?'

'Aye, I did, but there's our Ernie. I couldn't look after him full-time, I only wish I could.'

'No, but what if we did it between us? He's a good little lad, so placid. If you could just see to him while I do Miss Appleby's, I'd do the rest.

Or maybe she could find something part-time. After all, they're crying out for women workers. Just think about it.'

Jim and Tom organised a fire-watching team. Mr Firth, Bernard, Mr Dyson and even Alfie Ramsgate volunteered to work on a rota basis. The group were to watch the school, the football ground and the council estate. The school was considered the building most at risk as it was thought some children might hate the place so much they would have a go at setting it on fire, and blame the war.

Sally hoped this would help take Jim's mind off her suggestion that she should look after Ernie – her husband hadn't liked that at all. 'I thought we might have had a bit of peace when we moved across 'ere,' he'd said crossly. 'Now it looks like we're to be invaded again.'

Sally knew he would get over it, though, so she didn't take much notice.

'I don't know what I'm going to do about my bedding,' Ida Appleby fretted. She had seen a notice in the paper that laundry deliveries might be delayed.

'Well, as far as I can see, you've plenty of sheets upstairs. What does it matter if it's a bit late?'

'All this worrying'll see me in me grave . . .'

'Then stop worrying,' Sally told her.

'It's just so inconsiderate.'

Sally looked at her. 'You mean inconsiderate, I suppose, but we all have to put up with things like this during a war.'

'*She's* not come back yet.'

'Who?'

'Her, the music teacher. Two weeks they've been away, her and the young one. She ought to be ashamed of 'erself.'

'I'm sure there's a perfectly reasonable explanation.'

'She wants throwing out! She's a disgrace to the neighbourhood.'

'She hasn't done anything to hurt anyone, as far as I can see.'

'Well, you would stick up for 'er. None of you young ones 'ave any shame.'

'*I* haven't done anything to be ashamed of.' Sally took the long brush outside to scrub the flags, relieved to escape Ida's wicked tongue. No wonder the woman's nephew never came to visit! When she came back inside, Miss Appleby said, 'Do yer 'appen to be going to't market on Friday?'

'Why?'

'I wondered if you could bring me . . .' she lowered her voice '. . . two pairs of knickers.' Sally knew that would mean a visit to Old Misery's stall and her stomach lurched at the thought of it. Well, she supposed it was time she faced the poor man again. After all, she was cutting her nose off to spite her face, going to Judith McCall's and paying top prices.

'Yes,' she told Ida. 'I'll bring you some. What size?'

'Outsize, with elastic legs.'

'Oh! You're never outsize.'

'I am. I'm deceitful.'

'Aye, you are,' Sally muttered to herself. 'You mean deceiving,' she said out loud.

Thirty inches of snow fell in the New Year, causing chaos on the roads on top of the constant hold-ups due to shortage of public transport. Workers who usually used their own cars to travel into the city were now travelling by bus or tram, due to the unavailability of petrol. Snow-shifters were also in short supply and the roads became packed with hard snow. The only ones enjoying these conditions were the children. Tramping to school on top of the drifting snow was a game to them. One day Daisy came running home as fast as her wellingtons would allow.

'Mam, Mam, come quick!'

Sally, worried by her daughter's urgent cries, grabbed her coat.

'What's the matter?'

'It's an old man, he's fallen and can't get up. He's only got one leg. And half a leg,' she added.

'Where? Come on, show me.' Sally set off after her.

'On the estate, the second house.'

The poor man had obviously come out to fetch

in his milk. Sally blamed his milkman. Mr Harrison would never have left it outside for a crippled man in this weather. The poor man had fallen and one of his crutches had slipped out of his reach.

'Come on.' Sally bent to help him up but he seemed to be a dead weight. 'Let's see if we can get you in out of the cold.' She tried to lift him again but couldn't.

'If yer can get me me crutch, I can manage wi' a bit of 'elp,' the man said. Daisy gave him the wooden crutch and he managed to turn over and rise up on one knee, then with Sally supporting his arm, he got up on to his foot.

'There! Let's get you inside.'

The poor man was icy cold and couldn't stop trembling. Sally looked round for the kettle, filled it and put it on the gas ring. 'How long have you been lying there? Mr . . .'

'Powell, but call me Danny.' It was obvious he was struggling to hear her. Danny was in his sixties and as deaf as he was lame. He was a happy individual, though, and soon began to joke about his fall.

'I'm a daft owd devil!' he laughed. 'Going skating at my age.'

Sally raised her voice to speak to him this time. 'How long have you been out there?'

'Since about two.'

'Two hours?' She shuddered. 'It's a wonder you haven't got hypothermia.'

'Nay, I'm all right, lass. Strong as an ox, I am.'

Sally glanced around. It was a small kitchen and not an inch of space on the table or draining board was left unfilled. It was all a clutter of mucky pots, filthy dishcloths and pans. There was no sign of any cleaning materials except for a lump of brown carbolic soap. Sally found the tea caddy amongst the clutter and rinsed out a cup that should have been white but was stained brown.

'I'll wash these pots up before I go, if you like.'

'Eeh, lass, don't bother about that. A bit of muck never hurt anybody.'

Sally cringed. 'Maybe not, but I'll wash them anyway.' She thought Danny looked a bit better now. She glanced out of the window to see what Daisy was up to. She was tramping about the garden where none of the snow had been disturbed, making marks with her wellies. Sally thought she'd be happy enough for a while. She boiled the kettle again, deciding to wash the pots and pans so she could leave the old man more comfortable.

'Do you have any wire wool for the pans?' she asked.

'Ech, no, lass. My missis always used soap, as far as I can remember. She used it for everything: clothes, pots, floors . . . and bodies,' he laughed. 'Don't believe in new-fangled things meself.'

'Well, perhaps not, but this brown soap's a bit harsh. Doesn't it make your cups taste?'

'Aye, but yer get used to it.'

'Right!' Sally said. 'But I can't get these clean without a scrubber.' It didn't take her long to tidy the kitchen. Then she looked at the floor. 'Do you have a mop and bucket?' She would never sleep if she went home and left the poor old thing amongst all this filth.

'Eeh, no, lass. My missis all's used a floor clart.'

'Right.' Sally wondered how long his missis had been dead and if the floor had been touched since. 'Who's been looking after you since your wife died?'

'Fanny next-door, but then she died as well.'

'Hmm.' Fanny and Danny . . . Mary would no doubt find that amusing when Sally told her .

'How old was Fanny, then?'

'Oh, just a spring chicken, only sixty-six. A grand lass. Bosom on her better than any film star's. Had to 'ave one of 'em off, though, 'cos of cancer. A pity to spoil a pair like that!' Danny chuckled. 'A great couple we were, me wi' one leg and her wi' one tit.'

Sally stifled a giggle, deciding she'd better not encourage him.

'Poor Fanny. And what do you have for your dinner?'

'Depends. Me rations are delivered from Co-op once a week, and a woman from Salvation Army comes and does me some shopping. Nice-looking woman she is. I only 'ave to warm summat up. If she's time, she warms it for me. Wouldn't mind 'er warming *me* up, 'specially today when I've been out skating. Trouble is, she can't get here when it snows.'

His grin was infectious and Sally thought what a jolly old thing Danny Powell was compared to Ida Appleby.

'So what are you having today then?'

'Owt.'

Sally looked in the pantry but there was no sign of any fresh food, only a few slices of dry bread. Well, at least he had a good fire. She went to the door. 'Daisy, pop over to our house and fetch an egg – and don't drop it!' While Daisy was on the errand, Sally toasted a couple of slices of bread.

'I don't want to put you to any trouble,' Danny protested.

'No trouble,' Sally said, and she meant it. Despite all the mess she'd had to tackle, it was a pleasure to help Danny Powell. Even so, she wondered what Jim would have to say about it.

Charlotte had been drinking all day. Her husband hadn't put in an appearance for three nights now and she hadn't been to bed for twenty-four hours, not daring to venture upstairs because of the dogs. The night before that she had retired early, hoping to be asleep before one o'clock. She had been. Then the clock had chimed and woken her, and it had also woken the dogs. She had heard them pattering around the room. Then she had felt the bedspread being tugged, and for the first time they had actually jumped on to the bed, pawing at her face and licking her until she screamed. Then the whimpers changed to snarls as the dogs became aggressive.

Charlotte managed to run out and close the door behind her. Now she daren't even go upstairs. Where *was* Mark? She knew he wouldn't believe her, though. He would say she was insane. Deny there were any dogs or that the clock had chimed. They were all against her. Uncle Walter, Mark, that woman . . . they were all conspiring against her. Well, she would show them! She would show them all. Nobody would ever get the better of Charlotte Kaye.

She just needed Mark to remove the panel from the wall and take out the valuables. It was time to be rid of them. If no one had yet reported them missing it was obvious they had decided not to do so. Once she had the money from selling them safely in the bank, that woman had better watch out. Charlotte had already planned her revenge.

Betty Hayes had acquired a job, and she hadn't even to travel to the city. She'd never felt safe there since the blitz and worried about Ernie when she was so far away.

Enid Cartwright had put a good word in for her. She worked as a school cleaner, and with the announcement that the school was to start serving school dinners had volunteered the information to Sally. 'Put Betty's name down,' Sally told her. 'She loves cooking, it'll be ideal for her.'

Betty did love cooking: she also loved her new job. Mrs Radcliffe, the caretaker's wife, was the supervisor and declared herself well pleased with the effort Betty Hayes put into her work. Betty enjoyed serving the children, and never gave them anything they didn't like. Daisy for instance, detested mashed potatoes – just like Betty had when she had been the same age. So, unlike some of the dinner ladies, she soon found out the children's individual likes and dislikes and served them accordingly.

With little Ernie thriving and being well looked after by Amy and Sally in her absence, Betty was completely content for the first time in her life.

'Anybody in?' Nellie called as she popped her head round the door. 'A special today.' She held aloft a thin blue letter. Sally couldn't wait to open it and read Ernest's news. Actually, there never was much news of her brother in his letters, just a few lines to say he was fine and that his shoulder was back to normal. Most of the letter would be devoted to hoping Daisy was well and being a good girl, and this time he hoped Betty and the baby were both well too. Had they heard from Clarence? Ernest said he was hoping for some home leave soon. He hoped they liked the new house, and thank God they'd taken the bloody piano! Not a word about what was happening at his end. Still, the letter proved he was well and that was worth a lot.

Nellie was always delighted to bring news from servicemen. She had known most of the young men locally from the day they were born. If there was any bad news to be delivered, Nellie would go home almost as downhearted as the recipent of the letter. Today she went on her way with a spring in her step. She had a letter for the Harrisons, the first one since the day their son went away. She couldn't wait to see Mrs Harrison's face! Oh, Nellie did love her job sometimes, almost as much as she loved the friends on her round. She hoped she didn't come across the milkman this morning, though. She had learned over the years that the men never shared their letters, not like women did, and she did so want to be there to witness the joy on Mrs Harrison's face.

Apart from Physical Training there was another thing now that Daisy didn't like about school: the dinners. However, Sally said she must stay so every Monday morning, as well as her bank money, she now carried her fivepence dinner money in her little shoulder bag. If Aunty Betty happened to be one of the servers Daisy would be happy, knowing she wouldn't be served any mashed potatoes.

Today, however, Aunty Betty happened to be

serving the junior children. Miss Clarke the head-mistress, who always supervised their meals, noticed Daisy's untouched helping of mashed potatoes and came to stand beside her. Loading a fork with lukewarm white lumps, she forced them into Daisy's mouth. 'Come on,' she said. 'Your mother has paid for this and it will make you a big girl.'

Daisy made an effort to gulp it down and then managed to say, 'Please, Miss, I feel sick.'

'Nonsense!' Miss Clarke briskly shovelled in another mouthful – and up the whole lot came. All over Miss Clarke's flowered smock, all down her thick lisle stockings, and even into her shoes. The headmistress's face turned the same colour as the chewed-up carrots adorning her smock. 'Right then,' she said, 'go and ask Mr Radcliffe for some sawdust.'

Daisy had no idea where to find Mr Radcliffe or even what he looked like but she escaped willingly – and was never made to eat mashed potatoes again.

It was Daisy who told Jim about the old man with the one and a half legs. 'Well, you were a good girl for fetching your mam. It's good to help people,' he emphasised. He soon changed his tune, though, when Sally told him she had cleaned up the kitchen and made the old gent his tea.

'I hope you're not taking on another lame duck.'

'No, of course not! But I couldn't just leave him

there and walk away. I mean, he might have been suffering from shock or something.'

'Aye, I suppose so.'

'Anyway, I'd better just pop across tomorrow, see if he's all right.'

Jim didn't answer but the look he gave his wife spoke volumes. Sally would never alter, if she lived to be a hundred.

After Daisy had gone to bed, Jim asked, 'So what's he like then?'

'Who?'

'Your new old man?'

'He's not *my* old man.'

'Oh, no?'

'No. Anyway, he's extremely cheerful, considering he's lost half his leg and is as deaf as a doornail. Oh, and he seems to fancy the ladies, especially the ones with big tits.'

Jim couldn't help laughing. 'You'd better keep yer distance then, if he's the randy sort.'

'Oh, I don't know.' Sally glanced down at her chest. 'I doubt I'm well enough endowed to suit his tastes. Besides, he fancies the Sally Army woman.'

'What's the house like?'

'Don't even ask.'

'Oh, as bad as that?'

'Worse. I'd soon get it shipshape, though, if I had the chance. Once it was bottomed, it would be a doddle.'

'Don't dare think about it.'

'He hasn't asked.'

'But he might.'

'No! He's as happy as a pig in muck.'

'Good.'

'But if he did ask? I mean, if he needed a bit of help, would you mind?'

'Yes. You've got Ernie to look after.'

'Oh, only for three hours. Besides, Mary's started taking him out walking when the weather's fit. It's good for her. You know she's longing for another child. And your mother's so much better . . . I think it's because she's stopped worrying about Betty.'

'And what if *we* have another child?'

'Ah, now that would be different, I would never leave it for a minute. But it hasn't happened.'

'Well, we could go and have another try . . .' Jim glanced at the clock. 'Before the bloody fire-watching! I've at least two hours.'

'Is that all?' Sally grinned. 'Come on then, let's get on with it.'

The fire-watching, Danny Powell, and even little Ernie were all forgotten then. Trying for a baby was the best fun in the world. Especially when they'd two hours in which to do it.

'I heard that car draw up last night and then another following it. She ought to be hung, drawn and quartered! Nothing but a prostitute, that's what she is.'

'Don't tell me you're on about the music teacher again?'

''Course I am. And what about the day they came back together, carrying a case? Fair brazen, she is.'

A knock on the door silenced Ida then and Sally went to answer it. Emily Simms stood there, looking pale and drawn. 'Have yer heard?' she asked.

'Heard what?'

'About the poor woman on St George's.'

'What poor woman?' Ida looked puzzled.

'The music teacher. She passed away during the night. I saw them carry her out first thing this morning.'

'Oh, no, not another death. My mother always says they come in threes.'

'I'm sorry to tell yer, Sally love, on top of old Walter and yer friend's little baby.'

'I didn't know she were ill,' Ida Appleby mumbled.

'Well, not many did . . . she didn't want anyone to know except for Mrs Watson. She's been staying with 'er for a couple of nights. Could see she hadn't long, though, fading away before her eyes, she was. She rang the lady's brother but she'd gone by the time he got 'ere. It's a wonder you didn't hear the car.'

'I did, but I didn't know what he was there for.'

'Well, you wouldn't. Can't say it isn't a blessing,

though. Suffered for months, she has. According to Mrs Watson, she was the bravest woman she's ever known. Not an ounce of flesh left on 'er and in so much pain, but still determined to keep herself smart, dressing herself up, putting on her make up . . . all so nobody would know how ill she was.'

'I've only been saying recently how ill she looked,' Ida mumbled.

'What? You said she was slimming herself to look nice for all her men friends!' Sally protested.

'Can't say as she had any men friends,' Emily observed. 'That young brother of hers 'as been an angel, though. He even took her away for a holiday, but it was too late to do her any good.'

'He looks a nice young man,' said Ida unctuously.

'*You* said he was sleeping with her!' Sally couldn't believe the soft words gushing so easily from Miss Appleby's tongue.

'Ah! But what about the older one?'

'He was a spiritual healer, brought in as a last resort. Came every day. Kindness itself, so Mrs Watson says. The poor man sapped all his own energy, passing it out of his body through his hands and into her. No good, though. The cancer had spread from 'er stomach to 'er brain. If only she'd gone to the doctor sooner . . .'

'Can't say I blame 'er, the way doctors are nowadays.'

'It wasn't as if she'd owt against them. She

couldn't 'ave 'cos she's left all her money to 'em, for research. Now how about that? I've never heard of anybody doing that before, have you?' Emily wiped a tear away from her cheek. 'Thinking of others, right up to the end. I feel right proud to 'ave known 'er,' she sighed. 'Eeh, I bet it'll be a lovely funeral.'

'Hmm, I always thought she was a classy sort of person,' Ida said. 'It's a pity we 'aven't a few more like her in the neighbourhood.'

'Oh!' Sally could contain herself no longer. 'You two-faced old hypocrite! You called her a . . . well, I can't repeat what you called her. I've heard nothing else all the time I've been here, and now the poor lady's laid out on her death bed! You should be ashamed. You're the most miserable, self-centred person I've ever come across, and if it weren't for leaving you in the lurch, I'd have walked out of here long ago. No wonder your nephew never comes to see you – it's because you're a spiteful, wicked old woman.'

'Nephew?' Emily Simms looked askance at Ida.

'Yes! There's a photograph of him on the sideboard, and he looks very pleasant and nice.' With that Sally burst into tears. 'I'm sorry, it's just that with Mr Jessops and everything, it's all becoming a bit too much.'

'Well, it isn't surprising, love.' Emily stared at Ida then. 'What's all this nonsense about a nephew? Don't tell me you're still passing your Donald off as a nephew? Especially to Sally, who's looking after yer as well as any daughter would. You're a fool to yerself, Ida! Everybody in Millington knows 'e's your son . . . well, everybody apart from Sally, obviously, and we accepted it years ago. Why, you've only to look at the red hair and the cleft chin on him to know he's belonging to Doug Fletcher. Especially us who knew 'im when he were a lad. Young Donald's the image of 'is dad.'

'Get me my tablets!' Ida exclaimed, almost fainting with shock. 'I've got one of me turns coming on.' Sally ran to get Miss Appleby's medication and a glass of water.

'Nonsense!' Emily snapped at her. 'It's time yer faced facts, Ida. Everybody knew you were knocking about wi' Doug Fletcher. It nearly ended wi' that poor wife of his divorcing 'im. Mind you, she'd 'ave been better off if she had. Nobody blamed you, Ida, we all knew he'd taken advantage of an innocent young girl.

'People in the rows would 'ave stood by yer, if you'd come out in the open. But, oh, no, you 'ad to go running away to somewhere or other – and you almost six months gone by then. And what did yer come back with? A beautiful baby boy who yer tried to pass off as yer cousin's. A cousin everyone knew you hadn't got! That was the worst sin of all, Ida, taking everybody in the rows for fools. Then, to cap it all, you brought the little lad up to call yer "Aunty". Did yer really think you'd got away with it? If only you'd told the truth instead of always being ashamed of 'im.'

'I was never ashamed of 'im! He means everything to me.'

'Aye, well, I reckon it's time yer told 'im that. Tell 'im yer proud to be 'is mother, and a grandmother too. Aunt and great-aunt, indeed! Anyway, think about what I've said, I reckon you've wasted enough time living a lie. I'm off now before Mr Baraclough closes. Are you all right, Sally love?'

Sally couldn't answer her. She had never been so flabbergasted in all her life. Finally she managed to pull herself together.

'I'll make us some tea.' In the kitchen she splashed her burning face with cold water, took a few deep breaths and mashed the tea. Then she spilled half of it as she carried the tray with trembling hands back to the other room.

'Here, Miss Appleby, drink this. Oh, I *am* sorry for the things I said.'

'No! You were right, and Emily was right, too. I'm glad it's all out in the open at last. Eeh, this is a good cup of tea, Sally.'

She smiled. 'It ought to be, I've used two spoonfuls!'

When Sally plucked up courage to go to Old Misery's stall again she asked Mary to accompany her for moral support. They wheeled Ernie out in his pram and people paused to admire him. Sally found two pairs of outsize pink knickers with elastic legs and gave them to Mary, to pay the man.

'I hope he doesn't think they're for me,' she giggled.

'I bet his wife wears that sort,' Sally said, 'I bet that's why he's so miserable.' They also bought a windmill to fasten on to Ernie's pram, a paint book for Daisy, and stamps for Stanley's album. Both the older children had decided they were too big for windmills.

When Sally called at Ida Appleby's with the knickers, Ida told her to bring the pram inside and made a fuss of baby Ernie, giving him a biscuit which she said would help his teeth through. Sally went to put the underwear away and found another half-dozen pairs neatly folded in the drawer.

'Are you sure you needed any more? You seem to have plenty already,' Sally queried.

'Oh, aye. I've heard there's going to be clothes shortages and rationing any day. We don't know how long this is going to last and I don't want to be caught without knickers.' Ida even managed a smile of sorts.

'This little 'un reminds me of our Donald when he was a baby, except that he had red hair.' She'd lifted Ernie out of the pram and was bouncing him on her knee. Sally had a feeling Ida wanted to talk about her son but Daisy would be home from school soon and she hadn't much time. She would make time, though, on her next visit, she promised herself. It had already made a difference to Ida, having things out in the open. If she talked about Donald a bit more, she might even end up like a normal human being.

Daisy was doing so well at school, Miss Robinson considered she was being held back in the baby class. Miss Clarke decided she could be moved up to Miss Williams' instead. Fortunately Carol and Jean – the little girl with no toys – were to be moved too. It would have been unthinkable for Daisy and her best friend to be separated.

The second class was far more interesting, but Miss Williams wasn't too pleased to be lumbered with another three pupils and wasn't quite as patient as Miss Robinson – even if Miss Robinson had had a pimply, hairy face.

On the first day in the new class, Miss Williams asked the children what they would like to be when they grew up. The answers ranged from engine driver to cowboy. One boy said he would like to be a skeleton, and then it was Carol's turn.

'Please, Miss, I would like to be a film star.'

Miss Williams sniffed at that.

When she came to Daisy, the little girl said, 'Please, Miss, I would like to be a typewriter.'

All the teacher need have done was correct the child by saying, 'No, Daisy, you mean a typist.' But teachers can be cruel sometimes, and Miss

Williams said, 'Oh! So you want to be a machine made out of metal with letters on, do you?'

All the other children were delighted and highly amused as they laughed and pointed at the embarrassed little girl.

Daisy didn't think she was going to like Miss Williams.

Betty was taking Ernie for a walk to see Doreen and baby Alice. She was halfway down the Donkey Path when she saw a soldier jump off the bus down on the main road. He turned up the path towards her and Betty's heart seemed to skip a few beats.

'Clarence?' She called out his name and put the brake on the pram; she was trembling so much she didn't feel capable of holding it back on the steepest part of the hill.

'Betty!' He hurried towards his wife and son. He looked so smart in his uniform, but Betty was shocked to see how much weight he had lost and the gauntness of his face. Then he held out his arms to her and Betty went into them, still keeping one hand on the pram, not trusting the brake on so steep a gradient.

'Oh, Betty.' Clarence was almost in tears, and the sight of her husband had the same effect on Betty, who started to cry. Then he was kissing her, just the way he had in the early days of their courtship, except that now there was a deeper, truer feeling between them, one that had been missing before.

'You look beautiful, Betty.' He touched her hair, then glanced into the pram. Clarence couldn't speak then. The smiling little face gazing up at him was a replica of his own on the old photographs at his parents' house. 'My son!'

'Ernie,' Betty told him. 'I didn't know what name you wanted. Bloody 'ell, Clarence, you just left me, without a goodbye or anything!'

'Ernie's a fine name. You got the money, though? And the other money came through for you, at the Post Office?'

'Yes.' Betty turned the pram round. 'How are you really, Clarence? You don't look too well.'

'Oh, I'm okay, considering.' But Betty didn't believe him.

'Come on, let's get you home.'

Clarence wheeled the pram up the hill with one hand and carried his kit bag with the other. He wanted to hold Betty's hand but couldn't. She seemed to sense the way he felt and placed her hand over his on the pram handle.

'I'm sorry, Bet.'

'That's okay, I'm sorry too.'

'What for?'

'For being what I was. I've changed, Clarence.'

'So have I.'

'Well,' Betty said, 'maybe if we've both changed for the better, we might be able to start afresh.'

'So yer haven't met anyone else? Got a new love, I mean?'

'Oh, aye, I've got a new love.' Betty watched her husband's face fall. 'He's in the pram, you daft bat!'

They laughed as they crossed St George's Road and walked along the row, happier than they had ever been. Betty and Clarence Hayes had both grown up at last.

Ernest Denman was flying a Spitfire Mark 11 long range, and for the first time ever was apprehensive about his own capabilities. The uneven fuel tank made the plane difficult to handle. He told himself that with practice he'd be okay. Fortunately, this was a test flight, one of many taken in readiness for the real thing. Take-off had been difficult, and he suspected keeping it on an even keel for landing would be more so.

He looked down over the south of England. The smooth, green sweep of the Downs would have soothed his soul with their beauty in other circumstances – though no place, in Ernest's opinion, could compare with the rugged hills and valleys of Yorkshire.

He planned his route and found that, compared to the Standard Mark 11, the LR took longer to reach 20,000 feet, and because of its extra weight couldn't match the maximum speed of the standard plane. The advantage of the long range was the distance the Spitfire could cover. The pilot would be alone for many hours, though. Time to think, time to dream of the day when war would be over. In the case of Ernest Denman, time to visualise the face that had filled his thoughts since he'd returned from his last leave in Millington. The face of Betty Hayes.

Mr Barker from the farm came every Saturday morning to empty the pig bins on the three rows. Old peelings, cabbage stalks, in fact anything edible, would be fed to his pigs. Charles, Mr Barker's son, would accompany his father, and, being about the same age as Daisy, would invite himself into their house where she would bring out her picture books and read to him.

Charles was a strong lad, the size of a ten-year-old; unfortunately he didn't have the brain power to match his size or his age. He was mentally impaired, though whether from damage at birth or an inherited condition no one seemed to know.

Daisy loved Charlie and would sit there on her three-legged stool reading books to him that she had long left behind herself, such as *Red Riding Hood*, understanding that these were the stories Charlie enjoyed.

'Your little lass's a damn' good reader,' Mr Barker said when he came to collect Charles, who never wanted to leave.

'Yes,' said Sally. 'She loves her books.'

'I'm going to write one when I grow up,' said Daisy. Sally and Mr Barker laughed but Daisy wasn't joking. She gave Charlie *The Three Bears* to take home.

Charles carried the book carefully in front of him as though it was the most precious thing in the world, a grin stretching from ear to ear on his face. He muttered something then and Daisy answered him.

'What did Charles say?' Sally enquired after father and son had gone home.

'He said he likes books with no words in,' Daisy explained. 'He means like babies' picture books. That's because Charlie's still a little baby, even though he's a big boy.'

Sally marvelled at the six-year-old's understanding.

'He won't like the books I'm going to write,' she said. 'They'll have hundreds and millions of words.' Then Daisy went out to play.

'They're like love's young dream,' Amy told Sally and Jim on her daily visit. She was delighted that her son-in-law had come home, even if it was only for a week. Clarence was entranced by his son and willingly cared for him while Betty went to work. Then, on her daughter's return, Amy would take her grandson on a visit to Sally in order to give the young couple time alone together.

Amy was right about love's young dream: Betty

was in love for the first time in her life. Never before had she needed to be with someone as much as she did with Clarence. He listened while she talked to him about her childhood, about her dreams for the future and for Ernie. In return, she comforted her husband when the trembling and the panic attacks came on him in the night. She bathed his brow, held him, and afterwards they would make love with such intensity that Betty cried at the wonder of it all.

They never mentioned the day when he would leave, except once when Clarence took his wife and son to Sheffield and had photographs taken of the three of them. He gave one to Betty and placed the other carefully in the breast pocket of his tunic.

'This picture'll remain close to my heart all the time I'm away,' he told her.

Then he kissed her, right there in the middle of the shop, with little Ernie grinning and dozens of people looking on. Many of them envied the handsome young couple's obvious happiness.

1942 came in like a lion, with twelve inches of snow falling in a few hours in the middle of January. Pat Cartwright was delighted, as the extreme weather prevented her from reaching the grammar school. Any enthusiasm she had initially shown for it had now disappeared as she found herself struggling to keep up with the more diligent students.

Pat might have coped better if she had not suddenly become obsessed with the opposite sex. Her homework was rarely completed before she was titivated and off out to meet her gang. Three times a week they would go to the Palace. Films were changed Mondays, Wednesdays and Fridays, and it was considered a disaster if one of them happened to be missed. Although not much of any of the films was actually seen, the darkness of the cinema being just an opportunity to cuddle and pet with any of the opposite sex Pat and her friends happened to fancy.

Once or twice the usherette had caught the youngsters going too far and made the amorous teenagers leave. Pat had been amongst them on a number of occasions. Because she always told her parents she was going with a friend, they had no idea of their daughter's antics. If anyone had told Bernard Cartwright, it was doubtful he would have believed them. So it came as a shock to him when he came home one night from the afternoon shift and Enid said, 'Our Pat's getting a name for herself.'

'What? What sort of name?'

'Potters Row Pat, good for a feel.'

'What?' Bernard's face turned scarlet and Enid burst into tears.

'How do yer know?' Bernard asked his weeping wife.

'It was written on the wall in the lads' toilets.

I had to clean it off. I've never been so humiliated in all my life, or so ashamed.'

'Where is she?'

'Out. She'd already gone when I came home from work at six.'

'And she's *still* out? It's bloody ten-past ten, Enid!'

'I know. She's never been out this late before . . .'

Bernard put on the overcoat he'd just taken off and went storming out, down the row and on to St George's Road. He saw one of the Dawson boys come from the Donkey Path and enquired, 'Have yer seen our Pat, Trevor?'

He looked uncomfortable and glanced back the way he had come. That glance was enough for Bernard who set off down the path, fumbling his way in the darkness. He reached the place where one of the flags had been carved out in the shape of a donkey. Suddenly he heard giggling – his daughter's giggling – coming from the bushes on the edge of the Donkey Wood. He moved silently towards the sound.

'What the bloody 'ell do yer think yer playing at?' he asked then.

A youth shot past him like a hurricane and disappeared in the direction of the main road. Bernard grabbed his daughter by the shoulder, just in time to catch her buttoning up her blouse.

'I . . . we were just talking, that's all.'

'Aye, that's why yer name's written all over the walls up at the school, is it? Because they like to *talk* to yer? "Potters Row Pat, good for a feel"? You dirty little bitch!'

'No! I don't believe you.'

'Potters Row Pat, that's what the lads call you.' She started to cry. 'I don't let them feel.'

'Don't yer? Then why were you half-undressed?'

Pat just cried harder. She couldn't answer her dad. She had let that lad feel inside her bra, but that was all. She would never let anybody go any further.

'Who was he?'

But Pat didn't answer, she daren't, she wouldn't put it past her dad to go and find the lad. Well, she couldn't blame him. She knew she'd done wrong. It was just that she got carried away when she was kissed . . . but to write about her on the school wall, where everybody could read it! She'd thought he really liked her – and all the time he'd been telling everybody what they'd done. She would never dare show her face. All the gang would be laughing at her. Oh, and that name . . . Potters Row Pat!

She was still crying when she walked into the house, and cried all the harder when she saw how upset her mam was.

'I think you owe yer mam more of an apology than that.' Bernard glared at his daughter. 'Do yer realise what she must have felt like, seeing your name on that toilet wall?'

'I'm sorry, Mam, I really am. I just wanted to be part of the gang. They seem to have shut me out now I've gone to the grammar and they're still at Millington School.'

'So you decide to turn yerself into a cheap little slut to get back in again?'

'No! It wasn't like that. I really like him . . .'

'Well, he obviously doesn't think much of you, to write *that* on the wall.'

'He does! Well, I thought he did.' Pat looked so downcast that Enid felt sorry for her daughter then.

'Well, you bloody well won't be seeing him again if I've aught to do with it!' Bernard very rarely swore. 'Surely you've made friends at yer new school?'

'Yes, but not living round here. They all live in Cragstone.'

'But you knew that'd happen, surely. You worked really hard to get to that school. Nobody made you go.'

'I know, but I didn't think about it, I suppose. I didn't realise I'd be left out of everything here in Millington. Anyway, I don't want to be part of a gang who are as crude as that. From now on, I'm going to spend my time working. I really want to do well, Dad.'

'Well, it won't be as bad for you in summer. You'll be able to go into Cragstone to meet your friends and invite them here,' Enid said. 'Do you know what I think, love? I think the Millington School lot are just jealous.'

'Maybe, but that's no excuse for acting cheap,' Bernard growled.

'I'm sorry, Dad. It won't happen again. I'm going to work from now on, and I'm going to find a drama group and join that.'

Bernard laughed. 'You'll be lucky to find owt like that with a war on!'

'Well, I'm going to try. I really want to work in the theatre.'

Bernard frowned. 'I doubt if there's much of a future in that. But you work as hard as yer can, and we'll see.'

'I'm off to bed now. I'm going to school tomorrow, even if I've to walk it.' Pat hoped the roads would be clear so that the buses could get through. She didn't want to fall any further behind with her lessons.

She didn't know what qualifications she would need to work in a theatre, but whatever they were, she would work until she got them. She didn't want to perform, the stage wasn't for her. She wanted to organise things, or even work in the booking office. Pat just liked the atmosphere of a theatre: the sound of the orchestra tuning up; the audience in all their finery; the swish of the curtains as the lights dimmed; the applause. She wanted to be part of it all.

Pat Cartwright had chosen her career, now she must work towards achieving her aim and forget about the so-called friends who'd tried to distract her. She wound up her alarm clock determinedly. Mustn't be late in the morning.

Raids over Sheffield were less frequent as the year wore on. On only one occasion was Millington in the firing line, when three cottages in the west end of the town were hit by incendiary bombs. Joe Denman and John Thomas put out the fires and helped a deaf old lady escape from her damaged property. Fortunately no one was hurt.

'Where are you going?' Charlotte's eyes narrowed as she watched her husband pack a small overnight bag.

'London.'

'Who with?'

'Myself. The Town Hall won't pay two men's travelling expenses when one can do the work.'

'I don't believe you! You're going with a woman.'

'Well, if that's what you choose to think, there's not much I can do about it.' Much as Mark detested his wife these days, he couldn't help but feel sorry for her. She was nothing but a bag of nerves, jumping at the slightest sound. Then there were her constant nightmares about dogs.

He studied Charlotte's face. The black smudges

beneath her eyes stood out in contrast to her sallow, wrinkled skin. She really did seem ill.

'Look, Charlotte, you need to see a doctor. You look awful,' he told her.

'Thank you very much.' Charlotte's eyes filled with tears.

'No! You've got me wrong. I mean, you look ill.'

'I don't need a doctor. I need you to get rid of those pictures and the clocks!'

'And I've told you . . . when you feel better, I'll get them out and we'll ask a valuer in to price them. You're in no condition for all that just now. You'd only go and say something to make them suspicious. Go to the doctor and get some sleeping pills or something for your nerves. Make an appointment for Tuesday and I'll go with you, I promise.'

'You mean, you won't be back before then?'

'No, I won't. I've an appointment tomorrow and another on Monday.'

'But I can't stay here on my own for five nights, I shall go mad!'

'Charlotte, my love, you already are mad.'

Mark picked up his case and his overcoat and placed his trilby on his head. Then he gave his wife the obligatory kiss and gladly left.

'Right then, what's on the agenda for today?' Sally still felt uncomfortable in Ida Appleby's presence, and decided there and then to have it all out in the open, regardless of the consequences.

'Look,' she said, 'I'm sorry for the things I said on that awful day. Perhaps it'd be better if I didn't work for you any more?'

'Oh, I don't blame yer for wanting to leave. Who'd want to work for somebody who lied and talked about everybody the way I did? And me an unmarried mother too. I should think you'd be ashamed to be seen coming 'ere.'

Sally interrupted the woman before she could say any more. 'Oh, no, I don't want to leave. Only I thought that after the things I said . . . And why should I mind coming here? Having a baby is nothing to be ashamed of, especially when you brought your son up alone. I should say that's something to be proud of. I mean, you could have had him adopted . . . though that would have been much worse, in my opinion.' Sally went to fill the kettle. 'I'll make us some tea.'

When she came back Ida was wiping her eyes, her face red from crying.

'Come on, drink this. Oh, I am sorry for the things I said!' Sally went to fetch her a clean handkerchief.

'Come and sit down,' Ida told her. 'I want to explain to you. Oh, but what must you think of all the lies I've told? Lie upon lie. I never was a housekeeper – I was a skivvy at the White Hart. That's where I met Doug Fletcher. He said he loved me. I suppose he did, in a way. The trouble was, he loved his wife as well but I didn't know that. I didn't know he was married with children. Well, he didn't look much older than me . . . I don't think he was, really, except that I was immature for me age, and innocent. I just thought he was wonderful. Oh! What must his poor wife have thought of me?' Ida began to cry again and Sally took the woman's hand in her own.

'Well, if it's right what Mrs Simms says, I shouldn't think she'd have blamed a young girl.'

'Even so, it was wrong what I did. Even if he hadn't been married, it was still wrong. I couldn't seem to resist 'im, though. It was Easter. He bought me a dress of blue crêpe-de-Chine, he called me Ida Blue Gown when I put it on, and took me to Scarborough for the day. There we were, at the Grand Hotel! He bought me a gin and orange, then another. They made me feel all warm and lovely inside. I felt so grown-up in me blue dress. Then he said we'd missed the train home so we would have to stay the night. If I'm truthful I didn't care, after the gin and oranges.

'Then we came home, he to his wife, and me to discover I was pregnant. I didn't know what to do. It was a sin in those days . . . well, it still is . . . to have a baby out of wedlock. Me mother gave me two choices. Either go away and 'ave the baby adopted or pretend it belonged to someone else. She sent me to stay with a cousin of hers who made my life a misery all the time I was there.

'Well, you heard the rest from Emily. I couldn't part with Donald, I loved 'im too much, but me mother said if the other kids found out he was mine, they'd call 'im a bastard and I couldn't 'ave that. I tried to make it up to 'im, worked like a horse to give 'im the best. Oh, but if only I could once 'ave heard 'im call me Mother, instead of Aunty.'

'Come on, I bet you feel better now you've told me?'

'I can't say I feel any better, but I am relieved it's all out in the open. Oh, and that poor woman across the road, too. I'm so ashamed of all the things I said!'

'Yes, well, we all make mistakes. If you only knew what *I* said the other night! I said that if anybody would go to their grave an embittered old virgin, it would be Miss Appleby. I'm so glad you proved me wrong!' Sally giggled. 'In fact, I like you much better now I know you're human. Come on, Miss Appleby, cheer up, it's not the end of the world.' She cleared the cups away and washed up. Then she got out the carpet sweeper and began wheeling it back and forth. She could hear Miss Appleby speaking to her above the squeaks.

'You'd better start calling me Ida. If everything's going to come out into the open it won't seem right me being a Miss, not with grandchildren to consider.'

230

Sally smiled to herself. Things were looking better already.

'Do yer think they'll forgive me, when I explain to them about being their grandma? I'm going to write to them today and send them a ten-shilling note to buy something for themselves.'

'If you slip them a few shillings, they'll forgive you anything if they're like most kids. Anyway, they've probably guessed already, children don't miss much these days.'

Ida got up from her chair and went to the drawer for a writing pad and pen, never once complaining about her legs.

Betty was subdued after Clarence went back. Letters passed between them almost every day.

'That young husband of Betty Butler's must idolise her, with all the letters he sends her,' Nellie passed the word at every house in the rows.

Amy looked much better now that the ulcer on her leg was healing nicely. She told her daughter she would mind little Ernie if she wanted a night out. 'But not dancing in the city!' she said. 'I can't go through that worry again at my age.'

'Oh, I won't be going dancing. Why should I want to dance with anybody except Clarence?'

So Betty and Doreen went to the pictures. Sometimes, if the film was suitable, they would take Daisy with them, to prove to Amy that they were behaving themselves. They scrutinised the newsreels closely, hoping to catch a glimpse of Clarence or Doreen's husband, but of course it was like finding a needle in a haystack. With little Ernie to care for, her dinner lady work and an occasional night out, Betty Hayes had never been so happy, but she would be even happier when Clarence came home.

Daisy was writing a story to tell to Charlie Barker. It was about a magic horse that could fly anywhere in the world. It could even swim beneath the sea, and the boy on the horse, who was called Charlie, had all kinds of adventures. Charlie usually liked books with lots of pictures in but Daisy's story seemed so real to him that the pictures formed in his head without him needing to look at them.

'Where are we flying to today, Daisy?' he would ask in a language only a few children like Daisy seemed to understand.

'What's he saying?' Sally asked Charlie's father as they watched him jabbering on to Daisy.

'Don't ask me.' Mr Barker said, shaking his head sadly. 'Ask your little lass, she seems to know.'

Daisy was happiest when she was writing, and now she was in the big class Miss Clarke came in every Friday to give them a spelling test. Miss Clarke was extremely strict about spelling and anyone who got a word wrong had to write it out correctly fifty times, over the weekend. Daisy rarely needed to correct any of her spellings but some poor kids might have five or six mistakes and would need to spend hours over the weekend, writing endless lists.

One day Miss Williams said, 'This week, instead of correcting spellings, I want you all to write a poem. I shall read them on Monday morning.'

Daisy was busy that weekend, going to visit Uncle Jack and Aunty Jane. It was almost bedtime when she decided to write her poem.

'Where's the writing pad?' she asked Sally.

'In the drawer.'

'No, it isn't. I've looked.'

'I used the last page when I wrote to Uncle Jack,' Jim put in.

'Well, I need some paper to write my poem for school.'

'I'm sorry but we haven't any. You should have thought about homework before this time on a Sunday night.'

Daisy searched in all the drawers and cupboards but there was no sign of a scrap of paper. In desperation, she took one of Jim's Woodbine packets, opened it up, and wrote a poem about a garden, in writing so small even she could hardly read it. The next morning she placed the cigarette packet with the other poems on the teacher's desk.

Miss Clarke came in as she normally did, but this time to read the poems. When she saw the cigarette packet, she said, 'I don't know who's written this but you'd better come out and read it to me because I certainly can't.'

Daisy hated being the centre of attraction but she had no option but to stand in front of the class and read the six verses off the tiny packet.

When she had finished Miss Clarke said, 'Come with me.' Daisy thought about the cane hanging on the wall over the headmistress's desk. She didn't know anyone who had ever been caned and hoped she wouldn't be the first.

'Daisy,' Miss Clarke said, 'your poem is very good – exceptionally good, in fact, for someone of your age.' She went to a shelf and found a new blue exercise book. 'Now, I want you to spend the rest of the lesson copying out your poem into this book. Then I want you to promise me you'll write another every week. Will you promise me that?'

There was nothing Daisy would enjoy more.

'Yes, Miss,' she said eagerly. She loved new exercise books and couldn't wait to begin writing in hers!

'If you keep producing writing of this calibre, you will go far,' Miss Clarke told her.

Daisy went back to class, determined to keep her promise. She had told Charlie Barker she would write a book one day, and she would.

Normally Whit Monday meant new dresses for the girls and new suits or shirts for the boys, but this year the beginning of clothes rationing meant make do and mend for most families. Except for the children of people like Sally Butler, who had taken a leaf out of Miss Appleby's book and prepared for the future. She had bought a few dress lengths of material from Norfolk market and Daisy was dressed as smartly as ever, in a Shirley Temple-style dress in white with a blue pleated panel running from collar to hem. When Whit Monday arrived Daisy was up with the lark and couldn't wait to be dressed in all her finery. 'I want to go and show Mrs Firth and Aunty Enid and Mrs Porter,' she said excitedly. She set off along the row where Norah and Pat were ready and waiting, eager for once to go to Sunday school. Everyone in the row came out to admire the children in their glad rags, and to give each child a few pennies for the pockets of their new clothes, even Miss Appleby.

Then they were off, each carrying a plate and a spoon which would be left in the chapel lecture room, where lunch would be waiting for them following the Whit walk.

When they were all lined up, four abreast behind the chapel banner, each child was given a hymn sheet. Daisy carried hers proudly, and waited with the others in line. Suddenly the sound of the Millington Band reached them, adding to their excitement. Following the band up the hill were the congregations from the Primitive Methodist Chapel and the Mission.

'Hail, Smiling Morn' the band played, smartly dressed in their navy blue uniforms. The members this year mostly consisted of men in their fifties, together with a couple of youths still too young to have been called up.

The chapel members joined in behind. Daisy could see Grandma Denman waving them on their way. Grandma would no doubt have been in the procession herself had she not volunteered to help with the lunch. Off they went like a trail of ants, wending their way along the main road. Pavements were lined with proud parents and grandparents. Aunties and uncles all turned out to wave to the children, glad of an excuse to sport their own Sunday clothes. One mother ran into the procession and wiped her boy's nose; another came to pull up her son's socks. Daisy was glad her mam didn't show her up like that.

At the bottom of the Donkey Path, the children from the Parish Church joined in behind. Waiting, too, was the Salvation Army, with their own band ready to play. The Methodists were next, and by this time Daisy's new, black patent shoes were pinching her toes and Norah was developing a blister on her heel. Both girls were relieved when they reached the point where they would pause for their first hymn.

'I'm thirsty,' Daisy told her cousin Pat, but there was nothing Pat could do about it. So Daisy told the Sunday school teacher, 'I'm thirsty, Mrs Smith.'

'You can have a drink when we get back to Sunday school,' the woman promised Daisy, but they had to walk all the way back before then! Outside St Joan's the crowd was enormous. Voices swelled as they sang. Daisy wished she could sit down and take off her shoes but she didn't want to dirty her new dress. She began to think Whit Monday wasn't quite as interesting as she had expected. Being so little, all she could see was the legs of the taller people.

The crowd began to move on the second lap of the journey. The sun was hotter now and the journey uphill, all the way to the sports field where prayers would be prayed and more hymns sung. Daisy noticed none of it. All she could think of was the white ice-cream van parked outside the tall wooden gates. She felt up her dress to the pockets of her knickers to see if her pennies were still there.

'Norah!' she shouted to make herself heard above the singing of 'Sound The Battle Cry'. 'Norah, I want a cornet.'

'So do I,' Norah said. She clutched Daisy's hand and pushed her way through the crowd until they reached the van where one or two other impatient children were already being served. The ice-cream was delicious and they were so busy trying to avoid messing up their clothes that they became hopelessly lost in the crowd.

'We're lost, what are we going to do now?' Daisy worried.

'It's all right,' Norah consoled her cousin. 'I can still see our banner. All we have to do is join in behind and hope Mrs Smith doesn't notice our cornets.'

By the time they reached the chapel, Daisy's lovely new dress was stained all down the front, her bonnet strings stiff from hanging in the ice-cream. Even her socks were dripped on. However, the procession was over for another year so no one would care, and now for potted meat sand-wiches and a yummy iced bun, followed by jelly – not quite set – and custard. By the time lunch was over no doubt a few of them would be feeling rather sick, Daisy included, but it was Whitsuntide so nobody cared.

Sally could always expect some of her cousins to turn up on Whit Monday, so lunch would usually consist of sandwiches and pickles. Afterwards everyone would make their way to the sports field where games and skipping would be organised. The men, after a few pints to slaken the dust, would no doubt show themselves up in the sack race. The ladies would show off their stocking tops during the skipping games, and the children would have the time of their lives.

After the relatives had made their way home, some to walk several miles, Sally's best dress would be hung in mothballs, Jim's suit pressed and put away for the next special occasion, be it wedding or funeral, and Daisy's dress washed and ironed ready for next Sunday. Her blisters would be treated with Germolene and her shoes packed with damp paper to stretch them. The most exciting day of the year – apart from Christmas – would be over. It would perhaps be another year before Daisy tasted ice-cream again.

In fact, it was banned altogether four months later, for the duration of the war. Daisy and Norah had sneaked one just in time!

Chapter Seven

Charlotte Kaye went to the surgery on Tuesday morning. All she told Dr North was that she couldn't sleep, not mentioning her dread of night-time or the hauntings. He prescribed something to help her sleep, and a tonic. When Mark arrived home she begged him once again to remove the panelling and take away the pictures.

'All in good time,' he promised. His wife had to be satisfied with that for now. When the clock struck one she simply reached for the sleeping pills and took another. Mark didn't see her. He was in the other room, fast asleep.

Ernest Denman was celebrating with a lime juice, triumphant that their raid over Cologne had destroyed two hundred factories. Being a Yorkshire man, he considered it fair retribution for Hitler's bombing of the fifteenth-century Guildhall in York, a month earlier.

Ernest was the life and soul of the NAAFI. It was only later, in the privacy of his bed, that he gave in and cried for the loss of comrades he had grown to love and respect for their friendship and courage.

Ernest wanted to go home. He wanted his parents. He yearned to be back in Millington. This bugger of a war had gone on long enough and it wasn't over yet, not by a long chalk.

All Daisy's class were moving to the juniors. They were waiting at the end of the infants' corridor. Daisy and Carol waited together. They watched a class of junior children file out and into the next room. A teacher came out then and began calling names from a list. Daisy Butler was one of the first to be called and went to join a new line.

'Now,' said the teacher, 'my name is Miss Moran, you will come with me. Your new form is 1A. The rest of you will wait here until your teacher comes. Your form will be 1B.'

Horror of horrors, for the first time Carol and Daisy were separated! Daisy looked around her frantically and was relieved to see Jean, the girl with no toys, in the same line. They moved into their new classroom, apprehensive about this unknown teacher. Miss Moran turned out to be all right, though. Daisy studied hard and enjoyed the work, which seemed much more difficult than last year's.

On the other hand, she was filled with terror on approaching the assembly hall to see a buck and a horse in readiness for gymnastics, and a huge pile of mats for forward rolls. Her stomach lurched at the thought of more PT lessons, and she felt sick at the sight of all that apparatus. Apart from that, she enjoyed the juniors.

Little Miss Broadway was on at the Palace. Pat was taking Norah and Daisy, who couldn't wait to see Shirley Temple again. She had already seen *Poor Little Rich Girl* and *The Little Princess*. Shirley Temple was Daisy's heroine. She had scrutinised herself in Mam's wardrobe mirror and did indeed look like the film star, especially in her new frock. The first supporting picture was Abbott and Costello, and Daisy was so enthralled with the programme that she left her cardigan behind. It was brand new, knitted by Grandma Butler.

Sally was livid with her. 'You don't value anything!' she shouted at her daughter. 'The trouble is, you get too much. You lose one more thing and there'll be no more pictures, even if it *is* a Shirley Temple film.'

The following Monday Daisy was skipping to school, swinging her shoulder bag in the air, when suddenly the press stud snapped open. The two-shilling piece destined for the Yorkshire Penny Bank flew out of her bag and rolled into a drain by the side of the footpath. Daisy looked down into the water but the coin had disappeared. She knew how angry her mother would be. Losing money was even worse than losing cardigans and pixie hats. Daisy knew she would be shouted at and then there would be no more visits to the cinema.

She worried about it all day, then on the way home came up with a solution. If she entered the sum of two shillings in the bank book as usual, and copied Miss Moran's initials in the margin, her mam would never know. Of course, if Sally had checked the entry in the book she would have recognised the childish writing, but she didn't.

It was Miss Moran, the following Monday, who noticed. Daisy had joined the savings queue, having forgotten all about the lost money by now. Miss Moran took one look at the book, checked it against her ledger and walked out of the room. After a short while she came back.

'Go to Mr Bramwell's room,' she ordered Daisy.

A visit to Mr Bramwell, known as Daddy Bramwell by the boys, was a rarity, reserved for exceptionally good behaviour or extremely serious trouble. Daisy realised it could only be the latter and felt she wanted to be sick as she tapped on the headmaster's door.

'Enter!'

Daisy went in and stood white-faced before his desk. She could see a cane propped up in the corner and trembled as she wondered what a whipping would feel like. The ruler was bad enough, Miss Moran had rapped everybody across the knuckles one day when no one had owned up to drawing a picture of her on the blackboard. She was easily recognisable with her big nose and the wart on the end of it.

'Right.' Mr Bramwell glared from beneath his thick thatch of hairs combed forward in a fringe. 'Who wrote this in your savings book?'

'Me, sir.'

'Why?'

'I lost my money, sir.'

'That's no excuse for forgery.'

Daisy wondered what forgery meant, it sounded very serious.

'Why didn't you tell your mother?'

'I thought she'd be mad, sir.'

'Of course she'd be mad, but not half as mad as she will be now.' He began to write a note then handed it to Daisy.

'Take that to your mother. I wish to see her.'

'Now?'

'Yes, now.'

Daisy ran all the way home before remembering her mother would be at Miss Appleby's today. She couldn't face Miss Appleby after the incident with the rabbit. Instead she went to Grandma Butler's.

'What's to do, love?' Amy knew something was amiss by the look on her grand-daughter's face.

'I want me mam but she'll be at Miss Appleby's. Can you fetch her for me?'

'Not till ten. She'll be at home still now, I should think.' Daisy was off through the gap and across the field, desperate to find her mam and get back to school. She didn't want to make things worse for herself by taking a long time over it. She handed the note to Sally, so out of breath she couldn't speak. Sally enquired what was wrong, but Daisy was already dragging her mother by the hand back towards the school.

In his office Mr Bramwell told Sally to be seated. He explained what her daughter had done and asked why Daisy had been afraid to tell her mother about the lost florin. Sally told him she had no idea.

'I hope you don't think she has any reason to be afraid of me. I very rarely punish her since she very rarely needs it. Daisy's not a naughty child usually.' Then Sally thought about the incident at Miss Appleby's and wondered what possessed her daughter at times.

Mr Bramwell stared hard at Daisy. 'Did you really lose the money or did you spend it?'

'No, sir, I lost it down a grate on the estate.'

'Well, what you have done is extremely serious. If you were older you would be in grave trouble. However, since you are usually a quiet, well-behaved and studious child, we'll say no more about the incident. Go back to your class – and do not forge anyone's signature ever again!'

'No, I won't, sir.' And Daisy was off along the corridor before he could change his mind. Miss Moran never mentioned the incident again. Daisy dreaded hometime, though, afraid her visits to the Palace would be at an end. They were.

When Sally paid another visit to Danny Powell,

she was gratified to see his face light up at the sight of her.

'Eeh, lass, come in.' He hobbled over on his crutches to let her in and went back to his kitchen chair. 'I've just been sat 'ere thinking about when your little lass come to me aid. I should 'ave been laid theer still if she 'adn't fetched yer.'

'Well, I'm glad she did. Anyway, how are you?'

'Oh, I'm right enough. I told yer, I'm as fit as a fiddle, I am.'

'You must be. Some folk would have ended up with pneumonia, lying there for two hours.'

'Not me, though.'

'Has anybody been? The Salvation Army lady?'

'No, only the lass from the Co-op wi' me rations.' He indicated the door that led into the pantry. The rations were arranged on a shelf amongst an odd assortment of tools. The whole pantry looked more like a junk cupboard, containing as it did a stepladder, old rolls of wallpaper, a fishing rod and a rolled-up tent.

'Hasn't she brought you any vegetables or meat?'

'Aye, some corned beef and some sausages – I expect they're more bread than meat, though. I don't bother with vegetables.'

'Well, you should, they're good for you.'

Danny laughed. 'I'm good enough, wi'out vegetables!'

'Would you like me to tidy up for you?'

'Eeh, lass, I don't want to be a nuisance . . .'

'You won't be, it won't take me long.' Sally washed up, using the wire wool she'd brought, then she mopped the floor and scrubbed the oilcloth-covered table. 'Do you always sit in the kitchen?' she enquired.

'Oh, aye. It's warmer in 'ere.'

'Wouldn't you be more comfortable in an easy chair?'

'Aye, I would, but it's not easy moving furniture wi' me leg.'

'I could do it, though.'

'Nay, lass, it's no job for a woman.'

Sally went to the door she guessed led to the sitting-room.

'Do you mind if I go through?'

'Nay, lass, go wherever yer like.' Danny grinned. 'It's all't same to me.'

Sally thought the room could not have been used for years. It smelled of mildew and felt freezing cold. There were, however, some lovely pieces of furniture there and a leather-covered three-piece suite. She went back to the kitchen.

'I'm going to bring a comfortable chair in here for you.' Sally moved the table from the middle of the room to beside one wall, and carried two of the kitchen chairs in to the other room. Then she struggled with one of the easy chairs and manoeuvred it into the kitchen.

'Don't you go lugging heavy things about or yer'll end up wi' piles!' Danny sounded most concerned for her. Sally just smiled and wondered what he would come out with next. She placed the chair to one side of the fire. 'There, how's that?' She fluffed up the cushions and a cloud of dust pothered out, so she took them outside and beat them before placing them back in the chair. 'Come on then, let's have you settled before I go.'

Danny rose up on his crutches then sank down in the chair by the fire.

'Eeh, lass, that's a comfort to me owd back.'

Sally smiled. 'Good. Now let's sort you out something to eat . . .'

'Nay, I can manage me food, lass. It wouldn't be good for me, sitting on me arse all day.'

'Are you sure?'

'Oh, aye. Tha's done more than enough for one morning.'

'Well, I'll be going then. I've to go to Ida Appleby's at ten.'

'Ida Appleby, off Potters Row?'

'Yes. Do you know her?'

'Know 'er? I used to fancy 'er before I met my lass. Eeh, Ida Appleby. Smartest lass in Millington, she was.'

'Really?'

'Oh, ah. Could 'ave 'ad pick of all't lads in Millington, and she 'ad to get lumbered wi' Doug Fletcher. Still, I blamed her father.'

'Oh?'

'Oh, aye. Rottenest bugger in't place . . . pardon

me language but 'e were. It was said 'e used to beat her black and blue.'

'No!'

'Oh, aye, and her mother.' Danny looked thoughtful. 'I expect Doug Fletcher were nice to 'er so she fell for the first one who were. A good-natured lad were Doug . . . if 'e could 'ave kept his cock under control.'

Sally bit her lip to prevent herself from giggling. 'Well, I'm going now.'

'Here, let me pay yer.' Danny felt in his pocket and brought out a huge wad of notes. He offered two to Sally.

'No! I don't want paying.'

'Well, when you come again, we'll sort summat out.'

'I will come and see you again, but I won't want paying.' She went to the door.

'Give Ida my love, will yer?'

'I will.' But she wondered what Miss Appleby would have to say to *that*.

Sally was so taken aback by the sight of Ida she forgot all about Danny's message. Today she was dressed in her best frock and her Cuban-heeled shoes.

'Well! You look nice. Is it a special occasion?' Sally asked.

'I've decided I'm going down Millington.'

'What? To the shops?'

'Aye, if yer don't mind taking me?' Ida powdered her nose in front of the mirror. 'I want some more library books.'

'I can bring those for you.'

'Yes, but I've read most of the ones you bring. Besides, I want to go to Whitaker's and get me shoes soled and heeled.'

'Right, I'll not take my coat off then, if we're going out again.'

'Can yer fetch me my handbag?'

'Where is it?'

'Under the edge of me mattress. It's safe there.'

Sally fetched the handbag and Ida's coat, which hadn't seen daylight for months, if not years. She looked at the fancy shoes. 'Don't you have any flat ones? It's quite a walk down the hill and back again.'

'Aye, yer might be right, I'll wear me flat heels. Although if we go along St George's, it won't be as steep as the Donkey Path.'

'Right.' Sally helped her on with her coat and off they went. Ida never once complained about her legs and chatted all the way down to the main road. Sally couldn't believe the change in her. The strain of trying to cover up the secret of her illegitimate son must have been more than the poor woman could bear. No wonder she had been so embittered. If Danny Powell was right, she must have suffered terribly when she was young, and the relief of it all being out in the open must be tremendous.

'I could do with a cup of tea,' Ida said after they'd

chatted to Mr Whitaker and exchanged the library books.

'There's a little cafe down the hill by the smithy, but it's mostly used by the steelworkers.'

'I don't care who it's used by so long as they sell tea.'

'Right, let's go and have a look.' Sally was surprised to see that the cafe had started doing a wartime lunch for a shilling, consisting of roast beef, roast potatoes and peas, followed by gooseberry tart and custard.

She thought the rough and ready atmosphere would have put Ida off, but she only said, 'Well, now we're here we might as well have our dinners.' While they were eating, Ida said, 'I'm going to come here again when I fetch me shoes back. Will yer come with me? Just till I get used to coming out again. I'll pay.'

'You don't need to pay. It's just that I won't get much cleaning done if I'm sitting in here.'

'Oh . . .' Ida waved her hand in the air '. . . forget about the cleaning. I've wasted enough of me life worrying about things that don't matter, life's too short to be bothering about stuff like that. You're making an owd woman happy by just being me friend.' She wiped a tear from the corner of her eye then. 'The Lord knows, I haven't many. Never did have. Me father never let me make any friends.'

'Why not? That's terrible.'

'He was jealous of anyone me or me mother spoke to, and if I wanted to meet anyone it had to be in secret. He wouldn't even let me go to work. Thank God he died when I was seventeen!' She looked Sally in the eye then. 'Oh, don't look so shocked. He only got what he deserved.

'He'd bullied a young lad unmercifully, a lad in his employ. The lad's brothers found out and waited for him one dark night. They beat 'im up and dumped 'im in the stream down the Donkey Wood. By the time 'e was found, 'e was dead as a dodo. When the constable came to tell us, my mother breathed a sigh of relief. She asked if he was sure that my dad was dead, and when he said he was afraid so, my mother said, "Thank God for that!" That's when I went to work at the White Hart. I loved working there . . . all the lads fancied me. Well, I weren't bad-looking at that time.'

'You aren't now,' Sally answered, and it was true. Ida had barely a wrinkle on her face.

'And I had to go and fall for someone like Doug Fletcher,' Ida sighed. 'He was nice, though. I did love 'im. He was the first and the last. No other man has ever touched me in that way.'

'We'd better be going,' Sally said briskly, thinking the woman had said enough for one day and could regret confiding in her by the time she got home.

'Aye, let's get 'ome. I can't wait to start me new book. Mrs Brown in't library says it's a bit naughty.'

Ida was smiling again, which Sally considered a minor miracle.

Emily Simms woke in the middle of the night with a blinding headache. She heard the rumble of thunder in the distance. That was the trouble with being a bit psychic, storms always gave you an aching head. The thunder rumbled again, closer this time, and a streak of lightning lit up the room. She got out of bed and took out the metal curlers from her hair, then she went downstairs and removed all the stray items of cutlery which were lying about the kitchen. Emily had been struck by lightning once, at the age of seven, wheeling her little brother along St George's Road in his pram. Fortunately the baby had avoided any hurt and Emily had soon recovered, but the experience had been frightening and she had ever since been wary of being near metal objects during a storm.

She made a cup of tea and took a couple of Aspirin but still couldn't shake off the headache or the feeling of uneasiness. Something awful was about to happen . . . She hated these premonitions of hers but couldn't ignore them. She got out the tarot cards and sat up to the table, unfolded the silk scarf in which the cards were wrapped and shuffled them. Emily very rarely consulted the cards these days. After the death of her husband she hadn't seen much point in learning what the future might bring. Tonight, though, that feeling of uneasiness was too strong to ignore.

She cut the pack into three, shuffled them again and cut them into two piles. She placed the top pile to the bottom and chose three cards at random, placing them upside down on the table and turning them over, concentrating all the while.

The first card wasn't a good one. Emily didn't like the Moon card at all. From past experience, it meant that someone was up to no good, usually a woman. The second card suggested there was a neighbour in trouble. The third, the Tower, filled Emily with apprehension. This spread clearly indicated trouble in store for someone close to her.

She shivered as lightning illuminated the room, more feeble now. Thunder rolled some distance away. The storm was passing over. It would have been better if it had rained and cleared the air. Emily shivered. She might as well go back to bed. Whatever was about to happen, there was nothing she could do about it.

Nellie was almost as upset as Betty. For three weeks now she had delivered no letters from Clarence. Betty waited on the step every morning, anguished and sometimes in tears when Nellie apologised as if it was her fault. Amy tried consoling her daughter by reminding her about Mr Harrison's son, who seemed to have disappeared for months and was then found to be a prisoner-of-war, but that only made Betty more agitated than ever.

'You've got to stop worriting,' Amy said. 'You've got our Ernie to think about.'

'I *am* thinking about him. I don't want him to be fatherless.'

Little Ernie just grinned as he spooned oatmeal porridge into his mouth.

'Da-da,' he said, pointing at the photograph on the dresser and setting his mother off crying once again.

Charlotte found an old can of paraffin. It had once served to keep a lamp burning in the outside lavatory in winter, before a bedroom had been converted to an indoor bathroom. She dug out a bundle of old rags and rolled the can inside them. Then she tied a scarf round her head and put on her coat. It was a dark night but she was more afraid to stay in the house than to venture out into the darkness. She cut through the council estate where nothing stirred at two in the morning.

Uncle Walter's was also in darkness. She was sorry if the pretty little girl had to suffer for her mother's sins, but it couldn't be helped. The child reminded Charlotte of herself in years past. It was that woman she wanted to hurt. Charlotte would never rest until she'd had her revenge.

She knew Jim Butler was on night shift. She knew everything about the family, after watching the house for weeks. She poured paraffin on to the rags and crept up to the front door. She poured the rest of the oil through the letter box then dug a lighter from her pocket. Swiftly she stuffed the rags through the letter box and held the lighter to one end before letting it go. It was aflame even before she even let go of it, but what was a burned finger in comparison to the thrill of revenge? Charlotte hurried away in the direction of the Donkey Path; that way there would be less chance of being seen. There was no hurry, there would only be the dogs waiting for her at home.

The draught curtain behind the door was ablaze within seconds, the flames licking along the carpet towards the stairs. If it hadn't been for Dippy, Sally and her daughter would no doubt have died. The dog barked frantically, waking Sally upstairs. At about the same time, Alf Ramsgate was on fire-watching duty. He could see the red glow showing through the fanlight over the door, even from across the field.

'Sally!' he bawled as loud as he could, and saw the young woman at an upstairs window, her daughter in her arms.

'Stop where yer are!' he shouted. 'Don't open't winder, and make sure the bedroom door's shut.' Alfie ran to the shelter where he knew a ladder was kept for eventualities such as this. He also blew his whistle, alerting the neighbours. Mr Dawson was the first on the scene and began dealing with the fire. He sent young Trevor to ring for the fire brigade. Alfie was by this time up the ladder and carrying Daisy to safety. Sally was out of the sash window after him before he had reached the ground. Daisy was hysterical.

'I want Dippy! He'll be burned.'

Alfie made his way through the entry to the back door. He kicked at it until it gave way and Dippy almost knocked him over in his haste to escape. The stairs were well alight by now and the fire beginning to spread to the living-room, but with Alfie and Mr Dawson working together they were able to keep it under control until the fire brigade arrived.

'This looks as though it was lit deliberately,' Bobby Jones said when he arrived to investigate.

'It certainly was,' agreed the firemen. 'There was paraffin involved.'

'Who would do a thing like that?' Alfie looked askance.

'Not kids, surely?' Mr Dawson couldn't believe anyone local would do such a thing.

'Could be, but I doubt it at this time of the morning.'

Only Mrs Simms immediately suspected who was responsible. 'Can I 'ave a word?' she asked Bobby Jones. She told him of her suspicions and he immediately went off to investigate.

Charlotte Kaye was a good actress, though, as Mrs Simms had once said. She answered the door in her nighty, looking bewildered and full of sympathy for the victims of the fire. The police could prove nothing.

Bobby Jones was still troubled, though. Not once had Charlotte Kaye questioned him as to why they should have suspected her. Most unusual, that.

By the time Jim arrived home from the night shift, the fire was out, but the stair and living-room carpets were ruined, the walls black, and the whole house stinking of smoke. They would also need a new front door and a new lock on the back. Alfie, not knowing about the key hanging in the letterbox, had broken the lock in his haste to rescue Dippy.

Jim didn't care about the work that would need to be done, or the expense. He only cared that his wife and daughter were unhurt. But what of the future? If someone had intended hurting them once, it could happen again. If it hadn't been for Alfie Ramsgate, he would have lost them both. When he told Alfie he was a hero, his neighbour said, 'Nay, Jim, if it hadn't been for that dog o' yours they'd never 'ave 'ad a chance of getting out alive.'

Jim knew different. Never again would he grumble about Alf Ramsgate being a scrounger. To Jim he was a hero, and always would be.

Daisy was allowed to stay off school the day after the fire. Normally she would have insisted on going, but it was games day so she didn't need any persuading. In the afternoon the lady from the Salvation Army called at Sally's. 'Mr Powell told me about the fire,' she said, 'and I wondered if there was anything we could do?'

Sally wondered how Danny had heard. Considering he never went out, he didn't seem to miss much of what was going on.

'It's very kind of you but we're managing, with help from our sisters and friends.' Sally decided she liked this friendly-faced woman.

'Mr Powell really appreciates your help,' she told the visitor.

'And yours. If your little girl hadn't had the presence of mind to fetch help, he might have been lying out there all night.'

'Yes, I'm proud of my daughter.'

'Well, if there's nothing I can do, I'll let you get on. Just remember, that's what we're here for – to help at times like these.'

'I will, and thank you.'

When she'd gone, Sally carried on clearing up the mess caused by the smoke and water. It could have been worse. A shiver ran down Sally's spine as she realised how much worse. If the fire had been started deliberately – which it was believed to have been – she doubted she would ever be able to sleep here in peace again.

If Charlotte Kaye were responsible, as Mrs Simms seemed to suspect, Sally wondered if the woman would strike again. They would have to be vigilant at all times. Sally wished she had never inherited this house. They had been safe in their rented property on Potters Row.

Betty knuckled down to help her sister-in-law

scrub out the house on Taylors Row, hoping the hard work would help her forget her worries about Clarence, who still hadn't written. In fact, her husband was one of 25,000 men who had been taken prisoner by the enemy in Tobruk.

Joe Denman was feeling his age. Even though he had been given a lighter job on the pit head it was still not an easy one, and with the Home Guard duties and his allotment to tend to he seemed to be tiring more easily of late. Lizzie was worried about him. Combined with the worry about Ernest and now Sally's fire, she wondered where it would all end. Enid, too, had advised her father to take things a bit easier.

'Let Bernard and our Jim take over the garden, Dad. You must start slowing down a bit.'

'Slowing down? In war-time? What the hell do yer take me for? If everybody slowed down, the bloody war'd never be over. I'll get Lizzie to buy me some Phosferine, that'll help.'

'All right.' Enid knew nothing would change his mind, but she could see why her mother was worried. Her dad had lost weight and seemed different somehow, more withdrawn. When she voiced her fears to Bernard, he said, 'Well, he's never had a lot to say for himself. Says little and thinks a lot, that's your dad. Of course I'll give him a hand with the allotment.'

'Thanks. We'll just have to keep an eye on him.'

One thing Enid was thankful for was the change in Pat. If she went to the Palace now, she would take Norah with her and sometimes Daisy. Pat worked hard at school and never shirked her homework. Most important of all as far as she was concerned, she had got herself into a theatre. Not that she was being paid, but that didn't matter. She had gone to the Empire first but they'd had nothing for her there. Then she had tried the Lyceum.

'I'd like to speak to someone in charge, please,' she'd said. The doorman had wandered off and Pat was left wondering whether to go when a smartly dressed woman rushed towards her. 'Yes?' she queried eyeing Pat up and down.

The girl never paused for breath, afraid this brisk woman would turn away. 'I want to work in the theatre. I don't expect to be paid, I just want to learn about the work here. I'm not a starstruck little girl who wants to go on the stage. I'll do anything – clean, sell tickets, shine the torch . . .'

'Stop!' the woman said, laughing, and held up her hand. 'What's your name?'

'Patricia Cartwright.'

'Well, Patricia Cartwright, I'm glad you don't expect to be paid because our funds won't run to it. How old are you?'

'Nearly fifteen.' Pat had added a year on.

'Come with me then. You can call me Liz.' She led Pat through the foyer and into the auditorium. Pat, who had only seen inside the theatre from up in the Gods, couldn't believe the spaciousness and magnificence, and stood mesmerised. 'Come on!' Liz was leaving her behind. Pat ran to catch up and they were soon in the vicinity of the dressing-rooms.

'Can you iron?'

'Yes.' She could. Enid had taught her daughters from an early age.

'Right, iron that shirt, and if it's not done properly, you're out. Understood?'

'Understood.' Pat had no qualms about ironing a shirt. Enid had shown her how to iron all the seams inside first, then the cuffs and collar, then the sleeves, and lastly the shirt body. She saw a hanger and hung the shirt on a hook behind the door. She noticed another shirt, a blue one this time, and ironed that, too. When Liz bustled back in she examined both garments closely.

'Pat Cartwright, you've just earned yourself an unpaid job!' Pat jumped up and down in her excitement. 'And, even more importantly, you've just ironed a shirt for Noël Coward.'

Pat felt the colour drain from her face. 'The real Noël Coward?'

'Who else? This is the Lyceum, not a second-rate establishment. You'll have to get used to seeing important stars here.'

'Yes, but Noël Coward . . .'

Liz laughed. 'He's appearing here in *Blithe Spirit*. I promised his dresser I'd iron his shirt, but I hate ironing, even for Noël Coward.' Pat was speechless, not only at touching something belonging to a famous star but at actually landing herself a job at the Lyceum, even if it was an unpaid one.

Sally was feeling happier now the house was clean again. The staircase had been redecorated and the carpet thrown out. At least they hadn't bought a new one when they'd moved in. The living-room carpet would have to be replaced along with the lino. Long Sam the insurance man was sorting out the claim. A new door had already been fitted. Today Sally was taking Miss Appleby shopping.

'We'll go to the library first,' Ida decided. 'Then I'll fetch me shoes from Mr Whitaker's.'

'What do you want from the shops?' Sally asked her.

'Me rations from the Co-op and owt they've got extra. Oh, and a bottle of lemonade,' she whispered in Sally's ear. 'I've started 'aving a port and lemon sometimes, it helps me to sleep.'

Sally grinned. 'Well, I suppose it's as good an excuse as any.' They queued at the Co-op and managed to get a few cans of peas and another of Spam. As they were waiting for the change to come back through the tube system, Ida advised, 'You want to stock up wi' tinned stuff, there won't be any soon.'

'Right then, we'll go and have some dinner now,' Sally said.

Ida was excited at the thought of eating out again.

Laden with shopping, they found a table near the window where there was room to place their bags. Not that there was much to see out of it except the soot-coated roofs and chimneys of the steelworks.

'Eeh, let me get the weight off my feet, these shoes are killing me.' Ida slipped her feet out of the Cuban-heeled shoes she had insisted on wearing.

'Change into the ones you've had repaired then.'

Ida looked round. 'Oh, I can't, somebody might see me.' But there was only one man sitting in the corner, and he was hidden behind a newspaper. Not that it could hide much these days with only four pages allowed.

'Shall we have some tea while we're waiting for the meal?'

'I 'ope it's not like dishwater.'

Sally couldn't believe this coming from a woman who had insisted on making two cups out of one spoonful of tea!

'How long has this place been open then?' Ida enquired.

'Just before last Christmas,' Sally answered.

'Don't tell me it's so long since I used to come shopping?'

'Well, with your legs being bad . . .'

'There's nowt wrong with my legs that a bit of exercise won't cure! It's a wonder they 'aven't seized up altogether, the way I kept sitting there, day in, day out, with nowt to occupy me mind. It's a wonder me brain hasn't seized up as well.'

'Maybe Dr North was right, then.'

'Well, yes, but he'll never be as good a doctor as Dr Sellars.'

The waitress brought their lunches, steaming hot and smelling delicious. Ida sat gazing across the room at the man in the corner.

'Well, I'll go to the foot of our stairs!' she said.

'What? You look as though you've seen a ghost.'

'I feel as though I have. If I'm not mistaken, that's Doug Fletcher over there.'

'Who? Him who . . .'

'Our Donald's father,' Ida whispered.

Sally couldn't help but stare at the elderly man. His hair was grey and curling over his collar but Sally could see how handsome he had been in his youth. In fact, he was still good-looking in a way. He didn't look well, though, and his clothes were shabby and unwashed.

'Are you sure it's him?'

'There'll only ever be one Doug Fletcher. A more handsome man never walked the streets in his heyday, nor a more charming. You ought to 'ave heard him when he turned on the flatulence!'

'You mean flattery, Ida.'

'Well! Whatever it was he turned on, I was daft enough to fall for it. Eeh, just look at 'im now – 'e looks as though a good meal wouldn't do 'im any harm. Now where are my shoes?' Ida struggled to get them on under the table and patted her hair into place. 'Is my hair all right?'

'Yes, it's fine. But don't tell me you're titivating yourself because you fancy him?'

'Of course not, I do 'ave me pride, you know!'

'My mother always says pride comes before a fall, so watch out. Besides, he looks as though his face could do with a good wash. Your stew's getting cold.'

Ida took a mouthful of stew and was mortified when Doug Fletcher got up and came and sat down on the free chair beside her.

'I beg your pardon but I saw you looking, were you talking about me?'

Sally blushed crimson as she realised he must have overheard. 'Oh, no, I was just saying this place could do with a good wash. The floor, I mean.'

But, Doug was staring at Ida. 'It can't be . . . It is, though. I'd know that flawless complexion anywhere, and those eyes could only belong to Ida Appleby.'

'I . . . er . . . thought it were you, only your hair used to be red and now it's grey.'

Doug didn't like the way this conversation was going.

'Well, yes, it has changed. More distinguished, don't you think? Not bad for sixty-nine, eh?'

'Sixty-nine? Still the same old Doug, trying to fool the ladies! How yer poor wife put up wi' you all those years, I'll never know. How is she by the way?'

'Well, I haven't seen her for a while. We didn't get on, decided to go our separate ways. Twenty years ago, to be precise.'

'*We*! I'll bet it was *her* who decided, and not before time either. And what about yer son?'

'Canada. Been there ten years.'

'So you're all on yer own then? The irresistible Doug Fletcher left all on yer own. No one to black yer shoes or iron yer shirts. No wonder yer looking sorry for yerself! Eeh, it must 'ave been fate that got me out of me chair and brought me down 'ere today just for the pleasure of seeing the great Don Juan disbanded.'

'Abandoned,' corrected Sally.

'Dumped, that's what I mean. Just like he dumped me all those years ago. Do yer know, Sally love, I think I've come off best after all. I've got me lovely neph— son, and me beautiful grandchildren, and all without 'aving to put up with the likes of *him*. Eeh! You've made my day, bringing me down 'ere. Come on, let's go and buy a bunch of flowers, I feel like celebrating.'

'Can you manage?' asked Sally, picking up the shopping.

'Manage? I feel eighteen again. It's as though all the shame and bitterness have slipped away and I can see Doug Fletcher for the poor poetic creature he really is.'

'Pathetic,' Sally interrupted, but Ida carried straight on. 'With nothing at all to show for all his deceit and flatulence.'

Sally decided to ignore that one. Then Doug Fletcher stood up and touched Ida's arm.

'I thought we could perhaps see each other some-time, Ida. I always had a soft spot for you.'

'Soft spot? It was *me* who had a soft spot. I must 'ave been soft in me head! The only one you ever had a soft spot for was yerself. When you'd got innocent young girls into trouble, you didn't want to know.'

Sally ushered Ida out of the cafe, aware that the waitress and some other patrons who had just come in, mostly steelworkers, were listening in to this interesting conversation. Doug followed them out.

'I didn't know you were in trouble, Ida. You went away. By the time I found out what had happened, the boy was growing up and you were making out he was your nephew. I thought it better to leave well alone.'

'Aye, better for you, no doubt. Well, I'll tell you this, Doug Fletcher, I wouldn't get together with you if you were the last man on earth. Go back in and enjoy yer dinner. It's a far cry from the Grand Hotel! Come on, Sally, let's go and buy those flowers and go home.'

'Well, that certainly told him.'

Sally felt a bit dazed as they walked up to the main road. The shift-workers were flocking in for the afternoon shift, brought by bus from all areas of the city, Barnsley, and the surrounding villages.

Ida bought three bunches of chrysanthemums and gave one to Sally. I'm taking one for Emily Simms, too. She's been such a good friend to me over the years and I've never appreciated it, but I do now.'

Then, when they were passing Miss McCall's, Ida saw a frock in the shop window. 'Oh, I do like that!'

'Try it on then.'

'Oh, I couldn't . . . wasting all me coupons on a frock.'

'Go on.'

'All right! I 'aven't bought owt to wear for years.'

'Except knickers,' said Sally with a smile. They went in. Judith McCall's was the most exclusive shop outside the city.

'Good afternoon. May I be of assistance?' the proprietor enquired.

'My friend would like to try on the dress in the window.'

'Certainly. It's woven wool, most exclusive.' The dress was brought from the window and Ida was shown into a cubicle to try it on. Sally couldn't believe the change in her when she emerged. The frumpy old woman had been transformed into a smart middle-aged one.

'Oh! That's really you.' Miss McCall threw up her arms in admiration. 'I'm afraid it is fifty-three shillings and eleven pence . . .'

Ida gazed at herself in the mirror and decided. 'I'll take it,' she said.

Later, as they were climbing St George's Road, she asked, 'What colour did she say me new frock was?'

'Almond.'

'Blooming new-fangled colours! It'd 'ave been called fawn in my day.'

'Well, whatever colour it is, you look lovely in it. When your Donald comes he won't recognise you.'

'I told 'er I was an eighteen but she wouldn't believe me.'

'Well, you don't look it!'

'I know. Like I said, I'm deceitful.'

Daisy was composing a poem for a competition. She had seen the details in a magazine at Grandma Butler's. The subject had to be one which would remind the troops of home. She chose to write about buttercups. She knew all about them as she could look out of her bedroom window at a fieldful. She thought a lot of soldiers might have had a similar view from their windows at home.

The top half of the field had been taken over now by Dad and Tom Porter for an allotment. It was full of cabbages and Brussels sprouts, both of which Daisy hated. She had enjoyed the peas, though, which she and Norah had eaten straight from the allotment. Dad hadn't minded, said it was better for Daisy to eat them raw than not to eat any vegetables at all. First of all she made a list of all the rhyming words, such as 'green' and 'scene' and glee and sea. Then she began her poem.

Down the lane the buttercups grow
A glimmering sea of gold and green.
Reflecting the glow of the evening sun,
A shimmering, dancing scene.
Down the lane and over the wall,
Little Ernie, and Dippy and me,
Follow the path through the long tall grass,
And into the buttercup sea.

Daisy wrote six verses about the glory of the flowers and little Ernie's delight as he played amongst them. Then she wrote the final verse.

The summer won't last for ever,
The flowers will die away.
And leave but sunkissed images,
In memory of today.
When winter spoils the meadow,
With slush and freezing rain.
I'll remember a warm, small hand in mine,
And the buttercups down the lane.

'What are you writing now?' Sally asked.

'Nothing,' Daisy said, and ran across the field to Aunty Enid's to ask Pat for an envelope. She didn't want anyone to know about the competition and her cousin could keep a secret.

'I need a stamp as well,' Daisy told her.

'Well, I haven't got a stamp but I'll buy you one.' Pat wasn't being paid at the theatre but was earning quite a bit in tips from making herself useful. There were lots of things Liz didn't like doing, such as arranging the flowers in the dressing-rooms and sewing on buttons. Once Pat was even asked to stand in for a chorus girl who hadn't turned up at rehearsal. The choreographer had been thrilled by her singing voice but didn't think much of her dancing, accusing Pat of having two left feet. She didn't mind, she loved her work, especially the tips.

'Don't tell ánybody, will you, about the contest? Then if I don't win, no one will laugh,' Daisy pleaded with her.

'And if you do win, think of the surprise it'll be to them all!'

Pat thought her cousin had talent, she would encourage her. Maybe one day Daisy would be famous.

Mrs Miniver was on at the Palace. Amy was minding little Ernie, enabling Betty and Doreen to go. 'You'd better go early,' she warned them. 'There's bound to be a queue.' *Mrs Miniver* was one of the year's most successful films.

Amy undressed Ernie and put on his striped pyjamas, then she gave him a digestive biscuit and a drink of milk. She cuddled the little boy and rocked him in the old wooden chair that had been her mother's. She sang the same lullaby she had sung to all her babies, the ones she still missed as much as she had since the day they were laid to rest in their tiny graves.

Sometimes she wished she could turn back the clock and give her remaining two children the attention she had not been able to then. So grief-stricken herself, Amy had failed to appreciate the sadness of young Jim and Betty. She should have talked to them more, explained why their brothers and sisters had suddenly been taken out of their lives. Jim had been less affected, but Betty, poor girl had needed comfort from her mother and not received it. No wonder she had gone off the rails for a few years, especially after her adored father died too. Oh, well, the lass had turned out all right in the end. Amy just dreaded receiving news that something had happened to Clarence. The lass was already distraught at the recent lack of word from him and Amy herself was beginning to fear the worst. Well, she would be there for her daughter this time, and for little Ernie.

She carried the sleeping child up to his cot and tucked the covers round his fair head. The baby scent reminded her of her own children, lost and still here. Amy said a prayer to herself then: 'Please God, keep this child safe and bring us news of his father.'

Then she went down to her knitting: another pair of socks for Clarence. No point in being pessimistic. She had a lot for which to thank God. Her son was in a safe occupation, her grand-daughter had survived a fire, her own leg was finally healed, and she had a lovely daughter and grandson living with her. When Clarence came home, she would be the most fortunate woman in Millington. Please God, let it be soon.

Chapter Eight

Ida seemed quiet when Sally arrived.

'Are you all right?' she enquired.

'Aye.'

'Only you seem a bit preoccupied.'

'Aye, I am. I've had a letter from our Donald.' Ida's face brightened then. 'Guess what?'

'You've won the pools?'

Ida laughed. 'No, I don't send 'em.'

'Well, then, I give in.'

'They're coming, all of 'em . . . our Donald, Joyce and the kids. For the whole day. I'm going to do a Sunday dinner. That's if I can get a nice bit of beef.'

'Oh, I'm sure Mr Baraclough'll find you a bit. After all, it is a special occasion.'

'Aye, I'm glad I kept me meat ration with 'im. 'E's a good butcher, knows 'is trade.'

'When are they coming?'

'Saturday.'

'So why were you looking so glum when I came in?'

'It seems I misjudged Doug Fletcher.'

'Oh?'

'I wrote and poured it all out to our Donald, about

275

being his mother. Told 'im how sorry I was for keeping it from 'im and that I did it for his sake, to stop 'im from being picked on, like.'

'And what did he say?'

'He told me not to lose any sleep over it. Says 'e knew from being about six years old. This nice man called Doug kept coming to watch them on the playing field, apparently. Sometimes 'e would join in and play with 'em. Donald says one day another boy said, "That's yer dad, isn't it?" Our Donald says he supposed he already knew as 'e looked just like Doug. The other boy said, "Don't worry, me mam says I've not to tell anybody." And 'e never did."

'Well, and to think your Donald kept it to himself all these years!'

'He says Doug Fletcher bought 'im a new football once for Christmas, but he let his friend keep it at his house so I wouldn't ask where he'd got it from.'

'Your Doug sounds a very understanding man. Just like Donald.'

'Oh, aye, our Donald is. Well, I expect he's got that from his dad . . . Oh, but, Sally, 'aven't I been a fool all these years?'

'Yes, but a well-meaning one.'

'I shall wear me new frock.'

'You'll look lovely. It fits as though it was made to measure. What about your grandsons? Has Donald told them you're their grandma?'

'Yes, 'e talked to them the other night, explained everything. 'E says the youngest jumped up and down with excitement at 'aving a grandma.'

'Do they know they've got a grand-dad as well?'

'Oh, I don't know about that. Donald hasn't mentioned it in his letter.' Ida sighed then. 'Eeh, I didn't shut me eyes all night, thinking 'ow thin and poetic 'e looked.'

'Pathetic? Well, I don't suppose he's eating properly, with no woman about the place.'

'No. It's a shame. And he used to be so handsome . . .'

'He still is.' Sally put the top on the Brasso and replaced the ornaments on the mantelpiece.

'Aye, 'e is.'

'Well, I'll be off then. I want to call in and check on Mr Powell.'

'Danny Powell? He was another nice-looking lad. A shame about 'is leg.'

'What happened?'

'A piece of metal swung the wrong way on the crane, straight through 'is leg. Got a lot of compensation, but no amount of money can mek up for a leg. Thought the world of each other, him and his wife did.'

'He fancied you once,' Sally told her. Ida took this in her stride.

'Aye, most of the lads did. Could 'ave had my pick of 'em if it 'adn't been for me father. He ruled me life so much I fell for the first one who looked

277

at me, when I found meself free.' She stared into the fire. 'He was a bad bugger, my dad.' She looked so serious for a moment that Sally thought she'd better not laugh at Ida's use of the swear word.

'He beat me mother and me with a leather belt, every time he had too much to drink. I'll never forget the fear on a Saturday night, waiting for 'im to come home. That's why I told your Jim not to hit your little Daisy.'

'He hasn't, ever. I have, but only a slap on the leg, and only when she deserves it.'

'Doug Fletcher'd never hit kids. He was a womaniser, but a kind one. I'm sorry I cheated his wife, even if it was unknowingly. But I don't regret 'aving our Donald. He's a kind, handsome lad, just like his dad.'

'Aye, well, I'm off. Have a lovely day on Saturday. Do you want me to do your shopping for you?'

'Do I heck! I need to walk more. I don't want to put any weight on or me new frock won't fit me.'

Sally was still smiling when she reached Danny's.

The telegram they'd dreaded arrived on Monday morning: Clarence Hayes had died of dysentery in a German concentration camp. The news spread along the three rows before dinner-time. Betty was inconsolable. Sally took up residence at her mother-in-law's in order to look after little Ernie. Amy was almost as upset as her daughter. She had grown fond of Clarence during his last week's leave and dreaded the effect his death would have on Betty. Sally took over the care of Ernie for three days and then decided it was doing her sister-in-law more harm than good.

'Betty needs to get up and see to Ernie,' she told Amy.

'Well, I don't know what to do for the best.' Amy, too, was worried her daughter would go into a decline if she stayed in bed much longer.

'I think we should make her get up,' Sally suggested.

'Aye.'

Sally went upstairs, carrying little Ernie. 'Betty love, our Ernie wants his mam. You need to get up.'

'I know. It's just, I still can't believe that telegram. If I could see Clarence . . . his body, I mean . . . then I would know for sure.'

'Yes, I can understand that. But they don't send news that a man's dead if they aren't sure. The telegram would read that he was missing, believed dead, in that case. Clarence isn't missing, Betty, he's dead.'

'Yes.' She got up on shaky legs. 'But his son's still here. At least I've something of him remaining.' She lifted little Ernie on to the bed and sat down beside him, holding him close. The little boy wound his arms round his mother's neck. Betty started to cry again, her tears dampening her son's hair. Sally left the room, knowing that she would be all the better for letting go of her sorrow.

'Mammy not cry!' Ernie hugged Betty tighter.

'No! Mammy won't cry any more.' She smiled at her son. He was a thoughtful little boy. Like his father, in fact. She would bring him up to be a son Clarence would have been proud of. She owed her husband that.

'Come on, let's go and help Grandma.' She knew how worried her mother would be about her grieving.

There was still the war to get through, still the kids to feed. There were thousands of wives in her position so she'd better stop feeling sorry for herself and get on with things.

Daisy searched the house, every drawer and cupboard, but couldn't find anything to write on. She even looked inside the music stool that had come from Grand-dad Denman with the piano, but was disappointed. She ended up cutting a brown paper carrier bag into squares. What she did find, though, was a pixie hat, obviously put away for the colder weather. A large-sized pixie hat in horrible khaki wool, the sort that was all wiry and itchy. Well, she wouldn't wear it. Fancy wearing a pixie hat at her age! Everybody would make fun of her. Besides, she never had sore throats now she had had her tonsils removed. She would have to tell Grandma Butler not to knit any more, even if she did hurt her feelings.

When Daisy came home from school one day

there was a tramp in the kitchen. He was sitting at the table eating greengage jam sandwiches. Sally had felt sorry for him and invited him in for a pot of tea. Daisy couldn't take her eyes off him and sat down at the table with him so she could stare at him. He had hair down to his shoulders and a beard down to his chest.

'Hello, Curlylocks,' he said to her.

'Hello,' she said, fascinated by his long overcoat tied round the waist with an old pyjama cord. 'Where have you come from?' She knew it was cheeky to ask, but couldn't resist doing so.

'Where have I come from?' The tramp considered the question before answering, 'Well, originally I was a knight, in my past life that was, so I came from all over the place. Now I'm visiting all the castles, to try and find my spiritual home.'

'Where are you going next then?'

'Where my feet take me, little one.' He looked thoughtful. 'Maybe to Lancaster, I'm sure that's a wonderful castle.'

'I've been to a castle,' Daisy volunteered.

'Well, where was that then?'

'It's called Wentworth Castle. We walked there one day.'

'So you like castles?'

'Oh, yes.'

'Maybe you were a fine lady who resided in one once.'

'I don't think so. I can't remember it.'

'Ah, no, you won't remember until you see the place where you lived before. Only then will you recognise it as your spiritual home. Now when I visited Conway – that's a fine Welsh castle – I had the feeling I'd been there before. Then there was Colchester . . . a finer castle I never did see.'

'I wonder where my castle could be?' Daisy wondered.

'Here.'

She giggled. '*This* isn't a castle.'

'Yes, it is. Your home is your castle, especially a home such as this where the door is ever open and welcoming. Not many people would trust me to sit in their home, or be kind enough to give me their bread and a sup. Most folk'd be keeping an eye on me in case I stole their valuables.'

'We haven't got any.'

'Well, I can see two with my own eyes, hanging on the wall up there.' He pointed to the watercolours that had once belonged to Mr Jessops.

'They're of value, and don't you doubt that fact.' The tramp finished his tea. 'Ah, well, I'll be off then, little Curlylocks.'

Daisy suddenly had a brainwave. She went to the drawer in the living-room sideboard then she called to Sally, 'I'm just walking a little way with this man.'

'Don't go far,' her mother answered as she waved the tramp on his way.

'When you find your spiritual home, will you stay there?' Daisy queried.

'Ah, no, I'll be around these parts again some time or other. It's the wanderlust I was born with, to be sure.'

'Will you be cold when winter comes?'

'I shall be as cold as a penguin. I shall take shelter in a barn or two, but I shall be frozen to the marrow.'

'I've got a present for you then.' Daisy gave him the pixie hat. 'To keep your ears warm.'

The tramp looked at the hat and put it on his head, fastening it beneath the bush of his beard. He looked so odd that Daisy had to bite her lips to prevent herself from laughing. But the man was absolutely delighted.

'I shall treasure it always,' he told her.

Then he set off down the hill, maybe in the direction of Lancaster, Daisy wasn't sure. She couldn't wait to begin a story about a knight who died and came back to find his spiritual home. 'At least he'll have warm ears,' she muttered to herself as she went back into the house, the home the tramp had called a castle. It looked like an ordinary house to Daisy. A house without a pixie hat, much to her delight.

'Have you ever had your ears examined, Danny?'

'What?'

Sally moved closer and shouted, wondering if they could hear her next-door.

'Oh, no, I'm all right as I am, thanks.'

'Yes, but you would enjoy things more if you

283

did. You could listen to the wireless and enjoy conversations, properly.'

'No, I won't be going to the station.'

'You'd be able to chat up the lady from the Salvation Army . . .'

He must have heard that because he grinned.

'So shall I ask the doctor to look at your ears?'

'She won't be able to do owt, it's just owd age.'

'You're not *that* old.'

'It were't noise in't steel mill.'

'It might be, it might not. I'll ask the doctor to call.'

'I'll 'ave Dr Sellars, I like her.'

'All right, I'll make enquiries.'

'No, I 'aven't got a diary.'

'Sally looked round the kitchen. Everything was spotless now. Once she had bottomed it, he'd kept it nice and clean. He'd even washed his clothes and hung them on the rack over the fire.

He surprised her again when she put her coat on to go home by saying, 'I saw a new-fangled washer in a magazine the other day. You put the clothes in and turn a handle on't top. I'd like one of those.'

'Might cost a bit,' Sally said doubtfully.

'Oh, that wouldn't matter, I can afford it.' Danny frowned then. 'I can manage me clothes by hand, it's me bedding that beats me.'

'Well, it's up to you.' Sally almost offered to take his bedding home with her but knew Jim would be annoyed. 'Shall I see if I can find out about one?'

'Aye, if yer like.'

'We'll get your ears sorted out first. They might only need syringing.'

'No! I'm not much good at singing but I used to like dancing, when I had two legs.'

He was such a cheerful, game old soul that Sally went to change his bed after all and took the dirty sheets home with her to wash. It was windy, she could get them dry before Jim came off the afternoon shift.

A letter came from Ernest two weeks before Christmas. Nellie came hurrying in with it. 'Post! A special today.'

'Morning, Nellie. Would you like a cup of something warm?'

'No, it's all right, thanks all the same. I've just had one at Miss Appleby's. Nearly fainted from the shock.' Nellie grinned.

'Oh, she's not so bad really.' But Sally was concentrating on her brother's letter. As usual he was asking about all the family and giving nothing away about himself. She was to ask his mother for some of his savings to buy the three girls presents for Christmas. He also enquired about little Ernie Hayes and Betty, hoping Clarence was safe.

For the first time there was no mention of any girlfriends. This worried Sally at first but she realised he was probably too busy with the war in the skies as it was at the moment. With Nellie satisfied to have heard the contents of the letter and on her way, Sally went round to her sister's to reassure Enid that their brother was safe. They were, however, disappointed to think they would spend another Christmas without him.

'Should we tell him about Clarence, do you think?' Sally pondered.

'I don't think so,' Enid decided. 'No point in sending dismal news from home. Better to try and keep his spirits up.'

'When you've a bit of time to spare, will you come with me to Sheffield?' Ida Appleby enquired of Sally. 'Only I need to do some Christmas shopping.'

'Well! We could have gone now, if I'd known. I'd have put on my best coat and shoes.'

'You always look nice, Sally, there's nowt wrong with the things you're wearing. Oh, and I want to put some flowers on the music teacher's grave, while I'm down in the bottoms.'

'What about your legs? It's a fair walk to the churchyard if you're going tramping round Sheffield too.'

'The exercise'll do me legs good. Well, are we going or aren't we?'

'All right. I'll just nip home and fetch my purse.'

'No, yer won't. If you're going for my benefit, I'm paying.'

Ida had done the washing up herself and also

made the bed. It was obvious how much better she was feeling. Sally thought she might soon find herself redundant. Ida bustled about, putting on a bit of powder and titivating her hair. Then she put on her best hat and coat. She seemed to have shed ten years in the last few weeks.

'Right then, we'll go down the Donkey Path this morning, if I can hold on to yer arm? It'll save time.'

Sally thought Ida might find the slope difficult, but she set off at a steady pace and never stumbled once. She paused near the donkey stone to admire a hawthorn hedge adorned with spiders, webs and glistening with dewdrops.

'Now isn't that a sight for sore eyes? I haven't seen owt so beautiful in years. Oh, when I think of all the time I've wasted, sitting doing nothing instead of being useful.'

'Well, you can make up for it now.'

'The truth is I was ashamed, thought everybody were talking about me. That was because I was so soft-centred.'

'Self-centred. Soft centres are chocolates. So what do you think now?'

'I don't care. I'm too old to be bothered what anybody thinks, except our Donald. He and his family are the only ones who matter. And he's re-assured me that they all love me and aren't going to disband me.'

'What?' Sally was stumped for a moment. 'Oh,

you mean abandon you? Of course they won't do that.' They reached the churchyard and found the grave colourful with flowers. Sally removed a few that were dead and placed the new chrysanthemums that'd brought in one of the vases.

'I knew there'd be plenty of flowers on. That's because we all thought so much of her,' Ida declared.

Sally stifled a grin, relieved by the change in her but amused by it too. She'd be saying black was white next.

At the bus stop they sat on a bench to wait. On the wall facing them somebody had written that Hitler should be strung up in a particularly painful manner, and someone called Thelma had apparently been in the Donkey Wood with half the boys in the top form, with explicit details of exactly what had occurred. Ida either didn't understand half of it, or chose to ignore it, but Sally noticed the way her eyes kept straying to a drawing of an enormous penis. She was relieved when the bus arrived and they were finally on their way to the city.

Sheffield was almost unrecognisable to Ida, who hadn't visited the place for many years. Nevertheless she found gifts for Donald and his family. Ida was out of touch with the modern way of life and counted on Sally to help her choose something her small grandson and his teenage brother would enjoy. After the shopping spree they had lunch at the municipal restaurant before catching the bus home.

Ida had tears in her eyes as she noted the destruction of all the fine shops and old buildings.

'That lad was right,' she told Sally suddenly.

'What lad?'

'That lad who'd been writing on the bus shelter wall. Hitler does want stringing up by his balls.'

'Ida Appleby,' Sally spluttered, 'you'll never go to Heaven using language like that!'

'No,' said Ida. 'Neither will Hitler.'

Charlotte waited at the school gate for Daisy Butler to come out. The little girl was easily recognisable by her mop of curls. She knew Daisy would walk with her friend to the corner and then they would part company. The two girls were always the last to leave the school, and today they didn't vary from their routine. Carol left her friend and crossed the road to where she lived. Charlotte followed Daisy until she reached a part of the road that was secluded and tree-lined, then she caught up with the little girl.

'Daisy,' she called, 'you're to come with me.'

'No! I've to go straight home, I always have to.'

'Yes, usually, but today you've to come with me. Your mother's had to go to hospital and she's asked me to look after you.'

Daisy panicked at the thought of her mother being ill. What if she died?

'My dad'll look after me,' she cried, setting off as fast as she could, but Charlotte caught hold of her hand.

'No, we're going this way. Your mother says you're to be a good girl. Your dad's not at home, he's with her.'

'It's all right, I'll go to Aunty Enid's or Grandma's . . .'

But Charlotte tugged at the girl's hand, pulling her in the opposite direction. Daisy had no option but to go with the woman.

'What's wrong with my mam?' Daisy was tearful by this time. 'She was all right this morning.'

'Oh, she'll be fine in a day or two, nothing to worry about.'

Charlotte hurried away down the hill, imagining how the woman would feel when she realised her daughter was missing. Why hadn't she thought of it before? The obvious way to hurt the interloper was to take away her most treasured possession, the thing she loved most in the world.

'Where are we going?' Daisy enquired in a small voice.

'To my house, just until your mother gets better.'

'Yes, but I don't know you. Mam says I must never talk to strangers.'

'Oh, but I'm not a stranger. I'm your mother's friend.'

Daisy didn't know this part of Millington. The houses looked very posh. They passed a tennis court and a bowling green, and she noticed most of the houses had their own little shelter in the garden, not like the one in their field. They passed a street with little shops, a tiny Co-op and a post office. She'd never been here before. Charlotte turned up a long, tree-lined drive, still pulling Daisy by the hand. She was scared. She didn't know this woman and she didn't feel safe with her.

Charlotte unlocked a front door with coloured glass patterns in the top half of it. It reminded Daisy of the big chapel. When they got inside the woman locked the door and dropped the key into her pocket, which made Daisy even more nervous.

'Right then, what would you like for tea?'

Charlotte smiled at Daisy. She would actually enjoy the company of the little girl, she decided. Why should that Butler woman have everything: Uncle Walter's house, a husband who loved her, and most of all this lovely child? Well, she hadn't got her now. She would be Charlotte's for as long as she wanted her.

'Shall we have some beans on toast?'

'I'm not hungry.' Daisy shook her head.

'Oh! Well, I'll make some anyway. You may be hungry by the time it's ready.'

Charlotte was sick and tired of eating alone. Mark hadn't been home for two weeks now, she had no idea where he was. Not at work, that was for sure, not at night anyway. She set about making a meal and laid it out in the dining-room with a pretty lace cloth and the best crockery. She gave Daisy a glass of orange juice, too. One thing in her husband's favour was that he had friends in all the right places to provide them with a few little luxuries.

Daisy took a sip of the thick, sweet juice. She liked it and drank some more. She studied her surroundings. It was a lovely room with wallpaper that looked like patterned cloth and a thick, springy carpet with roses on it. In the corner there was a glass cabinet with lots of bottles, like the one Granddad Denman always brought over at Christmas. Daisy's tummy seemed to turn over then at the thought of Christmas without her mam.

'Will she die?' she said.

The woman looked shocked. 'What?'

'Will my mam die?' Daisy began to cry then.

Charlotte hadn't intended to hurt the little girl, closing her mind to the fact that setting fire to the house could have burned her to death.

'No! Oh, no, it's nothing serious, just a little operation.'

'Is it her tonsils and adenoids?'

'Yes, something like that.'

Charlotte set the hot meal in front of Daisy and sat down opposite the child. When the woman began to eat Daisy decided she was hungry after all. 'She'll be home by now then, won't she?'

'No. It'll be a few days before she's home.'

Daisy put down her fork. 'But I was home by teatime.'

'Ah, yes, but adults need to stay in hospital a little longer than children.'

'Tomorrow then? I can go home tomorrow, to my grandma's.'

'We'll have to see. I'll ring up and find out.'

'We don't have a phone.'

'No! I mean the hospital.' Charlotte was becoming annoyed by Daisy's questioning. 'Eat your tea.' The tone of voice told Daisy she'd better do as she was told. She decided that she didn't like this woman after all.

Charlotte cleared the table after tea and fetched a pack of Happy Families from the cupboard. Daisy considered herself too old for the game but didn't say so. After a few games, though, Charlotte became bored. 'What shall we do now?' she asked Daisy.

'Have you got any writing paper or books to read?' Daisy didn't expect any writing paper to be forthcoming but Charlotte said, 'Oh, we've got reams of the stuff. Come with me.'

She took Daisy upstairs to the study which had once been Brady Scott's. There was a desk full of stationery: pens, pencils, erasers. In fact, it was Daisy's idea of heaven.

'Help yourself,' Charlotte told her. Anything to keep her quiet! The novelty of entertaining a child had already abated. Daisy found a large lined pad and a pencil. The wall behind the desk was lined with shelves full of books, just like the Penny Library. Daisy decided that if she was to stay here, she might as well take advantage of the facilities.

The woman might even let her take some of the paper home with her, if she behaved.

By ten-past four Sally was worried. Glancing across the field, she noticed there were no children about. She knew Daisy was usually the last to come home, but never more than a few minutes after the others. Sally wondered if she had called in at Enid's and went to find out.

'Is our Daisy here?'

'No.' Enid called to Norah, 'Have you seen Daisy?'

'Not since playtime.'

'Maybe she's gone to her grandma's,' Enid suggested.

'Perhaps, but she knows she's to come straight home.'

Sally hurried to her mother-in-law's but Daisy wasn't there either. Next she went to Mary's. Stanley was sitting at the table, sorting out stamps for his album. 'Have you seen Daisy, love?' Sally was becoming more anxious by the minute.

'No. She never comes out till last.'

'Well, she'd better stop dawdling about in future.'

Sally hurried out and back across to her house, but Daisy still hadn't come home. Enid and Amy were on their way to search the field. Sally had decided to go in the direction of the school next. Daisy might have stayed at Carol's.

Daisy's friend lived in a large house. Her father

being something or other in the city, they were quite well off, one of the few families round about to possess a car and a phone. Carol's mother was rumoured to have a gentleman caller whom Carol called Uncle Harry, who only ever visited when Carol's father was at work.

Sally thought her a pleasant enough woman and was most grateful when she offered the use of both car and phone, should they be needed. They both questioned Carol but all she could tell them was that Daisy had gone straight home after leaving her.

'Have you any idea where she might have gone?' Sally asked. 'Anywhere special she might have wanted to play?'

Carol felt a bit scared when she thought about their hideaway in the doctor's garden, but Daisy would never have gone there again, she wouldn't dare.

Carol shook her head. 'We only ever play in the field, near the shelter,' she said. 'Or in our garden.' Sally hurried away, praying that her daughter had returned home by now. She couldn't just have vanished into thin air. Despite the cold, dismal day Sally could feel sweat break out at the back of her neck and her heart beating in her ears. Oh, God, if only Jim hadn't been on the afternoon shift!

Mrs Dawson had sent her boys out to look for Daisy, and Emily as usual had made a pot of tea. Sally wondered how anyone could be expected to stand drinking that when their daughter was missing! She set off again in the direction of the Donkey Wood. It was falling dusk by now, despite the extension of summer-time. What would they do if Daisy wasn't back before dark? She would have to notify the police.

Enid sent Norah down to Grandma Denman's, but Sally was almost sure the little girl wouldn't have gone there, and if she had her mother would have brought her back by now. Nobody could think of anywhere else to look. It was Ida Appleby who suggested checking on Danny Powell.

'She might 'ave gone to help him, she's a thoughtful little lass.'

'Aye, there's no harm in trying, I'll go,' Amy Butler said. She set off across the field, thankful that her leg was healed and she could be of use at times like this. She had hated sitting about like a lump of lard. She knocked on Danny's door and was just wondering if she should go in and save him getting up when he opened it.

'Amy! Amy Butler . . . eeh, lass, I 'aven't seen you since your better 'alf died. That was a sad day.'

'No sadder than when you lost yours, Danny. I'm not 'ere to socialise, though, I'm sorry to say. I wondered if you've seen our Daisy at all?'

'Daisy? No, I 'aven't seen her for a few days. She last came with 'er mam. She's a good little lass, Amy. You must be proud of 'er.'

'Aye, I am, but she's gone missing, Danny.' Then

Amy could control herself no longer. The past few hours had been a nightmare. 'We're at our wit's end,' she sobbed, and flopped down heavily in a kitchen chair. 'Eeh, I'm sorry.' She was embarrassed by her tears.

'Eeh, lass, there's no need to apologise. No wonder you're upset.'

Danny lifted the kettle off the fire and poured water into the brown teapot. He got two cups from the hooks underneath the cupboard, cups Sally had scrubbed till they were like new.

''Ere, come on, lass. Do yer take milk and sugar?'

Amy nodded. 'One sugar and just a drop of milk,' she managed to say between her sobs.

Danny poured the tea. 'How long has she been gone?'

'Since home time from school.'

'Aye, come to think of it, she didn't go past today.'

'Are yer sure?'

'Certain. I always watch the kids come 'ome. Some of 'em wave to me, and it passes the time. It's a long day on yer own, lass.' Danny grinned. 'Mind you, theer's one or two of the little buggers who chuck pebbles at me winders, but they don't mean no real harm.'

'They shouldn't plague you like that, Danny.'

'Oh, they don't mean owt. Besides, I can remember doing summat similar when I was their age.' He frowned. 'I wonder where Daisy can be? It's not like the little lass to be naughty.'

'I'm sure I've no idea. Well! I'd better go and see what's happening.'

'Aye, well, let me know, Amy lass. I shan't sleep tonight if I don't hear she's home safe.'

'We'll let you know as soon as she turns up. Thanks for the tea.'

'Come again, Amy. I like a bit of company. Like I said, it's a long day on yer own.'

The child was still missing and Betty had gone to fetch Jim from work. Sally was inconsolable. Her father had come as soon as Norah had given him the news. The house at Taylors Row was overflowing with well-meaning neighbours, but the only person Sally wanted to see was Daisy. She wondered briefly if the fire and this incident were connected, but dismissed the thought as too far-fetched. Jim came in then and immediately sent for the police. He didn't know who looked to be in a worse condition, Sally or her father. He gave them both a tot of brandy and then took one himself. He wished everybody would go home. He knew they all meant well, and had obviously been a comfort to Sally, but now he was here he needed to think and he couldn't with all these people mithering. It was like he'd always said: their house had an ever open bloody door, and all he wanted to do now was shut it, with them all outside and only Sally and him left inside.

Bobby Jones turned up with another constable. A missing child warranted two coppers, it wasn't like a few missing tins of paint. At this point Jim said he thought everyone else should go home so that they could talk in private. He promised to let them know what was happening and to call on them if they were needed.

Bobby Jones began at the beginning. When he heard that Daisy had left her friend on the corner, he sent his colleague off to make house-to-house enquiries along that road. When the other policeman came back, alone, Bobby Jones sent him off to organise a proper search party. At least a dozen men and boys were soon split into pairs and sent off in various directions.

At least Sally could see something being done, though it wasn't much consolation. In fact, she would never forget this day if she lived to be a hundred. She now knew exactly what Mary and Tom had gone through, losing their little daughter.

Charlotte filled the bath and sprinkled some scented salts into the water, which coloured it pink and made it smell of roses. Daisy lay back in the lovely, silky warmth and thought it wasn't so bad staying with Aunty Charlotte. When the water began to cool, she got out and dried herself on a fluffy, white towel. Charlotte had prepared well, and had bought the child a lovely flannel nighty with a pretty rosebud trim round the collar. Daisy marvelled at her warm bedroom and springy bed. She thought this woman must be ever so rich.

She had a little lamp on the table by her bed and Aunty Charlotte had said she could read for as long as she liked. She had found a book called *Nan the Circus Girl*. Aunty Charlotte brought her up some cocoa and real chocolate biscuits. Daisy hoped her mam would soon be home, but in the meantime it wasn't too bad staying here.

Bobby Jones had been uneasy after the fire at the Butlers and now he thought he would make further enquiries at the house of Charlotte Kaye.

Charlotte had anticipated a further visit and had prepared well for it. Any trace of the girl had disappeared from downstairs. Daisy was ensconced in a room at the back of the house, the one that used to be Charlotte's until the dogs took it over. She didn't think they would bother Daisy, though, it was Charlotte they were after. The door to the room was locked and she had donned her most glamorous housecoat, hoping to distract any caller's attention. When the bell rang she tried to answer the door looking suitably surprised.

'Oh! Has something happened to Mark?' Her hand rose to her throat with the expertise of a professional actress.

'No. We're making house-to-house enquiries about a missing girl.'

'Oh, how awful. How long has she been missing?'

'Since four o'clock.'

'Oh, my goodness, that's a long time. How old is she?'

'Do you mind if I come in and look round?'

'Not at all.' Charlotte hoped he wouldn't go upstairs. Bobby Jones went along the hall and into the kitchen. Everything was shipshape with only one setting of crockery draining on the board by the sink. He went through to the lounge, marvelling at the decor and the warm comfort of the place. The woman must be worth a bob or two to live in a house like this. Emily Simms must have been wrong to suggest that Mrs Kaye was envious of the Butlers' inheritance. This woman didn't need to be envious of anyone. She had it all.

He glanced up the darkened staircase. No sound from up there. He felt a bit of a fool now, trailing all this way for nothing. 'Right, Mrs Kaye. Sorry to have bothered you. I'll be on my way.'

Charlotte had let the top of her housecoat fall open, revealing an inviting cleavage. Bobby Jones blushed when she said, 'You're sure I can't offer you anything?'

The policeman hurried out as fast as he could. Women like that always made him feel uneasy, mainly because he didn't think he'd know what to do with one like her if he really did get the chance. Give him a comfortable, cuddly, plain Jane any day. Eeh, but he could imagine what a beauty Mrs Kaye must have been in her younger days. Oh, well! Another wild goose chase.

He hoped the little lass turned up soon, though. Missing children were the cases that upset Bobby Jones the most, especially with so many mucky-minded men about. He just hoped Daisy Butler hadn't ended up in the hands of one of them.

Daisy switched out the light like Aunty Charlotte had shown her. It had been lovely with it on, but as she tried to go to sleep she found the unfamiliar surroundings scary. The room didn't have a blackout blind, just a heavy velvet curtain, and every so often the moon escaped from behind the clouds and lit up her surroundings, showing the long black shadows by the porcelain figures on the dressing table. Daisy had admired them with the light on but now they were scary and strange. She could also see a long ghostly shape behind the door. She was sure it hadn't been there when the light was on. When the moon came out again she would peer hard and try to make out what it was. Something was tapping on the window and she could hear a thumping sound in her ears.

She screamed out then and heard someone hurrying up the stairs. The landing light was switched on. Soon she would see the thing behind the door . . .

Charlotte was even more afraid than Daisy. What if the dogs were waiting to pounce on her when she opened the door? Slowly she pushed it open and peered gingerly inside.

'I was scared of the thing behind the door,' Daisy announced, 'but it's only a dressing gown hanging there.' She realised now that the tapping on the window must have been the creeper on the wall. The thumping in her ears had ceased, for She felt silly and thought of an excuse. 'I felt a bit sick.'

'Do you need the bathroom?' Charlotte asked.

'No, I'm all right now.'

'Well, you'd better not go to school tomorrow.' Daisy had played right into her hands. Charlotte had been wondering what excuse she could make for keeping her away. Daisy was about to protest that she felt better, but changed her mind. It was games tomorrow, and that was almost as bad as PT.

Carol hadn't slept all night for worrying about Daisy. Where could she be? She ought to tell about the house in the bushes. What if Daisy had decided to fetch her teaset and had fallen or something? If she didn't come to school, Carol would tell them then.

But Daisy didn't come to school. The headmaster questioned all the children in assembly in case any of them had seen her or knew where she might be. Una Bacon said Daisy sometimes went to Barkers Farm to talk to Charlie so that information was relayed to Bobby Jones. Carol wondered if her father would punish her if he became aware of the painted bushes. She decided if there was no news about

Daisy today, she would definitely tell Daisy's mother.

When Jim and Tom Porter followed Carol through the wall and into Dr Sellars' garden after school that afternoon, they couldn't believe the two girls could have caused such havoc to someone's private property.

'Bloody hell, Jim.' Tom looked incredulous. Carol peered inside their hideaway to see if there was any sign of her friend, then she ran home, leaving the two men still mesmerised by what they were seeing. The hideous blue paint was daubed over every bush for a radius of about twenty yards. The old curtains hung forlorn, dirty and saturated, and sodden mats and boxes littered the ground.

'Well, at least Daisy isn't lying here injured, that's one consolation.'

'Aye, but where the hell is she?' Jim looked around him at the mess. 'We're going to have to tell Dr Sellars about this little lot.'

Tom cringed. 'Do we 'ave to? Nobody else knows about it, and I don't think young Carol's going to confess. She looked petrified, the poor kid.'

Jim glanced around, making sure nobody was looking, then made a dash for the broken bit of wall. 'Come on then, let's get out of here!'

Tom grinned and leaped after him. 'She never does owt by halves, your Daisy, does she?' Then he realised the remark was in poor taste with the little girl still missing.

'No, she doesn't. And I'll tell yer this, Tom. If our Daisy's disappearance is another of her escapades, she 'll see the back of my hand this time, that's for sure.'

'Nay, Jim. I don't like to say this but the little lass's been missing for almost twenty-four hours now. That can't be one of her escapades, as yer call 'em.'

'No. No, it can't.' Jim looked all in suddenly. He hadn't been to bed at all last night and it was doubtful he would go tonight either if his daughter hadn't been found.

'Come on, lad. Let's get thee home.' Tom knew exactly what it was like to lose a daughter. He said a silent prayer that this one wouldn't be lost for good, like their little Celia.

Sally was frantic. Mary had never left her side all day. Others were in and out all the time, bringing hot soup, coming up with ideas on where to look next. Emily Simms suggested searching Charlotte Kaye's house, and Bobby Jones was relieved he had thought of it first. He assured Sally that her child wasn't there.

At six o'clock more police arrived with the news that the reservoir was to be dragged. At this Sally fainted and was taken to bed. Dr Sellars was called then and bedrest prescribed, with hot bricks at her feet. Jim and Tom dare not look at each other in the doctor's presence lest their guilt about the damage to her garden showed on their faces. They were both relieved when she left.

More excuses were made when Daisy asked to go home. 'Can't I just go and see my mam and then come back?' she asked. She wanted to know why this strange woman was looking after her. Normally she would have been at Aunty Enid's or Grandma Denman's. This woman didn't seem like one of her mam's usual friends. Sometimes she was kind and let Daisy do anything she liked; at other times she became annoyed if Daisy even spoke to her, telling her to be quiet or to go to her room. She had thought about running away and in the middle of the night sneaked downstairs, but the door was locked. The back door was also locked and Daisy wondered why the key wasn't hanging in the letter box like it was at their house. She began to worry then that she had been kidnapped. She had read a story about a kidnapped boy once. She began to cry, imagining she would be here forever.

'What are you crying about? You're a big girl, and big girls don't cry.'

'I want to go home, just for a bit. I'll come back if you want me to.'

'You can go home when I say. I'll tell you what! Why don't I go and get a Christmas tree and you can trim it up? I'll get some holly too. We'll make the whole house look nice for Christmas.'

'But I won't be here at Christmas. I want to be in my own home by then.'

'We'll see.'

'That's what you said before.' Daisy knew she was a big girl but she couldn't help crying all the same.

When Amy Butler hadn't let Danny know about Daisy's whereabouts the man couldn't sleep for worrying, and when no news was forthcoming by the third day he decided to go and find out what was happening for himself. He put on a suit he hadn't worn for more years than he cared to remember, the shirt he had last worn for his wife's funeral, and his best shoe. Then he set off on his crutches for Potters Row and Amy's house.

When Betty opened the door to Danny she didn't know who he was. Amy came and helped him into the kitchen, pulling out a chair for him.

Little Ernie stared at the pinned up trouser leg, wondering where the man's leg had gone. Betty put the kettle on and Amy apologised for not keeping Danny informed. 'The truth is, there's nothing much to tell.' And then she broke down, as she had so often in the past four days. 'Our Daisy's still not turned up and I can't help fearing we've seen the last of 'er.'

'Mam, that's an awful thing to say!' Betty placed her mother's cup of tea on the table so forcefully that it slopped all over the white cloth.

'No, lass, yer mustn't give up hope. Yer know what they say, weer there's life there's 'ope,' Danny encouraged her.

'Yes, I know, but we don't even know if she's alive. Our Jim and Sally are frantic wi' worry. Where can she be, Danny? They're still searching the dam. Thank God they 'aven't found her body!'

'I 'ope yer don't mind me coming, Amy. Only I couldn't rest, and I didn't want to bother Sally.'

'No! It's nice of yer to be bothering.'

'Well, that little lass saved me life once. I don't think I'd 'ave survived out there much longer. Other folk'd passed me by and left me lying, but your little Daisy fetched her mam. I'll not forget that in a hurry.' Danny paused. 'I'd just like to say that if theer's owt to be done, money wise, I'm not without a bob or two, If they need owt, they're welcome to anything I've got.'

'That's very kind of yer. You're a good man, Danny Powell, you always were.'

'Well, I can't go roaming about, searching the hills and dales, not wi' only one leg, but I can put me hand in me pocket when needed. So if yer'll just pass the message on to yer son?'

'I will, with many thanks.'

Danny struggled to his foot and adjusted his crutches. 'I'll be off then, I'll not outstay me welcome.'

'Nay, stay a bit longer. Our Betty'll be off to work in a minute and I'd be glad of a bit of company.

Our Ernie keeps me busy enough but 'e's not a brilliant conversationalist as yet.' And Amy smiled for the first time in four days. Danny always had that effect on people. She remembered he had been a jolly lad at school. 'I'll tell yer what, Danny, you stay and have a bit of dinner with me. I've made some corned beef hash and it'll not get eaten otherwise.'

'Nay, I can't take your food, not with the rationing.'

'Oh! Sit yerself down, Danny. It were right, what yer said the other day. It is a long day by yerself, especially when you're worriting yerself to death about summat. I'd appreciate yer company, I really would.'

Danny grinned. 'Then I shouldn't like to disappoint yer, Amy. I like to give satisfaction to the ladies, especially a good-looking one like yerself.'

'Get away with yer! Yer always were a joker, even at school.'

'Aye, but I'm not joking today. Yer are a grand-looking woman, and always were.'

Amy blushed. It had been a long time since she had received a compliment of that nature. In other circumstances she might even enjoy Danny Powell's flirting, but today she was too worried about her grand-daughter. She turned to the gas ring so that he couldn't see her flushed cheeks. 'Aye, well, by the time I've set the table this'll be done.'

It was nice to be making dinner for a man. Men

always appreciated food more than women did. If only she could hear little Daisy was safe, she would right enjoy Danny Powell's visit.

Ida Appleby couldn't get over little Daisy's disappearance. It had even cast a damper on Donald's visit – or almost. She couldn't bring herself to stay miserable on such a special day. Donald had turned up with a lovely bunch of flowers for her. He had even attached a card which said 'To a Very Special Mother'. Ida was almost in tears when she read it.

'Come on, Ida. Don't spoil this special day,' said Joyce, and kissed her mother-in-law. 'We need to make up for lost time and get to know each other, without any pretence about aunties and nephews and all that silliness. Now then, lads, how about a kiss for yer grandma?' Peter and Paul gave Ida a cuddle and she got out the comics she had bought them. Donald asked if there was anything his mother needed doing.

'Aye, you can fetch me some holly from down the wood. I'd like to brighten the place up for Christmas.'

'Sure. We'll go after dinner, won't we, lads?'

Ida and Joyce chatted while they dished out the meal; there was even Yorkshire pudding to go with the beef. 'Mother,' Donald said when they had all finished eating, 'you look ten years younger than the last time I saw you. What have yer been doing to yerself?'

'Well! I've bought meself a new dress from Judith McCall's, and I've stopped feeling ashamed of meself.'

'Ashamed? Why ever should you feel ashamed?' Joyce looked askance at her.

'For pretending our Donald wasn't mine. That was an awful thing to do. I told meself it was for his sake, but I realise now it was for me own as well. I should have stood up to me mother. It were her who told me I had to either have him adopted or make out 'e belonged to somebody else.'

'It was a cruel thing to make you do, but you kept your baby. That was courageous of you in those days,' Joyce said.

'Mother, will you put it all behind you now? We'll all start afresh,' Donald told her. 'I know you want to trim the house up, but we've got a better idea. We want you to come and stay with us for Christmas, don't we, lads?'

'Yes!' Both boys jumped for joy at the suggestion.

'Oh, there's no need for that . . .'

'Oh, well, if you'd rather not?'

'No! no, I'd love to come, but I don't want to intrude on your holiday.'

'Right then, you're coming. That's settled.'

Ida felt a lump filling her throat. This would have been the happiest day of her life if it hadn't been for little Daisy's disappearance.

* * *

Daisy wasn't scared to go to bed any more. It was more scary in the daytime when Aunty Charlotte was liable to have one of her moods and shout or throw things about.

'Can I go to school?' she would ask every morning at first, but then she realised it only made the woman angry so she stopped asking.

Once Charlotte threw a cereal bowl across the table, narrowly missing Daisy's head. Another time she was kind and took her into the garden. They cut some holly branches which were heavy with scarlet berries and tucked them behind the pictures in the living-room. Charlotte locked her in one day and fetched a Christmas tree, and Daisy made stars and bells out of cardboard as usual. She felt no joy at the sight of the tree, all trimmed and twinkling, though. All it did was remind her of last Christmas when she was at home with Mam, Dad and Dippy.

Daisy had tried all the windows while Charlotte was out but they were jammed tight with paint. She had also tried to get to the phone, but Charlotte kept the door to the study locked all the time. Anyway, Daisy didn't know anyone's number, even if she had gained access. Maybe she would be here for ever. She passed most the day by writing.

She wrote about the day Carol's parents had taken them on a picnic to Longfield Beck. She wrote about the sun filtering through the trees and speckling the river with dancing reflections. She wrote about the insects and the fungi they had found amongst the gnarled tree roots, and the squirrels darting up and down the trees. She described the green of the beeches, and the fragrance of the blue-bells she'd helped Carol's little sister gather to take home.

Carol's father had offered to teach Daisy to swim but they hadn't any costumes. He had told her she didn't need a costume as no one except them would see her. Carol had been adamant that they were too old to go naked, even in front of her own parents. Daisy ended up by crying at the thought of never seeing Carol again. She could think of no way of escaping.

An Invasion Committee had been set up in Sheffield in case the city was invaded by land, which was considered likely after the raids on the French coast. Detailed plans had been made in co-operation with military authorities and Mark Kaye had chosen to remain in the city while these plans were completed. Now, with Christmas only a few days away, he decided he'd better go home. He hoped Charlotte had sorted herself out by now. Didn't fancy listening again to detailed accounts of non-existent dogs and rundown clocks that continued to chime.

He saw the strip of light where the curtains hadn't quite met as he drove up the drive. Secluded by tall trees, it was unlikely that those lights from the house would have been detected but he'd better put them out. He tried the key in the lock and found it wouldn't go in. Charlotte must have left her key in the lock on the inside. He rang the bell and waited. Where the hell was she? He rang again, and again. He was just about to go round the back when the front door opened, revealing a flustered Charlotte.

'What the hell did you leave the key in the lock for?'

'Well, seeing as you haven't been home for nearly a month, I wasn't expecting you. Has she thrown you out?'

'What? Who?'

'Whoever it is you've been sharing a bed with.'

'Oh, for God's sake, Charlotte! I've been working all the hours God sends, the last thing I wanted was a woman. Bloody hell, I've enough on with one. Look, can't we try and have a peaceful, amicable Christmas?'

Charlotte began to panic. 'You mean, you're home for Christmas?'

'Well, if it's going to put you out, I can go back where I came from?'

'No! I didn't mean that. It's just . . . I'm not prepared.'

'The house looks prepared to me. In fact, it looks quite festive. Are you feeling better? You look it.' She did, too. Having Daisy in the other room had protected her from the dogs. Besides, the girl had been company, someone to talk to. Now what was she to do? Daisy couldn't remain in her room all day, but neither could Charlotte let her go. Bloody

Mark! When she'd wanted him, he wasn't there. Now he couldn't have turned up at a worse time. She would have to get rid of Daisy, there was no other solution. But how?

Daisy heard voices. It was the first time she had detected any sign of a visitor since she had been brought here. She should scream, now, before they went away again. Aunty Charlotte had bundled her upstairs and shut her in her room, with a warning to keep quiet or else. The little girl knew by now that she was being held prisoner. The excuses the woman was making to keep her here didn't make sense. Besides, she knew she should have been at school. She must act. If not, the visitor might go away. So Daisy went and stood by the locked door and screamed as loud as she possibly could. Then again.

'What the . . . ?' Mark took the stairs two at a time. The screams were coming from Charlotte's room. His heart began to palpitate at the thought of the things she had told him about those dogs . . . but these screams were human, obviously screams of terror.

Daisy heard footsteps approaching.

'Help! Please, help me!'

She saw the knob turn but the door was locked. 'Please don't go away, I want to go home!' Daisy was crying by now. All the days of pent-up fear rose to the surface and she was almost hysterical.

Mark didn't bother about the key, he kicked at the door until the lock gave way. He couldn't believe what he was hearing as the little girl told him her story. He had known how irrational his wife could be, but now he realised that she was mentally ill.

He lifted the child in his arms and carried her downstairs. Charlotte was cowering in a corner of the lounge, fearful of what her husband might do. He would deal with her later, he decided, or the police could. His first priority was to get this child home.

'Where do you live, pet?'

'Taylors Row.'

Uncle Walter's house!

'Right, but first I have to use the phone. Do you have a coat?'

Daisy nodded and went to fetch her things. Mark called the police. He gave them his address and told them his wife would need an ambulance. He himself was taking the little girl home. 'She's desperate to be home, and no wonder! My wife is clearly mentally ill.'

Then he carried Daisy out to the car. 'What's that you've got?' he asked as he saw the foolscap pads under her arm.

'My writing books. Aunty Charlotte gave them to me.'

'So she looked after you all right?' he questioned Daisy as he drove her home.

'Oh, yes, except when she threw a dish at me. But she was a poor thrower, like me, so she missed.'

Mark smiled despite his anxiety. Daisy didn't seem much the worse for her adventure. Now she was on her way home she was actually chatting to him. The house was in darkness. Of course, it would be, because of the blackout. He was about to knock when Daisy said, 'Just open the door, it's never locked.'

When a strange man walked in with Daisy in his arms, Sally just stood there, mouth agape, for a few seconds. Then she made a grab for her daughter and held her so close she could hardly breathe.

Jim felt his fists clench ready to attack the stranger but Daisy said, 'This nice man rescued me. The woman kidnapped me, but he found me and rescued me.'

'Please sit down,' Jim asked Mark.

'I think we all should. You must have been out of your minds with worry. I'm so sorry I didn't go home before.' He explained why he had not and who he was. 'My wife is obviously in need of medical help. I can assure you, nothing like this will ever happen again,' he concluded.

'What about the fire?' Sally enquired.

'Fire?'

'Someone tried to burn this house down. The police went to question Mrs Kaye but found no evidence to show she had anything to do with it. Only now, I wonder . . . '

'I didn't know anything about that,' Mark insisted, looking very pale.

'They were supposed to have searched her house last week too,' Sally said. 'And they found nothing then either.'

'Somebody obviously slipped up somewhere,' Mark told her.

'Are you all right, Daisy? Did the woman hurt you?' Jim searched his daughter's face for signs of anything untoward, but she said, 'Oh, no. She gave me a lovely bedroom with a real electric light of my own, and lots of writing paper.'

'Well, Daisy doesn't seem to have come to any harm,' he said.

'She made me eat lots of things I didn't like, though.'

'Good!' laughed Jim.

'I'll have to go,' Mark told them. 'I rang for the police. They should be with Charlotte by now.'

'Thanks. You don't know what we've been going through this past week.'

'I've a damned good idea, though! If I had a daughter like Daisy, I know what I should have gone through if I'd lost her. I'm really sorry about this. Have a good Christmas.' He shook hands with Jim and Sally. 'I expect the police'll be in touch.'

'I don't suppose it's any good wishing you a

Happy Christmas,' Jim said. 'Not with your wife like she is. But thanks, anyway.'

'No. I doubt it'll be very festive.' A grim-faced Mark went out to his car. Bobby Jones was just turning the corner as he started the engine.

The PC wasn't very happy. His superiors had given him a right dressing-down for only half searching the house where Daisy Butler had been held captive. Right bloody way to start Christmas! he thought. Then he saw Sally Butler, holding her daughter in her arms. That was all that mattered really, Daisy was home. But what if Mark Kaye hadn't come back when he did? The possible consequences then didn't bear thinking about. He would have to be more thorough if a situation like this ever occurred again. Bobby Jones hoped and prayed it never would.

When Mark arrived home an ambulance was drawn up before the house. He hurried up the front steps and saw the ambulance men trying to resuscitate Charlotte!

'What's happened?' he said as he knelt beside his wife.

'Well, we can't be sure at this stage but it looks like a heart attack,' the medic said. 'Of course, they'll be a post mortem. I'm sorry, sir, but she'd gone by the time we arrived. There was nothing we could do.'

Mark felt the colour drain from his face.

'Are you all right, sir?' The ambulance man felt for Mark's pulse.

'Yes, it's the shock, that's all. What a home-coming!' He told them about the little girl then. 'My wife hasn't been right for some time,' he said, 'but I didn't realise just how ill she was or I would never have left her.'

'Aye, well, you weren't to know. We need to be on our way, sir. We'll take your wife now. You'll be notified when the funeral can be arranged. Will you be all right on your own?'

'Yes, thanks, I shall be okay.'

Mark cried when the ambulance had drawn away. Not because he would miss Charlotte, though. Oh, he was sorry things had turned out like this for her. She had been a good-looking woman when he had first met her. No! he was crying from relief that he would finally be free from her mood swings, free from her jealous rages. To be truthful, Mark Kaye was relieved to be free from his wife.

Chapter Nine

The house at Taylors Row was once again full to the seams. All the family were joining in the celebration of Daisy's return. Even Grandma Denman had climbed the hill to welcome home her granddaughter. For once Jim didn't mind. The relief of his daughter's return was worth all the visitors. News from Bobby Jones of Charlotte's death had put a bit of a dampener on things, but for a few minutes and no longer. The woman had obviously been insane. Maybe it was a welcome release for her.

A Christmas tree had immediately been brought up from the Donkey Wood and decorated with last year's ornaments. Rations were pooled in order to supply enough goodies for the party. 'Why wait for Christmas?' Sally said. 'Our Daisy's homecoming is far more important.'

Jim and Bernard went to the Sun and came back with as much beer as they could coax out of the landlord, who had been as upset as everybody else in Millington by the disappearance of the girl. All Sally's family were present with the exception of Pat, who was spending more and more time at the theatre. There were also Amy, Betty and little Ernie, and the house was already crowded, but then Jim invited Tom, Mary and Stanley. Then Amy blushed furiously as she plucked up the courage to ask if Danny Powell could be invited too.

'Danny?' Sally couldn't believe her ears. 'I didn't know he ever ventured out.'

'Well, 'e ventured out on our Daisy's behalf,' Amy said. 'And 'e even offered to pay for owt what was needed.'

'Of course he can come. Do I need to fetch him?' Jim asked.

'Oh, no, 'e can manage quite well.' Amy thought it was time Danny was welcomed by her family. He had been quite a comfort to her over the past week. 'Our Daisy can fetch 'im.'

'Oh, I don't know . . .' Sally was afraid to let her out of her sight.

'I'll go with her,' Norah said. She knew how Aunty Sally was feeling. Norah had cried herself to sleep every night her cousin had been away.

Danny was all dressed up. He never knew when Amy was going to turn up these days so had begun to smarten himself up a bit. 'Daisy, me precious!' he said, seeing her. 'Oh, it is good to see yer.' He even had tears in his eyes.

'We've come to take you to a party.'

'Party? I haven't been to a party since I was a young man.'

'Well, I want you to come to ours.'

'And who's this then?'

'It's my cousin Norah.'

'Well! Aren't I a lucky owd man, being escorted by the two prettiest girls in Millington?'

The two girls giggled and busied themselves passing him his coat, hat and crutches, and locking the door.

The table looked a picture. Betty had placed twigs of holly between the plates, and made a junket for the kids and a basin of Bird's custard. The cake meant to be eaten at Christmas had been brought out prematurely. Who cared about that when Daisy was safely home? Besides, Christmas was properly the celebration of Christ's birthday, and they could do that without all the frivolities. They would all go to chapel and thank God that He had seen fit to return their precious child.

Plates were half-empty when the door suddenly opened. Everyone stopped whatever they were doing except Jim, who choked on his beer. Daisy was the first to acknowledge the visitor.

'Uncle Ernest!' She ran towards him and jumped up into his arms. Joe Denman spoke the words on everyone's mind. 'Thank God!' Jim recovered from his choking and shifted Stanley from his chair, sitting Ernest down near the food. Lizzie prised herself up from the sofa and gave her son a hug and a kiss. 'Welcome home, son. Are you well?' She didn't think he looked at all well.

'I am now I'm here,' Ernest laughed. His eyes were scanning the room but the person he was looking for was nowhere in sight. Then Betty came from upstairs, with little Ernie still rosy and bleary-eyed from his nap. Ernest thought he had never seen such a beautiful sight and knew he never would again. He had thought of Betty Hayes every night since she had confided in him before giving birth to her little boy. Now here she was before his eyes, yet still as far out of reach as ever. He looked round the room for Clarence, but of course a soldier could be anywhere in the world.

'So this is little Ernie, eh?' He grinned and held out his arms for the little boy who was his name-sake but the child was timid and clung on to Betty's skirt.

'He'll come round, he's just shy,' she said.

Sally thought Ernest must be overwhelmed by the number of people here and began to explain.

'We're having our party early. I know Christmas Day isn't until Friday, but we've a better reason to celebrate so we've brought it forward.'

Danny Powell thought he was intruding now the airman had returned.

'This ought to be a family occasion. I don't want to outstay my welcome, so if you'll excuse me I'll just get me coat.'

'No!' Jim said. 'We've other days to spend with family, this is our Daisy's day. How long is it since you got drunk, Danny?'

'I'm not sure, but I do know I ended up in't middle of't undertaker's window display. Somebody'd stood an urn on me chest. I was fined five shillings for breaking and entering – and it weren't me who entered, it were me mates who took me! I know summat . . . when I woke up, I were glad it weren't my name on that gravestone.'

Amy thought Danny always knew how to cheer folks up. She was glad he was here.

'Right then, if we promise not to take yer down to the undertaker's, you can get drunk tonight. 'Ere, get this down yer.' And Jim gave Danny a tot of the last of old Walter's brandy.

Mary had made up some packages and the children were playing pass the parcel, with Grand-dad Denman playing the piano. Sally thought her father had shed a few years since Daisy's return, and another few in the short time Ernest had been in the house. She would probably never feel contentment such as this again. Not happiness, she daren't call it that since it would be tempting fate – and after what had happened to Daisy, she never intended to do that. No, all Sally needed was contentment, and today she was quite content.

Christmas was spent quietly, apart from the usual excitement on discovering that Father Christmas had been. Ernest Denman was glad to be home, and apart from treating all the family to tickets for the pantomime – *Aladdin* – at the Lyceum, was content to spend time quietly with his parents. Nobody had mentioned the death of Clarence Hayes and Ernest himself had decided to steer clear of Betty even though he was longing to spend time with her and Ernie.

Pat Cartwright was home very little over the holidays. The pantomime period was a hectic time at the theatre and she was dashing from costumes to cleaning, from tea-maker to prompter, in her element. With chorus girls in short supply, due to many young women being away in the services, the average age of the girls who performed was seventeen. Some were only fifteen, in fact, and Pat made friends of her own age. In fact, Pat Cartwright was having the time of her life. When her family turned up for the performance on Boxing Day they were all taken backstage to meet the stars, a treat indeed. Daisy told Pat that when she grew up she would write a pantomime. Uncle Ernest said he had every confidence in her doing so.

A few weeks after Christmas, Daisy, Carol, Una and Jean attended another performance, when Gypsy Petulengro paid a visit to the Palace Cinema. Sally was torn between wanting to go and fear of what he might predict.

'He told me about Charlotte taking away something of great value. He also told Daisy she would see the inside of a hospital. Both things came true.'

'So let's go. He might predict something good this time,' Mary said.

'Ah, but what if he says something terrible is

about to happen? I won't be able to shrug it off this time. Not now I know how accurate he can be.'

'Oh, come on, it'll be a laugh.' Mary really wanted to go but Sally still wasn't sure. In the end they did go but decided they would sit up in the circle, where he was less likely to pick them out.

Gypsy Petulengro remembered the little Shirley Temple lookalike though. How could he forget? That prediction was one of the strongest he had ever experienced, and it was the same again tonight. She was in the end seat, next to the right aisle.

'The girl with the curls,' he said, 'at the end of the fourth row upstairs. And the girl in the red coat, close to you . . . Most unusual, but you're both destined for fame. You with the curls will find fame in your home town, and at a very young age. You are most gifted but must work hard. Never give up your dream for one second. Go for what you want and you will acquire it. The girl in red . . .' That was Una Bacon. 'Do you sing?' Una nodded. 'Will you say yes or no to my questions, please? So that other people can hear.'

'Yes, and I dance.'

'The dancing may give you pleasure but the singing will give you fame beyond your wildest dreams. You will travel the length and breadth of the country. Forget the dancing and train your voice. Will you do that?'

'Yes, I will. Thank you.' Una's eyes sparkled in

the lights from the stage. She was to be a singer, he had told her so, and Daisy said he knew. He had told Daisy, too, though he hadn't told her how she would become famous. He had only told her.

'Isn't he good?' Daisy said.

'Yes, he's marvellous!' Una agreed.

'Well, I don't think much of him,' Jean mumbled.

'That's because he didn't tell you anything,' Carol said. 'You're just jealous. But he'll be right, Daisy will be famous when she writes her book.'

Whether it was the Phosferine or his son's leave it was hard to tell, but Joe Denman certainly looked better and was taking his Home Guard duties extremely seriously, especially the visits to the club to slaken the dust. Sally decided she could stop worrying about him.

With her niggling anxiety about what Charlotte Kaye might do next at an end, she was at last able to relax. Daisy had returned to school to face a profusion of questions and had taken advantage of finding herself in the limelight by exaggerating her experience. When Jim heard some of the tales she had told, he said to Sally, 'Our Daisy's a born story-teller, she can't half spin a yarn.'

'Well, she says that's what she's going to do with her life – write books.'

'Then I'm afraid she's going to be disappointed,' Jim laughed. 'People like us don't become authors.'

'Well, according to Gypsy what's his name, she's about to become famous . . .'

'What a load of rubbish! Yer surely don't believe all that stuff, do yer?'

'Well, he wasn't far out before.'

'Coincidence, that's all.'

'Well, we shall see. If she keeps writing like she is now, she might well be successful. Her teacher says she's outstanding for her age.'

'Aye, and pigs might fly.'

A few months later Jim was to eat his words. Nellie came one morning with a very official-looking envelope addressed to Miss Daisy Butler.

'What can it be?' Sally turned it over and considered opening it, but she couldn't, not when it was addressed to her daughter. She stood it in the centre of the mantelpiece, propped up by the clock. Nellie was most disappointed. When Jim came home off the morning shift he looked at the name on the envelope. 'What's this?' he asked his wife.

'I've no idea, I can't read through paper.'

'All right, no need to be sarcastic!'

'Well, I've been wondering and worrying all morning.'

When Daisy arrived home Jim handed her the envelope. 'You've got a letter. Do yer know what it's about?'

'Not till I open it.' She tore the envelope open and read the letter. Her face had turned the colour of beetroot.

'Well?'

'I've won! The competition in Grandma's magazine . . . I've won.' She handed the letter to Jim who began to read it.

Dear Miss Daisy Butler,
I am pleased to inform you that you are the winner of our writing competition. The adjudicators considered your poem 'Buttercups' was the most likely to remind our troops of home. For a competitor of your age, the poem is an outstanding composition.
The prize is on its way to you and we hope you find the typewriter useful in your writing. We wish you success in the future. Your poem will appear in the summer edition of the magazine. We shall, of course, forward a copy to you.
Yours sincerely,
Rosie Stem
Editor

'Well!' Sally said. 'Congratulations. A typewriter . . . why didn't you tell us you'd entered?'

'Because you'd only have laughed.'

'I wouldn't.'

'No, but Dad would.'

'I would not!' Jim was stunned.

'Yes, you would. You think I'm silly when I say I'm going to be a writer.'

'Well, I won't now. Are you going to show us this outstanding poem, then?'

'Not until it's in the magazine. It's only scribbled,

but it won't be when I get my typewriter. I shall be able to type up my story about my kidnapping, too.'

'Oh, Daisy, don't you think you ought to forget about that?'

'No! It makes a marvellous, exciting story. You just wait until you read it.'

'But do you think it's fair to Mr Kaye? It will only upset him.'

'Oh, I won't mention names, no one will recognise it, only me.'

'Anyway,' Jim said, 'don't yer think you ought to go and tell yer grandma? It isn't everybody who has a famous grand-daughter.'

'No! I'm going to tell our Pat first. She bought me the stamp so it's only fair. Besides, she believed in me.'

Jim felt ashamed that he had belittled his daughter. 'I believe in you, love,' he said.

'Right, I'll go and tell our Pat now. Then I'll tell Grandma Butler. I'm not a famous grand-daughter yet!' Daisy ran to the door, hugging her letter. As she went out she turned to her parents. 'But I will be,' she said.

Mark Kaye had removed the panel from the alcove and brought out the boxes containing Mr Jessops' belongings. He looked at the clocks which stood silent and run down, pendulums hanging motionless. The vases were pretty but reminded him of the cremation urns used for holding ashes.

He shuddered as he unwrapped one of the dog prints. 'You were right, Charlotte, there *is* something weird about these,' he murmured. He picked up a photograph from the dressing table of Charlotte in her younger days, and sighed. 'Well, it seems you got away with it, but it didn't do you much good, did it? Brady's house, your uncle's treasures, and all they did was drive you to suicide.'

He put down the photograph and walked round the room, running his hand over the expensive furniture. Then he smiled to himself. 'Seems I've done quite well out of our marriage, Charlotte.' He walked slowly downstairs and poured himself a drink. Lifting the glass, he declared, 'Bottoms up, old girl, wherever you are.'

Ida Appleby had not so far stopped talking about her family Christmas, but on this particular day, when Sally arrived, she said, 'I've been thinking . . . what if I invited Doug Fletcher up for a meal some time?' She paused, watching Sally for her reaction. 'Emily says he's always hanging around the cafe so I can always find 'im there. I could do a meat pie if you could get me some of that horse meat, like I used to make when I was housekeeper . . . I mean, when I worked at the White Hart.'

'I hope you're not planning a dirty weekend, you and Doug Fletcher?'

'Well, I think we're a bit past all that at our age.

Mind you, with a good dinner inside us, you never know.'

'What will Mrs Simms say?'

'Not much, she's not one to pass judgement. In fact, if I'd been a bit more like Emily, I'd 'ave been a happier woman. Oh, Sally, if only I hadn't taken any notice of me mother, our Donald might never 'ave moved away!'

'Now, Ida. He moved away when he was promoted, you should be proud of him for that.'

'Oh, I am! And our Paul and Peter as well, they're grand lads. So what do yer think I should do about Doug?'

'I think it's time you did what you want to do.'

'Aye, and bugger everybody else!'

Sally couldn't help laughing. 'Well, I'd better get on.'

'Oh, sit down and let's have a natter. Besides, you 'aven't read me letter yet. Me grandsons are going to come and stay for a week in their school holidays. Oh, it will be lovely 'aving somebody to make a fuss of, especially at bedtime. It's been a long time since I've given anybody a goodnight kiss and a cuddle.'

'Well, I shouldn't count on that if I were you. You might find the boys consider themselves too old for kissing. Still, you can always fall back on Doug. I'm sure he wouldn't object.'

Sally poured tea into the two cups. Ida got up and went to the cupboard, bringing back a bottle of whisky. 'Here, let's 'ave a drop of this in it. Our Donald bought it. 'E says a drop in me first cup of a morning'll be good for me. So let's drink to our families.'

'Yes, to our families. And to as many kisses and cuddles as we can get. Everybody needs affection, Ida, no matter how old they are.'

'Aye, Sally, you're right. And thank goodness I've realised it before it's too late.'

Daisy didn't know what was wrong with Carol. She had been miserable for weeks but wouldn't say why.

'I thought I was your friend, but you're always snapping at me,' Daisy complained.

'I know, I'm sorry. I don't mean to, and you *are* my friend, my very best friend.'

'Well, stop being so grumpy.'

'If you're my friend, why won't you go to the pictures?' Carol pleaded. 'It's Bob Hope and Dorothy Lamour, it's sure to be good.'

'I told you, I'll go with you tomorrow. I've got my piano lesson tonight.'

'Please, it's *got* to be tonight. Anyway, you said you're not bothered about playing the piano.'

'I'm not, but Mam says I've got to do something apart from writing all the time. Besides, I read somewhere that pianists can type faster than anyone else.'

'That's all you care about, your writing. If you

cared about me you'd come with me to the pictures. I'll just have to go by myself.'

'And then I'll have nobody to go with tomorrow.'

'I'm sorry but I have to go tonight. It's Monday and my mum goes out on Mondays. So I'll see you at school tomorrow then.'

Carol looked so sad as she set off for home, dragging her feet, that Daisy almost called her back and told her she'd changed her mind, but she knew her mam wouldn't let her miss her lesson.

She called after her friend, 'See you tomorrow, Carol.' But she didn't turn round. Daisy was really worried then. It was as though Carol didn't want to go home. She decided to tell Sally about it when she got home.

'Mam . . .' She didn't really know what to say. 'What would you do if your friend was unhappy and moody all the time?'

Sally considered the question for a moment then said, 'Well, I suppose I'd ask her what was worrying her.'

'I've done that. She says it's nothing, but I know there's something wrong.'

'Is this friend Carol, by any chance?'

'Yes, and she's always been so happy until now.'

Sally frowned. She wondered if the rumours had any truth in them, if Carol's mother actually *was* having an affair with the so-called Uncle Harry. If so, that could be the cause of the change in Carol. The girls were growing up fast and becoming perceptive enough to notice such things. Of course, Carol wouldn't feel able to confide in Daisy about her mother's infidelity, as she wouldn't want anyone to know. Sally herself couldn't talk about it to Daisy either, not when it might just be idle gossip. Instead she said, 'You're both growing up, love. You'll find that you feel a bit moody sometimes when your body starts to change. Just keep an eye on her and let her know you'll always be there for her if she needs you.'

Daisy went for her music lesson but couldn't concentrate on anything Miss Collins was saying. She played 'Home, Sweet Home' fluently, but that was only because she had practised it so much she could have played it in her sleep. When Miss Collins started going on about crotchets and quavers and semibreves it went in one ear and out of the other. Daisy didn't like it when her friend was so sad.

Dr Sellars came to see Danny. Mr Powell very rarely needed medical help and she doubted she would be here now if it hadn't been for Mrs Butler's intervention. 'Good morning, Danny.' She knew better than to give him the title of Mr Powell.

'Hello, Doctor Sellars.'

'I've been told you're slightly deaf.'

'Oh, nay, I'm not short of breath. I can breathe as well as anybody.'

'Let's take a look at your ears.' She shone a light

336

in each of them. 'Well, if we get rid of the wax we might get somewhere.'

'Aye, I know they're full of hair. My missis used to cut 'em but I can't do it meself.'

'Has Mrs Butler been putting the drops in?'

'Oh, aye. She drops in every day to put that stuff in me ears. I don't know what I would do without 'er.'

Dr Sellars smiled to herself. Danny was one of her most cheerful patients despite his disability. She got some water from the kettle and a dish from the sink and syringed his right ear. Nothing moved the first time, then a large plug of something hard fell into the dish.

'Have you been putting anything else in your ears, Danny?' she asked.

'Oh, aye, I used to put cotton wool in to stop the noise at work.'

'You heard me that time, didn't you?'

'Aye, I expect you were shouting a bit louder. People get fed up talking to me after a bit and start shouting.'

'I'm not shouting. Your ear's been completely blocked since you left work. You must have pushed the cotton wool right inside. Come on, let's do the other one.' The same thing happened again. A huge, black ball came tumbling out into the bowl.

Danny grinned. 'Eeh, fancy, I can hear the damned clock ticking. It sounds like Big Ben!'

'No wonder you were deaf, look what I've got out.'

'Bloody 'ell.' Danny couldn't believe it. 'Sorry, doctor, for swearing. I were just surprised, that's all.'

Dr Sellars got her things together. 'That's all right. Just promise me you won't put anything else in your ears?'

'Oh, I won't, lass. Eeh, listen to that, I can hear it raining. Eeh, thanks, love.'

'Don't thank me, thank Mrs Butler. She's the one who called me. Good morning then, I'll be off. Let's hope it's just as long until the next time we meet.'

'Aye, let's hope so. Good morning then, Doctor.'

Danny couldn't believe it. All those years with his ears blocked! He got his crutches and went to the bottom of the stairs. If he sat down on his bottom he could climb up fairly easily. When he got to the top he had another pair of crutches waiting. He managed to hop into the back bedroom. There on the tallboy stood the wireless. He knew the accumulators would need charging but it was a grand wireless set. He would get Sally to carry it down for him and ask little Daisy to take the accumulators to be charged, then he would be able to catch up on the news and a bit of music.

Next he remembered the gramophone. He found it in a corner and managed to slide it out to the middle of the room. The records were in a box in the bottom of the wardrobe. He wound the handle at the side and fitted a new needle, then he looked through the records, reading the labels. Tears came to Danny's eyes then as he remembered dancing to them with his beloved Rosie. He put on a record. 'Dancing with Tears in My Eyes' was about right. Danny wiped tears from his cheeks, not tears of sadness now but of joy as the memories flooded back.

They had lived for the day, had Danny and Rosie, enjoying every moment. The holidays where they had danced on the beach in the moonlight and ended up making love under the pier. The nights they had been content just to sit in the firelight, listening to these records. The summer days they had walked over to Longfield and picked bilberries to make a pie then lain hand in hand among the heather, listening to the grouse's call.

The record ended. Well, Danny might not be able to walk to Longfield any more, and he certainly couldn't dance, but he could still listen to the birdsong now he'd got his hearing back *and* he could listen to his records.

He could even buy some new ones. That Vera Lynn, he liked her.

He wondered what type of music Amy Butler liked. It would be nice sitting in the firelight with Amy. Eeh, life would be so much richer now he could hear summat. And it was all down to young Daisy. Danny blessed the day she had brought Sally

Butler into his life. He was a fortunate man, and nobody must ever try to tell him otherwise.

Sally was shocked one Sunday morning when she answered the door to find Mark Kaye standing on the step. 'Oh! she said. 'Won't you come in?'

'Yes, but I'll just get some things first.' He went back to his car. Inside the house Sally bustled about, tidying the living-room. Daisy had told her how posh the Kayes' house was. Mark came back carrying a box which he stood on the table, then he went out again and fetched the clocks, carrying them in one at a time, careful not to shake them about.

'Hello, Daisy, how are you?' He smiled at the little girl who seemed to look even prettier than the first time he'd seen her. 'I'm returning these things,' he told Sally. 'They are rightfully yours, and I'm sorry for all the trouble we've caused.'

Sally lifted the cardboard flaps of the box and found the vases. Then she lifted out the pictures, wrapped carefully in pieces of cloth. The books lay in the bottom, volumes of Dickens and Shakespeare amongst others.

Sally was overcome by the sight of Mr Jessops' treasured belongings and went to make some tea so that no one would see her tears. When she came back she said, 'Look, I've been thinking . . . they should have been Charlotte's by rights. I said so at the time. Why don't you take them? Oh, apart from the dog pictures . . . they're not worth much, but I'd like to keep those.' She unwrapped the framed prints and propped them up against the box.

Daisy couldn't believe her eyes. 'Hey, they're pictures of the dogs at Aunty Charlotte's!'

'What?' Mark exclaimed.

'The dogs . . . they came at night and slept on my bed. When I was scared they made me feel safe.' She frowned. 'I think I was dreaming, but I'm sure I wasn't asleep. Perhaps they were ghosts.'

Mark Kaye flopped into a chair. 'Daisy, Charlotte didn't have any dogs. There were never any dogs in our house.'

'Oh, well, she wouldn't talk about them, but they came at night and were gone by morning. They were the dogs in these pictures.'

Sally laughed. 'You must have been dreaming, like you said, or else imagining things. You know what a vivid imagination you have.'

'I wasn't, look . . .' Daisy ran upstairs and came back with a sheet of paper which she handed to her mother. 'Look, that's part of my story. The one I wrote when I was at the house.'

Sally read the paragraph Daisy was pointing to out loud so that Mark could hear.

'"On the first night I was afraid and didn't dare go to sleep, but then on the second night I heard a clock chime and something wondrous occurred. A pair of dogs entered the room, large dogs, which in most circumstances I would have feared. On this night, however, they lay one on either side of me, friendly and comforting. One was grey with a touch of white and was tall and thin. The other was just like Mr Baraclough's at the shop. After that, they came every night to protect me and I was no longer afraid."'

Mark Kaye was trembling. So Charlotte had been right! She probably wasn't insane at all. Strange, certainly, but not to the extent he had thought. It had probably been the shock of seeing the dogs that had brought on the heart attack. If only he'd got rid of the pictures. He examined them closely but could see nothing strange about them. Still, he would be relieved to be rid of them.

'Well, as I was saying,' Sally said, 'take any or all of these. They are yours by rights.'

'No, they're yours. After all the trouble Charlotte caused you, I wouldn't dream of taking anything.'

'But I got the house,' Sally told him. 'Please, at least take one of the clocks. What will we do with three wall clocks?'

Mark shuddered at the thought of living in a house with those clocks again. 'Well! Uncle Walter must have found room for them,' he told Sally.

'Yes, but we prefer things less cluttered.' Sally wrinkled her nose. 'Go on, take something. It'll make me feel better.'

Mark considered her offer. 'No,' he said finally, 'I don't want any of it. Sell whatever you don't want and put the money in the bank for Daisy. Call it compensation for her distress.'

'Well then, thanks. I never expected to see these again.' Sally took down the two watercolours and hung the prints in their place.

'Here,' she said to Mark. 'Take these two pictures. I never liked them.'

He grinned. 'Okay,' he said. 'But I definitely never want to see the dog pictures again. They give me the collywobbles! I just hope they don't decide to haunt your house too.' He wondered who had painted the originals.

'Oh, that's just our Daisy's imagination running riot again.'

Mark bade Sally goodbye and went home, thinking, if only you knew.

When he'd gone Sally stood looking at the pictures. She could have sworn the Alsatian used to be with the girl on the other picture. Goodness, she was becoming as bad as Daisy! Now, what were they going to do with three clocks?

Daisy was in the middle of an art lesson when Jean, who shared her desk, said to her, 'Your mum's having a baby, isn't she?'

Daisy felt herself blushing. How did Jean know something that Daisy herself should have known, but didn't? She said the first thing that came into her head. 'She is *not*.'

'Yes, she is. My mum saw her at the clinic.'

'Well, your mum shouldn't spread gossip!'

Now Daisy couldn't concentrate on the picture she was painting. She felt stupid. How could her mam have kept something like that from her? She must think Daisy herself was a baby. She couldn't wait for home time and hurried away without even waiting for Carol. She had to catch up with Norah, and the seniors always seemed to be out before the juniors. She waited at the gate for her cousin.

'Hiya, Daisy. What are you doing here?'

'Norah, is my mam having a baby?'

'I think so, she looks a bit fat.'

'Has your mam said anything?'

'No! But then, she wouldn't. They never tell us anything like that, do they?'

'Well, Jean's mother's told her. She said my mam was at the clinic. I felt so stupid, not knowing.'

'Oh, don't worry about it. Besides, I thought you wanted a baby?'

'I did when I was little, but not now I'm ten!'

'Are you going to tell yer mam that you know?'

'Why should I? If she can't be bothered to tell me, I shan't tell her.'

Daisy went to call for Carol later, she couldn't wait to confide in her, but when she saw her friend's face she was too concerned for Carol to think about herself.

'What's the matter?' she asked.

'Nothing, I'm all right.'

'No, you're not. You haven't been all right for a long time. You've got to tell me what's wrong.'

'I can't.'

'Why not? I thought I was your friend. Don't you trust me?'

'Yes, I do trust you. But I can't tell you . . .'

'Well! I've got something to tell *you*. My mam's having a baby and she's never told me! Besides, how could they do something like that?'

'Like what?'

'Well, you know. Doing things to each other. How can she let him put his thingy inside her? Like our Norah told us happens when you get married. I shall never get married if that's what you have to do.'

Before Daisy had finished speaking Carol had burst into tears. She was sobbing her heart out and Daisy didn't know what to do.

'What did I say to make you cry? Look, let's go to our house. If you can't tell me what's wrong, perhaps you can tell my mam.'

Carol shook her head but she didn't object to Daisy leading her by the hand to Taylors Row. Jim was at work and Sally was using the sewing machine, the treadle making so much noise that she didn't hear the girls enter the room. She jumped when she finally saw them and stopped pedalling when she saw the look of misery on Carol's face.

'Whatever's the matter, love? Here, come and sit down by the fire.' Sally sat down beside her daughter's friend.

'Mam, you've got to make her tell you what's wrong,' Daisy insisted.

'Do you want to tell me, Carol?' Sally asked in a soft voice.

'It's *him* . . . he does things to me! Every Monday, when my mum goes to her first-aid class, and any other time he gets the chance.'

'What sort of things, Carol?' Sally felt as though her blood was turning to ice.

'He . . . he touches me, up my dress, where he shouldn't . . .'

'Daisy, go and make some tea, love,' Sally ordered her, and for once her daughter did as she was told. She didn't like the sound of this.

Carol was shuddering with sobs, wrapping her arms around herself and shivering as she spoke.

'And he takes out his thing, you know, and makes me hold it until . . .'

She could say no more. When she'd finally calmed down she continued, 'He says it's what all big girls do and it's to be kept our secret or he'll tell everybody at school. I hate him, I do! I can't go home . . . I'm going to run away. I'll go to my grandma's in Leeds.'

'Look, Carol, he won't tell anybody, anybody at all, because if he does he'll go to prison. You've got to tell your mum and dad.'

Carol shrank away, horrified. 'Tell my dad? What are you talking about? It's *him* I'm telling you about.'

346

'What? I thought you were talking about your . . . your Uncle Harry?'

'Uncle Harry? He would never do anything to hurt anyone. He's good and kind. I think he might kill Dad if he finds out.'

Sally thought killing might be too good for someone who could do things like that to his own daughter.

'Listen, love, you've got to tell me something. Has he ever put his . . . his *thing* inside you?'

'No. But that's what I'm scared of. He says he's saving that for a treat. That's why I can't go home.'

'No, you definitely can't. We shall have to wait for Daisy's dad to come in from work and see what's to be done then. In the meantime you can stay here, all right? Daisy, are there any biscuits?' Her daughter looked almost as upset as her friend and was still trembling.

Sally know she had to comfort and reassure both the girls.

'Look, it's a horrible thing he's done, but it could have been worse and he won't do it again, I promise. What he's done to you, Carol, is something only grown-up people should do, when they love each other. When you love someone, it's something you do naturally and it's never horrible. But never, ever, should it be something anyone forces you to do. And never at your age. It's something to be treasured until you grow up.'

Sally didn't want Daisy or Carol to be put off

347

sex for the rest of their lives. The monster had already done enough damage. Carol was still shaking. Sally would have to let her mother know where the girl was. She decided to ask Mr Baraclough if she could use his phone. The good-hearted soul never minded so long as the caller paid. Luckily it was Carol's mother who answered.

'Hello, it's Sally Butler here . . . Daisy's mother. Is it all right if Carol stays the night with us?'

'Yes, of course, so long as she's no trouble?'

'No, she's no trouble at all. I'll see she gets to school in the morning. Goodbye.'

She hurriedly replaced the receiver, worried that the woman would detect something unusual about her voice.

Sally herself was still in shock from what Carol had revealed to her. Why in God's name had the girl not been able to confide in her own mother? Then she wondered if her own daughter would have felt able to confide in her. It wasn't as if she ever talked to Daisy like a grown-up. Perhaps it was time she began to do so. After all, the girls had seemed to be more worldly wise than she had imagined. She would begin by telling Daisy about the baby she expected. Tonight, though, there were far more important things to sort out. For now she must try and act as though things were normal in order to calm Carol down, but what would happen when her husband came home, she dreaded to think.

*   *   *

When Jim did come home, after his customary pint at the Sun, Daisy and Carol were already in bed. Sally could hear them chatting, and the occasional giggle reassured her. She served Jim his supper and then said, 'Carol's staying tonight.'

'Oh, that'll suit our Daisy.'

'Yes. I mean, no. It isn't a social visit . . .'

'What then?' Jim didn't really care so long as no one was ill. He ate another forkful of potatoes and onions.

'Something awful has happened to Carol, Jim. Her father's been interfering with her, using her for his own sexual gratification.'

'What?' Her husband jumped up, slamming the cutlery down on his plate. 'And has our Daisy been visiting that house?'

'Shush! We don't want Carol to hear. The girl's upset enough as it is. And, no, our Daisy hasn't been in the man's company. The thing is, what are we going to do about it?'

'Christ! Do we have to get involved in summat like this, Sally?'

'Well, seeing as Carol's plucked up courage to confide in me, yes, I think we do.'

'Bloody 'ell! What do we do . . . fetch Bobby Jones?'

'I think we need to tell her mother first. She'll need to know why Carol hasn't gone home. Besides, there's the baby sister to consider, too. I think we ought to confront the family, now.'

'What, tonight?'

'Well, yes. I was hoping you'd come with me.'

'Oh, aye. Well, you certainly can't go alone. The man might turn nasty.' Jim left the rest of his supper, his appetite deserting him. 'Come on then, let's get it over with.' Sally knocked on Emily's door and asked her to sit with the two girls.

They walked past Danny's house and reached the end of the road, passing under the tree-hung part where Daisy had been snatched by Charlotte. Sally's stomach turned a somersault as they rounded a corner and their destination came into view. There was a sliver of light showing beneath one blind.

'At least they're still up,' Sally whispered.

She rang the bell and it was Carol's father who answered. As soon as Jim saw the man standing there in his silk, paisley-patterned dressing gown, his pent-up anger rose to the surface. Jim clenched his fist and smashed the man right between the eyes, sending him flying backwards so that he landed on the third step of the staircase inside. The cry he let out brought his wife running to the scene. She let out a scream before hurrying to his aid.

'Jim, you shouldn't have done that!' Sally was trembling with shock.

'Oh, I think I should. In fact, somebody should've done it long ago. You dirty, filthy bugger!'

Sally felt sorry for Carol's mum. 'Look,' she said,

'I need to tell you something. I think you should sit down.'

The other woman looked bewildered but let Sally lead her through to the room where a light was glowing.

'Carol told me tonight that her father has been using her for sex, any time he got the chance but mostly on Mondays when you are often out.'

'What?' Her face turned ghostly white and she looked as though she might faint. 'Has he . . . ?'

'No,' Sally interrupted, knowing what the poor woman was thinking. 'He hasn't had full intercourse, told her he was saving that for a treat, but by the sound of it, he's done everything else.'

The other woman jumped up from her chair. Screeching like a banshee, she flew at her husband, still huddled on the stairs, scraping her long, painted nails down his already bleeding face. 'I'll kill you for this!' she hissed.

'Well, you weren't there! You and your first-aid class . . . You were with Harry, weren't you?'

'Of course I was with Harry. He's a real man, that's why. How often have you made love to me in all the years we've been married? Twice! And now I know why you forced yourself to rise to those two occasions . . . because you wanted children. Wanted *little girls*.'

There was a vase set on the turn of the stairs, about two feet tall and filled with pampas grass. If Jim hadn't caught her hand in time she would have brought it crashing down on her husband's head.

'Look,' he intervened, 'we're not interested in your marital problems. We just want to know that things are going to change, because there's one thing for sure – Carol's not coming back here until summat does.'

'Oh, something will change all right. *He* can pack his bags and get out of here.' She turned on her husband. 'I'll give you one hour, then I shall call the police.'

'You wouldn't?' His face was deathly white beneath the blood.

'Wouldn't I? Just try me! You've had five minutes already.'

The man staggered up the stairs, saying as he went, 'You'll miss my money, you'll never manage.'

'I'd rather scrub floors than live with a man who even thinks about touching his own daughter. And this house is mine, don't forget. My father saw to that. He never trusted you, did he? Now we know he was right. And don't go near my other daughter or I'll kill you!'

Sally thought she meant it, too.

'Well,' she said, looking at her visitors, 'now that's settled, I won't keep you any longer.'

'No,' Jim said. 'He hasn't gone yet. We'll wait until he has. He might change his mind.'

'Thanks, yes, best be on the safe side. I'd appreciate that.'

'Do you think he'll cause any problems?' Sally asked her.

'No. He's too much to lose. He's in a job where they won't tolerate any scandal, and I expect my friend Harry'll be here to watch over us. The truth is, I ought to have thrown him out years ago. It never was a proper marriage.' She looked embarrassed. 'You heard the whole sordid story, didn't you? I'm sorry, I shouldn't have inflicted it on you. Still, at least I know now why he didn't want me. Not that it's much consolation . . . my poor little Carol! Perhaps I should inform the police, to protect other children?'

'It's up to you. You've got to weigh up the harm it could do to Carol, if all the sordid details become common knowledge.'

'I know. Maybe I should protect her from that.'

They heard a couple of cases being trundled downstairs then and Carol's father stood, shame-faced, in the hall. He had cleaned himself up but it was obvious he would have a couple of black eyes for the next few weeks.

'I'm sorry, I don't want to be like I am . . . I need help.'

'You bloody well do,' Jim muttered.

'And I'm going to get it, I promise. I won't bother you again.' He turned at the door. 'And I'll send money for the girls . . .'

'No, I don't want anything! I'll manage. I shall be putting in for a divorce, then I shall marry Harry. He'll be a proper father to my girls.'

'I'll give you grounds then, I shan't fight it.'

353

'Thanks for that at least. Now, I'd like you to leave.'

'Are you all right?' Sally asked after they'd heard a car drive away.

'Yes, I'm fine. Apart from worrying about how to deal with Carol . . .'

'I should just leave it. She'll get over it sooner if it isn't mentioned. I'll tell her you know, and that if she wants to talk about it, you'll be there for her. Do you think that'll be best?'

'Yes, thank you. But *why* didn't she tell me what was happening? I would have dealt with it immediately.'

'I don't think any of our girls confide in their mothers. It was Daisy who persuaded her to speak up in the end.'

'I'll try and be a bit more approachable in future.'

'I think we all need to be that.'

And Sally would tell Daisy about the baby tomorrow, she vowed. If they didn't want their children to keep secrets, then parents shouldn't have them either.

On 14 February 1945 the RAF descended on Dresden, pulverising the city and leaving 130,000 believed dead. Ernest Butler flew back to base jubilant that the raid had been a success, but grieving for some of his comrades who were destined never to return. Six weeks later Allied troops crossed the Rhine to capture Cologne, and on 12 April the

354

concentration camp at Bergen-Belsen was liberated. By 7 May the war in Europe was at an end.

The next day Victory in Europe was celebrated throughout Britain. The children at Millington School were given a holiday, and everyone on the three rows joined together in the largest celebration any of the residents could remember. The men found enough wood and rubbish to build a bonfire on the field between Potters and Barkers Rows, while the ladies set to work preparing a street party. Even Ida and the Broomsgroves joined in the preparations. The Dawson lads found a Union Jack and some old red, white and blue rags to cut up for bunting, which they hung from the bedroom windows across to the clothes posts and the sycamore tree. It wasn't until the tables were set out and everyone ready to feast themselves that anyone had time to notice that in amongst all the flags and finery, hoisted on the end of the guttering on Potters Row, was another large, pink satin embellishment: Kitty Ramsgate's famous brassiere.

Amy Butler invited Danny to join the celebrations, and Tom, Jim and Bernard almost did themselves an injury trundling the iron-framed piano from Taylors Row across to the field.

Betty Hayes secretly felt like crying at the thought of all the lives sacrificed by brave men like Clarence so that today's celebration could take place. Nevertheless, she dressed little Ernie in his best clothes, put on her fanciest frock and a huge smile, and went to join the party. Even Pat stayed home to be with her family on such an important day, and as usual took charge of the entertainment. Grand-dad Denman had been invited 'specially to play the piano and the singing could be heard halfway down St George's Road. Danny Powell surprised everyone, and embarrassed Amy Butler, when he sang 'Amy, Wonderful Amy'.

'I think we've got a romance on our hands,' Betty confided in Jim.

'Well, by the looks of her it isn't doing her any harm.' Amy definitely looked better than she had in years.

'He's a good man, Jim.'

'Aye, so Sally tells me. It seems they've been 'aving cosy nights in, listening to records.'

'Well, it's as good an excuse as any, I suppose,' Betty giggled. Little Ernie came running towards them then, a hot potato in his hand.

'I like bonfires, mam! Can we have one every day?'

'No, son. Only on special occasions.'

'What's an occasion?'

'Oh, Ernie, go and find our Daisy, she'll tell you.' And Ernie ran off, stuffing the potato into his mouth.

'He's as bad as our Daisy for asking questions.'

'He's a grand little lad, Betty. Clarence would have been proud of him.'

'Yes, he would. I don't really know why we're celebrating, Jim. The city's almost destroyed; sons,

356

fathers and husbands either dead or half-dead. And it's not really finished yet, is it? There's still Japan.'

'Aye, love, but the worst is over, I reckon.'

'Well, let's hope so, and that there won't be another war in a hurry. Not in my son's lifetime anyway. I've lost my husband. I couldn't bear it if I lost my son.'

'Good Lord, Betty, let's hope it never comes to that! Come and get a drink, this is no night to be miserable.'

'No, I'm going to join the conga.' And Betty joined the long line dancing its way down towards the Donkey Path. 'Come on, Ernie!'

The little boy giggled as he tried to follow the footwork of the merrymakers in front of him.

'Where are we going, Mam?'

'Down to the works yard. There's a concert starting down there.'

'What's a concert?'

'Like a party, with people singing and dancing.'

Jim, Tom and Bernard had retired to a table in the corner along with Alfie Ramsgate, who bagged the seat nearest the beer. They were all rather inebriated. Then Jim said to Alfie, 'Who do yer reckon that parachute up on't roof belongs to, Alfie?'

'It belongs to our Kitty.'

'Who's responsible for it being up there then?'

'I reckon it was one of the Dawson lads,' Bernard said. 'They're always up to summat.'

'It wor me.' Alfie looked sheepish.

'You? Why?'

'Well, I'm fed up of the bloody thing. I reckon she's got another bloke since I bought 'er that brassiere.'

The other three men couldn't keep straight faces as they wondered what type of man could face a session with Kitty Ramsgate.

'What meks yer think that?' Tom enquired, trying to appear serious.

'Well, she started wearing fancy knickers to match the bloody brassiere. Pink french ones wi' lace on 'em.'

'Well, let's face it, Alfie, they'd 'ave to be french ones to fit round your Kitty's thighs.'

'Aye, well, it's costing me a bloody fortune. Besides, she goes flaunting 'erself to all and sundry now. I wish I'd never bought the bloody thing.'

'I thought you'd 'ave been proud of a pair like your Kitty's. There's not many like them.'

'Aye, well, that's not the problem really. No, it's more that she puts on them fancy undies, and they mek her feel all sexy, and I'm not getting any younger . . . I can't always get it up! And I'm thinking, if I can't do owt for 'er, somebody else might. Anyway, wi' a bit of luck the bloody thing might blow away, then we can get back to normal.' Alfie grinned. 'Don't tell our Kitty it were me who hung it up theer, will yer?'

'Oh, we won't, Alfie. We'll spread the rumour it were one of the Dawson lads. She's always the first to get hold of a bit of gossip, is your Kitty. Where is she, by the way?'

'Gone to 'er mother's, or so she says. And that's another thing – all the stuff she brings back wi' her when she reckons to 'ave been to 'er mother's: nylon stockings, two-pound bags of sugar, tins of bloody jam! She's not getting them from 'er mother's, is she?'

'So she 'asn't seen that up there yet then?'

'Not yet.'

Bernard looked puzzled. 'So if your Kitty's brassiere's up theer on the guttering, what's she wearing today?'

'She's only been and bought another one! Black this time. *That's* why I think she's got another man. That and all the presents.'

'Well, I'm sorry it's upsetting you, you being jealous.'

'Oh, it's not upsetting me, her 'aving another man. In fact, I wish she'd bugger off wi' one! It's the bloody price of all them fancy brassieres and things I'm upset about.'

The party ended with all the old folk singing the songs of their youth round the dying embers of the fire. The younger ones had taken off to the works yard where people from all over Millington had gathered. By the time the strains of 'God Save The King' had died away most folk had shed a tear or two, either for loved ones lost or others hopefully on their way home.

*　*　*

It was while the men from the rows were trying to sleep off their hangovers the next morning that Kitty went out to empty the ashes. It was there, right above her head, her precious brassiere. The wind had filled out the cups so that it floated, splendid and proud as the figurehead on a sailing ship.

Kitty didn't stay to gather gossip as she usually did but ran screaming up the stairs. She took off one of her dirty old slippers and gave poor Alfie's bare backside a beating he would remember long after the brassiere had blown away. Peace might reign over Europe but it hadn't yet been declared at the Ramsgates' on Potters Row!

On 19 August the celebrations were repeated and this time the war really was over. Victory over Japan had been declared.

Daisy hadn't wanted to go to grammar school, not after she had heard Pat talking about all the games such as tennis and hockey that had to be endured. She had the sense, though, to realise that a writer needed the best education possible. So she and Carol passed their exams and settled happily at their new school.

Una Bacon had no interest whatsoever in being educated. All she wanted was to go on the stage. Nevertheless, she was a bright girl and worked hard in the seniors at Millington School.

Jean knew that even if she had passed the eleven plus it would have been a waste of time; she would be expected to leave school at fifteen to start work and help keep her many brothers and sisters.

The four girls still remained friends out of school hours, though, and continued to meet most nights.

Kenneth Butler was born in October, a placid, beautiful baby whom Daisy adored from the first moment she set eyes on him. She helped bathe, dress and feed him, and if he cried in his cot she would lift him out and cuddle him till he fell asleep. She wrote a poem about an old wicker cradle, especially for her brother.

On Sunday afternoons, after Sunday school, the four girls would trundle prams containing brothers, sisters and cousins on walks to the common or to the west of Millington. They would giggle and start to show off if they should happen to meet any boys on the way. It wasn't long before gangs of youths would congregate in some beauty spot or other where the four lasses might happen to stroll. The truth was that the four friends were growing up to be beautiful, desirable girls.

Jim was delighted that Daisy took Kenneth off their hands. It gave Sally and him time to catch up on their lovemaking. He even considered locking the door to keep out any visitors, but his wife wouldn't hear of it.

'What will anybody think, if they find the door locked in the middle of the day?'

'They'll either think we're out or that we're lying naked on the bed, making mad, passionate love.

What the hell does it matter what anybody thinks?'
he answered.

'And what if our Daisy comes back and she's
locked out?'

So the door remained unlocked and ever open to
visitors, as usual.

Chapter Ten

'Did yer ever make any enquiries about them new-fangled washers?' Danny asked Sally one day.

'No, but I will. I'll ask Mr Brubeck on Friday.'

He was a salesman who travelled to three or four South Yorkshire towns, selling everything under the sun. If Mr Brubeck couldn't get it, he knew somebody who could. He lived in Cottenly and called every Friday after tea at Amy Butler's. If anyone on the rows needed anything, from prams to coal buckets, Mr Brubeck usually managed to locate it, even in wartime. His customers would pay him a fixed sum each week, so that by the time anything was needed there would be enough on the card to cover it and prevent anyone from finding themself in debt. In times of need, Mr Brubeck would bend the rules and allow the item to be paid for after the purchase, but none of the Butlers had ever found themselves in that situation. Danny knew about the payment system but was adamant that the new machine would be paid for, in full, on delivery.

All Potters Row looked forward to Mr Brubeck's visits and the neighbours would congregate in Amy's kitchen to see what new delights he had to offer. Sometimes it would be a lady's blouse or stockings, a man's working shirt or a fine linen tablecloth. Mr Brubeck never asked for coupons so nobody ever questioned where the goods had come from. On this occasion he had brought a little blue linen coat which would fit Kenneth in a few months' time. Sally was delighted that she had made enough payments to cover its cost. She then enquired about the washing machine for Danny and Mr Brubeck said he would see what he could do.

True to his word, a few weeks later he had found a washer. The contraption was a large, green metal container on four legs. A handle rotated a paddle inside the drum, and Mr Brubeck said the washing came out just as clean as if it had been scrubbed by hand. All the neighbours came in to admire the wonderful invention.

Kitty Ramsgate spread the rumour in Mr Baraclough's the next day that Amy Butler had turned all posh and got herself a new-fangled washer: 'She'll not want to talk to the likes of us now!'

She had to eat her words the next morning when she saw Jim Butler and Tom Porter carrying it away again, so she spread a further bit of gossip that Amy had bitten off more than she could chew and found she couldn't afford it after all. Meanwhile Danny was trying out his washing machine and finding it a marvellous, labour-saving invention.

* * *

Lizzie Denman was hanging out the washing when her son came into view. He had lost so much weight she had to look twice to make sure it was Ernest, then she dropped a handful of gipsy pegs on the ground and ran to meet him with open arms.

'Oh, son!' she exclaimed. 'Are yer here to stay this time?'

'Aye, Mother, I'm here to stay.' He could see the tears in Lizzie's eyes and tried to joke her out of the emotion they were both experiencing. 'Until yer either kick me out or I get meself a wife.'

'That'll be the day,' she joked back. 'Who'd 'ave yer?'

'Where's me dad?'

'Work. He'll be home at ten, or thereabouts.'

'How're the others? Our Enid and Sally?'

'All right. And our Pat's working now.'

'Oh! What's she doing?'

'The same thing she's been doing for the last few years, but now she's getting paid for it.'

'Good, it's what she's always wanted, a job in the theatre.'

'Aye, I reckon she'd made herself so useful they couldn't manage without her.'

'What about our Norah and Daisy?

'Oh, our Norah's doing all right. I reckon she'll end up in the offices at the works. She's usually top of the class. As for our Daisy . . . I worry about her. All she wants to do is write, and since she won that competition it's made her ever more determined.'

'Aye, I heard about that. She must 'ave been thrilled. I don't think yer need to worry about our Daisy, though, she's such a determined kid I dare say she'll do anything she sets her heart on.'

'Aye, but she's going to need a job in the meantime.'

Ernest had been longing to ask about Betty Hayes and little Ernie but couldn't think of an excuse. Instead he asked, 'Is Clarence home yet?' and saw the confusion on his mother's face. 'Clarence Hayes?'

'Nay, lad,' she said. 'Clarence Hayes won't be coming home again. He died in a concentration camp.'

'What? When?' Ernest felt a flutter of hope and then immediately a wave of guilt for his unworthy feeling.

'Eeh, it must be a couple of years now.'

'Nobody said.'

'I expect nobody liked to talk about somebody dying, not when you were at risk too.'

'But at Christmas when Betty was there . . . what must she have thought when I didn't even offer my condolences?'

'Don't know. lad. I don't suppose she'd 'ave wanted reminding, she was pretty cut up at the time.'

Ernest couldn't wait to see Betty now. He made an excuse that he was eager to visit his sisters and set off to Enid's on Potters Row. She was thrilled to have her brother home, but shocked by his appearance.

It seemed to be his mental state that had been worst affected. Ernest was blinking all the time and his left hand seemed to have developed a tremor.

'Sit down, love. Let's get you a drink and something to eat. You look like you could do with fattening up a bit.'

'No! No, thanks, I'm not hungry. I could murder a cuppa, though.'

Enid took the singing kettle from the hob and mashed the tea. When it was brewed she sat down opposite her brother and poured it into two cups.

'So how are you really?' She stirred her tea. 'And don't say you're fine.'

'No, Enid, I'm not fine. I'm a bloody nervous wreck and that's the truth. The worst thing about it was watching the planes of me mates going up in flames around me. Not just me mates either, the ones I had to shoot down too. The poor sods in 'em were lads my own age. It wasn't their fault they were fighting the bloody war, any more than it were mine.

'One of them was coming straight at me when one of our lads went for him. I saw his face, Enid. I could see the fear in his eyes. He no more wanted to kill me than I did him. I didn't have to on that occasion, me mate got him in the side, saved me life, but there were other times . . . we actually cheered when we got one of them. Can you imagine that, Enid, can you?'

'No, Ernest, I can't. I only know you did what you

had to do and it must have taken a lot of guts, but it's over now and you must put it behind you. Just like countless thousands of others will have to do.'

'Aye, I know that, but was any of it worth the carnage? All the men and women who lost their lives? I don't think so. And it *isn't* over, Enid. What about the people of Hiroshima and Nagasaki? The aftermath of what we did there won't be known for years. You're right, I shall have to put it behind me, but it'll still be in my head. I shall never forget . . . I can't.'

Ernest finally let go of the tears he had kept in check for so long. His sister held his hand and let him cry, knowing he would be all the better for doing so. When he had calmed down a bit he was more like his old self.

'So what's this about having another earner in the family?'

Enid laughed. 'I haven't seen any of it yet! Not that Pat's earning all that much, she'd be bringing home more from an office job.'

'Ah, but would she be happy?'

'Would she heck!'

'Well then, let her be happy, Enid. We only have one chance at life, we've got to make the most of it.'

'Oh, it made us realise that when our Daisy went missing. We've got to let our kids be happy while they can.'

'What about poor Clarence? What happened to him?'

'Dysentery. Betty was devastated.'

'How is she now?'

'Fine. You know Betty, gets on with things, makes the most of them. She's a wonderful mother . . . and I know you've got a thing about her, so what are you going to do about it?'

Ernest felt the colour rising in his cheeks. 'How do yer make that out?'

'How? By the way you never took your eyes off her at our Christmas get together.'

'Yes, but what if she doesn't fancy me?'

'If she doesn't, she'll tell you. If she does, you'll never know unless you ask her. Take her to the pictures or a dance. They still have them at the Victoria Club.'

'Will *you* ask her for me?'

'Will I heck! Where's the great lady-killer disappeared to? The one who went away?'

'He's still here, just sadly out of practice.'

'Yes, well, she'll be in if you wait another half an hour.'

'Right, I'll go and see our Sally while I'm waiting.'

Enid noticed the spring had come back to Ernest's step as he strode towards the gap in the wall. It could have been the letting go and having a good cry, but it was more likely the anticipation of a date with Betty Hayes.

Little Ernie had been enthralled in an old *Play-box Annual* that had once belonged to Uncle Jim, but then the gasman came and the book was forgotten.

Ernie thought the gasman was the cleverest person he knew. He would empty all the pennies from the meter on to the table, after which he would slide each penny to the edge and into his hand. This would be done so fast Ernie could hardly see his fingers moving. When he got twenty-four pennies he would stand them up in a pile on the table. When they were all done he would count the piles and take them away in his bag. The best bit was that there were always some pennies left on the table. Grandma called that the rebate and always gave Ernie a few to go and spend at Mr Baraclough's.

Sometimes he would buy a bag of lemon crystals, licking his finger and dipping it in, sucking off the crystals and leaving his finger bright yellow. Another time he might buy some aniseed balls or a licorice stick. He couldn't wait for Grandma to give him some pennies . . . but then something happened to distract him for a while. A man came. He knocked on the door and waited until Grandma opened it. That in itself was unusual, but then this man was a stranger.

'Ernest lad, bring yerself in! Don't stand there knocking. How are yer?'

'I'm not so bad, Mrs Butler.'

'Aye, well. I dare say yer'll be better when you've been in yer mother's care for a while.'

'I expect you're wondering why I'm here? Well,

I've come to apologise to Betty. Nobody told me about Clarence last time and I don't know what she thought of me, not offering my condolences.'

'Oh, I don't think she'd 'ave thought owt about it. Anyway, she'll be 'ome in a minute so yer can offer 'em then.' Amy took hold of Ernie's hand. 'Come on, Ernie, let's go and see what Mr Baraclough's got today, shall we?'

Ernie wasn't bothered about going, though. He liked the look of this man and wondered if he was his dad. He looked at the photograph on the mantelpiece. No, he wasn't the same man, but he looked all right. He liked him even better when he took a silver sixpence out of his pocket and gave it to Ernie, saying, 'Here, Ernie, see what Mr Baraclough's got for sixpence.'

'Ooh, thank you, mester.'

'Ernest . . . my name's the same as yours.'

But Ernie was already off across the field in the direction of the shop.

Betty was still in her cook's overall and wished she'd taken it off when she saw Ernest Denman waiting for her. He never even noticed the overall, all he saw was the way her face brightened at the sight of him.

'Ernest, what a surprise!'

'A nice one, I hope?' He grinned briefly and then his expression turned serious. 'I came to say how sorry I was to hear about Clarence.'

'Thank you, but I don't suppose he'll be the only one you knew who won't be coming home.' Betty's face had clouded over.

'No, but that's not much consolation. Anyway, I wondered if you'd do me a favour?'

'I will if I can.'

'Will you come out with me one night? I sort of feel a bit lost, after being away for so long.'

Betty's smile then looked like a ray of sunshine to Ernest. He couldn't take his eyes off her.

'I'd love to. It's ages since I've had a date . . . not since Clarence went back, in fact. Where would you like to go?'

'You choose. Pictures? Dancing?'

Betty privately wondered if a dance might be a bit of an ordeal for Ernie, who was obviously in a nervous state.

'Pictures,' she decided.

'Right.' Ernest was glad. He would have Betty to himself in the pictures. 'When . . . Saturday?'

'Sure.' Betty smiled at him again and Ernest thought he was in heaven. 'I'll meet you outside,' she told him.

'You will not! If I'm taking you, I'll pick you up here. Seven o'clock, okay?'

Betty nodded and waited for him to leave. The way he was gazing at her, she knew he wanted to kiss her. She wanted it too.

'Mam! Look what Mester Ernest bought me.' Ernie ran in, holding aloft a bag of pear drops.

'Did you say thank you?' Betty just managed to tear her eyes away from Ernest's.

''Course I did.'

'Yes, he did.' Ernest ruffled the little boy's hair. 'I'll see you another day, Ernie. 'Bye, Betty.'

'See you Saturday . . . don't be late!'

'Don't worry, I won't.' The smile Ernest flashed her then was the one the girls used to go wild about in the old days. It had the same effect on Betty.

When Mary came in for her morning chat she seemed fine, but halfway down her cup of tea she burst into tears.

'Whatever's the matter, Mary?'

'It's happened again.'

'What's happened again?'

'I really thought I was expecting this time, and now I've got my period again.'

'Oh, no, I'm sorry.'

Mary Porter had longed for another child since the day her daughter Celia had died. Ten years later she was still hoping.

'Oh, Mary, you'll have to stop torturing yourself like this,' Sally told her.

'It's all right for you, you've got Kenneth!' she sobbed.

'I know, but you've got Stanley. Maybe you'll have to be content with one child. Many a woman would give anything to have a healthy son.'

'I know, that's what Tom says.'

373

'Your Stanley's a son to be proud of. He's doing very well for himself.' Stanley had been employed by an electrician and was being given day release to attend college.

'I know, I realise how fortunate I am most of the time, it's just when my periods are late that I start hoping again.'

'Yes, I do understand. I just wish you'd stop upsetting yourself, that's all.'

'I'm better now. Best be off.'

'Mary,' Sally called as her friend reached the door, 'let's go to the pictures tonight. It's Frank Sinatra and Judy Garland.'

'Yes, okay, I'll see you later.'

Sally was troubled for her, though, as she went over to Ida Appleby's. Ida soon cheered her up. She seemed to get younger with each passing year, and it was all due to Doug Fletcher. She had sought him out at the cafe as she'd said she would, told him he looked like death warmed up, and invited him over to Sunday dinner. He had been visiting her twice a week ever since. He also took her to Sheffield on Saturdays for tea and sometimes the theatre. Today she looked as though she had lost a shilling and found a ten-bob note.

'Well!' Sally said. 'Come on, I can tell something's pleased you, what is it?'

'We're going to Scarborough, to the Grand Hotel, for a week!'

'Really? In a double room?'

Ida blushed. 'I don't know yet. Doug says it's entirely up to me, but I think I'm too old for all that 'anky-panky.'

Sally grinned. 'You're never too old for a cuddle, Ida.'

'No, but he might not want to stop at a cuddle.'

'You might not either.'

'Maybe you're right . . . but it's me body I'm worried about. All me flabby bits, and me breasts . . . they're not as firm as they were.'

'I'll tell you what, I'll go and borrow you one of Kitty's brassieres,' Sally chuckled, and Ida giggled too. 'Seriously, though,' Sally said, 'you've a better figure than some women half your age. Besides, Doug'll have some floppy bits as well. Ida, go and share a room with him. You can see what you feel like when the time comes, but at least you'll have the companionship. It'll be lovely having some-body's company, and if you feel like sharing his bed, go ahead. Nobody'll be any the wiser. And what does it matter if they are?' Sally paused then added, 'He's a nice man, Ida. He cares for you. I like Doug.'

'I know. I care for him as well.'

'Well then, go and enjoy yourselves. You're only young once.'

'All right, I will. And if I come back pregnant, I'll blame *you*.'

Daisy typed up all the poems she considered to be her best ones and placed them in a folder to show to her English teacher. He had selected one of her essays to be entered for the school prize and had asked to see some more of her work. Her heart was thumping as she placed them on his desk. 'Thank you, Daisy,' was all he said.

She waited nervously for a few days until he came to find her, one afternoon break. 'Will you come to my classroom, Daisy? I'd like to speak to you.'

He asked her to sit down then told her, 'I've read your poems and made some enquiries about where the best place is to send them.'

'Really? So you think they're good enough?'

'They're certainly good enough. Whether they'll be accepted is another matter. You've got to understand that publishers receive thousands of manuscripts a year. However, I have a friend who has a friend who is a literary agent. I think you should let him look at your work.

'Even if it is accepted – which is by no means certain – you won't make much money, poets rarely do, but it would be a breakthrough and a way of making your name recognisable to publishers. Then it will be time to submit your *real* work.'

'My real work?'

'Well, I'm surmising you write something other than poetry?'

'Yes!' Daisy had never told anyone outside the family this before. 'I'm writing a novel.'

'Good, good. And what are you thinking of doing

when you leave school?' The teacher frowned at her then. 'You're not thinking of depending on your writing to provide you with a living, are you?'

Daisy blushed. 'I don't know. I shall have to do something, I suppose, but I just want to write.'

'Even if your work is accepted, it takes a few years before the money starts to arrive. Keep writing by all means, but you need a job in the meantime to provide you with an income.' He sat back in his chair to show that this interview was at an end. 'Oh, and would you like me to deal with these for you?' He indicated the poems.

'Yes, please. If it isn't any trouble?'

'It will be my pleasure.'

Daisy couldn't believe some of her work was being sent to a literary agent. The teacher was right, though, she would have to start thinking about getting a job and wasn't sure how she felt about that.

One day the four friends were at Una Bacon's, playing her records. As usual the conversation turned to boys, and eventually sex.

'I'm never having any babies,' Una said. 'I want a career.'

'Don't you ever want to make love, then?' Jean asked.

'Yes, when I'm married.'

'Well, how will you not have babies then?' Carol wondered.

'I shall use contraceptives,' Una announced.

'What are they when they're at home?' Daisy had never heard of them.

'They're rubber things that fit over a man's willy.'

'You're having us on!' Daisy felt embarrassed.

'Don't tell me you've never heard of them? I've known about them for years,' Una boasted.

'How?'

'I found one in my mum and dad's room, under the bed-side table. Hang on, I'll show you.' Una disappeared upstairs. When she came back she was holding a small rubber thing that looked like a balloon. 'Look, this is one. It catches all the seeds in it so that they don't end up inside you.'

'Well, I wouldn't trust one of those.' Jean knew how easy it was for her mum to become pregnant. 'I wish Mum had one, though, it might help a bit.'

'She can't. You're Catholics and it isn't allowed.'

'I wouldn't trust one either,' Daisy said. 'I bet it would burst, it doesn't look very strong to me.'

'It is, look.' Una stretched it. 'I know, let's see how strong it really is . . . let's fill it with water!' She pressed the end over the tap and turned on the water. The girls giggled as more and more water stretched the condom until it took on the shape of a balloon.

'There must be pints in there,' Carol estimated.

'At least four,' Jean said as they watched the huge balloon spill over the edge of the white pot sink. 'I should turn off the tap, if I were you. What if it bursts?'

'No.' Una was fascinated to see how much it would hold. 'Let's just wait . . .' Suddenly the pressure became too much and the thing burst over the edge of the sink and flooded the kitchen floor.

'Oh, bloody 'ell!' Una wasn't the type to use bad language but she knew her mother would go crazy if she came in and saw this mess.

'Have you got a mop?' Daisy looked round the kitchen. It was the only one she had ever seen that had a carpet square on the floor instead of lino and a mat.

'I don't think a mop's going to dry that carpet.' Jean was more domesticated than the others. 'We'll have to take it outside to dry.' Jean and Daisy carried the carpet outside and threw it over the clothes line. Una and Carol tried rubbing it dry with old floor cloths but all that did was make the pattern run.

'We'd better stop, we're making things worse,' Carol said. 'Let's go out and pretend we don't know anything about it.'

'We can't, not now we've taken the carpet outside.'

'Well, let's bring it in again, then.'

'No.' Una had promised her dad she would never be dishonest again, after she had been in trouble once before. 'I'll tell the truth.'

'But what about the contraceptive?' Daisy felt sorry for her friend.

'Well, I can't put it back now. I shall have to tell

them what we were doing.' She looked close to tears. 'I think you'd better go.'

The other three didn't need telling twice. They wouldn't like to be Una, talking about contraceptives to her parents! 'Well, if you're sure?' Jean said, but they were already out of the door and away.

When Bill and Marjory Bacon came home they were greeted by the sight of a sopping wet carpet hanging on the line, and a saturated kitchen floor.

'What the hell's been going on here?' Bill thundered.

Una turned on the tears, hoping it might help. She explained that she had been curious about how safe contraceptives were. This only made her dad more furious as he wondered how a girl of Una's age even knew about such things, let alone would want to test them. Marjory was more worried about the carpet square and decided they would have to buy a new one as soon as they could afford it.

'The point is, what were you doing snooping in our bedroom?' she said, to Una.

'I wasn't snooping!'

'Then how did you know we used such things?'

'I've known since I was about six. When I used to help you dust, I saw them. I didn't know what they were, but I knew they were something I wasn't supposed to know about.'

'No! And yer shouldn't know about them now either,' Bill grumbled.

'Oh, Dad, I'm not a baby.'

'And yer not an adult either, so just you forget about such things for a few years.'

It wasn't until Bill and Marjory were in bed that night that they finally saw the funny side of it.

'Well, at least we shan't have to worry about telling her about contraception,' Marjory chuckled.

'No, and neither will Jim Butler or the others. Our Una's done it for 'em.'

Ernest Denman loved Betty and was impatient to be married, but she had insisted on waiting. At the back of her mind was the possibility that Clarence might still be alive, but even she realised that was most improbable. Amy thought it was time her daughter tied the knot.

'That lad'll not wait forever, yer can't expect 'im to. He's a good lad and yer'll lose 'im to another lass if yer not careful.'

'He doesn't want another lass, he loves me.'

'Well, marry 'im then! He'll make a good dad to our Ernie. The little lad idolises him.'

'We're saving for a house.'

'Aye, well, that's very admirable, I'm sure, but in the meantime you can live 'ere.'

'I know. You're right, Mam. We should be married. I don't know why I keep making excuses. I suppose I keep thinking Clarence might come home.'

'Oh, lass. You know he's dead. Yer can't waste

yer life waiting for summat that's never going to happen.'

'Right then, we'll get married, just as soon as we find a house. I'll tell Ernest tonight.'

Betty and he were going to a dance. The Victoria Hall was back to normal with the original Tony Tanner Band members. Doreen and her husband Steve were going with them.

They also went out most Sundays, together with the children, sometimes to Buxton on the train, sometimes to Bakewell or Castleton. Last Sunday they had taken the kids down Speedwell Cavern. It had been quite scary to Betty and Doreen, but the kids had loved it and squealed with delight as they descended the rocky steps and got into the boat, deep in the cave, which had to be propelled down the narrow tunnel by a boatman lying on his back and walking along the roof. At the end of the tunnel there'd been a pool of water that was thought to be bottomless.

The kids had been fascinated. Betty and Doreen had been freezing cold and relieved to be back in the open air. Later Ernest had bought Betty a figurine made out of the beautiful Blue John, a mineral only found in the Derbyshire hills.

Betty was almost ready to go out, wearing a new dress made of kingfisher blue jersey which showed off her trim figure. Amy thought she grew more beautiful every day.

'Eeh, lass, yer a sight for sore eyes,' she told her daughter fondly.

Betty kissed Ernie, who wiped her kiss away and told her he was too big to be kissed any more. Then she dabbed on a drop of Evening in Paris, put on her best coat with the nipped in waist, and went to meet Ernest.

The band was playing a valeta when the two couples entered the dance hall. Most of the dancers were girls dancing together. The men were either hanging round in groups, eyeing up the girls and deciding which one they would ask to dance later, or in the other room at one of the snooker tables. Ernest and Steve had already had a couple of pints so were in the mood for dancing.

'Come on, let's shake a leg!' Ernest suggested. He was a good dancer and they made an attractive couple as he twirled Betty in the Gay Gordons.

'Oh!' She was dizzy after all the spins. 'Let's sit the next one out.'

'Come on then, let's go and get some refreshment.' They went into the side room where tea and biscuits were available. They could hear the singer offering his version of 'Jezebel'. Ernest gazed at Betty. 'That's what you are,' he said. 'Your eyes promise paradise, and that's all I get . . . promises.'

Betty giggled. 'You daft devil! Anyway, what would you say if I asked you to marry me, Ernest Denman?'

He stared at her. 'Are you serious?'

'I wouldn't joke about something like that.'

'When? Tomorrow?'

'Well, not quite. I'd like time to buy a wedding dress and get me hair done first.'

'Well, you can buy a dress and anything else you want, but don't have yer hair done,' he said seriously. 'I like it the way it is. It's what the men at work call "Come to bed" hair.'

'Okay, I promise I won't have my hair done. But there is still the small problem of where to live. Unless you would like to begin married life at my mother's?'

Ernest pretended to consider this. 'No, I don't think so, the walls are too thin. So we'll find a house and then arrange the wedding.'

'We might be waiting a long time . . .'

'We won't. I've got my eye on one that's been for sale for a while. It'll need doing up but that won't take long.'

'For sale? Oh, Ernest, I don't know . . . I've never liked being in debt.'

'Buying property isn't really being in debt, love. It's an investment. Besides, I've got a decent deposit saved already so we won't be paying much more a week than we would be if we were renting.'

'How much would it be, do you think?' Betty sounded scared.

'No more than three hundred pounds, and as it's been for sale for a while I might beat the chap who's selling down a bit.'

'Where is it?'

'Overlooking the Memorial Gardens. His son works at the steelworks in the low yard fitters with me. He's taking his dad to live with them.'

'So is it empty now?'

'Will be as soon as we want it. That's if it hasn't already gone. Well! Are we going to dance or sit here nattering all night?'

Betty kissed his cheek and let him slide his arms round her waist and dance as close as he liked.

'My resistance is low,' Ernest sang along with the vocalist, then nuzzled his lips into Betty's neck. 'I'm not kidding either. You can do whatever you like with me . . . I'm all yours. Thanks for asking me to marry you.'

Jim arranged for the family to go away in the works holiday weeks. He booked two weeks at Scarborough in a small boarding house in Sepulchre Street. Daisy didn't want to go unless her friend could go too, so it was decided that Carol would accompany them.

Kenneth was so excited he made himself sick and Sally was up all night holding out a bucket and bathing his forehead. His recovery when Jim suggested cancelling the holiday was miraculous, and he was soon running on ahead, clutching the duffel bag holding his swimming trunks, bucket and spade.

The station was crowded with families from Millington taking advantage of the two weeks' shutdown of the steelworks. Most of the men would have been paying into a savings club, and with this on top of their three weeks' wages in hand would be feeling quite well off. By the time the family changed trains at York, Daisy – as usual – was feeling travel sick and spent the last twenty miles in the train toilet, wishing she were dead.

The rich Scarborough air immediately put her to rights and she and Carol were soon soaking up the holiday atmosphere of its South Bay. Sepulchre House was a jolly place, made more so by the many Scottish holiday guests who seemed a lively crowd. Every day they would gather on the beach with a piano accordion and soon other sunbathers would bring over their deckchairs and join in the merry-making.

Kenneth soon made a couple of friends and seemed to be the only one of the family who could understand half of what the Scots were talking about. He said his new friends were having the same problem understanding his funny Yorkshire accent too! This didn't prevent Jim and Sally from joining in the fun, which often carried on until well into the night.

Daisy and Carol were more interested in strolling round the harbour or over to the North Bay and Peasholme Park, where there were usually a group of soldier cadets to flirt with. On the second day the girls had arranged to meet two of them and go swimming at the nearby open-air pool.

Daisy quite fancied one of the boys and thought she would show off in a bathing suit borrowed from Pat. Her cousin said it had never been worn so she was not to lose it. It was made of beautiful crinkled nylon and Daisy really did look gorgeous in it, or so Carol told her in the changing room. Things weren't to turn out quite as well as they'd expected, though. As soon as the girls stepped into the water, the bathing suit – which happened to be white – turned completely transparent. It was Carol, fortunately, who noticed, just before the boys joined them.

'Daisy, get under the water!' She pushed her friend beneath the surface.

'What are you doing Carol?'

'Your cossie . . . it's see-through. I can see your nipples!'

Daisy looked down. 'Oh my God! What can I do?'

'Keep out of the shallow end and you'll be okay.'

'But how do I get out?'

'I'll fetch you a towel, don't worry.'

The soldier cadets thought Daisy was a bit peculiar, the way she was carrying on.

'What's up? Are yer scared of water?' Jimmy Thomson asked. 'Can't you swim?'

'No.'

'Well then, come and splash about a bit. Once

you're used to the water, I'll teach you.' But Daisy still cowered by the edge of the pool in the deeper part. 'Come on, I'll hold you under yer chin and show you how to move yer arms and legs.'

Daisy was devastated to miss her chance. 'No! I've got to get out,' she insisted.

'But we've only just got in,' Jimmy grumbled.

Daisy thought she would die if anyone saw her. She might as well be naked.

'I'll fetch you a towel.' Carol climbed up the steps.

Jimmy, who had spent all the previous night imagining what Daisy Butler would look like in a swimsuit, suddenly realised he was never going to find out when she wrapped herself in a towel even before leaving the pool.

'What's up with her?' his mate asked.

'Don't know, I reckon she's been brought up in a convent or something.'

'Shame, I thought she was gorgeous.'

Daisy and Carol never saw those two lads again.

'I'd kill your Pat if I were you,' Carol told her friend.

'No,' Daisy answered. 'I've thought of something better. I shan't tell her about the cossie – and then one day the same thing'll happen to her!'

Daisy didn't remain cross for long, though. They were two teenagers on holiday, and loving every minute of it. They lay on the beach every morning, hung around the amusement arcades in the afternoons and danced every night – and never stopped giggling.

Halfway through the holiday they went to the fair, Carol wearing a new yellow dirndl and Daisy flaunting her trim figure in a tight-fitting skirt. They showed off in front of a group of soldiers by bumping them on the dodgems, then they decided to make for the Esplanade Gardens. Daisy thought she felt the stitches of her skirt give as she climbed out of the dodgem car but didn't stop to check.

The girls could hear the lads giggling as they followed them along the Esplanade, then suddenly a woman came up behind them and tapped Daisy on the shoulder.

'Excuse me, love,' she said. 'Your skirt's coming unstitched up the back seam. You're leaving a trail of thread behind you. I wouldn't have said anything only somebody's trodden on it and the lads behind you can see your undies.'

Daisy almost fainted as she felt behind her and encountered bare flesh. Carol took off her cardigan and tied the sleeves round Daisy's waist so that her bare thighs were covered. The cadets behind them let out calls of 'Boo!' and 'Spoilsport!' Daisy dodged into the nearest cafe to escape the jeering gang and promptly burst into tears.

'I shan't dare come out again,' she wailed.

Carol went to the counter and ordered two knickerbocker glories. They had been promising themselves one before the holiday was over and she considered this was as good a time as any to indulge themselves. She went back to their table and sat down opposite her friend.

'I've just decided which job you should go for when we leave school,' she told Daisy.

'What are you talking about?'

'A stripper . . . you'll have had enough practice by the time we go home.'

Daisy smiled, then she started to see the funny side of what had happened and began to chuckle.

The cafe assistant, who looked rather effeminate, came over carrying a tall, delicious sundae in each hand. 'Two knickers coming down!' he quipped.

The two girls looked at each other and laughed until the tears ran down their cheeks. This was one holiday they wouldn't forget in a hurry.

Chapter Eleven

Jim decided they would have electricity installed and divide the largest bedroom into two, to make a bathroom. He had been putting the rent money they used to have to pay into the bank, and with a grant from the council should have enough to pay for the improvements.

While Sally was telling Danny Powell about their plans he said, 'Have yer enough money to pay for it, lass?'

'Well, we should have.'

'If you 'aven't, let me know and I'll give yer some.'

'I couldn't do that, Danny. It's ever so kind of you but I couldn't.'

''Course yer could. I've told yer before, I owe me present comfort to you and yer family. Your Daisy saved me life, you gave me me hearing back, and Amy's giving me companionship. She's a grand lass and I shouldn't like to be without 'er. In fact, I wish she'd marry me, Sally.'

She was taken by surprise. 'You've asked Amy to marry you?'

'Oh, aye, but she's refused me point blank. I expect it's me being a cripple that's putting her off.'

'Oh, I don't think it'll be that. I suppose she's so set in her ways that it'd be difficult for her to change.'

'Aye, I suppose it could be that. I'm thinking of 'aving electric put in as well.'

'Really?'

'Aye, and I'm wanting one of them television things.'

'You're getting all posh in your old age, aren't you?'

'Might as well spend it, being as nobody'll let me give 'em owt.'

'Well, it's really good of you to offer, but if I were you I'd spend it on yourself. Besides, my mother-in-law may change her mind, then you'd have a wedding to pay for.'

'Nowt'd please me more, lass, nowt'd please me more.'

Daisy received a letter from the literary agent to say he was accepting her as a client and had passed her poems on to a publisher to be appraised. This boosted Daisy's confidence so much that she left school a couple of hours early and made her way to the offices of the *Millington & Cragstone Gazette*.

The receptionist there looked down her nose at Daisy. 'Yes?' she snapped.

'I'd like to see the Editor,' Daisy said.

'Have you an appointment?'

'No. But I've taken time off school so I'd really like to see him!'

The girl got up and hobbled on three-inch heels through a door marked EDITOR, closing it behind her. When she came out, she looked Daisy up and down and told her he could spare her a few minutes.

The Editor seemed to be surprised when he saw his young visitor. 'Yes,' he said, 'and how can I help you?'

'I'm Daisy Butler. I'm a writer and I'm leaving school next year. The thing is, I'd like to gain some experience now so that, if possible, I can work as a reporter then.'

He smiled but said, 'We have lots of people wanting us to employ them. Why do you think we should consider a young girl like you?'

'Because I've already acquired a literary agent, I've won an important writing competition and I've got my own typewriter! Most of all, because writing is the only thing I've ever wanted to do.'

The Editor sat up straighter in his chair. Daisy showed him the letter telling her she'd won the competition, and the one from her agent. She also had a letter from her English teacher. The Editor put on his spectacles and glanced at all the letters. 'Hmm, most impressive. You'd no doubt be an asset to any newspaper. The thing is, we don't happen to have any vacancies at the moment.'

'Oh, I wouldn't expect you to employ me yet. I couldn't work anyway, I'm still at school. What I want is the experience . . . I wouldn't expect to be paid. If I could just do something out of school hours, that's all I ask.' Daisy fluttered her eyelashes, sure of how attractive men found her. 'Please,' she added.

'Where do you live?' he asked.

'Millington.'

'Mr Dennison is our reporter for your area. You'll have to see him.' He looked at the clock on the wall. 'Can you wait? He'll be in any time.'

'Sure, I'll wait all night if necessary.'

The Editor grinned, 'I don't think you'll have to do that.' He pressed a button and spoke to his secretary. 'Jane, two coffees, please.'

The girl's attitude had changed when she brought in the tray. 'Do you take sugar?' she asked politely.

'Yes, please.' Jane studied Daisy as she poured the coffee, wondering what made her so special. Daisy caught her eye and winked, and the other girl blushed bright red. At that moment they heard a sound from the outer office.

'Sam!' the editor called. 'Here a minute.' Sam was elderly, balding, looked as though his shirt had never been ironed. 'Sam, this is Daisy . . . ?'

'Butler,' she reminded him.

'What've you got on for this weekend, Sam?'

'Too much,' he grumbled. 'Wedding at Millington. St Catherine's. Cragstone Show to cover, and the football match at Sheffield Wednesday.'

'Do yer want to offload the wedding?'

'Do I! I hate bloody weddings. I'm hopeless at describing wedding frocks and bridesmaids' head-dresses. Never can tell blue from green, or roses from anemones.'

Daisy knew he was only joking and smiled nervously.

'Right, Daisy Butler. Wedding at St Catherine's. What time, Sam?'

'Three o'clock.'

The Editor took off his glasses and polished them on his hanky. 'On my desk by Tuesday morning, Make a decent job of it and you'll be paid the going freelance rate, per word. Make a bollocks of it and you're out that door. Right?'

'Right, thanks.' Daisy was so pleased with herself she even gave the stuck-up receptionist a radiant smile on her way out. When she got home she said to Sally, 'Mum, I'm not going to music lessons any more.'

Sally had been expecting this. Daisy had only learned in the first place to be the same as Carol. 'But you're doing so well, Daisy. What about the exams you've passed?'

'A waste of time,' she said. 'You spend weeks learning three pieces of music, over and over again, so that you can almost play them in your sleep. Then, when you get there they just ask you to play one and you know you'll never play any of them again. How can that prove you're a good pianist? Then there are the aural tests, but I'm no good at those. It was pure luck that I passed.'

Daisy thought the only good thing about sitting the exams was that they had meant a day out, with lunch in a cafe and a visit to the pictures afterwards. Sally was relieved in a way. It meant she wouldn't have to go traipsing to the other side of Sheffield and sit about in a cold, damp schoolroom again while Daisy sat her exams.

'Can I learn instead?' Kenneth said. 'I want to learn to play the piano.'

'Yes, when you can read properly your granddad'll teach you. It'll be something to pass his time on.' Joe Denman had been lost without the Home Guard meetings.

'I *can* read my name.'

'Yes, I know you can, you're a clever boy, but you need to be a bit bigger before you can read music.'

'Come on, Kenny, I'll teach you,' Daisy said. It was his sister who had taught him to read simple words and his name.

'Why have you suddenly gone off the music lessons?' Sally asked her daughter.

'I was never bothered about them really. Besides, I've got a job.'

'What?'

'I'm going to interview the bride for an article in the *Gazette*. Then I shall have to type it out in time to deliver it by Monday teatime.'

'Goodness! My daughter a newspaper reporter.' Sally was so proud of Daisy. 'Will you be paid?'

'Of course.' Daisy preened herself.

'Where's the wedding?'

'St Catherine's.'

'Are you taking photographs?'

Daisy hadn't thought about pictures and the Editor hadn't mentioned any. 'I don't know, do you think I should?'

'Well, it would show you have some initiative.'

'But I haven't a camera, only Dad's old box one. Besides, I couldn't get them developed in time.'

'What about Uncle Bernard? He develops his own. He might do one for you on Sunday. He's always experimenting in the cellar. He might lend you his camera, too. Just this once.'

'Oh, if only he would! If I make a success of this first report, I've got the job. If I'm useless, I lose it.'

'Go and ask then. I bet he'll jump at the chance.'

Bernard was just a keen amateur, but some of the photographs he'd taken of the kids and the local landscape were really professional.

'I'll not only develop the film, I'll lend you me camera.' Uncle Bernard seemed quite excited at the prospect.

He had invested in a good two-lens camera and turned the cellar into a dark room. Enid grumbled about developing tanks and dishes cluttering up her kitchen and lengths of negatives hanging from door handles to dry. She couldn't resist showing off the finished pictures to her friends at the school, though, and was actually quite proud of her husband's hobby.

Bernard spent the next half-hour happily explaining about light meters and exposure times. He wished his daughters would take an interest in his hobby, but Pat was interested in nothing but the theatre and Norah obsessed with her latest boyfriend.

Daisy couldn't sleep on Friday night. The questions she would need to ask were rehearsed over and over again in her head. Then she wondered if she should dress up a bit, being as it was a wedding. When should she do the interview? Perhaps she should take a picture as they left the church, make notes of the dresses and flowers, and then go back later to the reception. If only she had asked who was getting married . . . she didn't even know their names. Why hadn't she asked Mr Dennison? It just proved she wasn't up to the task.

On Saturday morning the sun was shining. Grandma Butler made her customary visit and, while they were chatting away, said, 'It's a lovely day for the wedding.'

'Whose wedding?' Daisy pricked up her ears.

'Young Molly Murphy's. It'll be a grand do, Catholic weddings always are. They all seem to have such big families.'

'Grandma, do you happen to know who she's marrying?'

'Oh, aye. Zillah Brown's grandson. Not sure about his first name, though.'

'Where does the bride live?' Daisy doubted her grandma would know, but she did.

'In the Co-op houses, the first one in the row behind the Co-op butcher's. I used to see her and her sisters skipping in the yard. Eeh, that doesn't seem two minutes since, and now she's getting wed.'

Daisy didn't stop to hear any more. She ran upstairs and put on a blue costume and a pink blouse, slipped a jotter and pencil into her bag, picked up the camera and ran downstairs.

'Daisy, where are you going?' Kenneth asked his sister.

'Not far, I won't be long.'

Molly Murphy lived with her parents and a houseful of sisters and brothers. Daisy knocked on the open door.

'Come in!' Mrs Murphy called.

Daisy went in. There were kids sliding down the one-ended settee. Another stood drying himself on the table, and one sat in a zinc bath in front of the fire. A clothes horse stood to one side, adorned with white shirts on hangers. Sitting up to the table was a small, thin woman with metal curlers in her hair. 'Come in. Joan, put the kettle on!' she called. 'Mek this lady a cup of tea.'

'No! Please, don't bother.' Daisy thought she'd better introduce herself, although nobody seemed to care who she was. 'I'm from the *Millington & Cragstone Gazette*. I wonder if I could ask Molly a few questions about her wedding?'

'Is our Molly going to be in the paper then?' Joan came and stood by Daisy, unnerving her with an unblinking stare.

'Well, I 'ope so,' Mrs Murphy said as she rocked in the creaking chair.

'Is Molly in?'

'Aye, she's upstairs. Joan, go fetch our Molly.' Joan went through a doorway that had once had a door on but now had only hinges. She could be heard clomping up the bare wooden stairs. 'Molly, yer've got to come. Me mam says.'

'It'll be funny, our Molly being a bride after all't times she's been a bridesmaid,' Mrs Murphy said.

'Has she been a bridesmaid a few times, then?'

'Seven.' Mrs Murphy smiled, obviously proud of their Molly. 'Well, yer see, I've ten brothers and sisters and they all wanted our Molly because she's so pretty.'

Molly came running downstairs with Joan following. Molly had obviously just washed her hair as she had a towel round her head. Mrs Murphy's comments had been an understatement even so. Molly was more than pretty, she was beautiful.

'This's the newspaper woman, Molly,' Mrs Murphy said. Daisy stood up and offered her hand to Molly, who held her fingers out of reach.

'Sorry. I've just varnished my nails, and they aren't dry.'

'I wondered if I could ask you a few questions?'

'Ask away.'

'Right. Can you describe your dress, the material and its style?'

'You might as well look at it, it's in the front room. Come on.' Daisy followed Molly, Joan and another sister who she learned was named June. Another snotty-nosed girl trailed behind. The dress was hanging on a picture hook on the wall. Four turquoise bridesmaids' dresses in various sizes were laid out over a threadbare three-piece suite.

'Oh, Molly, they're absolutely beautiful!' That was no exaggeration. Molly's dress was of white taffeta with a sweetheart neckline, puff sleeves and a tiny nipped in waist. A broad cummerbund trimmed with lace and rhinestones completed the ensemble. Daisy jotted down the cummerbund details and those of the bridesmaids' dresses.

'And what are the names of your bridesmaids?' she asked.

'Joan, June and Jean Murphy, and Stella Brown.'

'And what about the bridegroom's name? Can't have a wedding without a groom.'

'John Brown, and his best man's his brother, James.'

'Right. And what about your headdress? And flowers?'

'Full-length veil held by a wreath of rhinestones. These lot are 'aving ribbons trimmed with flowers.'

'And the flowers?'

'Red roses and lily-of-the-valley. My dad insisted on roses. To tell the truth, I don't know how he can afford this wedding but he's determined all his daughters are going to get a good send-off. He said he would give us all a good do on our wedding day, if we promised to give him and my mum a good one at their funerals.'

Molly looked pensive. 'Do you know, I think we were the poorest family in Millington at one time, but we were the richest when love was handed out.' She changed the subject then. 'The kids are carrying posies of pinks.'

'Well, you're all going to look beautiful.'

'Thanks to Mary Holmes.'

'Do you mean Mary Holmes on Barkers Row?'

'Yes. She's a fantastic dressmaker.'

'She certainly is, if she made these.'

'You can put down that she made 'em, I like to give credit where it's due.'

'What about the mothers, what will they be wearing?'

'My mam'll be in blue, with navy accessories. His mam navy with white.'

'And where will the reception be held?'

'St Catherine's Hall. There's supposed to be a hundred guests but I expect there'll be nearer two hundred when the dancing starts.'

'Dancing?'

'Aye, Mr Crossman from over Warrentickle.'

'Well, it certainly does look like being a good do. Are you going away?'

'No. We've got a house, we're moving straight in.'

'Where's that?'

'Main Road. Oh! You can put that the girls in the umbrella department 'ave bought us a canteen of cutlery – Sheffield steel, of course – and the billet mill men a clock.'

'My dad works in the billet mill too,' Daisy said. 'Would you mind if I take a picture at the church?'

'No, come to't reception after tea, if you like. Take as many as you need. Jean, don't you dare touch that dress!'

'Well, thanks, Molly. You've been most helpful.' When they went through to the kitchen, another little boy was just getting dried.

'Come on, Joan, you're next. Yer can't go to a wedding wi'out a bath,' Mrs Murphy said. 'June, you put some more watter in't boiler for when it's our Molly's turn. She can't be getting bathed in mucky watter on 'er wedding day.'

'Well, goodbye, everyone, and I hope you have a lovely wedding. Thank you very much.' Daisy put her jotter safely in her bag and left.

'Don't shut door!' Mrs Murphy called. 'We need to let steam out.'

Daisy wondered if the door would still be left open when it was Molly's turn to bathe. She wouldn't be at all surprised.

Daisy didn't attend the reception, she didn't like to gatecrash, but she got a lovely picture of the couple outside the church. She was going to love this job if it meant she would be in contact with people like the Murphys.

After school on Monday she got off the bus a stop early and handed her typed-up article to the Editor. He opened the envelope and was surprised to see the photograph.

'My, my, a picture too.' He looked pleased as his eyes scanned the neatly typed pages. 'Well, Daisy . . . ?'

'Butler,' she offered.

'Well, Daisy Butler, it looks like we've got ourselves a new part-time reporter. You don't need to come to the office on Fridays, you can ring Sam. I'll give you his number. Call him on Friday evening and he'll tell you what's going for the weekend.' He scribbled a number on a piece of paper and handed it to her. 'There might not be work for you every week, it'll depend on Sam. I can tell you this, though, he hates weddings and fancy dinner dances so you'll be sure of those.'

'I'd better buy myself a posh frock then,' she joked. She was walking on air for a few days.

When the weekly *Gazette* came out on Thursday, she almost snatched it out of the newsagent's hand. She couldn't believe it. There, at the bottom of the front page, was her photograph of the bride and groom, with the headline 'SEVEN TIMES A BRIDES-MAID, THIS TIME A BRIDE' by Daisy Butler.

She danced up and down amongst the bags of carrots and potatoes.

'I wrote that, Mr Baraclough!' She felt tears filling her eyes.

'Eeh, Daisy love. Let's 'ave a look.' He called to his wife who was weighing out half-pounds of butter, 'Come and 'ave a look at this what young Daisy's written. Eeh, and look at the picture, isn't that lovely? And you've even mentioned Mary Holmes. Now *she's* going to be making a frock for my missis, she's just put a card up on the adverts board.' He grinned at Daisy. 'Looks like we're surrounded by famous folk.'

'Oh, I'm not famous yet, Mr Baraclough.' Daisy giggled. 'But I shall be, one day.'

Daisy had noticed the car when they got off the bus from school. It was parked round the corner at the bottom of the Donkey Path and had been there on a few other occasions. She had thought she'd recognised the man in it, but now she was certain. It was Carol's father. She wondered if her friend had seen him too and chosen to ignore him. Daisy decided not to mention it.

He hadn't intended spying on his daughter but the old urge had got the better of him. He had been disappointed when she'd alighted from the bus, though. Carol had grown into a young woman, attractive but too mature for his taste. Daisy was a different matter. She still had that childish quality about her, had not filled out like his daughter.

He felt the familiar thrill as he imagined that

405

fresh young body . . . He would bide his time, he could wait, but not too long.

Betty and Ernest's wedding arrangements were progressing well. The wedding would take place the Saturday before Easter. It was supposed to be a quiet wedding but had developed into a large affair, what with the friends and relatives of both bride and groom and neighbours from both sides. Ernest said an Easter wedding would give them ample time to get the house ready. He had been disappointed that Betty had at first chosen to wear a nice costume and had managed to persuade her to wear a proper wedding dress instead. She had bought herself a large white picture hat, and the dress was being designed by Mary Holmes – on Daisy's recommendation.

None of her nieces was bothered about being a bridesmaid, preferring to wear something suitable for later, so Betty had written to Florence, who was to be her chief bridesmaid, along with Doreen's daughter, Alice. Bernard had offered to take the photographs and Betty had made her own wedding cake, icing it beautifully in white and gold, to match the roses in her bouquet.

It was her ambition to start her own catering service, and Ernest had promised to set her up with the necessary equipment, once they were settled in their new home.

'I'm glad you're not wearing a veil this time,

giving Kitty Ramsgate summat to gossip about,' Amy said.

'Oh, no, she won't be talking about me this time.' Betty managed to keep her face straight. 'She'll be too busy gossiping about *you*.'

'Me! What's she got to gossip about that involves me?'

'You and Danny. All those romantic nights in, listening to music in the firelight.' Betty had heard no gossip whatsoever about her mother but she knew it would give her something to think about. Betty also knew Amy would miss them when she and Ernie moved out, especially her grandson. Nowadays, though, her mother was spending most evenings over at Danny's, or inviting him over here where she would cook something tasty for his tea. Betty thought it was daft, living in two houses when they obviously wanted to be in one. She had already suggested to her mother that she and Danny would be better off married. She tried again.

'Why don't you and Danny get married, Mam?'

'Don't be ridiculous,' Amy protested. 'People my age don't get married.'

''Course they do.'

'Well, I should feel disloyal to yer dad.'

'Oh! So you think I'm being disloyal to Clarence, do you?'

'No, you're different, you're only young.'

'Yes, and you look years younger since you became friends with Danny.'

'Aye, well, he's a nice man. He makes me laugh.'

'So what more do you want? Is he not sexy enough for you, is that it?'

Amy's face turned the colour of beetroot. 'You want to wash yer mouth out, young lady.'

'Sorry. Anyway, it'll make Kitty Ramsgate happy. There hasn't been anything to gossip about round here since her brassiere blew away and ended up hanging off the flag pole at the Town Hall. Besides, think of all the scrubbing it'll save you.'

'What do yer mean?'

'Well, if you took on Danny, his washer would come with him.'

'Aye, well, if I did marry Danny it wouldn't be for his washer or owt else he possessed.'

'No, I know that. You'd be marrying him because you care for him and he cares for you. And high time you both admitted it! Oh, I just thought of something . . .'

'What?'

'I hope you won't even consider wearing a veil?'

Even Amy couldn't help laughing at that.

'Oh, I don't know,' she said at last. 'I'd certainly look a lot better wi' 'alf me face covered up!'

Daisy jumped off the bus and ran straight into the phone box. She dialled Sam's number and waited. When he answered she said, 'Hi, Sam. You know I'm covering my aunty's wedding tomorrow afternoon, but if you want me in the morning I'm available.'

'Would you like to cover the meeting to discuss local plans for the celebration of the Festival of Britain?'

'Sure, where?'

'The Town Hall, eleven o'clock. Shouldn't take long unless Councillor Grey turns up. He could be rambling on till midnight.'

'I hope not, I've a wedding to get ready for.'

'Thanks, Daisy. I've a busy schedule tomorrow.'

'It's a pleasure.' Thinking about the little cheque that would be waiting for her on Monday at the office, she put down the phone, pushed open the door – and a hand came out and grabbed her wrist. It was Carol's father!

The hairs on her neck bristled with fear but there was no time to be scared. Daisy swung her school bag hard and landed the side with the metal fastening straight in his face. He relaxed his hold for a second, and she wrenched herself away from him and ran straight up the Donkey Path.

She soon realised she should have kept to the main road and gone to seek help in one of the shops, but it was too late now. She heard him pounding along behind her but he was obviously less fit than a young girl, and she heard him turn back and away from her.

Daisy was still shaking and slowed down as she reached the steepest part of the hill, to regain her breath. She wondered what her dad would do now. He'd go to the police . . . Perhaps she shouldn't say anything. It was growing dusk and she wished she hadn't volunteered to give her teacher a hand with marking books from the first form. In her nervous state, she was relieved to be approaching St George's Road.

Then she saw the car, waiting by the turnstile. She could just see the front of its bonnet but she knew it was his. There was no way she could leave the path without him seeing her, and if she turned and ran back the way she had come, he might be waiting for her again at the bottom.

On impulse she ran to her left, through the wall and into the doctor's garden. She knew how well-hidden their old hideaway had been; no one had ever found them there. She made straight for it now, praying he hadn't seen her run in this direction. If he followed her here, nobody would ever know. He could murder her and no one would find her for weeks. She crouched among the blue-painted holly bushes, ashamed of the mess she and Carol had made of the place when they had been little girls.

Suddenly a car door slammed. Oh, God, he had got out of the car! She could imagine him climbing over the wall, coming towards her . . . Then she heard the door close again and waited for him to drive off. She thought he was starting the car, but then she heard another door slam. She was confused now. Perhaps it had been Mr Baraclough's van door she had heard the first time. She dare not move, not even a muscle. Daisy realised she was shivering, but whether it was from fear or because she was freezing cold she wasn't sure.

It was pitch dark and still she waited. She wondered why no one had come to look for her. If they had, they'd have seen Carol's dad and he would have driven away. Perhaps he'd already gone? But she couldn't risk it. Not when she knew what he wanted. The thought of him touching her made her skin crawl. She would stay here all night rather than be raped.

Sally was pacing the living-room, going to the window and back again. She went to Enid's in case Daisy had gone there, then to Amy's and Mrs Firth's. If only Jim was at home! Why did he always have to be on afternoon shift when he was most needed? By the time she knocked on Mary's door, she was in tears.

'Sally, what's wrong? Come on, sit down and tell me.'

'Our Daisy isn't home yet. Oh, Mary, it's like a nightmare, a repeat of last time.'

'Now, come on, Sally. She might have gone somewhere for the paper. It is on Fridays that she rings what's his name, isn't it?'

'Yes, but she'd have come home first.'

'Sally, she's growing up. She could be with a boy or anything.'

'No, she'd have let me know. She understands what I went through last time, she wouldn't put me through that again.' Sally rose restlessly to her feet. 'I'm going home . . . she might be back by now.'

'I'll come with you. Look, why don't you ring that reporter? Check that she made her regular call. At least you'll know then that she came home from school.'

'Yes, I will, if I can find his number . . . it might be in her bedroom.'

'If you know his name, it'll be in the phone book at Mr Baraclough's.'

'I don't like to bother them when they're closed for the night.'

'But this could be an emergency.'

'Oh, I hope to God it isn't, Mary!'

Daisy was having to shake herself to stay awake. She had no idea what time it was and her watch had stopped. She had thought she heard footsteps once, a cracking of twigs and creaking of branches, but she daren't move, it might be him. Her eyes were closing. If she fell asleep she might never wake up again. Aunty Betty's wedding would be spoiled and she would let Sam down by not covering the Town Hall meeting. She tried to make up a poem to keep herself awake. 'In the wild wood, dark and deep . . .' It was so boring, it was making her even more sleepy.

Daisy was in the house in the bushes, pouring tea from the tiny teaset. The pandas were sitting round the table made from a cardboard box. Daisy poured tea for the baby panda and Carol cut the cake. It was Mother panda's birthday and they were having a party. Then Carol's father came through the bushes. He was wearing a party hat and told Carol to go away. He wanted Daisy this time. He came closer and Father panda rose up towards him, protecting her, just like the dogs had protected her at Aunty Charlotte's. The panda lifted the man and tore him in two, separating his upper body from the rest. Blood splattered out and mixed with the bright blue paint, then the pandas went back into the tea set and Daisy was left with the corpse of the man. She knew she was dreaming, but if the man was dead here she would rather remain in her nightmare than wake up and find him alive.

Jim didn't call at the Sun, for which Sally gave thanks. She met him at the door and he knew something had happened straight away by the look on her face.

'Our Daisy's missing, Jim. She never came home from school.'

'Is she at Carol's?'

'No, apparently Carol didn't go to school, she wasn't well this morning. I don't know what to do. Jim. She rang Sam when she got off the bus.'

'Well, we know she wouldn't go off without saying so we'd better notify the police.'

'Mr Baraclough said there was a strange car parked at the top of the Donkey Path about that time.'

'Does he know what make or colour?'

'No, he doesn't. He said he saw it stop, and it seemed to be a while before it started up again.'

Jim was just about to go for the police when Tom and Stanley walked in. 'Is Daisy back yet?' his mate asked.

'No, I'm going to Baraclough's to call the police.'

'Oh, Jim, where the hell can she be?'

'God knows, I'm sure I don't. Well, at least we can't blame the Kaye woman this time.'

'Let's go and look round before we involve the cops.'

'Where? She can't be down the path or we'd 'ave seen 'er on our way home.'

'Aye, I've just come up that way from the darts match,' Stanley said.

'I'll tell you what, I'll go across and ask Una if she's seen her, then I'll go to Jean's. You take a look down in the direction of the wood,' Jim said.

The men set off and Sally continued pacing from one room to the next. She remembered that she should have gone to the hairdresser's in readiness for tomorrow's wedding. If Daisy was still missing then she had visions of the marriage being postponed. She knew neither Ernest nor Betty would get married with this hanging over their heads. She noticed Dippy had made a pool behind the door again. The poor thing had no control over his bladder these days. She cleaned it up automatically as the dog waited to be put outside in half-hearted punishment, but it didn't happen today so he settled himself comfortably on the pegged rug in front of the fire.

Suddenly Tom remembered the den Daisy had once made in the bushes. It was a long shot, but it was all he could think of. 'Come on,' he said to his son. 'It's through the wall, somewhere near here.'

'What would she be doing in Dr Sellars' garden?' Stanley wondered aloud.

'Just summat I've remembered.' Tom felt his way in the pitch darkness.

'Ouch!' Stanley had almost poked out an eye on a tree branch, but he didn't care as long as Daisy was safe. She was the only girl he had ever cared about, though he doubted she even thought about him, let alone cared. Why should she? Someone as beautiful and clever as Daisy.

Tom had found the place he was looking for. 'Daisy!' he called. There was no reply but he had a feeling in his gut that she was nearby. 'Daisy, are yer there?'

Stanley's ears were younger and sharper than his father's. 'She's here, I heard her.' The noise had been faint, like the mewing of a cat. He went in its direction. 'Daisy?'

'Stanley.' Daisy couldn't move. Her whole body was numb. She began to cry, almost silently, as if she was too weak to do more. He lifted her effortlessly and she clung to him as if afraid he would go away and leave her again.

'What were you doing here, love? Yer mam's nearly frantic worrying about yer, and yer dad.'

'I'm sorry.'

'Don't be sorry, Daisy, just tell us what happened?' Stanley couldn't bear seeing her so upset.

'I can't tell you, Stanley. I want my mam . . . I'll tell her.'

'All right, let's get you home.' He carried her the whole way back and laid her gently on the settee in the front room.

'Come on, Stanley. let's go. I think Daisy's got something to tell her mam,' said Tom then. Stanley was reluctant to leave, but followed his father towards the door.

'Stanley . . . thanks.' The look in Daisy's eyes told him that maybe, just maybe, she did care for him a little bit.

'Oh, Dad, I'm sorry!' Daisy had started crying again. 'It was *him* . . . Carol's dad.'

'What!' Jim's fists clenched at the mere thought of the man.

'He was waiting for me to get off the bus. Grabbed me when I came out of the phone kiosk. I ran away and thought I'd lost him, but then his car was there at the top of the path and I didn't know what to do.'

'Go and call the police, Sally! He's a danger to young girls. He can't get away with it this time . . .'

'What do you think, Daisy?'

'Dad's right, the next person might not get away.'

'I'm not going to Mr Baraclough's, I'm going to Carol's. It's only fair to warn them what's going to happen. We shall have to tell the police about the man's history. Besides, they might know where he can be found.'

'Yes, you're right.'

It was Carol who came down and let Sally in. 'Has Daisy come home?' she asked.

'Yes. But I need to talk to your mum, Carol.'

'She's getting dressed. She'll be down in a minute. We were both still awake, worrying about Daisy.'

Sally explained to them both what had happened. 'I'm really sorry but he needs reporting.'

'I know, we should have done it before. Ring the police now,' Carol's mum told her.

'Do you know where he'll be?'

'Yes, I have his address, but he'll probably have run away after what's happened.'

Sally phoned the police, who promised to do what they could. She was eager now to return to her daughter.

'Are you sure Daisy's all right?' Carol sounded worried.

'Yes, apart from being freezing cold, she's fine.'

'Well, then, I'll see you tomorrow, at the wedding.'

'Oh, yes, the wedding. Goodnight then, and

thanks.' The wedding was the last thing on Sally's mind.

Bobby Jones was already there by the time she got back, eager to make amends for last time he'd failed to find Daisy. She told him her story and watched a look of revulsion flood the policeman's face.

'Don't you worry, we'll find him! He won't bother any other youngsters for a while. If I had my way, the man'd be castrated. Unfortunately, it isn't up to me.'

He picked up his helmet and prepared to leave. 'Right then. I'll go and see what his poor wife and daughters have to say.' He smiled at Daisy. 'I hope I don't see you again, love, not for a long time anyway. Except that you'll probably have to give evidence in court. Do you mind that?'

'No! Not if it gets rid of him for a while.'

'Good girl.'

Daisy thought the experience of going to court would be good for a writer. If might come in handy for her novel . . .

'Come on,' her mother said. 'Let's get some sleep or we're going to look like death at that wedding. It's going to be a lie in for you in the morning, my love.'

'Oh, but I can't. I've to report on a meeting at the Town Hall.'

'Oh, Daisy, are you sure you're up to it?'

'Yes, I'm fine.' As she went sleepily upstairs, she

called to Sally, 'Mum, will Mary and Tom be at the wedding?'

'Yes, of course they will.'

'And Stanley?'

'Yes, why?'

'No reason. I just wondered.'

Chapter Twelve

Daisy was up and dressed in her blue costume, all ready for the Town Hall meeting, despite her ordeal the day before. She felt slightly apprehensive as she approached the Donkey Path but hurried on, intent upon putting the experience behind her.

On entering the Town Hall, she was relieved to see no sign of Councillor Grey and knew the meeting would stay a short one.

According to a spokesman, it seemed that tidying up the area in an attempt to make Millington more beautiful was the most important thing on the agenda for the Festival of Britain. There would also be an appeal to shop owners on the main road to plant out tubs of flowers and hanging baskets. Apparently the works management had offered to plant a line of trees, such as birches and willows, on the piece of land fronting the steelworks. The Victoria Club committee were also enthusiastic about tidying up and planting trees on the spare land adjoining their club. There was to be a revival of the arts and crafts exhibition which had been so successful before the war, and a concert in the Civic Hall. The Horse and

Pony Society were to organise a gymkhana, and the Scouts a pageant.

Councillor Scott said these were only a few of the many things to be arranged and another meeting would soon be called when further details would be announced. He thanked his colleagues and the press for coming, and said if there were no more questions, he would be on his way to a round of golf. If anyone *had* wished to ask questions they would have had little chance to do so – the man was out of the door and away, to the relief of most people present. They could all go home and enjoy their Saturday activities, and Daisy had a wedding to attend.

It was a lovely day for a wedding. Amy's house was in chaos, with visitors turning up every few minutes, the latest ones Aunt Jane and uncle Jack. When they saw the full house they decided to go and visit Jim and Sally instead, to the delight of Kenneth and Daisy, and the dismay of Sally who hadn't intended cooking on such a busy day. She promptly sent Kenneth off to the fish and chip shop for six lots, which they all ate from the paper to save on washing up. After the meal, Uncle Jack was eager to go for a pint or two at the Sun. Sally knew what his 'pint or two' meant and insisted Jim change into his wedding finery before leaving.

'And don't forget to be back here no later than two. Don't you dare let your Betty down!' Jim was to give his sister away.

'As if I would!'

It wasn't Jim Sally didn't trust, though, it was Uncle Jack, who was such a joker he tended to make other people lose all track of time. Once he had dressed up in one of Aunty Jane's dresses, a pair of high-heeled shoes, and tied a head scarf round his head. He had made up his face and donned some of her jewellery to accompany Jim and Tom to the Sun. People had stared all night at the funny woman with Tom Porter and Jim Butler, but not one of them had guessed he was a man. Jim and Tom had laughed for days afterwards at the looks on the men's faces when all had been revealed. Sally wondered what Jack had planned for today, and hoped it wouldn't be anything too outlandish.

At one o'clock Florence turned up at Amy's, to the relief of her friend. Betty had been waiting all morning. The dress Florence had brought to wear was in lemon chiffon: 'To match Betty's flowers,' she said. Little Alice was in white, with a flower in her hair to match her posy of spring blooms.

Betty had kept her dress a secret. When she came downstairs, Ernie said, 'Wow! You don't look like me mam, you look like a film star.' Even Amy had a tear in her eye at the sight of her lovely daughter.

Jim turned up then as promised, and only a little bit merry.

Amy sniffed his breath. 'I don't know how yer dare walk into't chapel, smelling of beer!'

'Oh, Mam,' Betty said. 'According to you, nobody

should go to chapel wearing a veil when pregnant, nobody should go after having a drink . . . it's a wonder anyone's allowed in at all!'

Just then a car drew up and Danny Powell got out, looking immaculate in a new suit and shirt. He eyed Amy up and down. She really did look nice in a beige suit and cream blouse and shoes. 'Eeh, Amy, yer look lovely. I wish it were our wedding we were going to,' he said, and she blushed prettily.

'No, Danny,' Betty teased, 'I think me mam would rather live over the brush.' Amy reddened even further at this.

'Nay, love, I respect yer mother too much for that.' Ernie had gone outside to play and Danny, joking as usual, quipped, 'Mind you, if she ever does decide to wed me, I'll tell yer summat – one of me outside legs might be buggered but there's still life in me middle one!'

Betty and Jim laughed with Danny, and Amy looked as though she would like to strangle him. 'See what yer missing, Mother,' Jim said.

Florence and little Alice were now ready and came downstairs in all their finery. 'Oh, my goodness! Where's this fairy come from?' Jim teased little Alice, who began to giggle. 'I bet you've got a boyfriend, a pretty girl like you?'

'Ernie's my boyfriend, isn't he, Aunty Betty?'

'Is he now? Right then, we'd better start saving up for another wedding then,' Betty said, and Alice giggled more than ever.

The taxi driver popped his head round the door. 'Are you ready, Mrs Butler? I'll take you, Danny and Ernie, and come back for the bridesmaids. I think everybody else is already there.' He was back in a couple of minutes for Alice and Florence.

When they had gone, Jim looked at his sister. 'Well, Betty,' he said, 'I'm sorry our dad isn't here, but I'm sure 'e's watching from wherever 'e is. And I'll tell you this – he'll be the proudest man in heaven today, just like I'm the proudest man on earth.' He kissed his sister just as the taxi drew to a halt outside. 'The best of everything, love.'

Then they were getting into the car observed by children from the estate and further afield. Betty noticed Mary Holmes's two standing shyly amongst the others. Jim threw a handful of coins for them in keeping with the old Yorkshire custom. Then they were sitting back and on their way to chapel, to meet the love of Betty's life.

Millington Chapel was more crowded than Amy had ever known it in all her years of attendance. She was proud that her family and Ernest's were well liked enough for so many people to turn out and watch. She could make out cousins and half-cousins she hadn't seen for years. It'd be nice to have a chin wag with them later on.

She hoped the reception would go off well. She had ordered the best ham salad teas with trifle to follow. Danny had insisted on supplying champagne for the toasts. When she had tried to refuse he had been upset, pointing out that he had no children of his own to see wed and that Betty's wedding would give him the pleasure he had otherwise been denied. Amy considered it a shame he had never become a father, he'd have made an excellent one. Just like he had made an excellent husband, and would do again, she supposed.

She glanced sideways at his handsome face and felt an unfamiliar feeling, one she had thought she would never experience again. He felt her eyes on him and turned to smile at her. He took Amy's hand then and held it firmly in his.

What if someone saw him? Holding hands at their age . . . what would folk think? Then Amy thought, To hell with what folk might think, and settled down to watch their Betty come in, looking like an angel, walking down the aisle to the man she loved.

Betty and Ernest thought Bernard would never stop clicking his camera. Ernie, Alice and Kenneth were becoming impatient. Actually Bernard was just making sure of perfect pictures, since Daisy had told him she would include his name in her report: Photographs by Bernard Cartwright. Fancy that. One of these days he might even become a professional.

'Right,' he said, 'that's all for now.'

'Betty whispered something to Ernest and they

went towards the far end of the graveyard. She plucked roses from her bouquet and placed them on the graves, one for each of her brothers and sisters and one for her father. Then another, in loving memory of her first husband.

'You're ruining your bouquet, love.' Ernest looked at the bouquet with half its flowers missing.

'I know, but it doesn't matter. None of this finery really matters, does it, Ernest? Only people matter. People who are still here, people who aren't here any more . . . what's the difference? They don't go away just because we can't see them. They're here in our hearts, in our minds, all around us. So I'm sharing the happiest day of my life with them, by giving them a rose.' She took his hand then. 'Come on, or they'll be holding a reception without the bride and groom.'

'That's okay.' Ernest grinned. 'We can just sneak off home to bed. They'll all be too inebriated to miss us.'

'I doubt it!' Betty laughed as they joined the merrymakers and were greeted with a shower of confetti.

The dancing was in full swing. Trevor Dyson had recommended a four-piece band and they were keeping everyone happy, from the teenagers to the oldies. Sally couldn't believe her eyes when Ida and Doug rose to their feet and joined in the Boston

Two Step. They had obviously had a bit of practice at the Grand Hotel in Scarborough. Sally
privately wondered if they had had a bit of anything
else while they were there, too. If they had, it
certainly hadn't done them any harm.

Mary had been subdued all day, she had even
refused a gin and orange – usually her favourite
tipple – and asked for just orange juice. Sally
couldn't keep quiet about any longer.

'For heaven's sake, Mary, is there anything the
matter?'

'No, why should there be?'

'Well, it's a wedding. Anyone looking at your
miserable face would mistake it for a funeral.'

'I'm not miserable! Oh, I might as well tell
you . . . I think I'm pregnant, and I don't know what
our Stanley'll say. I mean, it'll be embarrassing for
him at his age . . .'

'Mary, that's absolutely wonderful! How can you
be feeling miserable when it's what you've always
wanted?' Sally hugged her friend. 'What about
Tom?'

'Oh, he's bursting to tell everyone, but I won't
let him until our Stanley's been told.'

Sally looked round the room for Stanley. Daisy
was locked in his arms in the middle of the dance
floor. 'I shouldn't worry about him. I think he's too
much on his mind at the moment to worry about
anything.' She moved closer to her friend. 'Come
on, tell all. When is it to be?'

'Well! I think it happened on New Year's Eve. You know, after we'd been to the dinner dance? So it'll be September.'

'Oh, Mary, I'm *so* excited for you. You must tell Stanley. Tell him now, while he's starry-eyed about our Daisy. Go on.' She beckoned the young couple over to their table. 'Come with me, Daisy, Mary's got some news for Stanley.'

'What's going on?' Daisy enquired.

'Stanley'll tell you later I expect. Anyway, what's going on with you two?'

'Oh, Mam, I *really* like him. Well, I always have, but since last night it's different. Now I really, really like him.'

'Well, he's a nice boy, I've always thought so. Just watch his face when Mary talks to him. If he smiles, I approve of him. If he frowns, I don't. Okay?'

Daisy looked puzzled, but they both stood and watched. Suddenly Stanley's eyes widened. Then he grinned and picked up a bottle of wine and held it up, Mary picked up her glass, and they clinked them together and both smiled. Stanley walked over to his dad, patted him on the back and shook him by the hand.

'I defnitely approve,' Sally told Daisy, beaming.

'Good,' she said, 'because it wouldn't have made any difference if you hadn't.'

Tom and the other men were banded together, as usual. 'I've got summat to tell you all,' Tom announced. 'Our Mary's expecting a baby.'

'Bloody 'ell, Tom, you're a dark horse. How long 'ave yer known?'

'A month or two.' He grinned at Jim.

'Well! It's smashing news. After all the disappointments, Mary must be delighted?'

'Aye. Come on, sup up, we're celebrating.' Tom declared.

Alfie as always was the first to down his drink. 'Aye, I'm celebrating as well.'

'What're you celebrating, Alfie? Your Kitty's not expecting as well, is she?'

'No, she's left me.'

Nobody moved. Glasses were held suspended in mid-air.

'What?' Jim thought Alfie was joking.

'She's left me . . . at last! I'm getting the drinks in tonight.' And he stood up to go to the bar.

'Blimey, that's a first, Alfie, you going to get a round in,' Mr Firth commented.

'Aye, well! I can afford it now, can't I? Now she's gone.'

'*Where's* she gone?'

'Off wi' a little fat bloke. 'E came and fetched 'er in 'is car. Came and knocked on't door and apologised to me. 'E said they were well matched.'

'Did yer thump 'im?' Tom enquired.

'Did I 'ell as like! I gave 'im a pound note to buy some petrol with. I told 'im the further he took 'er, the happier I would be.'

All the men laughed, then Jim said, 'Who'll look after yer, Alfie?'

'Look after me? The only thing *she's* looked after is me money. I'll tell yer one who'll miss her, though, Judith McCall. No wonder she can afford to retire. She must 'ave made a fortune out of our Kitty, all them fancy brassieres and things. 'E'll get a shock when 'e finds how much her underwear costs 'im.'

'It might be that underwear that turns 'im on?' Tom suggested.

Alfie burst out laughing. 'Then he'll get a big shock when she teks it off!'

'Well, even so, it'll be funny living on yer own.'

'I won't be on me own.'

'Oh, aye, 'ave yer got a floozy lined up then?'

'No! I've done with women. Our Florence's coming home.'

The men were surprised, but glad for Alfie's sake.

'She only went away because of 'er mother. Now she's gone, our Florence says she'll be glad to come home.'

They were all happy for him then. Florence was a nice lass who had got off to a bad start. They'd both be better off without Kitty.

'Come on then, get 'em in, Alfie!' Mr Firth handed over his pint pot. Nobody could ever remember Alfie buying a round before.

Jim looked round the room at all the guests

enjoying themselves. Even his mother was almost splitting her sides laughing, and no wonder.

Uncle Jack had obviously come well prepared. There he was, wearing nothing but a grass skirt and a garland of flowers round his neck. He was wearing a long black wig and dancing the hula-hula. He'd succeeded in persuading Emily Simms to join him on the dance floor, and someone had placed Betty's large picture hat on her head and given her the remains of the bouquet.

'Emily looks as though she's had one too many,' laughed Ernest, who had come over to buy the men a pint, much to Alfie's relief.

'Aye, it's a grand wedding,' Jim said. 'Something for your Betty to remember in the future.'

'Well, let's hope we never get another war to ruin this marriage.'

Ernest thought then about what Betty had said in the graveyard, and wondered if Clarence were here in spirit. If so, no doubt he'd be thankful she was happy and that Ernie was to have a new dad.

Jim was thinking, too, about how fortunate he and Sally were. Daisy, despite all the ordeals she had faced in her young life, was a daughter to be proud of. Kenneth was quite a character too. He'd announced last night that when he grew up, he was going to be on television. If he was anything like his sister, Jim knew nothing would stop his son from achieving his goal. Aye, they were fortunate in their kids all right.

Jim caught sight of his mother then. He didn't think she would hold out much longer against Danny. It'd be strange having a new step-father at his age . . .

If he had but known it, Danny was at that moment proposing to Amy for the umpteenth time.

'Well, Amy, it's been a grand wedding but it'll be lonely now they've gone.'

'Aye, it will.'

'So how about marrying me, then we can keep each other company?'

'I'll say one thing for yer, Danny, you're persistent if nowt else.'

'Oh, come on, Amy. I know I'm a one-legged old fool, but I do love yer.'

'Yer not a fool at all, or I wouldn't be considering yer offer.'

'So yer considering marrying me at last?'

'I'm not leaving the row, mind. I was born there, and when I leave it'll be in me coffin.'

'So it looks like we'd better get electricity put in 'cos I'm not coming without me television set and me new electric washer.'

Amy felt close to tears. 'Would yer really give up yer home for me?'

Danny took hold of her hand. 'I'd give up everything for you, Amy.'

'Except yer television and yer washer?' She grinned.

'Even them. But I hope yer'll accept me, gadgets and all?'

'Well, as I've taken quite a liking to some of them programmes we've been watching together, I expect I'd better say yes.' She watched as joy lit up Danny's face.

'Eeh, Amy, I'm as happy as a pig in muck!'

'She laughed. 'Do yer know what I love most about you, Danny?'

'Me good looks, I expect,' he joked.

'No! Yer make me laugh – and it's a long time since anybody's done that.'

And then Danny kissed his future wife on the lips for the first time, and although Amy turned the colour of beetroot, she did not resist.

Chapter Thirteen

Daisy and Stanley caught the last bus from Sheffield. They'd had a smashing time dancing at the Cutler's Hall. The band had been great and she'd felt like a star in her new black taffeta circular skirt and white mandarin-collared blouse. That was until Stanley got a pass out and took her for a drink at the Grand Hotel close by.

The sight of all the women's diamanté-trimmed cocktail dresses and the man's bow ties made her six-inch-wide waspy belt feel rather tarty somehow. Stanley said none of these posh women ever had a waist worthy of a waspy belt, and Daisy told him he was the handsomest man in the room. He was, too, in his khaki Army uniform.

Daisy wasn't quite old enough to be drinking but ordered a gin and orange anyway. It cost Stanley an arm and a leg and made Daisy, who was unused to alcohol, feel quite woozy. After a visit to the ladies, she took a wrong turn, became quite lost, and ended up in a fit of giggles by the time she located Stanley.

'You're not fit to take anywhere!' He grinned at her. 'Come on, we're missing the dancing.' The rest of the night passed in a blur and they kissed and cuddled all the way home on the top deck of the bus.

The lights were out when they arrived at Taylors Row. 'Come in,' Daisy invited, 'I'll make some tea.'

They both had other things on their mind, though, and the tea never materialized. They didn't switch on the new electric light – installed by Stanley before he was called up on his National Service, Instead, Daisy broddled the fire until a warm glow filled the room. Stanley reached out for her then and she came eagerly into his arms.

They sank down on to the settee and Daisy undid her blouse and slipped out of it. Stanley undid her bra and it fell away, revealing her firm young breasts. He felt her nipples harden and brought his lips down to taste her. The scent of Evening in Paris inflamed his senses and he knew he should draw away and leave right now.

Daisy had other ideas. She undid the clasp of his webbing belt and the buttons of his trousers. She had thought long and hard about what she was going to do. She wanted to give Stanley something to remember when he went back to Germany, and memories to help her through the next year, too. She felt the iron hardness of his erection and her insides melted with an unbearable ache.

'Oh, God, Daisy. Are you sure about this?' Stanley removed his jerkin and fumbled with his

435

shoes and trousers. The touch of Daisy's hand was almost more than he could bear. Now she knew what Carol and Jean had meant by being carried away!

Sally had heard the front door being closed, and the whispering voices, then the silence. She was lying rigid, waiting for the sound of Daisy's feet on the stairs, but everything was so quiet. She had seen the way things were developing through Stanley's leave. She had noticed the new underwear, more fancy than Daisy had ever bought before. It wasn't that Sally didn't trust her daughter, or Stanley, it was just that she could remember her own courtship. Besides, with all the scrapes Daisy had landed herself in over the years, Sally wouldn't put it past her to land herself in the family way, too. Well, she wasn't going to lie here while that happened.

Sally jumped out of bed and stamped out on to the landing, switching on the light and coughing loudly.

'Bloody 'ell!' Stanley had just succeeded in untangling his trousers from his shoes. Now he became even more tangled as he rushed to get them on again. Daisy struggled with her blouse and hid her bra under the cushion. She hurried to switch on the light, expecting her mother to barge in at any moment.

Sally saw the light go on, and coughed again, then she went back to bed. She didn't mean to be a spoilsport, she just wanted to protect her daughter. She guessed their ardour would have been cooled now, for tonight at least.

'I could kill her!' Daisy fumed, then she grinned. 'I'm glad to see you've grown a bit since I last saw your you know what?'

Stanley fastened his buttons. 'I'd better go, she'll be listening for the door.' He drew Daisy towards him then and kissed her passionately. 'Better luck next time,' he said huskily. 'Oh, and by the way?'

'What?'

'What happened to those school knickers?'

Daisy pushed him towards the door. If what had happened tonight was a taste of things to come, she didn't mind waiting. Stan wasn't just a quick thrill, like Jean had described, he was for life.

Sally finally heard the door close and settled down to sleep.

Chapter Fourteen

It was Daisy's twenty-first birthday but she had postponed the celebrations in favour of a much more important event. She looked around the hall at the assembled guests. There were no posh frocks or bow ties, just the ordinary people of Millington and Cragstone. Her kind of people. Fancy all these folk turning out to see her! There were members of the History and Art Societies, and a literary group from Sheffield. She could see Carol and Jean standing near the double doors, looking even more nervous than Daisy herself. No doubt Una would have been here to support her, too, had she not been basking in the limelight herself, in a theatre somewhere on the east coast. Daisy could see her mother and father, and her aunts, uncles and cousins, were all here too. Even Pat had taken a night off. The Editor of the Gazette had turned up, and Sam, no doubt hoping for an interesting column in next week's edition.

Grand-dad Denman and Grandma were all dressed up in their Sunday best. Had he not been here, Grand-dad would have been playing the organ at the club, a pastime he had taken up in his old age in place of working on the allotment. He had even managed to persuade Grandma to accompany him to the club on Saturday nights; she and her friend Mrs Hoyle quite enjoyed watching the turns they had on, and the young folks dancing. Grandma Butler was looking smart too. Sitting beside her, Danny winked at Daisy as she caught his eye.

There were people here whom Daisy had never seen before, but most important of all, there on the front row, sitting with her brother, was Stan. He grinned at her and fingered the small velvet-covered box in his pocket. A box that held a solitaire diamond ring.

She looked over to where her parents were sitting, waiting expectantly for her to begin, and for the first time the realisation hit her. She was a novelist! Daisy Butler had always told them she would write a book, and now she had. She had not let them down. The Chairman beckoned her up on to the stage.

'Ladies and gentlemen, we come now to the main event of the evening. It isn't often we have a published novelist in our midst. In fact, it has never happened before. However, tonight we have not only a novelist, but a local novelist – and a very young one at that. I won't bore you any further but will let her tell you a bit about her new book, which will be in the bookshops in November. Then she has kindly offered to read an excerpt from it. Ladies and gentlemen, I give you, Daisy Butler.'

Daisy came to the mic then.

'Thank you so much for inviting me here tonight, it is a great honour for me. I'm not going to tell you too much about my book as I hope you will all rush out and buy a copy when it reaches the shops.' The audience laughed at this. 'Except I would like to say it is about the kind of people who have enriched my life so far. It's about down-to-earth people, like my parents and grandparents. People I love very much. Now I'm going to begin at the first page,' she said.

'"It was just an old house, with draughty windows, creaking doors and damp on the walls. It was a haven for the lost, a refuge for the needy, a home glowing with love. Just an old house, but with an ever open door."' She caught her father's eye then and smiled to see the colour in his cheeks.

'Hey, that's what I always say,' he whispered to Sally. 'I hope the cheeky young devil hasn't written a book about *us*.'

Sally couldn't answer, she had a lump in her throat as big as an egg – a hard-boiled one at that.